The Bendelbinders had been man and wife for nearly fifty years. They often understood each other's thoughts without speaking. Now Aaron's voice was gentle as he reflected, "California, the golden land. A long time already, a new century since we left Bluttah Street in that cursed Poland, and Little Gdansk, that damned *shtetl*."

Malka kissed his cheek. "It's a bad sign of getting old, Aaron, talking of the past."

He smiled; for all his material success, the chain of popular-priced bargain stores, his standing in the Jewish community, he felt that Malka was brighter, hardier. In Little Gdansk they had called her "the *starker*, the strong one." She had a natural perception of things, could face crises calmly while he agonized, shouted, bellowed, impaled himself on events.

How ephemeral life is, after all, he thought. All the pressures of the past, the tragic events, their escape from Poland, the struggles in the new land to earn one's bread. Plans, desires. All are like seeds in the wind; so few set down roots. . . .

As he chronicles the turbulent times between the Roaring Twenties and the eve of World War II, eloquent storyteller Stephen Longstreet confirms the hopes of a better tomorrow for those passionate survivors of yesterday . . . those proudhearted people who fought for their dream and their destiny, never forgetting the values their forefathers brought from the Old World to America—the Promised Land.

Also by Stephen Longstreet:

The Dream Seekers

WHEEL OF FORTUNE

Stephen Longstreet

PINNACLE BOOKS   LOS ANGELES

WHEEL OF FORTUNE

Copyright © 1981 by Stephen Longstreet

An original Pinnacle Books edition, published for the first time anywhere.

First printing, January 1981

ISBN: 0-523-40965-6

Cover illustration by Gary Ruddell

Printed in the United States of America

PINNACLE BOOKS, INC.
2029 Century Park East
Los Angeles, California 90067

I wish to thank those who have been most helpful in preparing this book: Lucas Webb, Gaye Tardy, Vici and Avrom Thomi, and express my gratitude for the kind encouragement of a friend and fellow writer, Irwin Blacker.

To my granddaughter,
STACY ROBIN,
Who thinks
Of the past
As the magic
Which created
Her

We spend our years as
a tale that is told.
Psalms

The tumult and the shouting dies;
    The Captains and the Kings depart:
Still stands Thine ancient sacrifice,
    An humble and a contrite heart.
        Rudyard Kipling, Recessional

WHEEL OF FORTUNE

Prologue

Paul Silverthorn got out of bed at the Hotel Lotti in Paris with a sense of expectation, some specific joy. He was delighted by the sunshine streaming in through the window, by the fact that he—at age 25—had survived the Great War (now being called the World War) with just a bad hip, a disability that gave him a slight, distinguished limp. He was having lunch with Joyce, the girl he was deeply in love with, at Brasserie Flo, where often during the war on leave in Paris, he had sat drinking cognac in fear that he would go down in flames flying for the RAF, that the goddamn war, in a deliberate plot against him, would never end.

He dressed with care in a good set of English tweeds, selected a regimental tie of red and tan he supposed he had no right to wear. Picking up his top coat and the solid blackwood cane, he went down to the lobby where Madame Baldon, the head clerk's wife—a *grosse femme*—greeted him, holding up a letter. He thanked her, and glanced at the envelope. It was from his uncle Sidney in California, another note, he supposed, offering him a job in his uncle's film studio. Paul put the letter away unopened in the pocket of his Burberry and signaled to a taxi loitering down the block for a fare.

Paul Silverthorn didn't want to be a film director; he just wanted to have lunch with Joyce, the dark-haired English girl he had met a week ago at a meeting of some foolish group that was supporting "a Jewish homeland in Palestine." Paul had been taken there by Charlie Greenberg, a reporter on the Paris *Trib*, who had insisted a war hero's appearance would help the Jews. "Hell, Paul, you're still a Heeb in good standing, aren't you?"

She had greeted him at the door of the rented hall near Galeries Lafayette, made him comfortable in a chair facing two dozen people, most of them with the look of fanatics or dreamers. He had left quickly after saying a few words, none of which he remembered, but the girl had agreed to lunch at Les Pubs to explain things more clearly, and dinner the next day, after his sending her Parma violets, at Les Deux Magots.

He was deeply in love, with the ardor of a man who had never expected it to happen this way. Lost were his worldly cockiness, his ironic view of the times, the memory of pain and agony of the war years. All that seemed to be erased. Only this overwhelming emotion dominated as they rode holding hands in the landaulet in the Bois de Boulogne. Forget Uncle Sidney claiming that love is a kind of madness, "you can't understand it, you can't push it aside." No, who wanted to push it away?

He glanced at the taxi driver, a White Russian refugee, no doubt, by the smell of vodka, and a prince, at least in the old days. Touching a finger to a greasy leather cap, the driver ground his gears to put the balky taxi in motion.

In the early years of the 1920s, Sidney Silverthorn would often take a new motion picture his studio had just produced to Atlantic City for a preview showing, away from the wisenheimers of Los Angeles. It was also an excuse to come East and jolly the money people, to

2

see the new shows, discover some pubescent talented actress who might become an S S WORLD PICTURES star. For in his secret heart, he was a romantic, still seeking the ephemeral, the capricious. *Back Home Again*, a film he had very carefully (and skillfully) produced, was the story of three soldiers of the AEF returning home. Good comedy, lots of heart, short skirts, and legs. He hoped it would make money, keep the studio open.

Standing this early morning on the boardwalk at Atlantic City, watching the waves walk in on the sands, he smoked his first cigar of the day. He was a handsome figure of a man, hair thinning, a bit of a paunch, and in his late 30s still striving—for what? he'd often ask himself, still wondering about the value of many things. He inhaled on the good Havana leaf, leaned on the railing and looked out at the gray sweep of sea as it hissed onto the beach and withdrew.

No more drowned sailors from convoys torpedoed by U-boats, no more wreckage of war supplies that never reached the Allies. Now, he thought, it's the rum boats, the hooch runners twelve miles out, unloading their cargoes into speed boats and the Coast Guard trying to catch them or taking payoffs. On a clear night in his room at The Breakers he could hear the rattle of tommy guns far out to sea, and one night when the young dancer, Winnie Parker, whom he was taking back to the coast for a screen test, was asleep, stuffed with lobster mousse and souffle, he had stood at the window and seen red-orange flashes flaring on the horizon. Prohibition was a great success, he thought, for the distillers, the bootleggers, the graft and bribe takers.

The horror and agony of war was gone forever, the world made safe for democracy, a time of progress. Only the bilious and the querulous regretted America hadn't joined the League of Nations, or resented the new president, Warren G. Harding, as a figurehead of banality, jovial and brainless.

Sidney—S.S. as the film industry called him in respectful affection or fear—had supported the new president, and had even been invited to lunch at the White House—and a lousy lunch it was, with a lot of red-faced golfing friends of the president. Later, in a house on H Street, S.S. had been happy to lose four hundred dollars in the official poker game to oil men and the political fat cats. The president played a good hand of poker. The whiskey had been bonded stuff from federal warehouses, and the president had said, "S.S., you old rascal, anything we kin do, why just ask."

Sidney thought of Nat Bendell, born Nathan Bendelbinder, his mother Malka related to the Silverthorns. Hadn't Nat tried to take over a New Jersey federal warehouse with two million dollars of bonded 90 proof fine brands in it? A Jewish boy working with those Sicilians and their gangs.

Since the death of his father, old Alex, Sidney felt the bridge to the past seemed pulled down; he had, however, made up with his father before the old man died, forgiven him for breaking up that early romance, Sidney's first love. He had been a happy young innocent chump in those early days in Boston. Happiness? He tossed the half-smoked cigar into the sands below. "Some addled philosopher," Alex had once told his son Sidney, "invented the principle of happiness out of pure reason, and, of course, forgot that logic, too, is an illusion."

Right to the end, the old boy still had some of that magnificent audacity that had brought him from being a millionaire in St. Petersburg, ruined by betrayal of his Christian partners, to start up a junk business in Boston, raise a family, grow in political power and in

4

wealth. Yet he was always aware of man's predicament in an indifferent universe.

How unlike the Bendelbinders—take Aaron, the husband of Malka, father of Nat. Aaron felt no security here, was an Orthodox shul goer, could on his last birthday—at 72?—say to Sidney: "I'm like the ghost in Gogol's story haunting his overcoat. It's for your generation or your children's generation this land, this hope."

"Come on, Aaron, you're not like all those old Yids sitting in their prayer shawls, turning reality into dreams."

"And what do you do with your motion pictures, Sid? You give millions of people dreams for their lives, and what are your dreams?" The old man waved a hand in rejection. "Naked *nafkas* and drinking cocktails from shakers, shootings, cowboys on horses."

"The dramas of simple people. Anyway, happy birthday, Aaron, here in the embrace of your family."

It certainly was a family affair; Nat in his forties, ex-Spanish-American War soldier, former gambling house partner, and now, it was said, in the rackets; Nat's son Teddy, a song writer, "a Tin Pan Alley genius," some said; the oldest Bendelbinder son, David the lawyer, the widower who had lost a son in the war—all of them under the beaming cheerful eye of Malka, seeing to the food, the drinks, the rewinding of the Victrola. A *family*.

It had depressed Sidney. The Siverthorns had no such gatherings of family gossip, intimate chatter, loud well-worn jests. Back on the coast S.S. had a wife and a son, Harry, he was very fond of, but somehow the film and studio business seemed to create an insatiable appetite for his energy and time. "Time's incessant passage bleeding away," as one of his film title writers had put into a version of a movie based vaguely on a Tolstoy story. The industry was tough tittie, and yet when a

5

movie was good, Sidney felt an ecstasy, a creative pride. He loved picture-making like some exquisite guilt.

The Atlantic City day would not turn sunny, the boardwalk was deserted but for a dog sniffing at discarded salt water taffy wrappings, and an old Negro polishing a brass store front plaque lettered *M. MUTTAH, TRUE GENUINE ANTIQUES*.

Back in the hotel room Sidney found Winnie the dancer finishing a huge breakfast brought up by room service; there were the remains of a ham steak smeared with egg yolk, a stack of pancakes, little jars of jam, a basket of hothouse fruit, and a glass of milk.

He took off topcoat and jacket, looked with admiration at the beautiful girl, blue-eyed, reddish mink-colored hair shingled and cut short in the latest fashion. She was twenty-two and claimed to be seventeen. He had first been attracted by her attitude of passive tolerance.

She stood up and her blue dressing gown opened, exposed her marvelous dancer's body, the golden fuzz of pubic triangle. She was unblemished, free of the estrangement of culture, and made his senses quiver.

"Get dressed. No games. I'll take you to the track."

She didn't close the robe but came to him and rubbed her cheek against his. She smelled of health, of bath lotion and a big breakfast.

"Don't you want some yum yum . . . ?"

He laughed and hugged her to him. "Don't you ever think of anything, honey, but yum yum?"

"Dancing, exercises, going to mass, sending money home, and *that*. I sure love you, S.S."

"Sure you do," he said. "Sure you do." It was good to hold this young wonderful body close, to inhale her readiness, press her provocative self closer to him. "That's what this fella needs. Love, Winnie, love. Never

6

enough of that." He looked into her periwinkle blue eyes, touched with his lips the naked shoulder and neck. In the hotel some place in the tea room below someone was playing an old war song, "Roses of Picardy," on a piano, and he thought I'm alive, this girl is alive, and so many other unlucky people are dead, either from the war or the great Spanish flu epidemic of '19. And with her for a short time I'm all alive. For some day, what will I leave? Miles of exposed film. True values are born in anxiety by foolish strivers like me. So there's the bed, here's this wonderful girl. A moment of passion merging into moments of fulfillment. The piano below was into long melodic phrases with a beat implied rather than fully explicit. He moved the girl toward the bed. If only he could ever be truly in love again, not just give way to desire.

The phone rang, and Winnie lifted the receiver. "Yayess, who's calling?"

"Hang up, honey."

"It's the studio, Hollywood, S.S. Boy, imagine all that distance, talking to us."

"Shit," Sidney said, taking the phone. "Hello, S.S. Who the hell is this?" He sat down on the bed, unbuttoning his waistcoat.

A thin voice full of electrical sounds in the background spoke. "Sorry, S.S., so sorry to break in on your vacation, but Agnes Waters has walked out on *Passionate Victory*. Wants a new director and an entire costume change. We don't know if—"

"Goddamn it! Nobody can do nothing." He turned to the girl. "Take my shoes off, Winnie." He spoke into the phone. "How many days we into shooting? . . . Two? Fire the bitch—let her sue . . . Keep the sets standing, I'm coming back. Now get cracking . . . How are things here?" He laughed, feeling cheerful and adequate. "I'm getting laid."

7

He removed his tie, began to unbutton his shirt. "Jesus, I hope your screen test turns out, honey—I'm putting you into a picture."

"Yummy."

Nat Bendell always tried to make the Saratoga racing season. It was a class track, ran good bloodline stock, and he liked to stroll the paddock, talk to the hot walkers, the trainers, gossip about the early horses, the Darley Arabian, the Godolphin Barb. He'd pass out cigars from a leather case taken from his impeccable tailoring, doff his tan bowler to Richard Canfield, Lillian Russell with Diamond Jim Brady, an Astor or a Whitney. Nat had missed a few seasons when he had that trouble with the Sicilians. But that was patched up, and he only rarely now looked around over his shoulder.

The war had changed the town—the Saratoga Clubhouse had retained some of its style, but Canfield was gone, and the new *new* money of the war profiteers was showing. There were more autos than carriages taking the natty betters to the track from the Grand Union. Nat had parked his own low-slung Mercer at the curb, his oversized binoculars slung over his shoulder. He looked as if he were about to become impatient with someone. Since his troubles he had developed a nervous, impetuous temperament.

There was a call from the curb in front of the hotel. It was his son, Teddy Binder. Nat thought how the Bendelbinder name had been cut up and rearranged in two generations. He himself had become Bendell in his early days when stage comics made fun of immigrant names, and his son Teddy (Roosevelt) Binder had been named that tail-end version by his mother Sonia, when the boy's first song was published.

("Go explain that to God," Aaron Bendelbinder had said to them about name changes at his birthday party.

8

"He doesn't keep a card index up there, *that* I'm sure.")

Teddy at twenty-one did not have his father's weight or handsome features. His head was too large, he was too thin, but he had a charming smile, a genteel yet blasé calmness. He dressed a bit like the actors who gathered in front of the Palace cutting up touches. A dotted bow tie, two-toned shoes, a straw boater all suggested his hero, George M. Cohan.

Father and son shook hands. "Damn train was late, Nat. And I missed the early one. Listen to this—Ziegfield, Ziggy, wants me to write three songs for his new show!"

"Great, kid, great. I'm happy for you. Now let's get to the track. I got something very special in the third." He looked around him and whispered, "A boatrace the jocks set up in the third. Red Robin, nice odds so far. Sixteen to one."

Teddy treated his father like a big, dangerous kid. "Who cares? I should of stayed in the city, begun work on the songs. But I promised you I'd be here. So—"

"Jesus, Teddy, have some fun. You've worked hard. All those cockamamy army shows, and now you jump right into show business again."

"I do my work, Nat, you do yours." He grinned. "Whatever *that* is."

Nat nodded to someone, tipped his bowler. As they got into the car, he remarked, "That was Bet-a-Million Gates . . . What I do? You know goddamn well I'm just serving the popular needs of the nation. An unpopular law is no law when it keeps a citizen from his natural rights."

"You read that in the New York *World*. Heywood Broun."

Nat glanced at his son, pressed his arm in affection. "Getting much?"

9

"If I want it."

Nat said, "Ha! Look, we're having a bit of shindig at one of the cottages tonight. Some of the real sports. There will be janes up from a show that closed in Boston yesterday. Fun and games."

"Thanks, but I want to work tonight. Besides, they get me to a piano at these parties and I'll just be banging away like the professor in a New Orleans whorehouse . . . Sonia has this nice girl she wants me to meet. She thinks I should seriously settle down."

Nat frowned at the mention of his wife's name. They'd been separated for years. He owed her some gratitude from the time he had been in trouble with the Sicilians, and that didn't sit well with him. He didn't like being obligated to anyone—especially to a woman, a discarded wife!

"Some damn Jewish princess she got on tap, I bet. Do you a favor to let you kiss her ass. Or one of those Yiddish Art Theatre actresses—some young *yenta* who does Ibsen, in Yiddish."

"I'm just going through the motions for Sonia. And I'm human—I could fall in love. Why don't you go see Sonia? Call her on the phone, send her flowers on her birthday? You're not just irresponsible, you're a shitheel about this, Nat."

His father swung the car around a tallyho with its four horses and a cluster of top hats and women in summer array on top. "Whitneys," Nat said. "They drive their own coach and four. They drink the stuff we bring down from Canada. The real McCoy, not the horsepiss the wops make in their bath tubs. And only I can call myself a shit-heel. Or get the hell out of the car!"

It was clear to Teddy his father didn't want to carry on a conversation about Sonia or his own shortcomings.

* * *

Years later Teddy was to think about how the Silverthorns and the Bendelbinders, three generations of them, seemed for a time not to focus properly on their lives, the joys, the chaos, the absurdities. Not until a stranger, a distant Silverthorn from Holland, Ira, entered their lives . . .

BOOK ONE

GENESIS

rolled from Sequanna. It never. He didn't have it
such as the color photos lined the yellow pale

1

Ira Silverthorn's father, Abraham Silverthorn, retired early from the family grain-importing business, in Amsterdam, claiming a weak heart, then spent his time collecting Callot prints and rare coins, lived a lonely widower's life. He claimed that Ira, at age sixteen, had "the manners of a baboon and the habits of a dockside boor." He never let Ira come into the room where the glass cases housed his rare coin collections.

As a child Ira spoke a careful English taught him by his English governess at Ramsdorp on the Zuider Zee. He was an impressive sight at sixteen, being six feet three, brown hair worn long, roached and carefully combed. He had what he admitted was a Jewish-Dutch face—solid, square, even handsome—and stubborn features. Ira moved well for such a large man, no slumping, but hardly (his father felt) a figure of grace.

As a youth, he had planned to become an engineer and design steam engines for city waterworks. After one wild year at the University of Leiden, he became an apprentice working at setting up pumping stations for the firm of DeBijenkorf and Vroom, whoring and drinking in his free time. The Silverthorn grain-importing uncles, incensed over his gambling debts, exiled him to Java, where the family had interests in a railroad from Semarang to Batavia. Ira didn't drink as much as the coffee planters, liked the yellow girls, smoked too much tobacco, and was hauled back to Amsterdam by Uncle Isaac to learn the family business under the uncles' watchful eyes.

At seventeen, Ira married a plump Dutch Jewish girl named Tina Rebecca Lisse. He had a house on the Molenstraat in Amsterdam, played cards, lost and won, joined the Kalverstraat shul, stayed fairly sober, and was dreadfully bored with the family, their pride, the good life, the row of houses of the best Jewish families bordering Keukenhof Gardens. Bored with Tina, who prayed in Hebrew *before* they made love and *after* they made love and felt it was not perhaps God's wish for a respectable Jewish wife to have orgasms, to enjoy copulation; she found herself liking it very much and guiltily suppressed her outcries.

By the time Ira was nineteen he had assumed the air of a knowledgeable young man in business, in cards, drink, the theatre.

He told Uncle Isaac he was not happy, that he was bored with cargoes of wheat, oats, rye, Java coffee, the tobacco bales from Sumatra that went into his cigars. He had become, for all his youth, skilled in handling people, but he did not feel any satisfaction in what other people called pleasure. When Tina was at her worst, whining, complaining of the servants, the snobbery of other women in their social set, Ira would often go up to the top floor of his house where Rembrandts, old Hebrew histories, leather trunks bursting with documents in Talmud lore were stored. Ira would drink good Dutch gin and curse his life and make long speeches to the spiders about the futility of human endeavor. It was all *doss*, crap. He was even more in despair when Tina announced she was with child. He saw no sense in bringing another human into a world of ledgers, his father's Callot prints, rare gold coins in stacks, the counting of sacks of coffee, and sniffing

16

racks of prime cigar leaf, golden or that special greenish Caro tone so liked by the cigar makers.

Tina died in childbirth, and the newborn son, called Pieter, was turned over to Uncle Isaac, the family patron, and Tante Hilda, his wife, to raise.

Ira didn't grieve. He had liked Tina, and at first had found her amusing and sensual. It had been a family-arranged marriage between old Jewish importing and banking families. He did not drink more. But as Uncle Isaac told him, "You're not drinking less either, Ira."

The Dutch Silverthorns considered themselves Sephardic-descended Jews, proud of the fact they had survived their expulsion from Spain centuries ago. They had settled as patriarchs in Holland as herring processors and grain and cloth importers and exporters. They did not, like distant relatives in St. Petersburg, the Silberdorns in Russia, work in precious metals, nor, as did some of the Amsterdam Jews, in polishing lens or cut gems. Their warehouses handled the demands for barreled fish and grains for bread and brewing.

While not given to mystical contemplation, they supported the Great Synagogue of red stone and rare woods, attended on High Holidays, were blessed at birth and ritually buried when their time came, sometimes with a *kaddish* for the soul of the dead in the Jewish cemetery. But the Dutch Silverthorns did not feel any special *Yiddishkeit*; few kept the kosher dietary rules.

Ira never thought much about religion. His family was Dutch, part of the Netherlands for generations. They felt none of the harrassment, the humiliation of the Eastern European Jews, tormented, bloodied by the pogroms of the Tsar and Polish anti-Semitism.

Yet it was an echo of that year of 1892 that turned Ira's destiny toward America.

17

2

Ira was this cold night drinking small glasses of Jenever gin at the Herring Club in Amsterdam, eating a dish of Rodekool mit Bloedworst, with raucous youths of his own age. The Herring Club was made up of funseekers, town sports, young men of good, solid middle-class families who at times drank a little too much, were active on the bowling greens, went after ducks with shotguns on the zees in the summer, in winter skated on the canals. They attended the livelier dance halls, bedded the bolder waitresses, milk maids, and barge women.

They were called wild by their elders, flibbertygibbets by the respectable, and considered themselves daring, full-blooded young men.

As Ira savored his red cabbage with black pudding and apples, a cousin of his, Chaim Hedrin, came in, a thin youth with a nose beet-red from the cold, tow-colored hair, and the red-rimmed eyes of a scholar who read too much.

"Ira, Ira! There are terrible things being done."

"I know, they're not publishing enough books for you to bury your head in."

Chaim looked over the table: two blond Dutchmen swallowing Zeeland oysters, and a black-headed Jewish bargee, Yossel the Barrel.

"Ira, listen, that Polish group in exile, they are printing the false *Protocols of Zion!*"

Ira blinked. "What the devil are those?"

Chaim gestured with a finger as if it were a dagger, gasped for breath, "You don't know? It's a dreadful document forged by the Tsar's secret police that states the Jews of the world are involved in a great plot to take over the world, a conspiracy to control all money and destroy Christianity. And much more. Lies, lies!"

Yossel the Barrel wrinkled his brow, laughed. "So let them, who would believe such drek?"

"Thousands do wherever it's distributed. Jews have been murdered." Chaim helped himself to a glass of gin, swallowed, coughed, gasped: "We must stop them!"

"There are the police," said one of the Dutchmen.

"Ha, it's a secret press, and by the time the police act the Protocols will be printed and distributed. The Poles have centuries of Jew-hating and Jew-killings behind them, and they also hate the Tsar. They are frustrated. They are outlawed and they need to attract attention."

Ira, who had stopped counting the number of gins he had drunk and who had hoped for an evening of a cozy card game out of the chilly weather blowing in from the wintery North Sea, slapped the tabletop. "So let's go break their Polak heads, smash their press, burn their damn Protocols."

"Why not?" asked Yossel the Barrel.

"It's not a lark," cautioned Chaim. "Hundreds of Jews have been murdered by people who read these things and believed them. Germany is flooded with them. They are even appearing in America, and they are believed not just by bigots or fanatics."

"Don't spit so when you talk, Chaim. Have another gin and we'll go smash them!"

Ira was feeling gay, ready for a caprice, the gin doing

its work on his mind and body. He picked up his heavy walking stick and said to the men around the table, "Who's with us?"

The two Dutchmen said, "Why not?"

Yossel found the club's crowbar. "Crush 'em like a blanc-mange."

Outside it was bone-chilling cold. A wet wind blew, rattling signs. People walked bent over, eyes to the cobblestones, the vapor of their breath preceding them.

The shutters were up on most of the shops on Roeterstraat, and the street was dark. Between a brass lamp shop and a sailmaker's loft was a low, yellow brick building given over to sailors' gear, rain capes, boots.

Chaim whispered, "The printing press is in back by the alley. Come, follow." There were barrels and crates in the alley smelling of tar and old rope. And a narrow plank door with one small pane of glass showing a yellow glow through a thin coat of paint.

Ira, sobering, his mind clearing, asked, "In there?"

Chaim, wiping his nose with the back of a glove, nodded. "In there."

Too late to turn back—and they were freezing. So without another word Ira smashed the glass with his cane and threw himself against the door. It gave with a tearing sound and he was in a small room smelling of a hot stove, machine oil, turps, and the paper stacked on raw lumber shelves. Three men were working a clanging hand press, one feeding sheets, one working a treadle, the other stacking printed paper under a hanging lamp.

With a loud cry of "*Smucks, goyische momzers!*" Yossel the Barrel attacked the press with his crowbar as Ira and the others charged the Poles, fists high. The cane flashed in the lamplight, striking a mighty blow.

"Polaks, Polaks!" cried Chaim.

The Poles were surprised but game. Still, in a few

minutes the press was scrap iron. One of the Poles had a broken leg, and Chaim was trying to stop a bleeding nose.

Ira had been hard put to gain an advantage over a wrench-swinging blond with a face deeply marked by smallpox, but exchanging blow for blow, with his cane, he at last hammered the Pole into a corner and heard the man's jaw snap as the cane got in a heavy blow.

Ira, panting, his hands shaking, looked about, saw the big, pot-bellied stove, and shouted, "Into the stove with everything!"

Chaim, blood pouring from one nostril, cried, "Everything!"

The walls were covered with crude drawings of hideous hook-nosed Jews with swollen circumcisions, Jewish women performing vile acts on nude men; over all were obscene slogans attacking Jewish rituals, habits with foul language in Polish, Dutch, and pidgin English:

Jews Rape Christian Wirgins . . . Hang all de Roth-schilders . . .

Chaim shouted, "We should burn the place!"

"No, no, the whole street would go up," said Ira. "Just smash everything, throw the type in the stove. Come on. I hear people gathering!"

They left, climbing a back wall, feeling good and also fearful. They needed, Yossel the Barrel said, a hot goodnight drink, which they got in a grog shop near a ship repair yard. A Bishoweyn punch-flavored drink with amboina cloves and Ceylon cinnamon.

The raid caused talk, an investigation, Ira had a black eye that turned rotten-egg purple on the second day. He was in awe at what he had done. The authorities questioned the Poles, except the one with the crushed jaw. The police found two of them were wanted for a political murder in Warsaw. The third was a nobleman who transported young girls to the Argentine for some sinister purpose. Dutch law was firm and serious.

Uncle Isaac felt it might be better for Ira not to be seen in the streets. Perhaps he should leave the country. Property was sacred to the frugal Dutch. The printing press had been owned by a local German who was an admirer of Grand Opera, particularly Wagner, and published a magazine on racial purity. He would begin legal criminal proceedings for the wrecking of the press, he told the police, once he was sure of the criminals. Yossel the Barrel and the two Dutchmen had signed in a hurry to take a string of barges to Kampen and Vollenhave. Chaim was in bed with a bad cold and a broken nose.

Ira was in Uncle Isaac's private office on van Stolkweg. "Maybe I'll travel to America. Life has turned to *pot-kesse.*"

Uncle Isaac, round, placid looking, who in his youth had kept a mistress in Paris, and wore a great ruby in his wide cravat, tapped a finger on a wine glass.

"You're what? Twenty? It's time you make up your mind. Stay here, get arrested. Yes, America. Become a *vrijbuiter*, a freebooter. I wish someone would have kicked my arse and said get away when I was a young man."

"Where did you want to go?"

"Like you, America. Ach, if only I had gone—gone to some log cabin, ridden a painted pony over great plains, shooting the bison and the red devils, impregnating beautiful squaws. Made myself an empire like Sutter did on the Sacramento, not *plock* down here."

"Sutter was ruined by the Gold Rush. You've been reading Fenimore Cooper, Uncle Isaac."

The old man chuckled, his chin shook. "Seriously, Ira, you can go to America and inspect a railroad gone to rack and near ruin. The family has invested in it."

23

"I didn't do too well in Java."

"Not bad either. You were young and foolish then, a head full of *rooleje*. You know how business is done. You're a good organizer, mean enough to coldcock a foreman or knock a fat-mouthed stevedore on his butt. Or Polish pogromist."

"A railroad in a wild land? It looks easy maybe sitting on your stoop here but . . ."

"It's a Lockridge Bank project. Papa and I and Uncle Aaron Brugger are shareholders. On our advice, the Zion Aid Society has most of their capital in the shares, and things have been going not too good for years. It pays, but not as expected. Lockridge people are looking for a sort of manager to report on things, to stiffen spines, kick arses. Gott, twenty years younger, and I'd be riding what they call there 'the high iron,' and pronging an Indian princess. Well, Ira?"

"They'll say I'm too young."

Uncle Isaac snorted as he lifted his glass of Jenever. "Nonsense, think on it! You'll have to say yes or you'll be arrested. I'm going to London for a stockholders' meeting at Lockridge."

"America."

"I'd give my right nut, nephew, to go myself," said Uncle Isaac."

Uncle, Ira recalled, was always offering his right nut in whispered confidences when something excited him. But, as far as Ira knew, he had not delivered.

Ira accompanied Uncle Isaac to London and sat under a row of darkening oil paintings of stern English portraits, dour Scottish faces, in a marble hallway while the inner oak doors of the private Lockridge Bank swallowed up his uncle. Ira watched a dandy in a fawn-colored coat taking snuff from a gold box while indolently lounging on a chair; an old lady with soiled dia-

24

monds and an ermine muff was talking to a small dog. The whole private banking establishment smelled of sea coal fires, ancient oak paneling, and old ledger paper giving off the odor of river damp and mold. Ira noticed the gold coins stacked behind grills that clerks counted and pushed into canvas bags. Somehow Ira felt the metal itself seemed indifferent to the business of trade, shares, trusts, estate holdings, stock issues.

Uncle Isaac came out to Ira with a glow that could only mean several glasses of port or sherry taken on.

"Come, come, Mr. Silas Attenstock wants to converse with you."

"Who the devil is Mr. Attenstock?" asked Ira, staring at a fecal-colored portrait on the wall.

"Director of Lockridge Bank's overseas investments. Oh, I've built you up to the skies—fifty percent profit in our interests in Java, 8,000 tons of cargo a month loaded in ports, strong as a *ploegpaard* when it comes to rail lines and . . ."

"Damn it, the Java Railroad is only three hundred miles."

"Jungle all the way, with crocodiles and poison dart guns."

"That's Borneo."

Uncle Isaac opened a carved oak door. "Ah, my nephew, Ira Silverthorn."

Mr. Silas Attenstock was a lean man with big blue eyes, a thin line for a mouth, and a habit of pressing the fingertips of both his hands together. He looked wise, amusing, and rather bored, but leaned forward solicitously as they talked.

"Ah, Mr. Silverthorn. Your uncle has supplied me information of your skills and your achievements. The Jewish House of Silverthorn is honorable, has always worked well with us . . . A spot of port? We also do some business with Alex Silverthorn of St. Petersburg."

Ira inspected a model of a ship-of-the-line on a table. "I've heard you also serve Scot whiskey."

"But of course. Scotch." He winked, reached for a cutglass decanter. "So you'd like to rub shoulders with the Americans?"

Ira knew from experience one must not seem eager, not to appear too fully to have made up one's mind. Yes, it would be good to get away to the wilds of that vast continent, to begin again, tear oneself away from one's life of too familiar surroundings. Some secret, unexplained potent urgency seemed to push him forward. "It's interesting, sir."

"Damn colonials are a driving lot."

After a half hour of parrying, nodding, sipping, burning some good Havana leaf, Silas Attenstock put a hand on Ira's shoulder, with an expression of near enthusiasm.

"We'll settle it then. You'll have to be in the West on the damn railroad. Try and see if our steam cars can really have a hope of reaching the Pacific, what?"

"If possible, Mr. Attenstock, can I see your reports?"

"Ah, we'll give you detailed tallies. We also have large land holdings along the California coast."

"You'll want me to look those over also?"

"They may be worthless. It's far from the eastern industrial scene."

It took another hour of talk for Ira's duties to be fully outlined, to be written out later in detail by lawyers. Payment to Ira, Uncle Isaac insisted, was to be of five thousand dollars a year, U.S.A. in gold coin, with allowances for living expenses. "Vittles, tucker and board," added Silas Attenstock, "as they call it there. All agreed then?"

Ira didn't feel too sure of himself when he shook Attenstock's firm, dry hand, and was told again he trusted Dutch Jews. As they left the banking house Ira was frowning. It all seemed the malleable stuff of dreams. Uncle Isaac sniffed the smoky London air; a pea-soup fog was already trying to blot out the lamplighter's glowing balls of orange flame being lit along Threadneedle Street.

"Ira, you will save the Zion Aid Society, it's orphans, old folk, the Jews escaping Russia." Hackney coaches and hansom cabs were passing with a clatter and a huge dray of ale kegs made a grinding noise. A lady with a head setting in velvet-and-moire stepped into a coach revealing a bit of leg. An old man sweeping the crossing—he was wearing Crimea War medals—touched his tattered cap as Ira handed him some copper coins.

"The best to you gents. Gaud bless."

Uncle Isaac was in a fine mood. "Well, Silverthorn, inspector of two streaks of rust in the wilderness. Let us have the best tonight. Beefsteaks, a brace of lobsters, crimped cod perhaps, and raspberry fool with a bit of Bar le Duc currant jelly for dessert. And champagne, of course."

"I hear that buffalo hump and raw gut is a delicacy west of the Mississippi."

"Not tonight." He tucked his nephew's arm under his. "We'll go see Madame Needle's banging shop later and look over the *nafkas*. No tits on them like a Dutch girl, but such *skin,* you never felt such skin."

"I don't see what there is to celebrate. We haven't seen their lawyers' contracts yet. Frankly, Uncle Isaac, do you like the English?"

Uncle Isaac held up a gloved hand, signaling a hansom cab with his gold-headed cane. "Yes and no. Your grandfather Mendel—rest in peace—used to say the only thing wrong about Westminster Abbey is that

27

there aren't enough English goyem buried there. He was cheated in a wool deal during the American civil war by a London firm."

"I suppose I'll need a brace of good pistols," said Ira.

"To go with you on this adventure, I'd give my . . ."

"Yes, Uncle, I know—your right nut."

3

The sleeping passenger in Cabin B2 of the Cunarder *Princonia,* moving in a fairly rough sea, was having a dream . . .

He was smiling as he turned from the mirror and said to the girl, "Well, you are a baggage, aren't you?

She smiled, admiring his nudeness. "Circumcision and all, look at you, like one of them gods they paint on theatre ceilings."

He became aware of his nakedness and reached for his robe, but the girl shed her green cloak with its red fox trimming and came to him and hugged him, all the time uttering little grunts of satisfaction. She was a raunchy, fiesty girl, and seemed always a ready woman. The passenger in B2 didn't mind. He was beginning to feel for this girl, and he responded more from pride in being able to prove his virility than actually from true desire . . .

The room changed to Baden Baden; she, fresh from the bath, aroused him, her hands cupping his behind. He sighed; it didn't take much to arouse him, only an appeal to his sexual vanity. In one way he felt sad at playing this game, without love, driven by mere lust, as now, carrying her to the leather sofa in an alcove off the bathroom. In another way, he decided, playfully kissing her neck, it was good to feel one's manhood flood one's loins. And this stranger—who was she?—

was desirable as she unbuttoned, unhooked, untied various undergarments, loosening the petticoats, the corset covers, the corset, the knee-length drawers. It was, he thought, ardent and eager, like peeling away layers of rinds to reach some succulent, well-guarded kernel . . .

Now they were in a tree top in the Swartzwald. She stood on a limb in red-striped stockings and high-button shoes, a very provocative and vital woman. They made love in a large bird's nest, violent, almost belligerent, in their exploring.

The passenger in Cabin B2 was close to awakening, pushing on the skin of dreams. He was out in a London street. Bond Street? Carriages, drays were splashing mud, people were coming out of pubs and shops. The sun shone and the town was going about in its confident manner as if every day a Dutchman was strolling there stark naked.

He swung a cane, banged it with resentment, even in doubt perhaps, against a horse rack as if (he smiled) the cane was a new extension of his sexual dream and as if he were punishing himself now.

Awakening, the sleeping recalled, "It is written in the Talmud—when I was at home I was in a better place."

The passenger in Cabin B2 of the Cunarder *Princonia* came fully out of his nightmare with a dry mouth and with a feeling in his stomach he had been eating hot coals. He was unaware of where he was for several moments, putting down the dizzy, twisting roll of the vessel to his own querulous condition, to some sort of sudden, shaking disease.

Ira Silverthorn tried to think, had a dim recollection of coming aboard in Liverpool, saying goodbye to some merry fellows, all much the worse from the wear of a night's carouse, of his being led down dark passages of a ship smelling of pea soup, engine oil, and bilge. But after that, nothing but the night's tattered remains of his indecent dreams.

He remained prone, legs braced so he would not roll off the hard, narrow bunk. He was in a cabin painted gray with one brass porthole showing a dipping and diving horizon, the glass streaked with salt spray. An oil lamp swung from the ceiling, and he gagged at the stale residue of seasicknesses long impregnated in the cabin. The ramifications of his condition came back. He was off to America. The new promised land of so many Jews escaping the horrors of Russia.

He sat up, saw he was wearing socks of brown wool, a shirt with a collar missing, his trousers nowhere in sight. He reached under the soggy pillow—it felt like some disagreeable small animal—and found the heavy leather wallet secured by a brass buckle. His papers, his money, his letters of credit to Starkweather & Company, Boston were all there by the feel of his wallet. A carpet bag slid across the floor of the cabin; the Cunarder was rolling badly. What fantasy had brought him this far? Visions of America? He set his feet on heaving floor, held on, and the cabin spun at an angle, in his vision. He closed his eyes and when he opened them again, the cabin wasn't spinning; just the heaving remained and the acid complaint of the last drink before embarking. He recalled Uncle Isaac and some Jewish resident importers from Liverpool. First a meal of mandlen soup, gefelte fish, piroshkis, strudel, fruit compote, then on the town. It was all a vague painting produced by memory: no, not a painting, just a pencil sketch of a cafe, of naked thighs dancing the can-can, and so much wine . . .

He saw a water pitcher deep set in a wooden stand and crossed the cabin to it. He drank gulps of tepid water from its mouth, swished more through his lips and teeth, and spit it out into the basin under the stand,

31

moaning all the time. Pitcher and basin were lettered in blue: *Princonia*, Cunard Steamship Line. At least he was on the right vessel, even with a skull-cracker of a headache resulting from that wild Gadarene leavetaking party.

The cabin door banged open, the ship seemed to stand on its beam end, and in came a tall, thin man with a head of curly black hair, eyes of a sad dog, a whip-thin moustache with curled-up ends. The man skillfully balanced a linen-covered tray. He had the narrow body, long bony arms, of an animated silhouette, a tragic-comic smile.

"Ah, you are up, Mr. Silverthorn?"

"No. I'm dead. It's Judgment Day."

"Hardly that."

The tray carrier was dressed in a collarless blue flannel shirt and a hammertail coat a bit too large, checked trousers, and polished sharp-toed shoes, a bit cracked. He pulled off the napkin, presenting a pot, a tea cup, and some thick-cut slices of bread smeared with yellow and red jams.

"Thought you'd like a cuppa and a bit of filler this morning."

"God, no. Maybe just some tea."

"Of course. It's still hot. Damn near took an arser—deck's very wet."

Ira managed to swallow half a cup of tea, his head paining as he looked at the man smiling at him.

"Thank you, Mr.—?"

"Kalman—Janos Kalman, *nebech* the headaches? Happy to be in your service."

"In *my* service?" He felt a hilarious spectacle in shirt, drawers, and socks.

"Yes, sir. Traveling secretary, bookkeeper, letter writer, a man of trouble." He gave a military salute and clicked his worn-down heels. Janos Kalman, who appeared in his late twenties, showed the wary resignation of an abused hound.

"I don't need a secretary."

"Your uncle felt you did."

"What the devil . . . Uncle Isaac."

"You're sure you'll not eat some bread and jam? Food would help you. Give you your sea well-being. There are kippers in the dining salon, coddled eggs, perhaps some tapioca pudding?"

"Damn you, no. Just how were you hired?"

The youth bit into a wedge of bread and chewed thoughtfully. "Jolly old *momzer*, with you at the Red Lion Inn on Queen Street. We were, as gentlemen, discussing rates of exchange, guldens, marks, liras, letters of credit. I was pleased, happy, actually, to take service with the inspector of the Great Plains and Pacific Steam Cars."

"Oh, were you?"

The man's English accent was slurred, a bit singsong. Ira searched his memory for a clue to its origin. Lyric, petulant, a tone of heightened perceptions.

"You're Austrian—Viennese."

"Close, sir. Magyar *yoi istenem* from Budapest, graduate of the Debrecen School of Accounting, former Hasidic rabbinical student in the Toaj yashiva. Much experience as bank shares clerk with Tobbins and Klagton in Manchester—and of late—" Janos Kalman shrugged his narrow shoulders—"this and that. *Oysgematert*—worn out."

Ira, whose head was clanging a bit less, handed back the cup. "Been in gaol?"

Janos rolled his big, dark, liquid eyes to the ceiling. "Gott forbid. Mistakenly held and released. As a student of the Mishnah and the Talmud and the systems of Adam Smith, my life is based on live and let live. If you follow me, sir."

33

Poor bastard, one of Europe's wandering, homeless Jewish intellects. Ira saw the youth trembling for all his cheerful expression.

"You're strapped, broke?"

"On the balls of my arse, sir, as the Limeys say. But you'll find me a *mensh* good with figures. I write a splendid hand. I am loyal. As the great Nebemiah said, 'The man whose bread I eat, that's whose man I am.' "

"All right, Kalman, stop trying to impress me. If Uncle Isaac hired you, and if he was fairly sober . . ."

"Fairly, sir, a good Dutch *kop* on him. Would you like what the Americans call some hair-of-the-dog?"

"Hair of the . . . ?"

Janos put down the tray and from under a bunk reached inside a worn, leather carrying case with repaired stitching and came up with a long-necked bottle.

"Slivowitz, Polish plum brandy. I haven't seen it raise the dead, sir, but it's shaken up the living."

Ira swallowed some of the fiery brandy in a tea cup and had to admit it perked him up, his stomach responding with a discreet gurgle.

"Ever been to America?"

"In a way, sir. By letters. My Uncle Simon trades in cattle in St. Louis, and a cousin of my mother—may she rest in peace—Ben Mandelman in Kansas City, has a livery stable—deals in wheat and other grains. You'll find I have connections everywhere, sir."

"I said stop impressing me. You have the damn position, and if you don't work out properly, I'll kick you out. Where the devil are my goddamn pants?"

Janos lifted a mattress from a bunk across the way and presented a pair of dark wool trousers. A student's trick of neatness, Ira recalled.

"I must say, sir, a fine bit of wool. And I'll rinse out some of your shirts. You have, I suppose, neglected your laundry in England."

"Only there six days. Where are my trunks?"

"Below. I think you'd feel better on deck, a brisk promenade, to bring color back to your cheeks."

"In this storm?"

"No storm. Just a bit of rocking. *Einer Herd ist Goldes wert.*"

"Where did you learn German?"

Janos held out a shirt toward Ira. "For a time, I was married to a woman who ran an inn near Reienbach. Cooked everything in lard. I nearly died. It's a period of my life I'd rather not talk about. Ah, here's your collar—needs starch. Will you wear the plum-colored cravat or the pale blue one?"

By the third day out there was a sky the blue of a Dutchman's pants. The ship was steady, the British cuisine not as bad as one expected. A mild flirtation with an Irish lady had no time to reach a climax. Ira enjoyed walking the deck, sharing his little Waldman cigars with Janos, studying maps of western America. Janos proved to be a good map reader, wrote in a neat, not-too-ornate hand, and could quickly decipher complicated columns of figures. A surviver of a hard world of Eastern European anti-Semitism.

Ira refused to let the man shave him, but he let himself be talked into an American drink Janos mixed in the bar salon. Janos claimed it was called a horse's neck. "Learned it from a New Orleans man traveling in the south of France. Yes, there was a time I was a waiter in a pension at St. Tropez. That is how I got these flat feet."

Janos also claimed to be a refugee from military service. His eyes at times were sad and weary, but mostly he displayed a wry humor, and his shabby wardrobe, what there was of it, did have a stylish cut.

35

Ira brooded over a three-foot-square map of the United States, its vast territories filling up in the West, and he wondered about what he would find of the assets of the PG&P. As the trip drew to a close he felt like a somnambulist walking through unknown halls.

When land came up in the west under a mackerel sky, just a scribble of earth and deep green, he stood on deck, the wind whistling through riggings, Janos by his side, offering him a pair of brass-bound field glasses.

"New England, sir." He said it as if making Ira a gift of it.

"I feel like Moses seeing the Promised Land."

"Boston, sir. They eat baked beans and codfish. Very strict set of sexual moral values. A tradition of living off one's interest, *never* off one's capital."

"Get my trunks up."

Boston presented a busy waterfront, wharves packed with kegs and crates, the streets narrow and stony, new houses side by side old ones, bells ringing. The citizens spoke as if from clogged bronchial tubes. Signs indicated merchants—Weltons, Kinglets, Kahns, Spinellis, Condons, Cohens (also Cohns), Stillwells, Caseys, Pembrokes. Blacks, too—Negroes of all shades of black to tan.

Cather Starkweather, the younger member of Starkweather & Company on State Street, was cheerful and helpful. He gave Ira U.S. gold coins and paper money in exchange for his pound notes and Dutch gulden.

"Don't take change in money we call shin plasters, or script, or notes issued by local banks. It's 1892, modern times. No danger. But I suppose you'll carry a pistol. The Western natives still use weapons with a certain provincial carelessness, and often."

"Lockridge's man spoke of detailed maps."

"Of course." Cather Starkweather took up a pen,

dipped the steel nib in a pewter inkwell, and began to write in an elegant hand on a sheet of pale yellow note paper.

"The firm is Blakewell and Blondell. Did maps for the Vanderbilt rail lines. The address 17 Clark Street. Don't be surprised," Cather Starkweather coughed and touched his lips with a finger, "if it's a bit rough yet in the West—hard men with their fists always ready. You'll find travel not frugal, the food on the trains high; on my last journey to Pittsburgh, oysters were fifty cents a dozen, steak sixty cents, a whole lobster fifty cents. Whiskey is still ten cents a shot glass, but you can't get a good madeira or claret west of Kansas City, not till you get to San Francisco."

"I hope to eat buffalo."

"Well, Mr. Silverthorn, it's everyone to his taste, isn't it? You will get venison on the trains, woodrock, plover. Oh, but they're not kosher."

"I'm not very ritual."

"Anything else I can be of help with, Mr. Silverthorn?"

"I'll use the mail if I need your splendid advice or the telegraph if I get in trouble."

"If you need attire, we have several fine emporiums. You do appear eager to start."

Ira smiled. "As I heard a sailor put it, you bet your sweet ass."

"Really?" Mr. Starkweather had offered no sherry or port as the English had over a business transaction. "I would suggest you see something of our city, the Arnold Arboretum, the Atheneum. Could I offer you a chowder with Indian pudding at Pattens? No? In a hurry. Well, to get where you want you take the steam cars south, connect with the Erie in Buffalo, to Chicago, then on the Chicago and Northwestern. Beyond there are several routes to where you're going. The GP&P is working rails in western Kansas. You'll find our firm alert to your needs. They should be in Colorado near mountains."

"Yes, they should."

When Ira joined Janos guarding their baggage, he said, "Damned unprejudiced, these Bostonians, at least when dealing in money."

Janos shooed some station pigeons away from Ira's hat box, "I've seen no painted savages. The women are rather *zoftig*, don't you think, sir? Long legs under the petticoats, one would guess."

Ira thought of the Irish lady on board the Cunarder and wished he had followed up his first advances.

The two men saw an impressive surge west as they journeyed in a busy nation. Most amazing were the packed immigrant trains carrying what a station master told Ira were "Slovaks, swenskies, bohunks, micks, and dagos hunting something. Also the land-boom lawyers, damn sharks—and the ragtag and rabble of gamblers, painted women."

Ira found them all traveling with hope of land, of gain. There were Jewish pack peddlers, also Slavs with bundles tied with ropes, and trunks and boxes of all kinds.

The great escape from the Czar's pogroms had begun. Most of the Jewish women wore head cloths; the more flashy females from Warsaw, Moscow, St. Petersburg dressed in finery a bit tattered or soiled but with feathered hats perched on odd-colored hair and froufrou of ribbons and buttons gallantly worn. A few families traveled in groups with servants and governesses. But most of the Jewish humanity was poor and earnest, packed in cars lit by smoking oil lamps and warmed by rusting iron stoves. Everyone became cinder-stained

38

when the windows had to be opened for air. Once Janos beat out a live cinder smoldering in someone's hair.

"They're all not going to build railroads?" said Janos chewing on a stale bread and cheese sandwich bought at a railroad restaurant.

"They're going to build something, these people," said Ira looking over a time table smudged with damp ink.

"They could be the children of Israel in the wilderness. Only with packets of herring and stale bread."

As Ira in later years told of his trip West, it was clear he had enjoyed it all.

Mingled with homesteaders and those in peasant clothing from the villages of Europe were rough men in red flannel shirts, often greasy from camp cooking. Even so, there were the boiled shirts and elegant waistcoats of the gamblers, land boomers, park packers, also folks called "God thumpers,"—"fanatic-eyed Methodists," Janos said, "deep-dip Baptists, cultists of vague new religions that don't kill Jews."

Ira noted flawed diamonds and tried to overlook the reek of unwashed bodies; sometimes the painted ladies added a sweetish, unhealthy scent.

A jolly Jewish German, plump in a red waistcoat, said to Ira as they neared Chicago, "The East, it's packing up and moving West, for sure. The cities are getting smoky and the slums rotting away. It's the last chance some feel to get away. Of course," the man smiled, showing a splendid gold tooth, "some of them are running from the law. You know, bankrupts, embezzlers, and black sheep. If you're smart, you buy land. They're not making it anymore, ha ha. My father *gesagt, getan* came to this country in '49 to fine gold, did well building wagons."

"Is there room for all these people?"

"Room, mister?" He pulled a broadside from his Prince Albert coat pocket. "Glad you asked. This here is town plans for the best little new city you ever seen. A smart man just gotta want to invest in this greenest sweetest acres Gott ever made. Out in Keinmeyer Center, Kansas. Not built up yet, but if you get in on the ground floor for say a hundred acres or some good corner lots right on Main Street, why, you'll double your money in five years. I'm no *luftmensh* but I say what's right for you. Fifty-fold in ten years. Let me show you."

But Ira didn't buy that land. He said to Janos, as the youth dusted him off from train cinders as they chugged into Chicago, "It's all to the good, this westward movement. I'll get the PG&P's rails over the damn mountains come hell or high water."

Chicago, Ira found, still had wooden sidewalks in some places and deep mud where streets had not yet been set with bricks. But the city was building at a fast pace and the air was smoky with progress.

The PG&P Railroad had a representative in the city, a Roy Minton, who was to turn over to Ira a report of the actual condition of the railroad's progress. Lockridge Bank had found him but Ira couldn't. The telephone company had no Roy Minton on their subscriber list. When Ira and Janos found the Rifkin Building on LaSalle Street, Minton's last known address, the Polish janitor said, "Not here long time. Maybe six, seben months. Don't know where he go."

Ira looked in a little notebook he carried. "The railroad has a shipping supply office on what they call the South Side. Maybe they'll know of the missing Roy Minton."

Janos said, "We're chasing a dybbuk's fart."

The shipping office was more like a long shed, haunted by crates and bundles of freight that seemed to have lost labels.

Jack Harper, in an office labeled MANAGER, was built for wear: large, with a wide paunch; he was smoking a corncob pipe and twirling a long yellow moustache.

"Roy? That yellow-bellied sonofabitch," he laughed and groaned. "He skedaddled, and I don't know nothin' about no report. But I think I can find him for you. He's a great lad for the fancy hurrs . . . *hurrs*—that's what I said."

4

"We are in the Levee district," said Jack Harper. "For the real hurr parlor, Roy Minton he likes the Bevin Girls' Club. Sisters they are. Took two big Chicago houses, made them one by cutting doors through and furnished them tiptop, no bullshit." The big man with the weathered moustache smiled and closed one blue eye. "Like a goddamn king's palace. Real marble bathtubs for two or four, a gold-plated piano, and swellsmelling fillies that respond to you and swaller only bubbly and can jabber in French. Real fancy hurrs."

They got out of the open carriage in front of a sedate building with a marble horse block out front at the curb. "We'll find Minton here?" said Ira.

"Almost any night. He runs some kinda racket. Now, Mr. Silverthorn, don't this street look ready for anything?"

Ira had to admit it did. The levee that came up from the river was, he had been informed by Jack Harper, the sporting district of the city where politics, gambling, and vice were major projects. He observed the saloons with their great gilt signs—malt-scented places lit by gas flares. A passing parade of carriages and hackney coaches filled the street rimmed by crowds of sporting gents, women in finery by their side or casually strolling.

"It's all protected by aldermen and judges, taking the

boodle here and taking it there," said Jack as they mounted the neat stone steps between ornate iron railings. "You're safer here than in your own home."

"You come here often, Jack?"

"Well, now, only if I'm showing someone the town."

The big white door with the brass knocker in the shape of a mermaid was opened by a black butler wearing white gloves. "Gentlemen, you are welcome to Bevins' Club. Your hats and outer garments, please."

The hall was hung with heavy gold-framed pictures, scenes of Roman orgies—painted, Ira suspected, by untalented but sensual sign painters. There were also bronzes of nymphs being carried off by goat-footed fauns.

The heavy scarlet carpeting was complemented by red velvet drapes and flaring gas jets behind etched crystal globes. The odor of wet cigars, starched linen, and overripe hothouse fruit permeated the house.

A redheaded woman, no longer young but still attractive, held out a gloved arm to Jack Harper.

"Aren't you the stranger, Jack."

"Lo, Nance. We're looking for Roy Minton. This here is Mr. Silverthorn, a business friend of Roy's, from Europe."

"Why of course, Roy usually drops in."

She showed them into an overornate small room of gold and red and left. A maid brought champagne and glasses. The chairs were comfortable, a small fire winked at them from a tiled fireplace. Whoremongering in America could be impressive, Ira mused.

"They don't come no finer than this place."

"How many miles a day of rail is the P G and P laying?"

Jack sipped the wine. "Damn this stuff. Rails, who knows?" He whispered confidentially, "Ring for whiskey. This is la-de-da stuff. I've been over this survey map. I've done a bit of nosing around here and there. It's going West over rough high places. And a rotten lot of bosses in charge.

"I know it's aggravating." Ira pulled a bell rope. "That bad?"

A maid came in. Ira said, "Oh, some whiskey and a terrine of foie gras if you have it."

"Kentucky sour mash," added Jack Harper. "Now don't buffalo-crap me. Is this a real railroad or just a bunko share-selling scheme from Europe?"

"I'm here to find out. You see a charity organization has invested its capital, hoping to continue to work from the income."

"Your people think they can set up a line to compete against the Central and Union Pacific?"

"They were talked into it."

"Some people, Mr. Silverthorn, could sell shit to a stockyard."

"Baldwin is building us bigger engines, and in London I was told of the designs for a Grant class C-16-60 that can take a 36-feet-to-the-mile grade."

"You really serious?"

"One should be, Jack. I've got to get all the facts."

"Yeah . . ."

They drank the whiskey and Ira tried the foie gras as Jack waved his arm around the room. "Now this is a business. The whole place is like this. Nance and Netta, they know how to make a gent comfortable. Businesswomen, both of them, right down to their lace drawers. Southern aristocrats, they claim. Come on, let's get Nance to show you around."

"Be delighted," said Nance when the maid informed her that the men wanted to see her. "Just now some of the best rooms are not engaged, you might say."

Jack patted her corseted rump. "Always the little businesswomen."

"And don't you forget it."

The Gold Room, Ira saw, had fish bowls on gold stands. "Solid gold spittoons at $700 each, and a gold piano priced at $15,000," Nance said.

Ira tried a few of the keys. The piano was in tune.

"We have thirty boudoirs for our ladies, mirrors on the ceiling for easy viewing of the guests' desires, a big bouncy bed, oil paintings of the usual subjects—fun in the woods and lots of flesh being chased."

Ira said, "Impressive."

"On some nights we let loose boxes of live butterflies in the parlors and boudoirs."

Jack said, "No man is going to forget he got his balls fanned by a butterfly here."

A maid whispered in Nance's ear.

"Gents, follow me. Roy is here."

Nance knocked on a paneled door and opened it. A naked girl stood at a large mirror adjusting a bit of blue ribbon in her hair; a young man in his shirt sleeves sat in a chair tossing playing cards into a hat on the floor.

"Roy," said Nance, "you got company. Julie, you get into a robe and go down to the Turkish Room."

Ira said, "I'm the man sent over by Lockridge Bank."

The young man sighed. "See you later, Julie. Hello, Jack. Find chairs. I been meaning to get in touch with London."

"I'm Ira Silverthorn."

"Sure, well . . ."

In the next half hour, in the room smelling of strong scent and sandalwood soap, Roy Minton told his story. Drink seemed to have oiled his tongue—he smiled, rocked back and forth in his chair, shook a finger in the air, and talked without much urging.

"All right, all right, I've been rambunctious, I've been neglecting my so-called duties to the P G and Piss

Railroad. But what the devil is it anyway? I was hired by Lockridge to oversee the building of the rail line as a watchdog and when I talk to the contractors, when I get in touch with London, what do I get, huh?"

"They withheld information from you?" Ira asked.

"Not altogether. But, oh, the buggers played it close to the vest. What information I got didn't jibe. I wasn't paid my salary last three months and my expense accounts were questioned. Fastidious bastards. Hell, I didn't pad much. I had debts. I had a family, two darling little girls, a wife. Well, they've gone off some place. I had to find something to do. Got a leg up as a beer broker for the saloons and selling the banging shops. But it's a pittance, I tell you. Is there water in that pitcher? I'll have a glass."

Jack Harper and Ira exchanged looks while Minton swallowed a glass of water with a gulping sound. He wiped his mouth with the back of a hand and smiled. "So, Silverthorn, how do smart Jews in Holland get taken in this kind of scam? Yes, sure there is close to three hundred miles of rails laid down. But no connections, junction points between the big transcontinental lines, for us to haul goods, crops, or encourage passengers. Do they really want to produce a carrier or just sell shares to you Europeans? That's the crux. Do they?"

"I don't know," said Ira. "Now about that report I'm to study."

"Report? Hell, it's just a basket of wastepaper. Nothing matches. I tried, God knows, flabbergasted or not. I tried to get something together. Drove me to drink and to the whores. Oh Julie is a nice girl. I don't claim I'm better than her, and . . ."

"Can I get this, this basket of paper?"

Minton made a querulous mouth. "If you want to. I'll bring it over to your hotel. Parker House? Tomorrow morning? But I demand my back pay. In full. Fair?"

"Fair," said Ira, "if there's anthing valid in it. Really informative."

"Ha. It's not really a calamity. You'll see it's got good prospects. But shoddy planning, grafting contractors, cooked books, but . . . God, I need a drink, gentlemen. Oh, do I need a drink."

Dear Uncle Isaac: From my last letter you know I am deep in this nation you call Amerika. (They spell it with a "c.") It's not at all what we think it is, and I'm learning more and more about it and the natives' characteristics and attitudes to progress.

As I wrote I have been going through the papers that were to be a deep, searching report by this Minton who was running the rail-line office here in Chicago but panicked and ran. He's a loose-living, weak character, demoralized, but I think honest in the sense he tried; in the ambiguity of the situation, it was all too much for him. Lockridge Bank wasn't interested enough in the actual material and of building a rail line and, I fear, only in selling shares. A Mr. J.P. Morgan of Wall Street has for some time been reorganizing the whole American rail system, which he founded, like the PG&P, in a dreadful mess of mismanagement, corruption, and dangerous, faulty rolling stock. Morgan is a diagnostician of money and banking power, doing a fine job, merging railroads, blending and cutting out the dead wood. But I fear our line is too small to interest him. However, I'll put out feelers.

I leave with my assistant Janos Kalman to visit the railhead at Sawtooth Mountain, someplace beyond Kansas City and over the Colorado border, near the outcroppings of the Rockies. I am learning to drink bourbon whiskey, smoke Pittsburg stogies, carry a pistol, a Smith & Wesson. Weapons here are often a balance in the perilous equilibrium of survival.

The other night I was in a posh brothel on what they call the Levee in Chicago, not to sample the rustle of taffeta of the merchandise, but to catch up with this Roy Minton. What an establishment—gold-plated pianos and long-legged girls in and out of frou-frou with large, slim bodies you don't see in Europe. You would have given your left you-know-what to have been there. Minton told me a great deal, which I am putting in shape for you.

I have decided one thing. I am becoming an American. It's a melting pot, as some writer put it, and it has made a strange foray into my bloodstream. Poles, Germans, Russian Jews, what they call "niggers," right out of *Uncle Tom's Cabin*. Overall a perilous veneer of Irish who in two generations have seized the political systems in most of the large American cities. They are called Bosses. You've heard of the Tweed Gang, Honey Fitz, Crocker and others? It's a free-for-all system, grab what you can and be democratic when you steal. Belmont, who used to be a Jew, is accepted by society. In Boston, Jews and Italians are helping form a political machine with the Irish to fully overthrow the last hint of power of the Pilgrims and puritans. Very interesting, how quickly things are done here and how everyone has hopes of good fortune. Chicago is a bellowing pandemonium of stockyards, dealers in commodities, and street traffic of carriages and wagon drays.

At the moment I have the idea the rail line can be salvaged, put in some sort of working condition. Then you and your friends and the Zion Aid Society can sell your shares at a better price than now, and may even turn a proft and help bring more people out of the hell of the Czar's Russia.

With love,

     Ira

  ("Big Dutch," as some call me here.)

5

The Canadian geese flying south and, along the Deer River, the cottonwoods and aspen were beginning to lose their leaves. It was the last burst of the earth's effort to keep its colors before winter came. Beyond Construction Camp 5, the bald tops of Sawtooth Mountain were already icy blue with snow in the creases. Camp 5 of the P G and P consisted of fifty shacks that could be taken apart and moved off on flat cars, three Baldwin locomotives, work engines, and two dozen railroad coaches, among them the private car *Aspen.*

Wood smoke hung over the hollow in which the camp was situated. Here Ira had found a rough camaraderie existed in spite of Saturday night brawls. Log roads had been laid out from the main blacksmith forge, the supply sites set up on the mired meadows of buffalo grass, mule bush, wild hay, and vetch grass. The track was coming near Sawtooth Pass, and Ira was told it hoped to get across the 1800-foot rise before the heavy snows came.

The engineer in charge, an Australian named Nobby White, was double-heading his work trains, using two engines for the pass approach. The crews were padding their work denims and quilted jackets with bits of blankets and sheepskins.

At the main forge they were working on a red-heated driving rod that had been bent. The flat cars' wheels bringing up the rails made shivery *yong yong* sounds as cold metal met cold metal.

Ira, wrapped in a wolfskin coat, came out of the private car into the blue chill of morning. The wind was driving the camp debris of old paper, bits of rags, and brown leaves along the paths between the shacks and against the gray canvas tent walls of the cookhouse. Men were chopping up logs for firewood, their axes flashing in the captured light of a wan sun.

Ira shivered in spite of the high fur collar and dug his hands deep into his pockets. Weather, damn it, to cause a disintegration of the work quotas Nobby White had set.

He watched a six-mule team strain for a rise toward the tracks; whips snapped to the foul language of the skinners riding a load of ties. Nobby White, perched on top of the load, was smoking a short clay pipe, his red leathery face unshaved, a heavy yellow scarf tied over his hat and ears.

"Great day, Mr. Silverthorn," he shouted, his breath producing a thin cloud of vapor. "For bloody polar bears."

"Damn cold."

"Cold as Kelsey's nuts. But good-o weather to get a day's work from the track layers."

"How far from the pass?"

"Ten miles, as the crow flies. Only we ain't crows. Gotta build two bridges, grade at least six ravines."

Ira nodded. "Lockridge hopes you'll be across before the winter."

"We'll give it our best try."

Ira entered the car and threw off his coat into the arms of Sam, the black valet. The car was filled with the warmth of a big pot-bellied with its silver-colored trim and the smell of unaired living. In the main section, Janos Kalman, wearing a green muffler around his head and neck, was rubbing his red hands together while seated at a wall table over a collection of papers stuck on a spindle.

"You cold, Janos? Try some Armagnac in black coffee."

"I can't get warm. At the Lubavitcher Yeshiva in Zatomer, the rabbi's wet nose always had a frozen drop on the end of it. But it never got as cold as this there."

"Well, is this a railroad or not?"

Janos pulled some papers from the spindle, shuffled them around, took up a piece of thin blue paper.

"White appears honest. But the contractors for ties, rails, and mules are not really delivering all they bill us for."

"If we cancel our present contractors, we'll not get new supplies delivered till spring. I telegraphed San Francisco."

"Can't we find contractors with steel rails in Kansas City, Chicago?"

"Yes, but they can't fill orders in a hurry."

Ira took a pot of coffee off the stove and poured two cups. He handed Janos one. "Well, to pass the time White says for winter warmth it's a nice fat squaw covered with bear grease and smelling of wild garlic."

Janos didn't respond.

"White, he'd screw a snake if somebody held it down."

Janos shuffled through a batch of mail. "Some of the Pawnee girls are very beautiful. Lots of French trapper blood there."

"What can I report on work here?"

Janos sipped his coffee. "As you said, sir, if we don't get through Sawtooth Pass by the first really big snowfall, we're stuck here till spring."

"The road will be bankrupt by then."

"Brought the mail train in by Gordon Creek. There's a letter marked *personal*."

"Oh?" Ira took the envelope. It had a Netherland stamp; the handwriting was Uncle Isaac's.

Ira sat down by the frost-etched main window on the right side of the car and opened the envelope. There was still in him the tug of memory of the past in Holland, even if he knew he would stay here and as an American:

Dear Ira:

Your news is not of the best. As you know, half of the Jewish businessmen encouraged our Zion Aid Society to invest heavily in those damn railroad shares, and Lockridge Bank—a solid firm—in good faith felt it had splendid prospects. But they have also become involved in Argentina cattle ranches and have built railroads there to carry the steers to the beef packing plants. So overextended as they are, and with hoof and mouth disease reported, there are strong hints they may close their doors. If this happens, there will be much lamenting at the High Holidays as support for the Orphan School, the Old Age Home, the Hebrew Immigration Society, which helps the miserable Jews escaping the Tsar's pogroms, all will be left without enough funds. Perhaps it was foolish to put the Zion Aid Society funds into Lockridge shares. But for fifty years the firm was solid as the stone tablets of the Ten Commandments. Now we can only hope for some miracle.

If the rail line can be made to show some progress, then the shares will stop falling in value and we may be able to sell them at somewhere near what they cost us, if we can find buyers. We have

54

had one offer to trade them for some land in California. Who knows?

What else is new? Your father is locked in with his collections of coins and prints. The outer world doesn't exist for him. The sea has broken a bit through the dikes at Ijssimeer, but was plugged without too much damage. Remember Yossel the Barrel, the bargee, with whom you broke the heads of some Polak anti-Semitic bigots? Yossel has married a rich elderly widow in the cheese export business and sports a double gold watch chain and has presented a Torah to the Beth Israel Doelen Street shul.

I am as well as an old man with stiff joints can be. Add a blasphemous liver and gout in one toe.

People are getting old who were never old before. But as the Chassidin chant tells us: *V'tahhair libanu l'avd choh beehmess*, purify our hearts to serve Thee in truth. Look forward to your return.

Isaac

The stab of homesickness was strong in Ira as he finished reading the letter; but he was more disturbed by the plight of the PG&P and its effect on the Zion Aid Society. As Uncle Isaac had written in his last letter, "Money isn't something you throw off the back of trains."

Nobby White and even Janos might go to the Indian girls down the line, but he himself just then had no time or the desire for anything but getting track over Sawtooth Mountain.

"Damn, goddamn," he said, hoarsely. Janos lifted his head from his work but said nothing. A man with trouble was only natural in the way the world rolled. Janos had come to see that one faced situations with trepidation and with often emotional mistakes. Janos sighed as he cleaned a pen point and thought of Willow, the Pawnee girl he was courting with canned salmon, and not getting much more out of it as yet than giggles and a blow across the face from time to time.

Ira put on his coat, burrowed his neck down into the wolf collar, and went again into the chilly day. With a truculent expression he walked past work crews piling ties and the mule pens where the braying and flying hoofs greeted men trying to harness the animals for a work shift. A foreman shouted, "Hit them with an axe handle to get their attention."

Ira said, "But don't kill them. They cost seventy-five dollars each."

Ira got onto a handcar set on the rails and pumped himself the two miles to the end of the line. Brooding on imminent and inevitable problems, he breathed hard, surrounded by the vapor pouring from his mouth.

It had seemed such a lark to escape from arrest in Holland, cross the sea, travel West. Now the fun of it was gone. He panted, pumped the car forward, and decided damn all obstacles, he'd get the rails through the pass.

The track ended by a cut of granite and crimson salicornia in a clutter of work cars, a lonely locomotive breathing black smoke from its high stack into the chilly blue, while overhead long Vs of ducks moved over Sawtooth's peaks. He recognized them as Shoveller and Cinnamon Teal from a blue textbook on American birds. The sound of earth scrapers and the grunt of twelve men lifting a six-hundred-pound rail into place on raw ties were the only other sounds.

Nobby White was marking the gauge spread on already laid ties and then, as the rail was put in place on its tie plates, six men with long-handled, forty-pound sledges drove in the spikes to fasten down the rail. The sledge men were Irish and Swedes—rough, burly fellows given to knock-down fights and weekend drinking, just right for the strong blows needed to drive spikes into prepared holes in the hard wood. The sledge men, red-faced and wet-nosed from the cold, sang as they lifted their tools and drove spikes:

"Nobby White was a fine man down to the ground,
He married a woman six feet round
She baked good bread, she baked it well,
Baked it hard as the doors of hell,
Bang, you terriers, bang!"

Nobby grinned, "Save your breath, boys. Mr. Silverthorn, help me with the gauge-measuring rod. We'll have to try and level more ahead or we'll have to double-head every time we approach the pass."

"If I read the graphs right, twenty-six percent grade to the mile will do."

"Will do on solid rock ballast. The ground here is broken up like Jackson Hole below the Grand Tetons."

"Now the Bossman was Nobby White,
By God, a man never to scoff,
Last week a bang went off,
A mile in the air went he!
Bang, you terriers, bang!"

"Better come inside, Mr. Silverthorn, your cheek is frostbit."

They entered a supply shed where barrels of spikes and stacks of tail plates were stored. An iron pot with holes jabbed into it held burning chunks of wood on a bed of red embers. Both men pulled off their dog-skin gloves and held their hands near the glowing sides of the pot.

Ira became aware the cold was getting worse—his

57

bones seemed filled with ice water. He moved closer to the fire. Still his teeth chattered a bit. "Can we get through the pass before winter?"

"Up Shit Creek with no paddle, unless we get over Sawtooth before deep snow."

"Let me quote you a goddamn letter from London: 'The news of a direct line through the pass will keep the shares up and we could make a temporary deal with the Great Falls and Green River lines to connect us with the corn and cattle shipments east or the Copper Plate and Wahoe timber and coal and ore gondolas west to the coast.' "

"I'll work the arse off the crews, Mr. S."

"Goddamn it, Nobby. We'll have this line built." Ira pulled on his dog-skin gloves. "Maybe. And my name is Ira. Cut the Mr. S."

"Sure, Ira. It all depends on how late the heavy winter snow comes. It piles up as solid ice and tough snow twelve feet deep in the pass, the Indians tell me."

"We can build train sheds over tracks like the Central Pacific did."

"Not here. Not enough big timber grows hereabouts. We'd need thirty miles of shed."

Outside, Ira stared up at the dark gap that was Sawtooth Pass. A hawk circled in the cold blue air, moving in great gliding sweeps, hunting for prey. Tightening the circle, the bird hovered on unmoving wings over a group of lightning-scorched pines. Again and again the hawk searched the juniper bush in the rock fissures, making his circling glide. Nothing. Ira thought, the hawk is having no luck. A project often is never finished, he decided. But no use showing a woebegone face to the work crews. He waved to the men straining at the rails.

There was one telegraph line extended to Camp 5, not always in working order. The connection went by way of Council Bluffs down to St. Joe, where there was usually a drunken Morse operator. Ira had Janos write out several telegraph messages to be clicked east for information—to Boston to the bank of Cather Starkweather, to a Dutch steel importer on Wall Street. He also wrote to Uncle Isaac to pray for them getting through Sawtooth mountain. That night the temperature fell to 40 below—work had to halt. Ira dreamed he was skating on the main canal of Amsterdam and awoke at dawn, his feet ice cold, to find Janos in his prayer shawl doing his morning devotions.

In three days the work began again.

For some years there were stories told of how through ice and snow the PG&P rails went through the mountain pass. How six men were killed by early snow slides, how Ira and Nobby White put down a mutiny of the work crews with a weekend of free whiskey and a five-dollar-a-month raise in pay.

One Baldwin locomotive was lost, plunging nine hundred feet into a ravine. But in the end there were rails through the mountain, even if six hundred feet of them were laid directly on ice and packed snow and in the spring thaw had to be relaid on ballasted earth.

Lockridge Bank shares remained shaky, but it, too, survived. The shares in the PG&P rose some ten points but not to the price at which the Zion Aid Society had bought them.

Uncle Isaac wrote:

Now done with the railroad, so what will you do? Go out to the West Coast and see the land. It's a growing state of milk and honey, some say, and fortunes are being created in citrus groves, in ranching, in port frontage. But be wary of bankers, their interest rate is often more deadly than

59

Gatling guns. Everything is in the hands of God.
Were I younger and had two good legs I'd buy a
fur hat and join you.

    I made a prayer for you last High Holidays:
The God of Israel neither slumbers nor sleeps.
My life is bound up with my people,
With those who love me and whom I love.
Love is the shade on my right hand;
The sun shall not strike me by day nor the
    moon by night.
Love shall watch over my going out and my
    coming in,
From this time forth and forever.

Your Uncle I.

6

Of Ira Silverthorn's next four years in the American West, there are very few records but for the memories of old settlers and some letters to his Uncle Isaac; also what he himself told various people, some of which must be taken, as he sometimes said, smiling deprecatingly, "with a pound of salt."

He spent two preposterous years on the matter of the railroad shares of the Lockridge Bank. In the end the Zion Aid Society recovered sixty percent of its outlay of funds.

By 1896 he had turned his interest fully to land holdings, feeling that while the railroad was a project that could end any season a disaster, land was permanent and as yet was fairly cheap. He had taken to heart Mark Twain's remark, "Buy land, they aren't making it anymore." He saw many possibilities in the harbor area around San Francisco, in the vineyards in Napa and Sonoma counties that grew splendid grapes, but as yet had not developed a good vintage. He saw around Los Angeles hillsides, arroys surrounding orange orchards and lemon groves, cattle herds. Ira sensed a coming together of progress and wealth.

Amazingly, he found that there were established Jewish families in the West going back to before the Gold Rush of '49. People named Harris, Sterns, even a Levi Strauss who made the first popular work pants from the blue denim cloth he had brought around the Horn as material for tents. The endeavor to endure and prosper was a pleasing prospect.

In San Diego he hunted out, in a hired buckboard, a raucous old Jew who had come out with the mountain men hunting beaver, who now owned wagon routes to areas where the Southern Pacific rails had not yet probed. He also owned a chain of general stores far into desert country around Flagstaff, Kingman, and Phoenix, and was rebuilding his establishments in Los Angeles and San Francisco into department stores.

Moses Handler was a man of intrigue and vision with a tuft of nanny goat beard and a head of white hair that seemed always uncombed. He had powerful shoulders and a wide torso, but was short in the legs. He had begun in California as a pack peddler, then sold pots and pans, from a wagon, going into importing kitchen ware from China and Japan. He also had developed a taste for whiskey but still donned the *tallis* and *tefillin* and kept the Shulkhan Arakh, and had given two Torahs to the first shul in Pasadena.

Moses was a profane, tobacco-chewing, feisty old man in his sixties when Ira came in a hired buckboard to his large Spanish house in San Diego overlooking the Naval Station in the bay.

After greetings he set out a bottle of good brandy and sipped a glass after pouring one for Ira, studying his visitor, this big Dutchman.

"So you want to buy land down here?"

"Not just land, Mr. Handler. I want an option on some acres of shore line above La Jolla. Not just for myself; for some relatives back in Holland."

The old man grinned, sipped his drink, tugged on his little beard. "Ah, you have a good eye, *yingel*. A fine eye. You like the schnapps, the real thing, not local horse piss. That land you want, I'm holding. Hotels. In twenty years more eastern people will come here for the winter and the shore. Believe me, you got the eye for it. Where else you buying, if you don't mind saying?"

"Around Morro Bay, and some orange acres."

"Merchandising, no? Dry goods, department stores. You don't see a Wanamaker's, a Macy's out here?"

Ira refilled his glass. "Not for me. You, I know. But for me, dishes, rags, are not something I know."

The man touched his nose with a finger. "I have some shore frontage near Del Mar—maybe we can work out something. Stay for supper. I got a Chinese cook that makes the best sauerbrauten, a bean cholent to give God himself heartburn, and the best gefilte fish west of the Mississippi. Now I can afford it, I set a good table."

It was as Moses Handler had promised, a Chinese-cooked European-Jewish meal. The raftered dining room looked down through large windows on the bay. The other diners consisted of an old aunt, Mummeh Feigel, who wore a head cloth and seemed addled but dignified, and a young dark girl with jet black hair worn in two braids. She had large, amused eyes and was wearing silver- and blue-stoned jewels around her neck and on both wrists. She was introduced to Ira as Rita. She wore a white blouse and a tan skirt held up by a man's leather belt around her hips. She joked with the Chinese boy who was serving. A girl of ebullience, contrariness, Ira decided, hardly his type.

"You ride, Mr. Silverbush?" she asked him over the cold schav soup.

"Silverthorn, not Silverbush. I ride most anything on four feet but buffalos."

"So stay for tomorrow and we'll get you up on one of Papa's best critters."

"I have to be north for some business."

"Stay, stay," Moses agreed. "I have some Morgan

63

quarter horses and Rita will show you some hill acres you might like."

"I'm interested in La Jolla."

"I might weaken," said Moses, "sell a *little* section."

Ira was aware of the old bastard's interest in him. He was looking for a husband for the dark, silver-trimmed girl. Give her feathers and you'd have an Indian. But he now suspected she was the old man's daughter. That far onto the fly paper Ira didn't intend to put his foot, not for all the shore frontage in Southern California. There had been women in his life in the last few years, no protestations of love, but casual, amusing, satisfying relationships. But marriage! He had had enough of that with Tina.

Leberklose came in a tureen, followed by hot potato salad with pastrami. When the apple-carrot tzimmes was being put before him he faltered. Such Jewish cuisine he hadn't been faced with since a Dutch wedding ten years before. He caught an amused look on his host's face.

"How, Mr. Handler," Ira said, "do you get a Chinaman to cook like this?"

Rita laughed. "Papa stood over Wu Dong and his wife with a buggy whip for a couple of months and beat their asses every time they didn't get a dish right."

The aunt wiped her mouth. "A coarse man, my nephew."

"Nonsense! Wu is a genius. I'm extending his skills into the French—sole marguery, a lamb d'Agneau, a caneton bigarade."

"Papa is a glutton," said his daughter.

"Shut your face. Respect. Silverthorn, I'm a gourmet. What else is there in the world but good food, good whiskey, and something *zaftig* to take to bed, eh?"

"You're bragging, Papa."

"Eat," said the aunt.

"I've been on the scrounge so long. I don't often eat so well." Ira was feeling bloated, and the Chinese boy was bringing in a Nesselrode pie. "Do you eat this fancy every day, Mr. Handler?"

"Fancy? A little of this, some of that. Tomorrow I'll order Essic-fleish from our own beef, a simple goulash too with the real paprika. We don't often get a Jewish traveler who repects the cooking of the *kashrut*."

They are amused at me, thought Ira. They are making some sort of sport of me. Or they're all mad. This wicked old millionaire and this strange daughter. Mexican? Half Mexican or Indian. Maybe a touch of darkie?

Ira tried to force down a bit more food with the red wine, a Burgundy his host was praising, as a huge silver bowl of fruit and a platter of nuts were brought in. The Chinese boy was sweating, and no wonder, Ira thought, as he wiped his own damp face with a crisp linen napkin.

" 'Fruit,' the prophet Isaiah said, 'the eating of which is the only true love'—a pineapple direct from the Sandwich Islands. Bartlett pears from my own orchards."

"I must insist, Mr. Handler, I'm full. I'm out of practice for such a real Jewish meal. *Rachmones,* have pity."

Rita, smiling at his ordeal, stood up. "Come, we'll have the coffee on the veranda. The sunset is something."

The aunt spoke. "Like a bloodshot eye."

What a family. The aunt, so ready to blow away, thin, dried out, had been eating steadily, slowly, her mouth full of large teeth that clearly were not her own.

"A cigar?" asked Moses Handler as they walked through the open iron-studded oak doors to a vast veranda. "Belindas, Monte Cristos, maybe an Uppmann?"

Ira said not just now. Moses turned to talk to the

65

Chinese boy. "Tell Wu for breakfast, fried matzo, onions, and herring." He turned toward Ira. "We breakfast at eight. But you'll sleep good. The beds have goose feather mattresses."

Ira wondered if he should bolt—just dash for the stairs and run. But his stomach protested.

The sunset was a spreading chaos of run-together colors, like a child's splashed painting; it gave Ira a headache. Moses' cigar sent a wave of nausea through Ira. His stomach was trying to escape up through his throat.

Later he had to listen in the high ceilinged living room to an early gramophone playing a cylinder recording of a Docstedders Minstrel Show. Also Caruso singing in "Rigoletto." Piñon logs burned in a stone fireplace. The aunt dozed. Rita kept changing the gramophone records. Ira vacillated between discomfort and hopes of escape to bed.

Moses, apparently happy to have a captive visitor, explained how one ran a general store: "Most items you sell at low profits. Volume is what you're after. Always offer to take back any purchase cheerfully, mind you. No dirty looks, and when an item is in stock more than sixty days and not moving, out on its ass. Keep cutting its price ten percent a week till it's carried off. Always discount your bills for prompt payment . . . You're yawning. A hard day, Silverthorn? You'll sleep like an innocent child."

Ira, feeling loggy, miserable, packed with food, and now taking a last tot of brandy, said yes, he was ready for bed.

Rita said, "We'll be ready and saddled up right after breakfast."

In the bedroom there were chicken sandwiches under a napkin by his bedside, a wedge of strudel, a small bottle of white wine. He took two digestive tablets and fell into bed—a deep bed that embraced him—and he fell asleep to the hoo-hoo-hoo of a night owl drifting from the stables.

His sleep was troubled by a persistent dream: he turned a doorknob slowly and came into a room in Java papered with a pale green design of some sort of Asian demons. Bluish drapes were drawn. A small table held a gilt clock and two Chinese stone dogs with glass eyes. Facing him, in a blue and gold robe, was Wind Cloud, she out of his past, so long ago.

Oddly enough he was struck first not by the girl's amazing beauty, but rather by the warmth he felt at seeing her again, the pleasure he took in this intimate dream. He took her hand in his. It was warm, soft, with amazingly delicate bones. But it was a firm grip she gave him. He kissed her, as he used to, almost without thinking, as if it were the most natural thing; why shouldn't it be? he felt. Her arms went around him, she standing on tip toes; for while tall for a Javanese girl, against his big, long body she seemed petite, without in any way suggesting a need for protection.

Her mouth was searching for his and they continued to kiss, holding each other closer and closer. He stroked the black chignon, knotted behind her right ear. Now they were suddenly transported to a teak forest and heard elephants.

Wind Cloud made a soft throat sound and stepped away from him, dropped her robe. She stood naked. No shyness, not a hint of coyness to her stance. Just a naked girl, her body color a pale terra cotta touched with ivory. He noticed the pubic area was shaved (or had it never produced hair?). He didn't feel this was the time to question her disrobing—the pose was neither innocent or wanton; it had a natural, unassuming grace.

She said, "There is a bed."

"Yes." He saw the bed beyond a Dutch doorway. A brass bed piled high with pillows, a nightstand holding a pitcher and basin, towels, all dominated by a huge mirror.

He never could recall in full detail the next few moments before they were on the bed. He did disrobe—the undignified gesture of getting out of his white linen trousers—there, a naked man twin to the one in the mirror. He became aware of her eyes, blue instead of brown, wide open, staring at him, the mouth firm, trembling at the corners. Her breasts bobbed up and down as she lay and inhaled with excitement. He muttered, "Tina!" Then fiercely: "Tina!"

"You must hurt me," said his dead wife.

"Why?"

He tried to escape back into the first dream . . .

Ira gave an old Chinese hag a twenty guilder and in the street wondered if all Java would know of this. He felt, as he walked, slightly drunk on pineapple rum, there clung to him the body odor of the girl. He trembled. Dazed, he stepped in the way of a dray hauling herring kegs. The white Dutch driver shouted, "Look where you're going! You want to get your fucking head busted open?"

No, he decided he certainly didn't want that, and he jumped back onto a sidewalk.

He came awake in a great sweat and sat up with the feeling of a loss of stability and purpose. It was the too large intake of food—better to awake to smells of a barnyard and crocus and jonquil in a garden below the window.

7

Ira's visit to Moses Handler's lasted not for a day but for a week. The host sent back the hired buckboard to the livery stable, refused to get down to bargaining, insisting he so enjoyed Ira's company that tomorrow they would talk of some small sale: "Mañana, as the Mexicans say, is time enough. Go enjoy my horses, my landscape. Let Rita show you the best parcels of land, properties I *might* let go."

Ira saw he was trapped between his desire (call it greed) for land and a fear of the overwhelming hospitality offered by the Handlers, who seemed isolated in their huge Spanish house. Moses explained that they had little to do with fellow Jews in the community, "greasy tailors and dung shovelers, not given our habits of reading books, listening to music, laying a splendid table."

They were offering everything but what Ira had come for. Rita, who rode astride in a divided skirt, impressed him with her skill and daring in leaping ditches rimmed in mesquite and cottonwoods. He also had to take the jumps or seem less *macho*, as the natives put it, than this obstreperous girl of nineteen or twenty. It was impressive, this brown and yellow land of brush-covered hills, its ravines of prickly pear, the neat rows of citrus groves. Best for riding was the lonely shoreline of white sand with the growl of waves attacking the coast and pulling back as the riders' horses splashed hoofs in the foaming surf. Offshore, in the iodine-smelling kelp, sea lions basked and barked; Ira was told by Rita not to call them seals as most visitors did.

They sat on bluffs in the shade of live oaks and wild brush eating a lunch that Wu Dong the cook had packed for them. They spurred their horses up the rocky hillside and saw fires on the far horizon scribble their smoke on the blue moire sky.

"Aren't you afraid the whole damn countryside will burn?"

"Oh," said Rita crossing her picktoed riding boots under her fringed buckskin riding skirt, "it burns off the brush and Papa says the ash is good for the soil."

They were in a grassy glade with a wide stream running below it, happy after a dry season. The live oaks made gold-stippled shade while ants scavengered the lunch crumbs. It was the third day they had been out and Ira sensed he was becoming emotionally involved with this girl and her father, an impulsive pair full of a healthy perversity—Americans, clearly, not tied to the poignancy and pain of the Old World, its fears and problems.

It was a hot day, a solemn soothing heat stirred by a little breeze. They did not feel in the mood for finishing the food. Ira looked at Rita lying in the grass, hands crossed behind her head of dark shiny hair. Clearly she was more than a country girl, not the kind of women he sometimes dreamed of—a northern blonde or a girl with mink-colored hair, pink like a Rubens painting Uncle Issac owned, blue-eyed, shy, demure. But this dark-skinned girl was bold, muscled yet slim, with ironic eyes and pert mouth that suggested a corrosive fierceness. No, *not* this girl, even if there was building a communicable enthusiasm between them. What had that old skirt-lifter Goethe written? *"Zwer Sellen woknen, acr meiner Brust."* Two souls in my bosom, ach.

"You're a wanderer, Ira."

"I'm doing business for people on the other side."

"And cutting yourself a slice of the melon." She turned, swiveled on her hips to study his face closer. "You mind being a Jew?"

"Don't think about it much. It's like having green eyes or big ears. It's there, you can't repudiate it. Why the hell think about it?"

She beat off some ants with her wide-brimmed hat. "You think I'm half nigger?"

Ira laughed, as if the idea were preposterous. "Now that's a crazy question. You're you, you're a hell of a rider and . . . and . . ."

"And good company? You know Papa said last night you have too much dignity and think the whole world is conniving against you."

"The world, as an uncle of mine puts it, is not dropping roast larks into our mouths."

She sat up with a preoccupied expression. "My mother was a Shoshone. Papa bought her in Oklahoma for a pinto pony and two blankets. He said he couldn't afford her but she fascinated him."

Rita stood up, arms folded across her breasts, and there was suddenly a youthful gentleness about her; gone was the aggressive stance, the boisterous laughter, the quizzical smile.

"Would you believe Papa had her converted to Judaism, the whole thing, the ritual *mikvah* bath, the Hebrew prayers? He married her. Papa always does things with class."

"He must have liked her very much."

"He loved her, Ira. Very much. You people may think Papa is a bit 'teched in the haid,' as they say here, a mite crazy. He's odd, sure, but sane, believe me. It's

71

just he doesn't accept the same world most people do. He does things like teaching a Chinaman to cook French cuisine. He really sees the darkies, the peons, the town drunks as just like the rest of us. He's mean, too. A hard bargainer. He'll take your right eye in a deal, but he's honest, he keeps his word. Papa is one fancy sonofabitch. No one likes him."

"You love him."

"No, I don't. I never said that. I respect him. Oh, hell, it's too hot to talk. Let's go for a swim." She opened her wide, silver-studded belt and began to shuck her skirt and unbutton her pale yellow silk blouse.

Ira said, "Look, I mean, oh shit . . ."

She had her blouse open, exposing fine hard breasts with nipple areas the size of silver dollars. She grinned. "Come on, mister. You're no schoolboy. Here, pull off my boots."

What was he to do? he thought. It's like a cockeyed dream, no logic, or too much logic. She half-reclined, half-sat at his feet. He pulled off her boots and she leaped up and discarded everything else, stood nude there, a lovely golden color skin, her hair loose from its confining braids. She turned and ran down toward the stream, crying over her shoulder, "Come on, shuck."

An insistent inner voice said no and it was right but he stood watching her buttocks whip through the shrub oak, her torso twisting and turning as she ran. Almost solicitously, there was a response by his body, an erection.

Rita ran into the stream, splashing up shards of water, then partly submerged beyond a reed bed.

Ira began to loosen his belt, thinking all the time the situation was extremely exasperating. I have some scruples, he thought, and the man should make the first gesture. He hadn't been with a woman for a month now, and that had had no rapturous triumph of sensuality, not by a long shot.

So here he was, naked, so much white limb showing, sweat on the hair on his chest, under his armpits.

It was hot walking barefooted on the stones and grit down to the stream. He stood there, toes in the water, feeling suddenly like some disembodied soul. He stepped forward. The water was cold; he plunged in and swam with clumsy overhand strokes toward the frolicking girl, out to where the stream ran quicker and the water was deeper.

Rita shot up like trout for a cast fly and whirled around; her golden body varnished wet. She came to his side, kicked at his ribs with a long slim leg.

"Oh it's so goddamn fine, isn't it?"

"It's cooling." He tread water and she swam around him, laughing. "My, you're a big man. That chest is wide as a stagecoach. And the rest—I should blush . . ."

"Don't look."

She didn't turn away but said softly, "I like to come here and think of drowning. But Papa says death leaves you with nobody, not even yourself. You know like in that play, 'get thee to a nunnery'."

"Ophelia floating in her weeds."

"She was a bubble-headed fool, you know. Hamlet, he was a milksop, a tinhorn sport. She should have shown him her ass and jumped on him—what was *that?*"

There had been a splash from the other side of the stream and now a widening ripple advanced toward them on the surface of the stream.

Ira said, "It's something like a muskrat or an otter."

Yes, there was a sleek head and a black nose and suggestion of eyes.

The girl shivered, "I hate them. They're rats . . ." She came to him and put her arms around his body, her

73

eyes searching his face. "They're so slinky and nasty. *Ugh!*"

He held her close, touching at knees, bellies, chests, skin to skin, moving their legs to stay afloat, "A girl who will ride anything, jump any obstacle, scared of a little critter? Come on, it's just a bitty thing and now it's swimming away from us."

She lowered her head onto his shoulder. "You can't be brave about everything. Let's go get out of the water. I'm all goose pimples."

On the pebbled stream bank they stood naked and watched the creature swim, then dart ashore and disappear.

She, so lately vulnerable, kissed him; her arms held him and his encircled her. He was aware their breath was coming with difficulty and he again became aroused satyr style, extending between her thighs. It didn't matter to hide it, for they were intricate warm, damp flesh. Some fragment of verse came to him, verse heard long ago on some night of cavorting at the Herring Club.

" 'It was for this that I might Cynthia see, washing the waters with her beauties white . . .' "

"Hey," said Rita, flogging him with her wet loose hair, "What's that?"

"Something I heard once."

They were kissing in a great crushing of lips, wet mouths active, heads rolling. She managed to say, "Beauties white? Not me."

"More like gold."

Her heart was, he felt, beating against him like a watch and he brought her to her knees, bending over her. He knew he was near the point of no return. She was clawing at his back. "Not here. In the shade."

He lifted her and carried her to the dappled ground of the live oaks. The path on this return journey didn't

74

burn the soles of his feet. He put her down on the turf and there was an unspoken communication of bodies, nerve ends, galvanized by emotion. Rita was already a woman. He entered her with relentless, cruel urgency, not thinking much about her not being a virgin, just their moving together in the quivering light under the live oaks. They meshed, rolled about, their moans intensifying. Her eyes, as she stared up at him, were black as basalt. Now she, so lithe and supple, cried yes; yes, he answered. She bit his shoulder and he cruelly thrust on, spaced his urgent fervor, lavished in her his final frenzy; yes, she said again, oh, oh, fine, fine. He felt the enormous upsurge of passion come to a point of pleasure and pain and he cried something he did not remember later and they climaxed.

The horses once or twice lifted their heads at this distraction, then returned to noisily cropping grass with large yellow teeth.

The two naked bodies lay in an absolute completeness of sated wonder in the glory of their deed. Their center of gravity was returning but they were held in a kind of immolation as breath returned, nerve ends went back to their normal procedures.

She stirred against him. "We sure as hell wasted two whole days."

"We did?"

"Like some Yanqui schoolgirl I was loco over you, Ira, from the minute you came in the door."

"I'd lie if I said I felt that way. It was so odd, stuffing in all that goddamn food. My stomach, not my balls, ached."

"I have to explain." She raised herself on one elbow. He circled one of her breasts with a cupped hand, rotated it. "Um, Ira, look, this business of no virgin . . ."

"I didn't ask."

"Here's the honest-Abe truth. It's nothing much.

This Irish horse wrangler Papa hired last year. It was just I wanted to know, to find out what the devil is all the excitement. So a few times, three, and I didn't care for him or for that. It wasn't with any meaning. Just fucking like a boar and a sow. See . . ."

"Shut up."

"Papa found out and had the man run off the place. Funny, Papa wasn't angry. Sad, maybe, not angry. He thinks this thing is natural, and a girl is a human being."

"Will you shut up?" He felt her pubic area, slid a finger into moisture and smoothness.

"Papa made me promise I'd wait, wait until there was someone of, as he put it, of our sense of feeling . . . like you."

Ira felt the trap shut with a clang of steel spring. He put her on her back and they made a more leisurely love, even more ardently with no reticence, no pangs of conscience. As they reached the orgasm, his ears seemed filled with the sounds of cymbals and drums. This was all so splendid, so zestful, one could be tempted to love this girl, love her very much. Tomorrow he would make his escape.

8

After a heavy dinner of roast goose, and potato kugel, Ira and Moses sat on the veranda watching the swallows take over the old barn for the night and fruit bats slip out of some place on their leather wings to flit among the orchards.

The two men sat in the gathering twilight, the odor of the glowing end of their cigars mixed with the scent of citronella with which the Chinese boy had sprayed the air to keep off mosquitos.

Moses gave Ira a quizzical look. "You know, Silverthorn, we Jews are a naturally buoyant people. We have to be to bear all the burdens put on us by an inscrutable God. We mold situations to fit our needs to remain alive."

Ira said, "Is that why we are baffled and truculent?"

"As Spinoza said, 'Because I love God that doesn't mean God must love me in return.' Who knows? Tomorrow I want to show you something you'll never suspect. I raise orchids."

"I believe it." Ira stirred in his chair, knocked cigar ash into an abalone shell. "I'm leaving in the morning. I've been here much too long."

"Too long, too long, the man says! Your company has been a soothing ointment to me among the human cattle I live with." He placed a hand on Ira's knee. "It's time we put all the cards on the table. *Tocus offen tish*, as they used to say—put your ass on the table, eh? I have a daughter prime and lovely. You are a son of Zion. Between us is a mutual sympathy. I'm talking of a wedding. *There*, it is out in the open."

Ira sat very still hearing the peeping sound of the fruit bats. When he spoke it was with a sense of apprehension, of trepidation, as if there were some spell on him and he was fearful he couldn't break free of it. "I'm not thinking of marrying."

"Ha, what man really does? He thinks he needs it like a fish needs a bath. But there is also an awareness in a woman. Devil take them, that knows when the fruit is ripe, the harvest is near. Rita will make you a fine wife, a Jewish maiden." The old man chuckled. "Technically a worthy woman, for in the wisdom of the body is a true answer. Look, I don't promise you a *noddin*, a dowry, like King Solomon would. But enough, enough."

"I wasn't thinking of . . ."

"Some of the shoreline you want I'll give a sliver. I'm in worldly matters a rich man. Who knows how rich? I have a son, a hot-tempered *momzer*. He's away in college. He and Rita are all I have, so some day you and your children, blessed be the future, will have a good slice of the cake."

Ira said, "You've misunderstood, I'm afraid. I came to buy some land and somehow things have gotten out of hand. You're a hell of a fine host. I'm stuffed like a Passover goose. I've drunk your brandy, smoked your cigars . . ."

"And lain with my daughter . . . Oh, I'm not condemning. As it's only natural—as King David said to Beersheba, who can stop the conceit of young people matching parts?" The old man was getting feisty again. "It's not a matter of honor, doing the right thing. That's for romantics and the pious. I like you, Ira, very much I like you."

It was the first time the old bluffer had called him Ira. Ira answered in a staccato monotone, "No, it's too sudden, it's too . . . planned. Worked out by you, by Rita. A fool could see it. I could see it."

"Who tried to hide anything? I sensed a rapport. So stop your agitation. I have made a good offer. You have to see me for a father, a man getting old. I'm no poltroon or scoundrel, and Rita is no dishonored, seduced maiden out of Charles Dickens. No, I'll announce plans for the a true *chuppah* wedding and get Rabbi Beirbaum away from his scratching himself."

"And if . . ."

"If not, I'll send down to O'Donald's livery stable to bring back the buckboard. And it's goodbye Charlie, with the text from the Book of Numbers: 'Rise up, Lord, and let their enemies be scattered . . . and let them that hate thee flee before thee . . .' "

Ira didn't think the words somehow fitted the situation. He spoke slowly. "I love her, Moses Handler. It wasn't something I wanted. It was no sudden damn thing. It just came about. I've had a wife. She died years ago. It wasn't something I wanted to go along with again. And if I seem to draw back, believe me it isn't because of the Sioux strain in her."

"Shoshone. A fine people. One of the Ten Lost Tribes of Israel, the Mormons think."

"That never entered my mind . . . " Ira felt drained, warm; the cigar tasted bitter and he choked, coughed into the palm of a hand. "I do want to marry your daughter. That's what I'm fighting."

The evening had come down and there was only wan moonlight to light the veranda, but Ira could make out Moses' faint smile.

"My son, don't fight. Give in . . ."

He turned his head and yelled, "Chu, Chu! Where the hell are you?"

The Chinese boy, as in a well-rehearsed play, appeared with a silver tray with an ice bucket holding a napkin-wrapped wine bottle and two crystal goblets.

"A Steinberg Cabernet '87. So rare a vintage even that bastard Huntington or his gang, Crocker and Stanford, don't have it in their cellars." He twirled the bottle by its neck, then lifted it out and began to press out the cork. "I only had four bottles. This is the last." The cork popped, a white gaseous foam escaped. Moses poured the two goblets half full. He handed one to Ira, then lifted his chest high.

"To our joy and our pride in doing God's will and fear is the refusal to find a solution. Drink to survival in a world of wolves and let us and ours be spared for the coming twentieth century, where our children will sit beneath our arbors with their generations. *O-main.*"

"Amen," said Ira, gulping the wine to slack a burning thirst, drinking with a sense of failure, fully aware he had fallen among the strong and his own strength would be tested. Could he still escape?

Silver Spur Ranch
San Joaquin Valley
Kern County, California
April 18, 1897

Dear Uncle Isaac,

I am a married man, a newly married man. Much to my surprise with no pomposity or pretense, I may add.

I know you want to know about my wife Rita. She is nineteen, dark, independent, has a rich contralto voice, a sense of mischief, given to indulged

80

impulses, and—*and* her mother was a Shoshone Indian woman it would appear. At times I doubt that; as others I accept her as related to the Ten Lost Tribes of Israel, so some think.

Rita is the daughter of a Moses Handler, an Orthodox Jew long settled here who has prospered in land holdings and the establishment of general stores. He offered us part of his hacienda, as he calls his big Spanish-styled house, to live in. I thanked him, said no, that I was setting up a ranch of my own east of Bakersfield, far enough away, frankly, so we shall be plagued only by his visits.

Now that you and the Zion Aid Society are clear of your shares of the PG&P, if you again invest, I'd strongly recommend something dull and safe. Here in the American West, in fact all over this remarkable nation, men of daring and hard-nutted drive are taking chances, seizing control of steel, coal, oil, steamship lines, mines. Already they are called either "empire builders" or "robber barons." They set up controlling cartels called trusts to dominate the trolley lines, whiskey and distilling, gamble on futures in pigs and steers not yet born, and on crops not yet planted.

Cities are expanding overnight and land that was for the taking by the homesteaders is now selling at huge sums, in the cities by the square foot. So I have been going in for land dealing, carefully picking sites around the towns and cities here that must grow, will grow. My capital is strained, of course. Moses gave us as dowry bank credits for twenty thousand dollars which, as they say here, is peanuts. Janos Kalman, who has a keen Talmudic eye for property values, is aiding me in working out plans for land sales. We plan to buy, with as

81

small a down payment as we can, acreage cut up into building sites called lots, and with band music and free food, sell off section by section at auction, or through salesman showing off the sites.

If it doesn't work out, I'm a pauper; the ranch, two thousand acres of shrub and gullies, is mortgaged down to the last calf. So wish me—us—well. I asked my father for some of my share of the estate. He didn't answer but did send me a Callot etching and two Greek coins with the head of Alexander the Great on them as a wedding present. I have made them into cufflinks.

I am well but must watch my weight because of eating too much at Moses' table. We don't plan children just yet. No first Silverthorn born in America this or next year. There is a family of our name in Boston, I believe, and they may have already filled a cradle.

Come and visit us and I'll buy you a John Stetson hat and Spanish spurs.

Your nephew,
Ira

By 1900, when Joel Silverthorn was born, the S&K Land Company had sold off sites for what became the city of Greenview between Glendale and Pasadena; and in 1904, the year of Leah Silverthorn's birth, the seaside colony of Clam Beach was a success till an autumnal tidal wave swept much of it away. By the time Joel Silverthorn was seven, the S&K Land Company was deeply involved in ranches and town developments; held mortgages on orange groves in Ventura County; was partners with Moses Handler in vineyards in Napa County and was producing a popular wine, Grape Maiden Rosé, and a pale golden sherry.

With the passing years Ira tried to improve the quality of the wine. In 1905, when there was a good vintage, he had printed on the bottles' labels the lines of Euripides that Janos Kalman found for him: *"Where there is no wine, love perishes, and everything else that is pleasant to man."*

9

On their tenth wedding anniversary Ira and Rita gave a party at their Silver Spur Ranch.

Two huge oxen were slaughtered and set to roasting in pits of hardwood charcoal by the Mexican ranch hands. Forty guests arrived by buckboards and carriages from the railroad station in Bakersfield. Moses Handler, attired in a long linen duster and goggles, drove up in a snorting monster called a Falcon Knight.

"Call these roads? Call it a travel system? I tell you," he shouted, "we will have to surface with tar every damn cow trail before the auto car will be popular."

He lifted his goggles from his dusty face and kissed his daughter, who had grown plump, he told her, and hugged his grandchildren Joel and Leah. Then he shook the hand of his son-in-law after removing his driving gauntlets.

"So, a *gadilla*, eh? A fine spread of ranch you have here. A land of milk and honey, maybe not, but you dine under your own grape arbor like Abraham and Sarah."

He looked over the wide one-story ranch house, its hedges and trees, the guests seated under the grape trellis sipping drinks. Off by the corral he observed the oxen, drenched in sop sauce, turning over the hardwood fire.

"Kosher? If not, don't tell me."

Dogs and children frolicked underfoot.

"Moisha, Moisha!" came a cry from inside the auto. A woman wrapped in a linen duster, her head enveloped in a hat tied down by several veils, leaned out of the window. "Goddamn you, Moisha, you break my bones, you smother me in dust, and then forget me." She sneezed. "Get me down and pour me a drink."

"*Ah-tah,*" said Moses. "Mrs. Murry, forgive me."

The woman descended from the steaming auto car and shed her outer garments. She was a large woman with red hair—a bright color, perhaps a bit chemically aided, Rita whispered to Ira.

"Hanna Murry, that's me," she said, accepting a glass of wine from Rita. There was a self-righteous complacency about her. "The old turkey-buzzard said it was better than train travel, his motor car. But I ate a pound of dust and I may never use my ass again, unless I take off my corsets."

Rita smiled benevolently. "They're killers, aren't they? Come inside, Mrs. Murry."

"Hanna will do fine. And I need something stronger than this wop wine."

Later, seated in Ira's den, Moses said, "Mrs. Murry, she's a marvelous *shicksa*, owns some of the biggest citrus groves in Mexico, a widow lady married to a Sol Murry-Stein. We're going partners in a cannery up in Monterey."

Ira grinned. "She must like you, to ride in your bonebreaker."

"That's the problem. I'm a businessman and Hanna she wants to cuddle. But for you, congratulations, ten years? I expected at least six grandchildren, at the very least."

"Rita likes to ride too much to have too many pregnancies. Two is enough right now. There's talk of a tightness in the money market."

Moses Handler inspected a stuffed elk's head. "It's those *momzers* in Wall Street. Morgan, Rockefellers, Carnegie. But this Mark Hanna, the boss politican, he'll keep them under control. How's the land company?"

"The best two years yet. The 'Frisco banks are lending me nearly all I want, steer prices are holding. But Swift and Armour in Chicago are worried over federal investigations since that damn book by this Upton Sinclair came out."

"*The Jungle.* I read it. Lost my appetite. It's a scare booger. *Never* eat cold storage meat, believe me."

There was a knock on the door and Janos Kalman came in, no longer the lean, dried-out scholar but a well-filled-out man wearing a high collar and cravat with a pearl stick pin, red-stoned cufflinks, waistcoat, and a gold chain with a Klondike nugget attached.

"Ah, Janos," said Moses, "Every time I see you, more jewelry."

"It's James now—Janos is too Magyar. How's everything?"

"The goose hangs high. America, it's been good to us . . . Our fathers ate bitter bread and trembled in their sleep."

The former seminary student recited, " 'And the king sent for them, and they gathered unto him all the elders of Judah and of Jerusalem . . .' "

Moses grinned, "The Second Book of the Kings. But remember, 'the rowers have brought thee into great waters, the east wind hath broken thee in the mist of the seas. Thy riches . . . thy merchandise, thy mariners and thy pilots . . .' "

Ira produced a flagon of reddish wine and some hand-blown, pale green fluted glasses.

"The product of my own grapes."

"*Mazel-tov.*"

"There is a Hebrew *broche*, a prayer for wine," added Janos.

"So what are you waiting for?" asked Moses as Ira poured the glasses half full and handed them around.

"I'll do it in English for the unlettered. 'Blessed art Thou, O Lord our God, King of the Universe, who bringeth forth this harvest of the vine . . .'"

"*O-main*," said Moses as they all sipped. Ira smacked his lips. "It's the first batch. What do you think?"

Moses smiled. "A fine little domestic wine." He lifted his glass level with his eyes. "*L'chaim.*"

"*L'chaim*," they chorused.

"We are settled at last," said Janos. "Here perhaps we can take off our packs."

Moses looked thoughtful. "Let us hope so. Every place in the past the Jew could never become complacent, never be sure of peace, always put in more of himself than he took out."

Outside in the patio and by the corral, they could hear the ragtime music, children and the dogs romping, the click of glasses under the grape arbor—sounds of pleasure, enjoyment.

Ira refilled the glasses. "I have an uncle, a wise old duffer, a bit of a hedonist but no *zlub*. You catch him in the right mood and he'll point out that the shape of things to come will be basically the same as in the past. 'Don't unpack,' he would say when the gin reached his sad side, 'we must be self-contained, like an egg.'"

"There is," Moses agreed, "a disturbance in our two-thousand-year-old dream of taking roots. Always we are aware of the slowness of hope. But drink up, laugh, this is not the time to hunt shadows. We celebrate a fulfillment."

Janos frowned. "Yet, as the Cabala hints, we are all

directed by a twitch of a thread in God's hand directing a puppet."

Joel, a handsome boy with a dark cowlick over his left eye, and with just a bit of buckness to his front teeth, came rushing in. "Mama says, come on out, the band is playing."

They could already hear the oompah of the music, aided by the excited barking of the dogs.

"Yes," said Moses, draining his glass, "enough of the deep thinking."

Janos, now James, nodded. "Ah, Ira, it's a long way from that ocean trip we took together."

Ira put an arm around his friend. "Damn it, you didn't get seasick. I did."

"Chickens, I don't see enough chickens," said Moses.

"They are in the henhouse."

"A Jew keeps chickens, not dogs."

"So you keep saying."

They were full of wine and the sun was just slanting to the west through lion-colored clouds. They felt older than when they had first met, and time, Moses decided, had not as yet given a full definition to all their values.

Rita, up since an hour before dawn, viewed the bustle, addressed the servants. "*Avanti, Cristo*, don't drop the glasses—bravissimo—and now see to the napkins, the clean plates."

Ten years of simplifying myself, she thought. I am satisfied. So why on this happy day, this self-reproachfulness? I like parties, I like the gay chatter.

She yelled at two barefoot Chicano girls carrying a roast turkey on a platter, "Don't spill the trimmings, and more chairs!"

It was an animated scene to her liking—her children, yes, she had birthed them casually and easy, she had made love so often with her big wonderful hulk of a husband. But time and marriage had not sated her curiosity about life. Perhaps this was all there was to life, and was it enough? When a feisty girl, she had imagined another world of stronger drama and color. Was it Papa's fault? He and his games, his life so full of spectacular conceits and arrogance. He also had his religion to console him. That concept of Messianic faith she lacked.

She had hoped for a lovelier and more lasting reality. From the medley of her related experiences no absolute world was forming. She liked music without understanding its fine points but she still hoped to find, as in a symphony, that perfect chord in herself, an affirmation and a personal deliverance that music sometimes suggested to her.

Rita smiled at her distracting thoughts, lit a thin black cigarillo, and went to inspect the roasting oxen. I must count my blessings, she thought, the validity of my marriage, the beauty of my children, the grace and speed of my horse Diana, and look—those bastards are not basting the steers enough . . . *"No me gusta!"*

The past did not dissolve in her but remained in little pockets of memory that she did not shake out because she was busy—a past like the loose tobacco in the corners of one of her riding jackets.

It was a grand festive day and evening. There still exists yellowing photographs in a leather album, provocative images of the guests around the tables, of couples dancing—Mrs. Murry and Ira, Moses with his daughter; a scene of Joel and Leah carrying in a huge cake with the lettering smeared a bit: HAPPY TEN YEARS, MOM AND POP.

Almost everyone drank a lot, ate too much, laughed a great deal, toasted the happy couple, the prosperity the Lord had given them. Everyone, with intense buoyancy, agreed it was the best of times.

In six months, the great Panic of 1907 overwhelmed them, swallowed up most of their overextended enterprises, mocked their faith in their expectations.

Most became bankrupt and even the exceptions were as they had been in the beginning, desperately endeavoring to survive.

BOOK TWO

KINGS

10

First you are very small and the nurse says, oh, he is a wetty-wetty baby boy, and then you are learning to handle a spoon; rocka-bye baby in the treetop. You know Papa and Mama by sight and you are Harry Silverthorn, only they call you Hershey after the Yum Yum Chocolate Bar. Papa is S.S. and his hair is as thin as your own was when you were a wetty-wetty. Papa makes moon pitchers (*Pobrecita,* Inez, the Mexican maid, says). Mama is dear and always smelling very good when she tickles your belly button and asks *whose good little baby boy are you?* But she really knows.

When you are four you see Charlie Chaplin flickering on the wall and so with an old umbrella handle and a kitchen pot on your head you are copying the funny man. By the time they bring in the birthday cake with six candles and an extra to grow on, you know everything in sight is called California, and the people who come to dance and drink the hooch at the big house on Yucca Drive mostly talk of making movies and of President Harding. And sometimes they hold each other close, breath hard, standing. In the corners of the big house and in the garden you find them putting their hands here and there and tickling. Once in the daisy bed two of them played tickle on the ground and ate each other's noses.

Mama-dear is also called Nora-dear and the hostess

and she has headaches and talks of the servant problems—they tot and are sassy. Papa yells a lot when she
asks about lipstick on his collar and once he knocked a
man down and said "sonofabitch," which you are not
allowed to say; it is only for grownups.

Best of all the people who come to Yucca Drive is
Uncle Ira. He was the first Silverthorn in America, but
not related. He and Papa are in acreage. Uncle Ira is
Papa's real estate agent. Uncle Ira is tall and wide,
mostly laughing a lot. He feels the muscles of your arms
and says "wow, a starker!" He has more time to do what
he calls "loaf and invite his soul," more than Mama and
S. S. When you are seven, Uncle Ira takes you riding in
Griffith Park and makes his big black horse Prince
prance about.

Eating hot dogs from a three-wheeled cart under an
umbrella, Uncle Ira says, "Christ, Hershey, I wish we
could get S.S. out riding. He's stuck in that goddamn
[another no-no word] studio making leaping snapshots
and stripping a bathing beauty, and he doesn't see it's a
good marriage that counts, the only sure thing, kiddo."

S.S. and Mama yell a lot at each other, and Uncle
Ira tells you of hunting tigers in Java and cutting Doug-
las firs in the Northwest for railroad ties. And about his
ranch east of Bakersfield—the Silver Spur—and his
steam yacht in San Diego. Uncle Ira seems to be always
laughing, talking very loud about Herbert Hoover, also
of a Florida land boom. He and Papa look over plans
for rebuilding a studio or talk of Papa taking options on
theatres or escrows for hundreds of acres of land. Being
a Silverthorn seems to be very important when people
give affairs for collecting money for causes, and Mama
wears the triple string of pearls.

There is also the matter of the Jews. It isn't like
being a darkie like Jimjam, the chauffeur, or a chinky-
chinky like Hip Lee, the cook. Even if you are like

most everybody else, being a Jew, Jewboy, Heeb, somehow that is a set-aside type of people.

Uncle Ira, who knows everything ("and if I don't know it, it's not worth knowing") is having what he calls a hangover, seated, or rather reclining, in a canvas patio chair by the pool. His hands are over his eyes, folded, and he is moaning a bit when you ask him what does it mean, *Jew*?

Uncle Ira takes his hands away from his face and moans again and opens one big eye to look at you standing there in your bathing trunks by the side of the chair.

"Hershey," (he blinks in the sunlight) "simply put by a man with a brain-busting head this morning, a Jew is somebody that somebody else thinks of as a Jew."

"Is it like being cockeyed—like Charlie Wilson?"

"No, it's not something that always shows. It's just that everybody has to be somebody. Me and Sid, S.S., and Nora, your mama, we are Jews."

Uncle Ira is too brain-bushed to say anymore, and so you just accept it as something you'll know about—as the grownups say—when you're older.

Of course you are also something else. Papa was born in Russia, Mama in Austria, and Uncle Ira in Holland. That's why some people call him "Big Dutch." Also for his size. But they are all Americans.

For ten years, starting in 1912, the natives of Los Angeles—"the city of the Angels," as the Sunday newspapers sometimes called it—had been aware of an invasion of easterners who were not retired couples, fugitives from justice, or seekers of health in the perpetual sunshine.

There was some antagonism toward men with caps often worn peak to the back, carrying strange cameras on long-legged tripods; women in Gibson Girl blouses and fashionable "Lazy Daisy" hobble skirts. By the 1920s on the outskirts of the Pacific bluffs, or in Culver City, on Western Avenue, even in a hay barn at Gower and Sunset Boulevard, these newcomers played out dramas for something once called the Nickelodeons, but were now erecting neo-Babylonian palaces where one had to lay out a dollar to see Mr. Griffith's epic *Birth of A Nation*.

Names like Lasky Famous Players, DeMille, Ince, Zukor, Sennett, Laemmle, strange-sounding names and clearly in most cases Jews; Goldfish becoming Goldwyn; a street car conductor, Harry Cohn, a filmmaker. Odd, how these invaders laughed and drank, cavorted and drove their fancy roadsters, racing the Big Red Trolley cars to the beach, where bathing beauties in daring black stockings and beribboned swimsuits never went near the water. A pie in the face and kicks in the ass of a fat man were made as funny as crossed eyes. One talked of Griffith, the dour tall Shakespearean ham turned genius, of the sexual glare of Valentino, and one also heard in hotel lobbies and saw on posters the name of S.S. Silverthorn, President and Founder of Silverthorn World Picures—"Our Movies Circle the Globe." His domain extended south of Pico Boulevard in what a few years before had been bean fields with Japanese silently erecting poles for their climbing crops. Now, on sixty acres, were huge barnlike stages, a back lot containing a manmade lake around which Bagdad and Little Old New York stood cheek-by-jowl with Port Said (or Hong Kong, if called for), a Fifth Avenue mansion (a mere facade), a peasant village, half an ocean liner, a western Main Street "with real horse shit."

S.S. Silverthorn's chauffeured car, an overpolished Franklin, arrived at the studio at eight o'clock every weekday morning, usually also on Saturdays, and at least two Sundays a month when S.S. was facing some difficult studio problem.

The one-armed chief of studio guards, Matt Brady (a great war hero), would open the gates, give a military salute with his remaining arm, and S.S., a morning cigar between his teeth, would wave without looking up from the script or box office reports he was reading.

Already this morning activity was taking place: extras, harem girls, Red Cross nurses, frontier types, playboys in top hats and tails were coming out of wardrobe and makeup. Camera men were proceeding with their gear to the stages. From the commisary the odor of bacon and eggs and coffee attracted those employees who had the right to be a bit late; press department people, film cutters, bookkeepers, smocked members of the art department.

S.S. was deposited at the administration building, a new four-story stucco box, its six stone front steps guarded by two cement statues of Atlas carrying globes on their shoulders, the company's trademark; a wrestler of local fame, Turk McCann, painted and oiled, photographed with the globe, preceded the main titles of all studio pictures with a scroll reading: SILVERTHORN WORLD PICTURES *Presents*.

On the top floor of the tower was the suite of the president and founder. The pale, paneled walls held framed pictures of the dozen most famous stars under studio contract, posters of the studio's pictures that had made money and had been called classics: *The Great Plains* (the first million-dollar Western epic), *Vienna Nights* (the vices and passions of a sin-filled romantic city), *Marching Men* (the doughboys' true drama in the Great War, the realism of a battle-torn world).

S.S. Silverthorn disposed of his Panama hat and his cigar in the outer office. He nodded to Miss Wilton, his trusted secretary, a faded blond, serious-faced with rimless glasses. She was already sorting out the morning mail on the ornate black ebony desk by the bank of windows that overlooked the working stages, the back lot with its Tower-of-Babel confusion. She did her work with an unostentatious zeal.

S.S., as usual, gave a quick glance through the windows over his kingdom, noting the prop department chimney was smoking thickly, meaning they were burning props that might be salvaged, that some individual in overalls was smoking near the film vaults while coupling up a hose to water a flower bed.

"Take a note, Miss Winton. Have the workshop boss check what's being burned every morning. And fire the gardener smoking near the film vaults. Sonofabitch tosses a spark in the wrong direction and the work of the last dozen years will go up in flames, maybe burn down the whole fucking studio, pardon my language."

"S.S., here are the New York and Chicago weekend box office reports, here are the bank statements and Miss Rosalind Clay has not reported for work. Her agent wants you to call him."

"When hell freezes over. I'll talk to Lou Zucker."

In 1922 Sidney Silverthorn was in his late thirties, balding, thickening around the middle—still a handsome man but for his often puckered-up face or when he was scowling. "When he was feeling no pain," as some put it, he could be charming. Yet he cultivated a reputation of being a sonofabitch, a hard man in a deal, but one who kept his word. He was reputed to be a notorious lecher among his starlets, some of whom he had made into stars. Actually he was not an oversensual man, hardly bothered the females in his employ as often as town legend had it. True, he would sometimes take a young actress or would-be actress to San Francisco for a weekend and if impressed by a set of bouncy tits, a pair of gams, well-curved buttocks, he could be away for a night at the Alexandria Hotel. But usually his energies were dedicated to his fanatical love of making motion pictures, to amazing the industry by his daring in discovering some garage mechanic or waitress whom he would then make into a star. It was not all done by publicity buildups or invented glamorous pasts. S.S. had a mysterious gift of looking at some pimply youth or rattle-brained shop girl, trolley conductor or dissatisfied housewife, and seeing something magical, a femininity, a creature of caprices, a star quality that could be placed before a camera and taught to walk, emote, weep or snarl effectively. But he also had a strong business sense that was feared and respected.

"Ask Mr. North to come in," he told his secretary.

Colin North was a simpering, yellow-haired Princeton graduate known as S.S.'s "Shabbous Goy" (a reference to the goyem who used to come in to light the stoves in Jewish homes on Saturday when the Orthodox were not permitted to handle fire). Colin had served several other producers as their pet goy. He admitted he had read Walter Pater and H.G. Wells, and he escorted well-known visitors around the studio.

Smiling, Colin came in wearing an open-necked Brooks Brothers shirt, an apple-green college sweater, gray flannel pants, and two-toned shoes; he imagined himself as resembling a John Held, Jr. drawing, a popular image of the period.

"How is the stock doing?" S.S. asked.

"Twenty-two and a fourth opening price, S.S., on the New York Stock Exchange. Up almost two points this week."

S.S. began to go through the letters on his desk. "Who's buying in big lots?"

"Can't seem to see a trend in any big buying."

"Baloney, screw around with some of the Fox and

Universal crowd. Goddamn it, earn your keep. Spend."

"Okay, S.S., get right on it. I'll let someone put the arm on me for a hundred." He winked at Miss Wilton and went out.

Miss Wilton looked at her notes. "We're running the dailies on *Daisy Steps Out* at ten, and Von Kogan should have the footage we shot yesterday at San Pedro here by noon."

"Christ, that Heinie genius is three days behind. Oh, I don't want to see anybody. No agents, no reporters. Send in Zucker."

Lou Zucker headed the studio's press department (it was not yet called Public Relations). Lou was an unpressed middle-aged man with a crop of rust-colored hair and wearing a wrinkled, not-too-clean shirt; his trousers kept slipping down off his hips and he would hitch them up and tighten his belt. Lou Zucker was S.S.'s confidante, a loyal company man, ironic but not cynical. He had files on motion picture scandals, vice, and also of people one could trust, and he had often aided some rummy or has-been with a ten-dollar bill. A noted bad dresser, Lou Zucker was respected as the best handler of the press, the planting of news items (many of them true) in the local press, the wire services and the fan magazines. Lou, a widower, lived on Beachwood Drive with an old aunt who baked cakes for S.S. and often sent over a pan of blintzes to be heated in S.S.'s private kitchen.

Lou sat down and attempted to retie a worn, knotted shoelace.

"We got our ass in a sling, S.S."

"I figured that." S.S. tossed aside the letters.

"Somebody is selling S.S. World Pix short, that much I nosed out."

"You think Carl or Fox is trying to take us over?"

"They're horny enough. News is around we owe the

bank five million. Of course I issued a statement our European income is so high we're buying caviar from the damn Bolsies, and Eyetalian art for our theatre lobbies."

"It's closer to four million. We're not getting cash returns from the theatres fast enough. I'm thinking of selling states rights—cash up front."

"No, it only would bring in a few bob. We could send out two hundred more prints."

"Prints cost money, Lou, and Conversion Labs will balk at more credit for prints. We're into them for over four hundred thousand now."

"We should process our own prints." Lou grimaced as a shoelace broke.

S.S. nodded, walked to a cabinet, eyed the bottles of whiskey supplied by the best bootlegger in town, Claude Borgani—"the real good stuff, S.S., no malarkey."

S.S. turned away; his hard rule was never to drink any form of alcohol before six o'clock. From below on the lot a gramophone was playing, "I Got a Bimbo Down on a Bamboo Isle."

"Lou, I want you to take a limo out to Pasadena and pick up Mr. and Mrs. Aaron Bendelbinder at the station. They're coming in on the *Coast Special*. Get them to the Beverly Wilshire Hotel. Have them driven out to dinner at my house at 7:30."

"Bendelbinder? The Great Bargain Stores?"

"Fine people. A grandson of theirs, Karl, was killed in the war, was married to Vera, my sister Rose's daughter."

Lou gave S.S. a searching look. "That the sister who didn't come up with a loan last year?"

S.S. laughed. "That's my sister Rosie, a Hetty Green on the stock market, but can't forgive the fact that I

103

spent my part of our father's estate making what she calls moving snapshots."

Zucker went to the humidor on the golden oak desk where the best cigars were kept and took two out, sniffed them. One he lit from a gold-plated lighter; the other he put away in a vest pocket. He always insisted this kept S.S. from smoking too much.

"When you make the pitch, S.S., don't bullshit. Give it to Bendelbinder straight. *Capise*?"

S.S. scowled and beat a fist on his desk top. "What the hell you talking about?"

Lou made smoke rings and watched them rise. "I'm talking about keeping all this Taj Mahal of dreams—the studio not being sold up to become a bean field again. Bendelbinder has a couple hundred stores. His credit alone is worth millions." Lou looked at S.S. still with a fist on the desk.

"Come on, level with old Lou. You don't need the innocent stare of a baby that just crapped in a diaper."

S.S. smiled sadly, gave a self-deprecatory shrug. He sat way back in his high-backed swivel chair and placed the tips of his fingers together. "When I was East to open at the Empire with *Elephant Island*, I had dinner with them and they seemed interested in movie making. After all, thirty years selling pots and pans and house dresses, Aaron told me, can become damn dull."

"I know, my old man sold shoes."

"Old Aaron and Malka, his wife, they been through the mill, came here without a cent, through Ellis Island in 1894. He was a pack peddler before he started his first bargain store selling bankrupt and odd lots of trash stock. It wasn't like my father who came a solid citizen from Russia, with me and my two sisters with trunks and a fancy social past behind us. Same year, too, we landed in Boston, not the east side of New York. And my father got in with the Irish big shots that ran the state, took it away from the proper Bostonians. It was easier for us than for the Bendelbinders."

"The German Heebs had it the best."

Lou picked up a desk phone and ordered a limo.

"I heard that Nat Bendell, the bigtime gambler involved in the Becker-Rosenthal mess, is their son. This Nat I remember was mixed in with the big hooch mobs. The Moustache Pete's, old Black Hands. Showed lots of moxie when the Naples hoods got run out by the Sicilian gang."

"Never mind that. We have a rambunctious star, Rosalind Clay, who hasn't reported for shooting. Her fucking agent, Nico Pagani, is trying to jack up her price."

"I know. Do I kiss ass or cut her throat? A little item to the press, and it's either way."

"No, she's all right. She's not the usual studio gash. We had some hard years together till we had that big hit in *Irish Annie O'Neil.*"

"I'll just cut Nico's throat. Winchell would like an item as to who's limp-wristed and lavender-scented."

S.S. shook his head, "I don't hurt anybody with not giving them a chance to be good. Just give him a *klop*, scare him. I want her on the set ready to shoot by two o'clock."

When Lou Zucker was gone, S.S. took his pulse, then shook two pills out of a small bottle and swallowed them with half a glass of water.

God, the duplicity, he thought. The wear and tear. Since 1915 he had been flogging himself, always in a hurry, always tying up loose ends, shaking off dishonest partners. Building, expanding, borrowing, merging. Always one step ahead of the collapse of his beloved studio. He was addicted to making motion pictures. Catch him alone and he'd say he wanted to make the most successful films ever made; he wanted to make great

105

films of honest emotional content, to elicit from the audience tears and gasps of admiration. He didn't dare think of art, although in his private projection room he ran the motion pictures of Eisenstein, Pudovkin, Vertov, Turin. His pleasure in a well-made scene, he said, was better than an orgasm. He had gifts for film editing, lighting, sets, and story selection without claiming that abused word "genius." He had an ability for staying solvent where a dozen others had already gone under. In public he showed a pride of achievement; in private he was a brooder with a touch of melancholy, but some crisis was always on hand to give him little time for indulging in self-appraisal.

S.S. became aware of Miss Wilton, prim, neat, sun on her eyeglasses, standing patiently before him.

"S.S., they're waiting for you in the projection room."

He nodded, reached for a cigar. Miss Wilton followed him out with her notebook and his silver ash tray.

11

All night the train had been rushing past the ruby and emerald signal lights at the switching points, coming with dusty windows out of Nevada and climbing down into California, picking its way, Aaron Bendelbinder thought, like a sure-footed mule on a perilous mountain trail. Hard to believe that so many people and oxen pulling covered wagons had once managed the courage to come this way. The great driving wheels of the locomotive were leading the train past the gold and green orchards and field crops, flashing by houses lit by early risers preparing for the day.

In his Pullman car, Aaron Bendelbinder was reciting the morning prayers, standing in his striped shul shawl, wearing *tefillim*, the little black box containing the holy text held against his forehead, the prescribed band binding on arm and fingers, witness to his daily voicing of his faith as an Orthodox Jew. An old man deep in his seventies, joints stiffening, as was clearly shown by the way he swayed, as was proper during prayer.

"Thou shalt love the Lord thy God with all thy heart, with all thy soul . . ."

Malka, his wife, dressed in a blue loose dressing gown over her laced corset, was viewing herself with placid satisfaction in the oval mirror of the washstand, holding on as the train navigated a curve.

Here she was, in a luxury train that for the two days

107

since leaving Chicago had been moving southwest across a vastness of land she had never suspected. Such miles of growing corn, rivers burly with barges and traffic, the excitement of the Mississippi. Her children had years ago come back from school talking of such a river with such a name, and beyond it what an expansion of land, its miles of forests, men harrowing, burning brush, sending up smoke signals while a horse slowly pulled a plow, and so many isolated farm houses, left so quicky behind by a hoot of the engine.

It touched her, all this life she had never been a part of, never would be. Then she was awed by the brown, red and umber deserts, such empty isolation, grim, yet somehow of great beauty, and the horizons of sawtoothed mountains so much further than the horizons of the east she knew.

Swaying in time as the great train circled another curve, she saw the cars behind theirs, segmented like a tail of dusty glass and steel. Now the train slowed to the *ding-dong* of a crossing bell where Model-T autos and horse-drawn wagons waited. She saw the smoke from the train like a dark veil being torn apart as it left the locomotive. She felt again how intensely pathetic it is we can't ever know the lives of towns we pass by.

Aaron finished his prayers, complacent and detached.

Malka adjusted a lock of gray hair. "We can eat in the diner."

"Why not?" He reached for collar and tie. She waited, holding his jacket.

They had been man and wife for nearly fifty years (he preferred to call it "a half a century, a monument of tolerance"). They often understood each other's thoughts without speaking.

He spoke, adjusting the stiff collar. "California, the golden land. A long time already, a new century since we left Bluttah Street in that cursed Poland, and Little Gdansk, that damned *shtetl*."

His wife adjusted his tie, kissed his cheek. "It's a bad sign of getting old, Aaron, talking of the past."

He smiled; for all his material success, the chain of popular-priced bargain stores, his standing in the Jewish community, the Zatomer Burial Society, he felt that Malka was brighter, hardier. In Little Gdansk they had called her the *starker*, the strong one. She had a natural perception of things, could face crises calmly while he agonized, shouted, bellowed, impaled himself on events. How ephemeral life is, after all. All the pressures of the past, the tragic events, their escape from Poland, the struggles in the new land to earn one's bread. Plans, desires. All are like seeds in the wind, so few set down roots.

A son, Nahum, calling himself Nathan, then Nat, first a soldier in the Spanish-American war, a sport, part owner of a notorious New York gambling house until that scandal. Then, with those Italians, bootlegging until it nearly cost him his life as the Sicilians took over.

Now what? A roving life now, better not to know, selling Florida land in some kind of boom down there. But David, the older son (a bit of pride can't harm), a judge on the New York State Supreme Court; unhappy with the injustice he saw, a widower, his son Karl lost in the Great War. Grandchildren, great-grandchildren—Malka had their pictures in her luggage.

Then they were seated in the diner under the fans at the crisp table cloth with at least three Negro waiters, also in crisp white, attending, adjusting silverware, pouring water, Aaron writing out his order of hard-boiled eggs, rolls and no butter, black coffee, no cream.

As he had aged he had become more and more a respecter of the kosher dietary rules. Could one trust black men not to serve *trief*? Malka, who was not so firm about food rituals, ordered scrambled eggs, toast, waffles, cream for her coffee. She didn't care if the food was goyish, but because of Aaron she never mixed meat with dairy dishes.

It was a pleasant journey full of piquant details. Malka, as she aged, was taking joy in just existing, tasting, experiencing. Train travel in the 1920s was a luxury that in a generation or so would disappear, become degraded and limited, but as yet with its *20th Century Limited* that had carried them to Chicago, then crossing town to the Dearborn Station and getting on this grand train—it was a delight. She was determined to enjoy this trip to its fullest.

"Just look, Aaron, those trees have oranges and lemons on them."

"Did you think they grew in the boxes they are sold in?"

He chewed on a roll, cracked and removed the shell of the hard-boiled egg, waving off the service of a waiter.

"Sidney is doing very well with these movies," Malka said, watching another waiter move a pewter cover from a steaming dish of scrambled eggs.

"So it seems." Aaron was still in a bit of awe of the Boston Silverthorns. Malka was distantly related to the late Alex Silverthorn, Sidney's father; David's son Karl had married Sidney's niece Rosa. Yet Aaron never felt the close kinship with the Silverthorns that Malka seemed to assume without doubts or shyness.

They were not making the trip to just visit Sidney Silverthorn, but rather to spare themselves a bone-chilling winter on West End Avenue. For Malka, visiting California had always been a dream, so here they were, rushing through landscapes more highly colored than in the East, with mountains, people in backyards,

110

and patches of red and burned-out desert—the kind, Aaron thought, that Moses must have led the Children of Israel through for forty years. "No trains then," Aaron said out loud and his wife asked, "What?" and he said "Nothing."

Later, while Malka packed and repacked their baggage, Aaron sat in the club car smoking his pipe and reading a raucous *Los Angeles Times* that had been brought aboard at San Bernardino. It featured a society murder, a bit of corruption in city hall, the selection of a queen for the Pasadena Rose Parade, and some kind of a fish called grunion that would come ashore in the moonlight, dance on its tail, lay eggs to be fertilized by the action of the tide. Also the local Zionist Society was having a meeting to support the organizing of a new settlement in Palestine and to demand that the Balfour Declaration for a Jewish homeland, as promised, be put in force. Aaron took out a small notebook and marked down the date and place of the meeting. As he aged, more and more his thoughts had turned toward moving away from the world of business, politics, corruption, the daily struggles going on all around him in the postwar world of the twenties. Perhaps going to visit Palestine, see the school for orphans he helped support in Haifa, pray at the Wailing Wall, all that remained of the great temple destroyed by the Romans.

The porter was at his elbow. "We be in Pasadena in twenty minutes, sir."

That's the world, Aaron thought, as he knocked out his pipe—you dream of Jerusalem and you get Pasadena.

There were palm trees near the station—tall, naked trunks with frond clusters like heads of hair—and the scent of orchards, and horse droppings. A comforting warmth filled the air. A shaggy fellow came up to them

111

and wrung their hands. "I'm Lou Zucker. S.S. sent me. Welcome."

"S.S.?" asked Malka, carrying a heavy coat on her arm, and a large handbag on a glittery bronze chain. "And why did we get off here?"

"Mr. Silverthorn. Here he's S.S. Important people get off here. The rest go on to Los Angeles. A good trip?"

"Fine," said Aaron, counting their baggage. "These sleeping cars are really marvelous."

Down by the engine, a group of reporters and photographers had surrounded a slim young man in a belted tan topcoat; he was wearing a hat with the brim pulled way down on one side.

"Who's that?" asked Malka. "Einstein, it isn't."

Lou Zucker motioned to a chauffeur to take over the baggage and slipped a dollar into the porter's hand. "You can tell your grandchildren, Mrs. Bendelbinder, you saw Rudy Valentino, the kid himself, in the flesh . . ."

"He's that actor?" Aaron asked, "the tango where he knocks his heels on the floor, smokes long cigarettes?"

"He's a fine *mensh*, really, Mr. Bendelbinder. Not a *putz* like so many of these actors. My Rachel, she knew some Bendelbinders in Bialystok. But I don't suppose . . ."

"A distant cousin. We came over from Little Gdansk. But I'll accept you as a *Landsmann*."

Lou Zucker laughed, "If we don't accept each other, who will? Mr. Silverthorn had me get you a suite at the Beverly Wilshire Hotel, and I can put this car at your service."

"No, no, they have taxis?"

"S.S., Mr. Silverthorn, wouldn't like that. Anyway, you're having dinner at his house tonight. I'll have you picked up at seven o'clock."

112

"Very kind," said Malka. Fine as the three-day train ride had been, she was shaking as if still in the compartment. All she wanted was a real bath and wide bed.

The suite was a mixture of Louis Quinze and art moderne in gold and blue. The twin beds were soft, and there was a huge basket of fruit in a straw basket trimmed with red ribbons: oranges as big as grapefruit, apples redder than most and highly polished, grapes like pigeon eggs; a pineapple regally dominated the collection.

A card in an envelope was marked in a bold handwriting:

Sorry I couldn't meet you. We'll all be together this evening. Meanwhile enjoy the products of this part of the country.

Sidney

Malka palmed an orange. "When the Jews stop offering each other fruit you can be sure, Aaron, the Messiah is about to appear."

12

Social and material success for S.S. meant changing his place of residence. What had been good enough in his early days—a small, snug house on Beachwood Drive overlooking Hollywood—soon yielded to a more ample house on Yucca Drive. But now, with the continuing success of Silverthorn World Films, there had to be a mansion on North Elm in Beverly Hills, still a new scene for the well-off. The palm trees and other varieties of lush, tropical plants were still young; just as Beverly Hills had yet to mature to its full growth. But already the perpetual social climbers were looking to the west to the Bel Air hills, which were even more of a status symbol. Still in the future was the final high plateau in the social order, Palm Springs; then it was little more than a dusty, sunburnt village owned by an Indian tribe.

S.S. had built on his two lots a Spanish-style house—a style just coming back to popularity, since a cultural fair of a few years before in San Diego had made Hispanic shapes and detail the most desired style. S.S.'s residence had two-feet-thick walls, red tile roofs and Alhambra windows with cast-iron grills hammered into various forms by a local forge. Inside were high-ceilinged rooms with painted rafters; twisting staircases with black iron railings; rounded Moorish arches that opened to spaces of pegged oak floors; and Iberian tiles waist high in many places. Overhead brass lamps hung on chains. A fountain in the patio was surrounded by rare hibiscus plants and cacti set in colorfully painted Mexican pots. Hanging baskets contained cape primrose and begonias, other flowering plants, and staghorn ferns. There was a swimming pool, of course, but S.S. had not yet gone as far as a private tennis court or a steam bath; croquet on a smooth-shaved lawn and bathrooms with gold-plated faucets would have to do. In the four-car garage, disguised as a mission chapel, were two Cadillacs, a Pierce Arrow, and S.S.'s favorite, a cream-colored Dusenberg with red leather trim.

The status symbols of the automobile were still in a formative stage. As Harry Silverthorn was to write later in a high school essay, "The second-hand Cadillac is now the car for Negro servants; the Lincoln is still okay, but to cut the mustard you have to have a Daimler, Mercedes, or Rolls. Of course, for a kid to have a pony was the same as for some college boy to drive a Stutz Bearcat."

The age of the Cord and the Porsche was yet to come, but a few Jaguars were soon to be heard on Sunset Boulevard, mufflers wide open. Gasoline prices were rising: it was seventeen cents a gallon.

When Aaron and Malka Bendelbinder arrived at the Silverthorn's Elm Drive residence, a dozen people were having drinks out on the patio. Hispanic servants were passing around trays of hors-d'oeuvres, the splashing of the fountain under a spotlight in the gathering dusk adding its sound to the murmur of small talk and short bursts of laughter.

S.S., in a dark, sporting-cut jacket, shook the hands of the Bendelbinders, covering Malka's with two hands.

"Ah, Mrs. B., meet my wife Nora. Aaron and Malka Bendelbinder, my dear."

"How pleased," said Nora Silverthorn. She had been the star of an early Hungarian film, *Queen of Babylon*, a picture in seven reels that S.S. had imported early in his career, and her with it. Her career had foundered in America as fashions in films changed. She had gained weight but still retained that dark, heavy head of hair, the moon face of mysterious features that had given her European films their intrinsic charm. She was the daughter of a Jewish cattle dealer and butcher from Miskole named Baruch. She and S.S. had two children, Harry and Shari.

Nora had never fully learned to understand English, and while she had a good mind and an enigmatic resiliency, in Budapest she had been assertive and aggressive. In Hollywood, as a permanent exile, she had accepted isolation, resignation, and her husband's unfaithfulness. She lived in a chronic anxiety of making a social faux pas—the wrong seatings at a dinner, the "French chef" (actually from Luxembourg) spoiling the Beef Wellington, or laughing at the wrong time at a guest's remark (or not laughing at some joke that she failed to understand).

"Fine place you have here, Mrs. Silverthorn," said Malka, eyeing the guests as if they were exotic animals in a zoo.

"Is big, very big."

"Everything is Spanish," said Aaron.

"That's right," said S.S. "The tiles are from Madrid, the rafters I grabbed from an old mission that was torn down."

To show the strength of the floor, he stood on his toes and bounced up and down. "Solid floors, pegged, not a nail. Came from the Philippines. Those chairs from a church Pancho Villa knocked over in Mexico."

"They have crosses on them," Malka observed.

"Decor," said Nora, "dey was made by Christian Indians."

"Show Mrs. B. here the powder room, dear," said the host to his wife. "The plumbing we made here, it's from the set of *The French Widow*, our biggest grossing picture last year. So, come meet some people, Aaron."

The men seemed to Aaron like mannequins: two actors, a German director with a monocle, and Lou Zucker, whom he knew. The women seemed a bit less formal in bobbed hair, all showing a great deal of leg, wearing the popular tube dresses with the very low belts; they seemed breastless and hipless. One handled a jade green cigarette holder with enthusiastic stabbing gestures. "Nifty, real nifty."

S.S. introduced a tall, broad, middle-aged man holding a highball in each hand. He had a handsome, weathered face with a graying Buffalo Bill moustache and Van Dyke beard.

"Aaron, I want you to meet Ira Silverthorn. No relative, maybe, but I trust him anyway. Ira, Aaron Bendelbinder."

Aaron nodded. "You make pictures too?"

"Not me, no sirree. I'm in real estate. Land, orchards, and if you're staying I'll show you something nice in a house near the ocean."

"Just visiting."

"Say," Ira said, sipping a drink, "met your son Nat in Saratoga couple years back. Took me in poker for a hundred."

Aaron nodded. "He's like you now, interested in land in Florida. Says there's a big boom coming."

S.S. helped himself to a plate of baby-pink shrimp, offered it to Aaron who said no, they weren't kosher. S.S., in his own defense, pointed out that he did keep the dietary laws in the house by not mixing dairy and meat dishes.

118

Ira Silverthorn, still holding the two highballs and sipping from each in turn, grinned. "What the hell, those taboos were all right for a tribe of wandering desert shepherds four thousands years ago, but here in the West, Mr. Bendelbinder, if it doesn't eat you, you eat it."

"Ira is sort of a native son, been here since Christ was a cowboy. Came with the missions and the Mexicans. Used to own half this county."

"Not half, but a hell of a lot of it. Some good Long Beach frontage. West of LaBrea on Sunset out to the bean fields. But come the money panic of '07, I was overextended. It went like the wind in a leaky balloon."

"You wouldn't believe it what he owned once. He and his father-in-law, rest in peace, old Moe Handler . . . I found Ira couple years back in a little office on Fairfax renting stores and selling lots in Redondo. But he had an option on some failed lumber yard next to the studio that I needed for a new film stage. So he hunts land for me now."

"Sid still likes bargains." Ira was the only acquaintance of the founder of Silverthorn Wold Pictures who called him Sid and not S.S.

The relationship of the two men was strong, even if S.S. felt Ira had let too many opportunities slip away. The drive and ambitions of Ira's youth had been dented by failure, but he had retained an elasticity of spirit and was amused at human fallibility.

Actually only S.S. knew what had turned away the big Dutchman from pursuit of material success. His wife Rita had been killed in 1911 while riding; her horse had stepped into a gopher hole and fell with a shattered foreleg; she had been flung to the ground and broken her neck.

There had been a restless, tragic period of drinking

and wandering through Europe. His two children were cared for by his father-in-law. In 1912, sobered up somewhat after settling his meager estate, Ira had booked passage to America on the *Titanic* but was delayed by a three-day card game at Brown's Hotel in London. He took his escape from death in the icy waters of the north Atlantic as an omen that God was favoring him again.

But he never had any new interest in making a fortune or getting married again. When drinking, he would hide the agony of his loss with levity. "No, don't take a wife. You get to love her so much you lose your sense of balance, forget you can't win. It's like losing a dog you're crazy over. Maybe you can replace a dog but not really a wife, if you're finicky."

Even sober, he said very little about his past. He lived off his small real estate business, the commissions from the land deals he found for S.S.

The fortune of his father-in-law Moses Handler had mostly disappeared in early recessions and panics and changing merchandising methods, and the old man's neglect as he grew older. Moses seemed to think more of his Chinese cook, of his collection of Indian pottery than of trying to save his dwindling empire of general stores and shops. When he died a victim of the 1919 Spanish influenza epidemic, there was just a small trust fund left for Ira's children that would see them through college. "The lawyers came out best," Ira said. "Trust the shysters for that."

Someplace inside S.S.'s Spanish house a dinner gong was being struck. S.S. began to wave his guests indoors to the dining room, "My bootlegger sent over half a case of Clos-Vougeot and Chateau-Lafite."

Ira lifted two more highball glasses off a tray and said to Aaron, "You can trust Sid's bootlegger. It's safe to get swacked here."

"I'll remember that," said Aaron. He liked this big man, his directness and irreverence. He must talk to him about the Zionist movement.

13

Most of the dinner guests had left—two had to be helped out—and from the patio garden the night scent of magnolia and trumpet vine was strong as it came through the double windows of S.S.'s den. Ira and Aaron sat deep in red leather club chairs facing S.S. who, in a substantial black chair, was fingering an unlit cigar. Behind him, screen scripts and trade journals were scattered about or piled on shelves to dangerous heights. The pine-knotted walls held plaques and awards, few of any importance, but impressive. A large oil painting of Nora and the two children by an admirer of John Singer Sargent, but without his skill, took up nearly an entire wall—its artistic deficiencies accentuated by overbold color.

S.S. reached for a lighter on an end table and slowly lit his cigar, rotating its end carefully into the flame. "That's it, Aaron. It's only the beginning. I'm a man of a boldness, yes. Not rashness, no. Movies haven't reached yet half their viewers. Why in a few years they'll be in color, may even talk. Don't look so bug-eyed, Ira."

Ira was holding a snifter of brandy. "Talking? Feeling pictures maybe too, Sid?"

"Edison had pictures talking years ago. He put a record disc and film strip together in 1904. But none of the geezers wanted it then. I tell you there's no limit.

123

The world is on its bended knees, like Jolson, for story-telling, hungry to see their dreams on a screen."

Aaron felt like a guest who had been asked to sing for his supper. Yet Sidney Silverthorn was no snake oil salesman or medicine show spieler. You could see the man was really carried away with this obsession for making motion pictures.

"I tell you, Sidney, your offer to have me come in with you is an interesting one. I think you could be right that the industry can only grow."

"Can! It's already racing around the world. Hell, the man-eating natives in Borneo, the Indians in Peru, they know Mary Pickford, Doug, Tom Mix, like they know their fingers; in Russia they teach D.W. Griffith's *Intolerance* in the film schools as if it were holy Bolshevik text."

"Do they pay?" asked Ira.

"They'll pay to keep the *mojiks* happy, even if at times in only rugs and camels. Merchandise, right, Aaron?"

Aaron tried to find simple words. "The Great Bargain Stores, as you know, are now listed on the Stock Exchange. We have stockholders and must operate under the rules of the Exchange."

"You're president, chairman, the whole *macher*."

"Yes, but at a board meeting I can't get up and say, 'gentlemen, ladies, we're making moving pictures' . . . We are in the business of pots and pans and yard goods."

"You're the major stockholder, Aaron. Any bank will take your holdings as collateral, and—"

"Right, Sidney. And I've done just that. I'm with my son Nat in Florida land development. He and his partners are planning a whole city called Diamond Coves below Palm Beach and Miami. They're dredging, rooting out the mangroves, pumping sand and coral."

"You're in deep?" asked S.S.

"I am. The boom is coming, people who know say. Now if all things work out I could sell off some of my shares in Diamond Coves if there really is profit to be made, and take a flier in pictures. But right now . . ."

S.S. was thinking, puffing on his cigar as if trying to create a cloud of burning Havana leaf. "What do you think, Ira, of this Florida talk? Real, or sharpies going for broke?"

"Look around you—everybody is buying stock, burning it up, dancing the bunny hug; people are drinking oceans of bootleg booze—by the way, this brandy isn't bad. I'd say it's going to be a good long ride of prosperity. This Coolidge is keeping hands off. Land values will skyrocket."

Aaron said, "What spare cash I have I'm giving help to a home for orphans in Jerusalem and to the Zionists working for a homeland."

S.S. grimaced. He picked up a photograph in a silver frame of a young man in an RAF uniform standing by the wreckage of a plane with German crosses on its smashed wings.

"Another Zionist dreamer. That's my sister Rose's son Paul. An ace with the British he was and now he's working collecting funds in Europe for a Jewish homeland."

"Good for him."

"Yes? Also travels around doing what? Buying up weapons for the settlements in Palestine to defend themselves against attacks. An American! Crazy, I call it."

Ira winked at Aaron. "Not so crazy. The Balfour Declaration promised a Jewish state on what had been Jewish land for thousands of years."

S.S. waved off the idea. "The British aren't letting Jews in for long. This crazy nephew of mine is also involved in the smuggling of Russian refugees into Palestine. I offered him a job here in my studio, as story editor; he's a kind of half-assed writer. No, he's chasing something that can harm us here. We're Americans! We're no fuckin' Polish ghetto herring peddlers."

Aaron decided to change the conversation. Clearly Zionism was a subject that angered S.S. "So, Sidney, you believe in Florida land?"

S.S. stood up and walked to the windows. The spotlight on the fountain had been turned off and the white plume of gushing water was a dancing ghost. He turned and stood in thought, twisting his shoulders as if his clothes were too tight.

"If this Florida land thing looks good we don't need cash. Suppose, just suppose, we traded shares, your Florida shares for Silverthorn World Pictures stock— sort of merged the two enterprises? Who needs cash? Does Morgan or Rockefeller use cash? No."

Ira smiled. "Sid, sometimes you're a cockeyed sixteen-jewel genius."

Aaron looked in wonder from one man to the other. He had a reputation as a hard-headed businessman; one had to be ruthless as a hungry shark to have established over a hundred bargain stores. He could make sudden decisions, bluff when he had to, but in a business he knew from its hardships and the painful years of struggle. However, this making of motion pictures, this talk of land developers merging with film makers, was crazy. He would have to take it slowly, walk warily. "What advantage would a merger be to you, Sidney?"

Ira finished his drink. "Advantage? Both movies and land are growth industries. And best of all, with Silverthorn Pictures in such a merger, Sid can get bank credits for expansion, bigger and better pictures. Is he a genius or isn't he?"

"Thirty, forty more features a year, Aaron. A new

series of two-reel comedies like Sennett's. And I've this idea for a film newspaper, a better newsreel, with cameramen all over the world, not just pictures of cute baby contests or Elks' parades. Already I'm going to take pictures of this new Miss America thing in Atlantic City."

Aaron observed that S.S. was becoming more animated by the moment by his visions, gripped by a maniacal intensity, a driving, tenacious faith in the future.

"Ira, go to Florida," said S.S. "We'll talk it all over. He turned to a disordered shelf of books and bound scripts, tossed off a few, and dug up a batch of blue-covered pages.

"Here it is—*Pagan Islands*, a South Seas romance we can shoot in Diamond Coves."

"It's just mangroves and sand."

"We'll tie together the picture and the development." He handed the pages to Aaron. "Read it. If I'm any judge—and I am a good judge of solid commercial stories—this is it, simple, direct. Beachcombers, pearl diving, a native girl, a half breed, of course. They have sharks in Florida?"

Ira just shook his head as the adrenalin pumped quicker in S.S.'s body.

Aaron waved off the offer of the screenplay. "I'm no judge of these things. Let's not get carried away, Sidney. We'll talk. We're here for two weeks." He stood up. "It's been a good dinner, good company. Now, I'll find Malka and we'll get a good night's sleep."

Ira said, "You'll sleep like a top. Keep a window open—fine air."

Behind the house dogs had turned up some small night creature and were thrashing about in the back gardens of the house, hunting for it.

* * *

127

Later, at the hotel, Aaron stood at the double windows in his long night shirt, looking down on the night city, winding his heavy, double-lidded gold watch. Behind him Malka was remaking the bed, she being of the impression hotel maids never did it properly.

"They live a little crazy here, Aaron. You think Sidney's wife is happy? I tell you, he leads her a fancy dance."

Aaron finished winding the watch; he knew from years of caring for it just when the spring was tight enough. He put the watch carefully on the night table, added his reading glasses, his wallet, a handkerchief folded four times.

"It's a new world, the fruit is too red and no taste. Everything with orange juice, and drinking, and jazz babies dancing to saxophones. Is that music?"

"Don't be an *alter kocker*. New York is no different." She smoothed the pillows and then thumped them into a proper shape. "What was so long among you men?"

"Sidney wants me to become a kind of partner in making these movie pictures."

"Always you were against something you didn't know."

"I said I'd think it over."

"Think a long time."

He slid off his yellow slippers. "I wonder about this twentieth century. It doesn't connect with the world we were young in. I worry where it's rushing in such a hurry. Nobody stops to breathe, to be polite."

Malka said, "If I lived here I'd play tennis every day, like Nora . . ."

Searching, Aaron thought, we're still searching. Tennis! I am still a stranger in a strange land. I have tried not to commit the sin of feeling that I am better than anyone else; snobbery in its worse sense doesn't come from me. I like people—sometimes those that were bad

128

for me; I believe in work, in prayer, and doing what I have to on a job. I haven't outgrown pity and mercy. To ourselves each of us is a peculiar private person.

He nodded as if agreeing with his thoughts. He, a man who had need for God's word but not being trained in Talmudic lore, avoided much of the dogmatic hair-splitting that was often the game of scholars and other endowed loafers. His life had been lived in a simplicity of means, and he sadly suspected, standing there in his long night gown, that the true Paradise is often Paradise Lost. He expected no glittering reward for his faith. There was, he had long sensed, a natural instability to the world. He recalled the words of the learned Rabbi of Lutzvina: "Think of yourself as the new autumn apple hurrying to mature before the winter freeze."

Out loud he said, "I look around, everybody is in a hurry making money or thinking of making it."

"Didn't you?" Malka got into the bed, twisting the two gray braids of her hair into shape for sleeping. "I think I'll bob my hair. What do you think?"

"You want to be a *maydella*, a flapper, a young girl again?"

"Wouldn't you want to be a *yingel* if you could?"

Stiffly, he got into bed beside her. "No, not to go through it all again. Maybe it would be different, but sometimes I think God is indifferent to human concerns, and unlike Him we are obsessed by mortality. We seem to be living on the wrong side of the looking glass. Is it happening right side out? Then I feel there is nothing certain but uncertainty. You agree?"

Malka, eyes closed, head on pillow, grunted.

"I'm an old man. I think what if I go to Palestine, pray at the Wall of the Second Temple, see the citron growing, and if I die there what better place for a Jew to salt down in his bones in the old homeland, just to be with Solomon, David, Isaiah, Jeremiah." Aaron realized the brandy was still purring in his bloodstream; he was talking as if he were Job with his bare ass in the cactus patch.

"Sleep well, Malka," he said, turning off the night table lamp. But she was already asleep, making her nocturnal breathing. In the streets some jazz baby driving by leaned on an auto horn.

14

During the night, the *Sunshine Flier* had passed through Washington D.C., in the cold, window-pelting rain, whistled for crossings in Maryland, touched Richmond, Charleston, Savannah. It had stopped to take on water and add some special people at Daytona Beach, then raced beside the gem-blue ocean for Miami.

Laura North had risen early and breakfasted on French toast and coffee. After three years on the *New York Evening Sun*, she no longer found Pullman travel to be the novelty it had been when at twenty she had left Vassar to write the paper's minor obituaries and cover ethnic weddings ("not Negroes, of course, unless it's Ethel Waters or Josephine Baker"). She wasn't important enough to follow the drawn-out torture of Sacco and Vanzetti, but she had gotten a byline on some second-rate gangster killings, and Mr. Jenkins, the feature editor, had taken her to lunch at Keen's Chop House in the McAlpin Hotel.

Mr. Jenkins, it was rumored, led a maladjusted home life—with three unmarried daughters.

Now she was heading south to do a series on the fabulous, unbelievable Florida land boom.

"Now remember we're not the *World* or the *Journal*; no flashy prose, just straight facts, get what I mean?" Jenkins told her.

Later some gossip columnists were to say Jerry T.

131

Jenkins had been the basis of one of the characters in the play *The Front Page*; that was when he was a young hell-raiser in Chicago. But when he hired Laura North he was fifty—not drinking much, but going on a bender twice a year when he looked closely at his three ugly, motherless daughters, and thought of the unfinished novel in some desk drawer.

They were sitting in Louie's Place the day before she left. "In the 1920s it was a tradition," he told Laura, "that a newspaperman drink, lap up the sauce like nobody else, and must be writing a novel. But you stick to reporting. I know they call it journalism, honey, but journalists change their socks more than once a month. Now, you being a little lady, college degree, New England blood line, let me give you a few tips." He leaned forward. "All horse players don't die broke. So, remember in writing of Jews avoid the stereotypes—don't depict all of them as a little comical and pious, unless they're gangsters, and all aren't dominated by their wives and mothers."

"Isn't that true?"

"No, it isn't. Maybe our readers think so. The *Sun* is a conservative Republican rag so they like stereotypes of Abey and Moe and Max. To them no Italian speaks good English, the Germans are all fat and eat sauerkraut, and the dinges—"

"Dinges?" asked Laura, watching the speakeasy cat, bored with her six kittens in a box by the phone booth, wander off.

"Smokes, coons, burrheads. Negroes. They have them in Salem, don't they?"

"Only a few families. They are auto mechanics. One is a doctor who is a snob, and Mrs. Wallace is a trained nurse."

"You're spoiling the picture. A Negro is supposed to

be always jigging, has a soul for the blues, Dixieland jazz and loves watermelon and—"

"Fried chicken," added Laura. "Yes, there are stereotypes. I'll avoid them."

"Now you'll find a lot of Jews down there in Florida. New Yorkers mostly, so get names."

"Yes, Mr. Jenkins."

Back in the city room he gave her some notes. "Facts, local color, and if you get close to a real Rum Row story, the bootleggers running in the stuff from the West Indies, give me a couple of columns, but don't drink the damn stuff, it might be Jamaica ginger and you'll go blind. You can cover Colonel Parker and his gambling club in Palm Beach, but stay away from the Capone boys in Miami. You'll lose your virginity."

"Mr. Jenkins, I was married."

He looked up at her from his pile of galley proofs, his blue eyes slightly bloodshot, the green eyeshade he always wore coloring his jowls a graveyard tone. "So you were, Laura, so you were. Well, keep your nose and expense account clean. And pare the copy down to two thousand words a story. If we get ten good features I'll take you to dinner at McShorley's Saloon for a sampling of the brew."

"No girl could ask for more." Bed would be next on the agenda with Mr. Jenkins.

As the *Sunset Flier* passed seaside houses with red tile roofs and barbered palm trees, she opened the yellow-covered *Complete Florida Guide* at a marked passage; but it was no good, just a booster's handout. Mr. Jenkins expected something better. She hadn't lied about her marriage, but for all her genteel bourgeois past, she was still a virgin and ashamed of it. In early 1924 she had gone uptown to the New York School of Fine and Applied Arts to do a story on Frank Alvin

133

Parsons and had been shown around the place by Ralph Pointer—tall, blond, very British, in his forties, clean fingernails (Christian Scientists and insurance salesmen, her grandmother up in Salem had always insisted, look to their fingernails first—if they're not clean, a sign of bad character). Ralph's nails had been very clean and he took her to a high-class speak over on 54th Street with its paper grape leaves and a smell of sour mash and grain alcohol. They had a good pasta dinner and a bottle of red after two scotch-and-sodas at the bar. Then a nuzzling ride on the top of a double-decker Fifth Avenue bus right up to the Cloisters and a hasty kiss at the door of her East 72nd Street rooming house. Missing a father, she trusted older men. They were married a week later and it turned out in the next two weeks he was unable to deflower her, as he had strained himself at handball at the English Arts Club. He was neat and found too much affection embarrassing. When not teaching dynamic symmetry at the art school, he spent a lot of his time with Ossie, a red-headed young man from Virginia who worked in the rug department at Bloomingdale's. Laura walked in one Saturday afternoon, her interview with Bishop Hayes in New Brunswick having been canceled by the churchman's sudden collapse and death at morning mass, and found Ralph and Ossie locked together in the big bed, attempting to strangle each other with their cocks. It seemed that Ralph, in the country on a student's visa, needed an American wife to stay on in the U.S.

The train had increased its speed and she gulped, hiccupped, very sad. Her grandmother had written from Salem, "City men tend to take up the vices of wily Orientals, Greeks, Jews, and of course, the English Church, army, and navy are given to buggery. Cultivate your soul. Keep your bowels open."

So she was a divorced virgin. What the hell. She'd do a crackerjack series of articles and finish that book of poems, *Love And All That Stuff*. She had in the Village met some of Ralph's friends: Edna, Bunny, Dos, Floyd, all poets and writers. She had cut her hair into bangs like Dorothy Parker.

Laura took out her wad of research notes on Florida and reread them. Yes, she'd go to bed with Mr. Jenkins (his fingernails were bitten off) and learn to like needle beer, develop a stability of purpose. The notes were neat, slanting to the right, the T's firmly crossed.

Miami, Florida, as we know it. In 1870, Henry B. Lum tried to settle in Miami to grow cocoanuts, with a land-selling scheme on the side, but the project was a failure. Then in 1890 Henry Flagler began to inch his railroad south, first to Palm Beach, then to Miami, building hotels, casinos, and churches along the way. By 1912 there was a bridge from Miami to a sand spit, Miami Beach. By mid 1920s this great lush land boom had begun.

No gambling of any size in the early days, just small bets on yacht races, lawn games, private card games. Then post-war progress. First gambling house in Miami run by two characters, McCall and Morris, the Beach and Tennis Club. Featured no outdoor sports but did have Helen Morgan singing, usually seated sadly on a piano. "A class joint." Gourmet tropical food—one had to have a bankroll to get in. Town expanded to other gambling places, Embassy Club, the Brook Club; the mob has a share of many of these enterprises and in hotels that run gambling, mob often takes as much as one-fourth share of the gambling income. Tried to muscle in to the Villa Venice, the

Deauville Casino. Talk of Chicago-style warfare. Some townies who refused demands brought down own gunmen to protect interests. Sheriff's office enormously profitable; one gambling house owner claimed he pays sheriff's people a thousand a week for the right to run wide open. Local law has an insatiable appetite for graft.

The young porter (she was one of the few in the car who hadn't called him George or boy) told her, "Be in Miami half an hour. You want to get to Miami Beach you hurry to get a taxi to cross the Causeway. Very busy times in Miami."

"Where is Coral Gables, Diamond Coves?"

"Oh, just to the south. Not far down. Thank you, ma'am."

He put away the two dollars she handed him. Laura carefully noted that amount on her expense account beside the cost of her meals. She did not pad her account. The Norths were an old New England family who were going downhill in the twentieth century but still proudly sticking to old moral values. Laura's great-grandfather had owned fabric mills. Her grandfather had been ruined playing the market in grain futures and cotton and wool speculations. Her father, dead many years now, had ended his career as a barber, the second chair on the left, in the Somerset Hotel. Grandma had raised Laura and sent her through college and preached moral courage, fresh air, and wholesome thoughts.

Laura located the small notebook in her handbag:

Stay at Biscayne House on Collins Avenue. Moderate rates. Contacts: Mr. Cecil Wright, Miami Beach Chamber of Commerce; Gloria Henley, press rep, Miami Hotel Association; Carter Brooks, feature editor, Miami Herald; Nat Bendell, builder,

Damond Coves; Montez Tjaden, publicity for Greater Florida Real Estate Guild.

The train pulled in. The sun was dazzling lime-white, and there were fuchsia, camellias, phlox. Men in linen suits and Panama hats greeted men in northern tailoring. Taxis were doing a brisk trade carrying off people and luggage. A great many tanned faces, a few with noses peeling. She was shocked by the loud colors, the men without jackets or ties—in New York, even to go without a vest was daring.

On an Adams Express station cart a casket was being pushed toward the open door on a baggage car across the tracks. Laura averted her eyes. She had always, for all her obituary writing, feared the idea of dying, of death, funeral trimmings, graveyards and mourning bands. Grandma had never sold her on the church's dogma—there is no death, no evil, no pain. Carrying her portable typewriter and her battered suitcase, she went to hunt up a taxi. The only dogma she wanted to believe in at the moment was: there is no heat rash, but already her neck was red and was itching.

15

In her collecting of information, Laura found that Diamond Coves had originally been called Crab Inlet, an insect-infested place set among thick mangrove growths, Spanish bayonet plants, and wild bitter oranges. Before the Civil War, Abolitionists smuggled out runaway slaves by small schooners. After the war, until Prohibition came in, it had been a village of lopsided shacks and patched, unpainted fishing boats. Once in a while the boats brought in great goggle-eyed turtles that they slaughtered on the shore and stewed in an iron cauldron. Checking old records, Laura found the people were a mixture of beaten-down whites with a high yellow complexion, either from mixing breeds or a persistent fever they called "the ol' shakes."

When the rum runners in their fast boats began to appear in 1920, Crab Inlet had a few months of prosperity; new shoes, store teeth and flivvers appeared as sacks of whiskey, rum, and brandy were brought ashore, and trucks came through the cane breaks on a new secret road cut through for them to load and carry off the landed cargoes. But that had not lasted for long. Federal agents began a series of raids; there were gun fights all along the Inlet. After several seizures of cargo from the West Indies ports of the bootleggers, the good times were over.

The only recall of that period Laura found were reports of the remains of a crab-eaten body turning up in a fisherman's net and the rusting shape of a discarded flivver used by the shaggy children as a hiding place in their savage games. Crab Inlet went back to its smoky, disreputable way of survival—odorous, noxious, definitely subnormal.

It became Diamond Coves when agents began to appear in crumpled linen suits wiping out the sweat bands of their Panamas with silk handkerchiefs, beating at the biting insects on their damp necks, and offering low prices for the mangrove swamps, cane breaks, and the crescent of shacks along the only cleared area.

The Diamons Coves Estates sent in tractors to clear the wild growths; the mangroves and their obscene, probing roots were sawed off close to the water and then great hoses began to suck up from the Inlet sand of crushed coral to cover the roots. Roads and streets were cut through shrub, more sand was sucked up, and acres of beach front were created. What had been neglected drainage canals became waterways, and ingratiating colored billboards and signs went up on the still raw land.

Laura North's taxi brought her to the Civic Center of Diamond Coves, as yet not completed. On planks laid across an unpaved section of sidewalk bordered by poplars, roses, and amaranth, she walked to the Land and Sales Office. The walls of its outer room were taken up with land plats, sales charts, and some ostentatious watercolor paintings of the projected City of Diamond Coves, with its ten-story hotel, rows of Riviera villas, Spanish haciendas, two- to five-acre Ponce de Leon tracts, and a tile and brick city hall topped by an Italian bell tower.

Several men sat around at card tables making phone calls, pouring out a sales pitch. Two girls with shingled

140

hair and heavy earrings were busy at Underwood type-writers.

"Go right in, honey," said one of the men when Laura asked for Mr. Bendell.

She tapped on a frosted glass panel, and went into a square room with a wooden floor, a draftsman's tilted table, a scale model of a city, looking like children's toys set on a work bench. A handsome man in his middle forties was holding a sandwich in one hand, a cup of coffee in the other.

"Hello, hello, come right in. You're Miss Laura North of *New York Evening Sun.*"

"I've interrupted your lunch."

"Everybody does. Coffee?" He pointed to a pot on a hot plate.

"Black."

"Grab a seat. We're still not furnished."

They sat on two folding chairs sipping the coffee, a half-eaten sandwich set aside on a pile of blueprints.

"We're six weeks behind on everything. Furniture still in New York. These crackers work real slow. Half our streets laid out but water mains, gas lines, curbing still to do and people crazy to move in."

"You believe in this boom, Mr. Bendell?"

"Cross my heart, hope to die, I do."

She was impressed with what she knew of him from the *Sun's* files—an immigrant boy who set up a stove and shoe polish business in his early teens, a volunteer soldier in Cuba and the Philippines in the Spanish American War, a partner in a plush New York City gambling house, a noted sport at Saratoga, forced to give up his gambling interests after the Rosenthal-Becker scandal that exposed payoffs to city hall and the police, later involved in dealings in illegal alcohol with some Italian gangs.

141

This background seemed impossible of this well-dressed man smiling at her, so neat in a pale gray silk shirt, dark tie, ivory-colored linen suit cut just a bit tight; narrow, off-white, well-fitted oxfords, not the two-tones popular among the Florida dandies.

" 'World history is city history,' some guy said. So it's no boom, Miss North. This is a solid expansion of what I hate to call the American Dream, but what else is it? A vacation land for just folks from the middle class, a playground for the well-off."

"I read in one of your folders that Florida has always been for the rich."

"No more. Anyone can afford to build on a lot, his own bit of land to put up a cottage or a villa. You want to take notes?"

"I'll remember. Just who is the Diamond Coves Estates Corporation?"

He smiled blandly at her, took one of her hands in his. She noted a diamond ring on one finger. "Ah, Miss North, right to the point. We're properly charted by the state, approved by the county, strictly kosher all along the line."

"*Who* is the company? It's a costly project."

"Ten million. I'm president, director, and we have shareholders, important people, smart investors."

"How many million did you yourself put in?"

He smiled like a parent at a sassy child. "Come on, sweetie, you want a full report on the setup, right? The by-laws, the financing, the bank credits that back us up?"

"If I'm to write a good story, yes."

"The whole *magillah*, right? Right. You have dinner with me tonight at the Clover Club and I'll bring the full shareholders report. You like dancing?"

"I dance." She smiled at his gaucherie, his informality. He had charm—oh boy, did he—and that boldness,

142

a directness as if he were willing to tell you all. She'd hate, however, to get into a poker game with him . . . She and Grandma, on rainy days or when snowed in, used to play cut-throat poker for matchsticks.

"Good, Laura. Here's a scoop for you. We're in the process of merging with Silverthorn World Pictures. They're going to shoot features here, build a studio. Who's your favorite movie star?"

"Milton Sills." (With what ease he had slipped in that "Laura.")

"No kidding? Mine is Clara Bow. You look like her; anyone ever tell you that?"

"I thought people felt I was more like Dorothy Parker."

"Don't know her. Look, I'll have one of my boys show you around. I'd do it myself, only I've got this meeting in Miami."

"Can I get a taxi late?"

"Skip it, sweetie. I'll have one of the boys take you back. Just leave your address outside with one of the girls. I'll pick you up at seven, okay?"

She said okay, feeling herself a pilgrim in a new land. She had met Jews in New York in her newspaper work but had seen them as a people sufficient unto themselves. Grandma talked as if they had horns, but that they were much like anyone else was clear, or so it seemed to her as she left to inspect Diamond Coves with a young man with splendid teeth, a military moustache, and a British accent to match.

Laura did like dancing. Sometimes when depressed in her tiny room at the Martha Washington Hotel (women only), she would wind up her small Victrola, put on "Tea for Two" or "Alice Blue Gown" and dance in her stockinged feet around the room, eyes closed, avoiding the few sticks of furniture. She had dated young men at college dances, and sometimes was aware of their erections. At a New Year's party at the *Sun's* city room, she had danced—after two jolts of bootleg gin—on Mr. Jenkins's desk.

The Clover Club was darkly lit and crowded with small tables. A band played Paul Whiteman-style on a platform, and a girl with loose breasts who mistook herself for a Montmartre *chansonnier* sang in a too-tight gold lamé gown.

Nat Bendell ordered the club's whiskey, but asked for extra glasses and produced a large silver flask.

"Marty runs a ritzy club here and his hooch isn't bad. But mine is better. One of the boat captains from Cuba brings in special stuff for me, right out of a limey-bonded warehouse in England."

She suspected Nat Bendell preferred special items. He danced well. He had a way of whispering close to her ear and laughing that put her at ease. He drove her back to her hotel in his white Packard roadster, kissed her cheek casually, blatantly, as he left her, adding he'd see her for lunch at the Miami Yacht Club.

"You can't write about Miami without going there."

Larua went to sleep with the fancy printed Diamond Coves Estates prospectus on her stomach, unread.

It had been a pleasant evening; she was a bit woozy from the potent stuff in the silver flask. Yet how good to dance. It didn't mean anything but clearly Nat Bendell was a man, a *macho*, as they said in the West. Women had spoiled him.

That week she saw Nat Bendell twice more. Then she went down to Coral Gables; that development was presenting William Jennings Bryan in person to the Florida land rush.

She was typing away on her portable every night till two in the morning, and Jenkins sent a Western Union

144

message: KEEP IT FLOWING. KEEP IT TIGHT.
LAY ON THE LOCAL COLOR.

The rat infested, insect-riddled Dixie Cabins
Fishing Parties have been tractored out [her third
article began] and foundations poured for what is
to be the Gulf Stream Hotel, with 200 rooms and
200 baths, and a radio in every room. The hotel is
scheduled to open in October, 1926. Meanwhile a
garish Moorish building of two stories is being
erected, the Land and Sales Office. Signs can be
seen every place: Winter Homes, Diamond Coves
Acres—Beach   Front—Business   Properties—
Home Lots—

Salesmen in natty tan and tropical helmets meet
all visitors with maps of the choice locations, show
off a sample home being erected and sports and
shopping areas around which the asphalt streets
are still soft and the sound of the steam roller ac-
companies a jazz orchestra, Benny Mohawk and
His Original Dixieland Band. They play on weekends in what is shaping up as the town square.

It was a typical scene, Laura North found out, as she
moved about up and down the coast, developments
being repeated in a hundred variations of the boom in
Florida land. They had names like Coral Gables, Sunset
Point, Palm Harbor, and Green Seas, and a bit inland,
Home Acres, Tropical City, and Sun Gardens.

As she tramped the rail terminals, she discovered
that day and night freight trains were unloading cargoes
of timber, bathtubs and toilets (often pink), cement,
kegs of nails, plate glass, plumbing pipe by the mile,
roofing material, and tiles in all shades of red, yellow,
and blue.

Along the roads and highways around Miami she

145

passed signs that announced: LAND, LOTS, SHORE FRONT, DEED AND TITLE SEARCH. The rich and the poor mixed in a frenzy to get deed and title to something pointed out to them on a wall map. Some took it across the street to a land broker or waiting buyers in a hotel lobby and sold it quickly at a small profit. (Nat Bendell insists they are fools—it's going up-up-up!) She wrote:

In a way it is like the tulip madness in Holland where a couple of centuries ago people paid fortunes in gold coins for some rare tulip bulb. Here they may be buying a 100 by 100 lot from a map—a lot that's under water at high tide.

I mix with gamblers, ladies of easy virtue [Mr. Jenkins would blue-pencil "whores"], high pressure types with plans for beauty salons, car dealerships, or race tracks; all are rushing for deals "in the proper locations." The speakeasies run wide open, drinking is heavy—rum runners lie just outside the twelve-mile limit. The county sheriff's office seems to move slowly and enjoy the prosperity of the boom.

A friend [no need to mention N.B. again] pointed out Toots Magana, who controls the coastal bootlegging, and Hilda Kissingeer, the popular madam with a brothel on the outskirts of nearly every new development. The bookies openly take bets on all horse races being run around the country. A Chicago wire service of the Anikstem brothers runs it. The city fathers of various communities say they don't know what to do with all the new tax money, income from permits to build, subdivide, and incorporate as a community. But my friend says they "drop a lot of it into private bank accounts."

At night the signs of leaping neon singe the sky-line in various colors offering food, music, dancing, movies, barbeque. I have found the nightclubs are at their most boisterous at 2 A.M. [Better cut that line—it's not on my expense account.]

Florida today is like the opening of the Oklahoma land rush together with the wildest night on the Barbary Coast; only the costs and the profits here run into millions and millions of dollars.

Some of the makers and shakers of this boom are honest dreamers who see a paradise for the middle class; some are tricksters who used to stand on windy street corners selling magic can openers out of kesters; others could have been gold-brick salesmen. There are even some Bible Belt fundamentalists bringing in the converts to buy their way into a New Zion; Come-Be-Saved-By-Jesus cults are active.

She rubbed her eyes as she finished typing. Then she added a line without thinking: I AM IN LOVE WITH A JEW.

Carefully she X'ed it out.

16

Outside the office of the Diamond Coves Estates the tropical night sounds had begun—a frog's throaty mating call, the buzz of biting insects, the crickets' penetrating music.

In the last two weeks the office of Nat Bendell had acquired a large dark desk deeply carved on all sides with motifs of fish and small game—turtles, beaver, wild turkey. The antique dealer had sworn it had once belonged to Andrew Jackson. On the floor was a good copy of a Persian rug of pale rose and sharp greens. From nearby in one of the cabins where part of the construction crews lived came the nasal radio whine of Rudy Vallee singing "The Maine Stein Song."

Ira Silverthorn and Lou Zucker were drinking beer with Nat Bendell, taking it directly from the bottle, Adam's apples bobbing. It had been a thirst-producing day. Lou was wearing his blue double-breasted pinstriped suit that he usually wore in Los Angeles, but he had adopted a plaid golfing cap. Ira propped up his cowboy boots on an extra chair and relished his drink.

"This is good beer."

Nat agreed. "It's not needled, shot full of ether . . . Now it's been a couple months since when we were to do a big bitch of a layout on the merger of Diamond and World Pictures. What gives?"

Ira watched the moths bumping against the screens

trying to get in at the lights. "You know lawyers. They'll fuck their own clients six ways from Sunday running up fees."

Lou said, "They're still looking over, you know."

Nat pressed a fist against his chin and looked over the two men from Silverthorn World Pictures. "It's all kosher. You saw what I owe banks, what is due to contractors, how many shares are out. So give it to me straight. What's the goddamn bottleneck?"

Ira took out an envelope and slowly removed a sheet of paper. Then he placed a pair of old-fashioned silver-rimmed glasses low on his nose. He made a sucking sound with teeth and lips. "You're into the banks for over three million—a million more to your father. You hold or listed for yourself a third of the shares. We'll go into how much you put or still owe on them later. Nat, the nigger in the woodpile is Global-Horizon Corporation, listed as owning nearly two-thirds of the shares in Diamond Coves Estates."

"So it's all proper by the charter."

"Sid's lawyers, Kornblue and Cassidy, and the accountants, the CPA shmucks, want to know what's the Global-Horizon Corp?"

Nat smiled. "What did your CPA bloodhounds find?"

"G-H is incorporated in Delaware, owns or controls the Spinelli Transportation Company, Dockside Stowage and Warehousing on the Brooklyn and Jersey City waterfronts, and the Harvest Italia Olive Oil and Pasta Importing Company."

"Hardly," said Lou, "a fly-by-night outfit. But that's the kick in the *tocus*, Nat. You see the Spinelli Brothers, Monte and Gino, are also big-time bootleggers and run the waterfront rackets."

Nat stood up. "Wait just a cockeyed minute. Let's get it right. Monte and Gino Spinelli lend money

150

through their import-export firm to captains or leasers of boats that bring the booze in, sure. But they're lenders, not operators. They do business mostly with boat owners out of the Bahamas. As for the New York waterfront, they haul and warehouse, and their nephew Cesar is head of the local of the Packers and Shippers Union, duly elected."

"He's been indicted twice for kickbacks for dock looting, busting a few legs and arms of shippers."

"Anybody can sue, and does, but he's never convicted for more than a parking violation. Global-Horizon is legit. They have about three mill in this development right now. Tell you what I'll do to convince S.S.—I'll get the Spinellis to put, say, two million more in the Diamond Coves Estates account at Amsterdam-Manhattan Bank and Trust. How's that?"

Lou stood up and stretched; his bones creaked. "Damn climate's too damp for me. Give me Hollywood and Vine any day and the corned beef sandwiches at the Brown Derby. All right, Nat, you give S.S. an official statement from Amsterdam-Manhattan like you say, and we'll try it out on our shysters. Fair?"

"Fair," said Nat. "May take a week or so. Ira, I got some personal matter—nothing about the project—I need advice on. You mind staying?"

"No, of course not. If you have more beer in that icebox."

"I need my sleep," said Lou. "Been scouting some of the nightclub acts for S.S. every night for a week."

When Lou Zucker had left, Ira went to the icebox and took out two bottles of beer—"in case you get long-winded."

A moth had somehow gotten past the screen barriers and was fluttering against the light bulb hanging from the ceiling. Nat rose and went over and stood under the light, hands lifted, palms inches apart, then slapped them together, attempting to crush the darting light-mad moth.

"A man, Ira, no matter how smart he thinks he is, and how sure he is, has learned more than blowing his nose from experience, that there comes a time when logic and reason don't matter."

He clapped his hands and caught the moth, looked at the results, and wiped his hands by rubbing them together. "In a nutshell, I'm thinking of getting married."

Ira took a long pull from his beer. "You've got the right. Who's stopping you?"

"I got the right. As for Sonia, the wife, she went out to Reno two years ago and got one of those quickie divorces. So I'm not walking out on anybody, not breaking up a happy home. Understand?"

"It's that *shicksa* you've been up and down the coast with?"

Nat returned to his chair and wiped his hands on a handkerchief, nodding. "Laura hit me like a ton of bricks right from the start. If you ask me why, I have to say I don't know. It was not just hot nuts. I've known society broads, floozies, a lot of really beautiful janes. So why this one? And a goy?"

Ira shrugged. "Look, Nat, when I was just a Dutch tenderfoot, I married a girl whose mother was a Shoshone Indian. Nobody would want a better marriage. Nobody. It transcended everything in my life."

"Ira, if it was that cozy, how come you never married again?"

"How come that moth isn't going to look for a light again? Doing it all again would have spoiled the memory for me. Besides, I'm no spring chicken. This Laura, she's what—middle twenties? I'd guess give a year or so, either way. You're deep in the forties. Oh, it doesn't show, not if you don't come close."

"She likes older men. Maybe Laura sees me as her

152

old man. He died when she was six. I told her I don't want to play papa."

"You've known her, what, a little over two weeks? Maybe it's just temporary insanity like everybody in Florida these days. Ever think she's all wound up by this candy-colored three-ring circus? And I gather you've really been showing her the high life, the big spending, the Gold Coast. Once back in New York, however, in her one room, three pairs of shoes, her thirty-five-dollar-a-week job, this enchantment will all melt like snowflakes."

"You say no? Easy as that?"

"She that good in bed?"

"We haven't been, she's no slut. Your advice is no?"

"That's right."

"Thanks, Ira, but I'm going to marry her."

Ira studied the determined frown on Nat's face. "I'm not twisting your arm to make you say no."

"I didn't feel I would go this far."

"Maybe that's what Juliet said to Romeo, or the other way around. All you need now is an official piece of paper and a judge."

"I'm going to have a rabbi. I can't hurt my mother and father."

"Here you'll not find a rabbi for a mixed marriage. They're all Orthodox here. They'll not marry a Jew and a Gentile. However, I have this rabbi, an old friend up in Atlanta. Used to be partners with him long time ago. He studied in the seminary and finally decided he'd be a rabbi. I could get him to come down."

"He Orthodox too?"

"Yes, but don't worry—Rabbi Kalman owes me a few favors."

Nat seemed lost in thought when he looked up. "I'll let you know."

153

Ira said, "My advice is, don't. But if you do, the best of luck."

Ira finished the second bottle of beer in one gulp, patted Nat's shoulder, and left for the cabin he was sharing with Lou Zucker. Nat sat staring at the pattern in the rug; it seemed to have faces, tree shapes, squares and triangles; perhaps the pattern had a meaning, like life, or perhaps it meant nothing, like life. He was worried over this love thing. He felt like the residue you find in the bottom of a bottle of wine. It was not that he was going against the ideas of his parents, Aaron and Malka. He had paid lip service to the Torah, High Holidays, would go on like that from habit. He had prided himself in being a systematic thinker, a man who looked out for Number Uno. Now he wanted to comfort, protect this girl. He was as much in love, perhaps even more, than he had been as a youth with Sonia in the days she was an actress in the Jewish theatre on Second Avenue, playing in a Yiddish version of *The Cherry Orchard*. The past was no help; too often he had acted selfishly, avoided the consequences of emotional acts. Laura was like a new view of the world, a life-enhancing force, in her gentility and constancy so different from the women he had known.

Since his escape from death in the early gang wars of Prohibition, he had felt a great loneliness that bought sex could not solve. He had severed the umbilical cord to the faith of the Jews in their God, their morality. He lived a gaudy life but was aware of its shadows, like the matter of taking up with the Spinellis. Before Laura had appeared he had felt a demoralizing weariness at becoming involved in an enterprise based on shaky assumptions (the Florida boom *had* to continue, values *had* to inflate, Diamond Coves would make him a millionaire). And Sidney Silverthorn had made promises but was now acting as if he were walking on hot coals.

154

All they wanted in Hollywood was cloying adulation.

Here he was getting the heebie-jeebies and Laura was typing up a story of the day to send on to her paper and so couldn't be with him. To hear her voice would dispel that deep-down anxiety he hid from the world. He phoned her hotel and asked for her room. He waited, heard the ringing. For a moment he thought she was out with some other guy. Then her voice, clear and simple: "Hello?"

"Hello, sweetie. Just want to say good night."

He liked her silvery laugh. "Good night, darling. I've got two thousand words yet to bang out. Good night."

Nat felt better, reassured. Love—some laugh at it, kick it around, wisecrack about it like Winchell. But love exists and could be better than a contract to loot the mint. Why deny this? He was a clever man, a very clever man, but in the matter of emotional responses he understood only the most elementary drives.

He had lived a great deal of the time outside the law. It didn't make much difference to him. It would, however, have to be different with Laura—a little more care, a sloughing off the hoodlums and big shots.

Once clear of the Spinellis, he'd take on a car agency from Detroit, maybe get interstate trucking contracts, a taxi franchise, all legit. He thought of Laura typing away, sitting there in her slip, a Lucky Strike smoldering in one corner of her mouth. He had told her something of his past, not all, but enough. She had quoted some character, William Blake: "Man has no body distinct from soul."

He decided to go for a midnight swim. The beer was all gone. Outside the frog had found what he had wanted and was still.

She had intended to finish the article on the Negroes' part in the land boom; they, too, were speculating, buying and selling, if on a lesser scale. But the phone call from Nat had broken her determination to continue with her work in the damp heat. She had smoked more than she intended and her throat was raspy; the last cigarette was gone from the pack. The little room was hot. A night breeze, warm and smelling of overripe fruit, fought the small brass electric fan on the dresser. Getting into bed, Laura engaged in a kind of self-reproachful introspection: why had she fallen in love after her bad experience with Ralph Pointer, the roaring sissy? She had to bring her writing for the *Sun* and Mr. Jenkins to a successful climax and not brood over personal emotions. She had carefully planned a career—what had forced it off the track? The requirements of her body, its insatiable but virgin curiosity? An indulged impulse? For all her innate shyness in her relationship with a man, she did seem to be again attracted with that doubtful nervous intensity. And was Nat really the true object of her new affection?

A strange man, fascinating, tender with her for all his brusqueness toward the world. And what of her new attraction to Jewishness? Did she aspire to a realization of faith? Somehow all her leaning toward a godhead so far had been a failure in producing that desired moment of revelation. Her family has been Episcopalian, good high church people. As a small child, she had enjoyed the ceremony, the stained glass, the candles, the chants, without fully understanding. Grandma had taken her away from that and introduced her to Mary Baker Eddy's texts, and while Laura obligingly had read *Science and Health*, it had been too prim for her, a mindless turning away from sins and pleasures. Grandma's gardener, a Catholic (she was fifteen and he was drunk), had exposed himself to her in the hothouse. "Nose to arse we play the dog games of nature." She had run from him, too ashamed to tell Grandma.

156

In college Laura had avoided sex, sublimating her drives by writing poetry in the style of Edna St. Vincent Millay. But then she went to work on the *Sun* and met some of the heros of the Village. They were a godless lot. It was Bunny who told her, "God is not dead, merely castrated."

The fan and the breeze failed to cool the room. Hunting a stub of a cigarette, she found on the shelf beneath the night table the usual hotel Bible.

There were ring marks from wet glasses set down on the cover, and silverfish, those strange insects, had eaten away some of the text. Laura opened it at random:

> How godly are thy tents, O Jacob,
> Thy tabernacles, O Israel!
> As the valley are they spread forth . . .
> As garden by the river's side
> He shall pour the water out of his buckets
> And his seed shall be in many waters . . .

She must have slept, for she awoke with a dry mouth in the warm morning, no breeze coming through the window. Her heat rash was back.

She sensed she had come to a kind of deliverance—a garden by the river's side—that was a summons from within. Something that could offer permanence, stability, an assurance of her own worthiness to exist.

17

In the city of Atlanta, addressing the Hadassah in the Jewish community, Rabbi Kalman said, "Some think you are more loyal to Robert E. Lee than to Moses." He added with a serene radiance, smiling, "I have met at least two Jefferson Davis Cohens, but the names Abraham and Solomon have not come to my notice." The audience of matrons applauded. You expected this from this rabbi.

The Jews still supported a few Orthodox shuls, but in Atlanta the Reform temples were becoming increasingly popular with their young well-shaved rabbis, who felt that folk dancing and modern art released a spontaneity of feeling. The droning intensity of Hebrew prayer puzzled the younger generation, which repeated it by rote without understanding.

Rabbi Kalman was the leader of a small synagogue in a suburb called Stanton, rabbi to plumbers, dairy farmers, roofers, tailors; here the rabbi and his wife Surrah "the *rebbitzen*" took care of the spiritual needs of twenty-four families.

Rabbi Kalman was leaner than he had been when he was just Janos Kalman, vagabond seminary student, working with Ira Silverthorn, a time of prosperity and loss. He had never been a vain man, and when at last he had been accepted and then came out of the Ohio Hebrew Seminary as a rabbi, he was no longer a young man. He had gone to the red clay country in the South, grown a salt-and-pepper beard, and in a black alpaca jacket and dark flat hat had gone out to Stanton Center where there was no rabbi, just a Torah in a closet in the home of Mendal Rice, a dairy farmer.

In a short time there was a converted ice cream factory that became the shul Oheb Scholom. The rabbi married Surrah Bogan, the daughter of a pious bookbinder and job printer. She was plump as he was lean; she was jolly, while he was often given to deep sighs as he read Bar-Hebraeus and Maimonides. A perfect couple, agreed the congregation, very much in harmony and at such a low salary.

When the phone call came from Ira Silverthorn in Miami Beach (the new Babylon, if not the Sodom and Gomorrah of the Yiddish tourists), it was good to hear the old ardor with which Ira spoke.

"So how are you, Rabbi? Or can I still call you Janos?"

"Call me what you will. You sound healthy, you pork eater."

"I confess even to lobster and a dozen Blue Point oysters. I need a great favor. I want you to perform a wedding ceremony."

"Yours, Ira?"

"No, the Bendelbinders, the Great Bargain Store people have a son, Nat Bendell . . ."

"A name changer."

"Just a shortener. Can you come in about a week for a proper Orthodox wedding, the *chuppah* ceremony, the smashing of the wine glass, the whole *magilla*?"

"In Miami the rabbis aren't circumcised? Or they're too busy playing tennis?"

"Rebbe, he's marrying a *shicksa*. And the rabbis here will not perform a mixed marriage ceremony."

Rabbi Kalman, who had been drinking a glass of tea,

160

now took a sip, made a deep, throaty noise, "And I will?"

"Of course you will. I brought you to the New World, didn't I?"

"And beset me with temptations. Ah, Ira, Ira," he laughed, "of course I will. You'll pay the fare and board for me and Surrah. I have no Rothschilds or Otto Kahns in my shul."

There was a silence on the Florida end of the phone line. Rabbi Kalman asked, "Are you still there?"

"Yes, of course. I knew you'd do me this favor. There may be one other thing."

"What more—a *briss*, they have a boy baby?"

"No, no. Laura, that's her name, is thinking seriously of converting to Judaism. She's been talking to some local rabbi and she's read up on it—"

"Jews don't seek out converts. That's for the pope."

"Come down Monday. We'll talk it all over. How is Surrah?"

"She's fine." He turned his head. "Ira Silverthorn sends his regards. We're going to Miami. A wedding."

"Give him my love. I'll bring a honey cake."

"Hello, Ira? Surrah sends her love and will bake a *lakeoch*."

After the call, Rabbi Kalman sat a long time thinking of the past, had another glass of tea, hummed the "*Havanagila*." Somehow he felt sad for all his affection for Ira Silverthorn. A lonely widower, his children grown away from him, in schools. He was living a sort of parasitical life attached to that movie maker with his half-naked bathing beauty girls and passionate kisses shown at the local Bijou Theatre. A world of abomination on a silver screen and all in a frenzy of making fortunes, playing the stock market; even his farmers and workers were talking of their holdings in RKO Radio, Goldman Sachs, U.S. Steel. And the land speculation; good farms being cut up to produce those flimsy new suburbs. But he too had had his years of grave delinquencies, had lusted after Mammon.

"Surrah, we're going to Miami Monday. A wedding, and before that, maybe a conversion ritual."

"Why, Rebbe, would anyone who isn't a Jew want to become one?"

"Why does a wife badger a husband with foolish questions? Go get the broom and I'll beat you."

"You'll wear the new alpaca jacket."

He said he would . . . vanity, vanity, all is vanity. He would even trim his beard. Beyond that he wouldn't go. There were times when the old rover's life still drew him, and so far he had the strength to resist. *Danken Gott.*

Laura North was stubborn, her mind made up. She would become a convert to Judaism, to the Orthodox faith. Sitting with Nat, she chewed on a blade of grass, spoke firmly. It came to a head as they sat this evening on the beach of Diamond Coves. "I join the original firm. Why should I join the Reform group?"

"Memorizing a lot of Hebrew prayers. Memorizing the *brochas* in Hebrew. There's that ritual bath you'll have to go through."

"I know, the *mikveh.* Nat"—she caught his arm—"you want me to become a Jew or don't you?"

"Rabbi Kalman says the final answer has to come from you."

"All right. I've been practicing the prayers, by ear, from a recording I made in a Hebrew school."

Laura began to recite: "*Boruch es adonoi hamvoroch . . .*"

"You'll take the ritual bath?"

"Can I drown?"

162

"The bath is three feet deep. But there will be rabbinical observers . . ."

"What! Observers?"

"Your sponsors must hear you splash, go under, and recite when you come up."

"Can I wear a bathing suit? It doesn't sound holy."

"Bathing suits are not Orthodox. The children of Moses had no bathing suits."

"Oh, God!"

"No male witnesses. However, Mrs. Kalman will help you dip under."

He patted her shoulder. "The male witnesses will be outside by an open door. They listen, don't look, are not supposed to—they're men and . . ."

"You're not taking this seriously. I am very serious."

"All right. You're serious."

"Where is the pool? At the YMHA?"

"Once each shul had its own *mikveh*. You can't use city water. It must be pure water from heaven."

"Oh."

"Rain water is collected from runoffs on the roof. There are almost no true *mikvehs* in Florida. But arrangements for the use of one at the Congregation Shearith Israel in Blutonville have been made by Rabbi Kalman."

Laura shook her head. "I'm scared. But don't let me back out."

Surrah Kalman in a flowered hat, a loose blue dress, her Sabbath best, sat with Laura as they drank coffee in her hotel room.

"Don't you worry, Laura, I'll be with you all the way."

"In the pool?"

"In the *mikveh*, out of the *mikveh*."

"The witnesses?"

"They stand outside the door. It is cracked open. Drink, it's time."

"I'm doing right?"

"What you feel is right. In Judaism, the woman, she is nothing. She is just to serve a man; takes care of house, raises children, lights candles on the Sabbath. Truth is, without us they'd blow away. Let them think they are everything."

Laura saw her face, free of makeup and lipstick, had a bit of a shock as she looked into a mirror.

Nat came in, and standing behind her, looked at her. "Good, no makeup. We've picked up Rabbi Esserick and Rabbi Kalman for your other two witnesses."

"God," she said feeling her breakfast turn over. "You a witness?"

"Yes."

"Just let me get a few sheets and towels."

"They have them."

Nat and the two rabbis, one small and bent, his nostrils stained with snuff, and the other stick-thin, beard at a cocky angle, his blackwood cane held between his knees, all sat in his Packard, the top up. "What are we waiting for, the Red Sea to open?"

"Rabbi," said Nat, "this is Miss North. Rabbi Esserick will be one of your witnesses."

The little rabbi held out a knobby hand. "Welcome to Zion."

The ride across town was at first silent. Then Rabbi Esserick broke into song, banging down on his stick:

> *"Zol ich zine a koval*
> *Hob ich nit kine kovadleh."*

Laura whispered to Nat, "What's he singing?"

Nat translated as he drove around a twelve-wheel rig carrying oranges:

"Should I be a blacksmith
I don't have an anvil."

Surrah patted Laura's hand. "Show some respect for
the ritual, you men."

Nat joined the singing:

"Should I run a tavern
My wife is drunk."

Surrah turned around. "It's a scandal, Janos, this
lightness of yours.

"Keep quiet." He sang two more verses.

So they came to Congregation Sheareth Israel, a red
brick structure of Moorish design dating back to the
1890s when Jewish farmers from Russia, Poland, and
Romania came to grow grapes and apricots for the raisin
and dried fruit trade. They added oranges, went to
chicken farms, then to carpentry work. They did not
grow rich, but neither were they poor. They added a
big cement-block annex to the back of the temple for
the ritual pool for the monthly plunge that a pious wife
made, according to the laws of the creed. It was a community of righteous moral superiority.

The party of five went through a blue-painted fire
door, came into a low hall. An elderly woman with gray
hair handed Surrah a set of keys with a nod. Laura
looked after Nat with something like panic as he and
the two rabbis followed the old woman down another
hallway. She braced herself, swallowed hard, felt heavy
and a frivolity out of keeping with the event.

Surrah unlocked a small room and pushed her in,
then pulled on a naked light bulb set in the ceiling. "So
here you are. Off with the clothes."

She undressed and when she was nude Surrah draped

165

a sheet around her shoulders and motioned her to sit down before a narrow wedge of mirror on the wall.

"That's fine. No makeup. No jewelry. Take off the wristwatch. Let's see the nails. Not short enough. So, left hand first."

Surrah clipped the fingernails very short, then the nails of the toes. Laura looked at herself in the flawed mirror and wondered just who it was she was staring at. She was a stranger there, naked—a body no one had used.

"You remember the *brochas*?"

"I think I do."

"So come." Surrah kissed her. "For *mazel*."

She stood, a sheet around her, legs somehow escaping no matter how she folded or turned the linen square. The little room led to a short hall, then to a plain pine door. Surrah opened this and below were four blue-tiled steps leading down to the pool. The walls were blue-green and windowless. Glaring yellow lights in mesh holders were set in the ceiling. Surrah held her back as she began to go down the steps to the pool.

"No, first a shower."

"I showered two hours ago."

"Not in a *mikveh*."

There was a shower booth, grim, gray. Surrah turned on the water and Laura soaked herself under the tepid flow. Surrah dried her and held up a comb. "Bend down the head. The hair must be combed every place, but *every* place."

Laura felt her short hair being combed. Surrah handed her the comb. "Do it yourself. In the pubic part, please."

"Oh!"

"So that every inch of skin will be wet, not covered dry by matted hair."

"Damn! Pardon me." She combed her pubic area and stood again in the sheet. She was led back to the pool. Surrah said, "Now you go in—all the way under. Each time recite the proper prayer. You understand?"

"Yes, yes."

"You will be washed clean of any other religion you may have known. Go."

"I'm going." Surrah pulled the sheet from her. Then she turned her head to the partly open door and shouted, "Starting."

Laura heard footsteps outside the door. She stepped into the water. It was warm and crystal clear. She ventured in slowly, knees, thighs, belly, ribs; went deeper, until it lapped at her breasts, covered her nipples. She sank into a squat, put her head under, holding her breath. A singing sound in her ears, a thumping noise as if someone were hammering. She rose, blew water from her nose, recited the prayer:

"Blessed art Thou, O Lord our God, King of the universe, Who has hallowed us with Thy commandments and commanded us concerning immersion."

"O-main!" shouted Surrah.

"O-main!" came from the three behind the slightly open door. Laura sucked in air, dipped, stayed down five seconds, came up and delivered the second prayer:

"Blessed art Thou, O Lord our God, King of the universe, Who has kept us in life and sustained us and enabled us to reach this significant moment. Amen."

The *O-mains* were louder.
Once more she dipped and came up trembling.

"Mazel, with *glick,"* cried Surrah, eyes tearing as she held up a big bath towel. Laura ran up the steps and was enfolded in the bath towel. She felt Surrah kissing her and saw tears on the rosy cheeks. *"Mazel-tov."*

Laura clung to the older woman.

Dried, dressed, her hair damply combed, she followed Surrah from the room where old books smelled of decaying calf and piled-up papers. Folding chairs were set on a faded rug. Nat, grim and pale; Noah Esserick, smiling and plucking at his little beard; Rabbi Kalman, rolling his head, tapping on his chest, withholding himself from a pinch of snuff.

He stood up, suddenly fierce. "Will you love the Lord your God with all your heart and with all your soul and with all your strength?"

She said firmly, "Yes."

"And the words which I command to you this day shall be engraved upon your heart, and you shall teach them diligently to your children, and you shall talk of them when you sit in your house and when you walk by the way, and when you lie down and when you rise up. So it is commanded."

She dared to look at Nat. He was chewing on his lower lip. She felt pity for him, suddenly love. He was a fellow Jew, she thought, and smiled.

"And you find them for a sign upon your hand and they shall be as covers between your eyes. And you shall write them upon the doorpost of your house and upon the gates, that you may remember and do all my commandments and be holy to your God."

She nodded.

"In token of your admission into the household of Israel, this rabbinical gathering welcomes you by bestowing upon you the name, Leah bas Hebron, by which you will henceforth be called in Israel.

"May He, Who blessed our mothers, Sarah, Re-

168

becca, Rachel, and Leah, bless you our sister on the occasion of your acceptance into the heritage of Israel and your becoming a true proselyte in the midst of the people of the God of Abraham. May you, under God, prosper in all your ways and may all the work of your hands be much blessed. Amen."

They all kissed her.

There was a red wine and some little cakes. They sipped. Rabbi Kalman held up a crisp paper and he began to read. His voice was low:

"I read you this conversion certificate to which you agree. I stand here in the presence of God and this rabbinical group to declare my desire to accept the principles of Judaism, to adhere to its practices and ceremonies, and to become one of the Jewish People.

"I do this of my own free will and with a full realization of the true significance of the tenets and practices of Judaism.

"I pray that my determination guide me through life so that I may be worthy of the sacred fellowship which I am now to join. I pray that I may ever remain conscious of the privileges and duties that my joining with the House of Israel imposes upon me. I declare my firm determination to live a Jewish life and a Jewish home.

"If blessed with male children, I promise to have them brought into the Covenant of Abraham. I promise to bring up all the children with whom God shall bless me in Jewish beliefs and practices and in faithfulness to Jewish hopes and the Jewish way of life."

Rabbi Esserick recited: "Hear O Israel, the Lord our God, the Lord is one! Blessed is His glorious sovereign Name forever and ever."

There were more *O-mains* and handshaking. Nat slipped some folded bills into the hands of the old *mikveh* woman who had appeared as they filed out into the clear sunlight. In the car Laura sat staring ahead at the traffic; now her very marrow seemed to tremble. Nat held her hand. Rabbi Esserick no longer sang. He was at first wrapped in thought and then began a whispered conversation with Rabbi Kalman on atheists.

As they came to Laura's hotel she said, "I want to be alone a little bit. You understand, don't you? You're all wonderful. I'm in love with you all."

"Wonderful?" said Rabbi Esserick. "And love, that large and sad province?"

There was a hugged farewell, a pressure of Nat's arm, and she was off, running.

Rabbi Esserick nudged him in the back of the neck with his cane. "It's a day of rejoicing. She's better off, believe me, than with Kierkegaard, Freud, or Mary Baker Eddy. No, yes, Rebbe Kalman?"

Rabbi Kalman shrugged. "There are times I feel the nerve is dead in American Judaism. So many shallow certainties and such stylish games."

Surrah turned half around. "Rebbe, it went well."

"Woman, be still," said Rabbi Esserick, winking.

Rabbi Kalman said, "I was thinking of what the poet said: 'there is more faith in honest doubt than in half the creeds.' "

"Shame on you!" said Surrah. She made as if to spit twice, an old wives' gesture to keep off evil spirits.

Rabbi Kalman said, "Sometimes I feel the Torah is the idolatry of the Jews, a credulity before a divine charisma, or a feather from a bird that doesn't exist."

Rabbi Esserick was quoting Ecclesiastes:

"He has put eternity into man's heart."

Laura sat on the bed, taut, nerves quivering. The shakes weren't bad; she was feeling now all she had held back during the day during the ritual. All those absurd or vital metaphysics? Should she feel holy? She was aware that now she was Jewish she must sense the

170

isolation, being outside the world—the enemy camp—she had just left. She had added to herself, she hoped, a stern fidelity; she wanted the wedding to take place quickly so as to belong fully to what she had chosen, not to be left alone, not yet inside a narrowed circle. Marriage would bring her fully over to the way she would go. If there was fear in her, there was nothing maudlin. She could use a drink, and she hunted up the bottle of Three Star Nat had brought over and took a sip.

Now to practical matters. She would phone Grandma and get the cold reception she expected. To Grandma she had desecrated some noble vision of the true godhead, alienated herself from her birthright, inextricably become lost among outsiders. No matter, she could bear all that. Since childhood she had resisted Grandma's one true way—the only path to bland perfection. It had in a way hardened her, polished her, made her contrary and able to face what the world handed out. It would be harder to talk to her editor, Jenkins. For him the only reality was a newspaper. He would see her as a soldier with no fidelity, deserting under fire, leaving some gap in the front lines undefended.

No matter; she had achieved a rapproachment she hoped with something stronger, more satisfying, than the confusion of her life till now. "No doubts, no doubts!" she cried out loud as she finished her drink, sprang up and thought of the wedding in three days in the small ballroom of the Everglades Hotel. Nat's mother and father were coming down, Mr. and Mrs. Bendelbinder, Nat's son the songwriter, Teddy Binder (how that family made free with names, names cut apart, changed).

She had danced at college dances to a Binder tune, "Come A Little Closer." She'd have a stepson a few years older than herself! And family: Bendelbinders, the Silverthorns; no Adams, Norths, Bancrofts, Islees.

A visceral intensity overcame her. Laura went into the bathroom, gagged, stomach flapping like a flag in the wind, stood with her mouth open. But she didn't vomit. A nice Jewish lady didn't toss her cookies; maybe she yelled a bit.

"Oi gevalt!" said Laura to the mirror, and laughed.

18

The wedding was a small afternoon affair with a *chuppah*, canopy of flowers that Surrah approved of, in the small Orchid Room's monstrous tropical decor at the Everglades Hotel. The guests included Aaron and Malka Bendelbinder, and the songwriter Teddy Binder, the product of Nat's first wife Sonia, who did not attend. Teddy, looking very handsome in London tailoring, played the "Wedding March" following a few passages of Bach's "Partita in A Minor" on a hotel upright. Ira Silverthorn and Lou Zucker saw to the catering, the hotel permitting kosher food brought in from Mama Klein's Kosher Restaurant to be spread out on buffet tables.

Also present were two of Nat's salesmen and their girls from the Diamond Coves sales office, and Rabbi Esserick, his wife and two daughters—girls who spoke in faint chortles.

Laura held tight to a stoic smile. Rabbi Kalman did not linger over the Hebrew ritual, but voiced it with proper rolling tones, then translated for Laura's benefit into English. Laura looked beautiful in an off-white dress, no orange blossoms. She stood very still, spine straight, by Nat's side, smiling when he seemed to wilt a bit. He was wearing an unaccustomed yarmulka and sweating lightly; with a thrust of his shoe heel he broke the glass on the rug that ended the ritual. As Ira explained it to Laura over cold cuts, fish in aspic, hot knishes and fruit stew, the glass breaking was either a symbol of the destruction of the Second Temple by the Romans or the deflowering of the bride: "Take your pick."

Laura, cheerfully drinking champagne from a goblet, said, "Local customs all observed."

Teddy came over and kissed her cheek. "Hello, Ma."

"I didn't know we'd have a celebrity at the wedding."

She was trying to see it all as simple and gay, to pump herself full of buoyancy, but inside her heart was pounding and her legs seemed filled with jelly.

Her past was lost irretrievably. Grandma hadn't sounded too upset in the phone call. "I have a sense, my girl, that in this world all can be for the best. Even half-Jew babies." It added to Laura's feeling of parting, the end of other things.

Mr. Jenkins had sent a telegram:

LOST A GOOD REPORTER TO MAKE A LOUSY HOUSEWIFE. WILL RETIRE YOUR TYPEWRITER WITH HONORS. THE BEST. HONEY. THE VERY BEST. JERRY J.

In one corner of the ballroom, Aaron and Malka were seated with Rabbi Kalman and Surrah, sipping champagne. Rabbi Esserick and his family had left for another tribal wedding.

Malka said, "It's no shame anymore to marry a Christian. Pardon, former Christian. In cursed Poland, of course, the goyem are monsters, have been for thousands of years, to the Jews a plague."

Aaron smiled. "I can remember a dozen decent Poles, but I'd have to think hard. I'm not too sure about mixed marriage." He moaned softly; the ceremony had stiffened his crackling joints. "I'm more and

174

more, as I get older and stiffer, seeing Palestine as a solution for we who had to run. Perhaps only for my generation, the immigrants."

Rabbi Kalman stroked his beard. "Everyone picks his corner to feel safe in. For me, as an American, this is the place to be as the Lord made us. Palestine I leave to Surrah here. She has a *pushka* collecting funds for the Homeland, if the British ever live up to their promises and make it so. The sun never sets on the British Empire; maybe God doesn't trust it in the dark."

Surrah, inspecting a tray of little cakes set before her, looked up. "I don't say Eretz Israel is for us, but the ghettos of Poland, Russia, Romania are filled with people looking for escape. The Bolsheviks are as big anti-Semites under the skin as the Tsars were. Look at poor Trotsky. He saved the revolution with his Red Army, fought on forty fronts, and—enough of history." She touched Aaron's hand. "You help the group, the ORT, that is training young Jews as farmers, machinists."

"I gave, I gave."

Malka said, "What is needed right now are weapons. The Arabs are massacring men, women, and children."

Ira sipped black coffee. "S.S.'s nephew Paul is involved in a project to arm the settlers. Lots of World War surplus arms are floating around in the Middle East."

Malka shook her head. "That one? A dilettante in Paris with artists and writer *schleppers*. I met him. He collects arms? A sad day for the Jews."

Ira poured a dollop of cream into his coffee. "That's why he is so effective. Everyone thinks like you: 'Another art bum'."

Rabbi Kalman stood up. "They're leaving."

Nat and Laura were standing by the double doors, waving, and Teddy at the piano was banging out "The Wedding of the Painted Doll."

175

Surrah sniffed, wiped her nose; Malka permitted herself a tear or two. A waiter moved about trying to empty as many bottles of champagne as he could. The hotel had the wine concession. Nat and Laura disappeared.

"You'll stay for a few days as our guest?" asked Aaron of Rabbi Kalman.

The joyous sense of common achievement was fading with the scent of dying flowers.

"Believe me, Bendelbinder, I like the sun here and I would stay but I have two other weddings this week in Stanton, and a bar mitzvah boy to teach some Hebrew, monkey fashion, by ear."

"Come and visit us in New York," said Malka. "I'll see you get a real Jewish meal, not this deli trash."

Surrah was collecting cakes and other portable items of food into a large napkin. "You don't mind? It would only go to waste."

"No, no, of course not," said Malka.

"Only to be thrown out, and we have so many poor children who will have a fine *nosh*."

Rabbi Kalman was buttoning his alpaca jacket. "My wife is a genius *schnorror*."

"And so what if I am? A little here, a little there or we'd be bare-assed at what they pay you."

Rabbi Kalman winked at Ira. "What does a man need? The tail of a herring, six olives."

Teddy was playing a Hebrew melody. Cheerfully they all began to sing:

> Hava nagila v'nism cha!
> Hava n'rana v'nism cha!
> Luru achim b'lev samayach!
>
> Let us rejoice and jubilate.
> Awake brothers, with joyful hearts,
> Let us sing and rejoice.

176

The surface of Biscayne Bay reflected the moon in gentle, golden ripples. On shore the large houses of the early tycoons of rubber, railroads, and meat packing were being taken over by the newer invaders, the first of the crime lords, and a new kind of retired middle class riding the tide of prosperity. The yachts and houseboats on the bay, spaced carefully apart, showed as red and green mooring lights, but for a late party on a pale blue yacht, lit up with strings of colored mast lights. A band on board sent out the strains of "I'm Always Blowing Bubbles" over the alcoholic laughter of its guests.

The houseboat *Maria*, owned by a corporation controlled by the Spinelli brothers, showed only a dim light from its aft bedroom. Nat and Laura had been amorously active in the wide bed for an hour. The bride was silently seasick from the gentle roll of the houseboat. The motion and her last series of orgasms produced a woozy sense of floating.

They lay side by side, Nat's body tanned, hers almost milk white in the lamp light but for her arms and face that had been exposed to the Florida sun.

She hugged him to her. "I'm sorry, darling, you had such a hard time at first."

"It's sure true what they say about virgins. God, sweetie, it was like a kid with his first lay."

"Want to talk about it?"

"What?" He turned to face her.

"Your first lay."

He laughed and slapped her ass. "We need a refill."

He got out of bed—he looked huge without clothes—and held on to a bedpost as the boat heeled a bit. He lifted the champagne bottle from its container of melting ice and poured two glasses.

"You know we nearly killed the whole bottle."

"That and the rolling of the boat and the fucking, I'm kind of floating halfway to the ceiling."

Nat frowned at her. "Look, sweetie, don't say those words. I'm no goddamn prude, but that's whore talk, not sweetheart-wife talk."

"Would I make a good whore?" Giggling, she rolled over in bed, took the glass, and sipped. "Come on, tell me, would I?"

Nat wiped the spilled wine off his chin. "Let me tell you something. I met this actor, John Barrymore, one night in Nell Kimball's sporting house in New Orleans. And he told me about the time he picked up this nice young Jewish woman, no tart, in the lobby of the St. Charles. A respectable woman, you know, but alone in town."

"I bet it happened to you, not John Barrymore."

"So he goes to her room, spends the night with her. In the morning she asked like you, was she as good as a high-class hooker? He said, of course, and she says, 'If I'm as good, please leave a hundred dollars on the fireplace.' And he said, 'Lady, my dear lady, from a clearly respectable woman like you I didn't expect so gross a request.' What do you think she answered?"

"Tell me."

"She said, 'Oh, it's not for me. It's for Hadassah.'"

Laura joined his laughter, then rolled onto her back again, put out her arms. "Darling, I think I can earn a hundred dollars myself, right now."

They made love tenderly, leisurely, ending in a great passionate climax. Laura, recovering her breath, thought of what Grandma had told her once, "Motivate yourself." Well, she was certainly doing that. She wondered if Nat too felt some new-found sensitivity on this, their first night as a married pair. She looked at him, he on his side, eyes closed; poor baby, perhaps she had demanded too much, and, you know, a man is unrelenting in trying to prove he is the insatiable stud. Or so she had heard in the ladies' toilet from some of the sob sisters on the *Sun*.

For all his brusque manners in public, Laura knew he was different when free for a time from projects, his problems; all that fell away and he became like he must have been as a boy in a mean, pre-war ghetto in Poland, a boy of sixteen reading Dumas against the advice of the shul elders. Surviving a pogrom by the peasants, in which Jews were killed, homes looted, a few burned, and the village policeman bribed to bring some sort of order . . . Nat was due for the brutal military service in the Tsar's army, and so after great hardships he had escaped with his father Aaron to America and years of dreadful poverty on the East Side of New York, saving to bring over the rest of the family.

As a brash young boy, he set up his own stove and shoe polish business while Aaron, a burdened pack peddler, roamed the country roads, savaged by farm dogs sleeping in hedges. Nat volunteered for the Spanish American War, was decorated, then began his days as a partner in a fine gambling house, ending in near tragedy when he had come close to a gang death during the early Volstead whiskey highjacking.

How strange that she, a Pilgrim-descended New Englander, should be in bed now with such a man whose struggle to survive could bring him this far, to a luxury houseboat, even if borrowed. No matter, he was an earnest person, capable of deep-felt love when you were alone with him. He hated pomposity and pretense, was a bit too stylish, overneat in his dress, and careless with his grammar. Oh, how she loved him, loved being a wife and loved being what he called a good lay. She had this sense of mischief, that she'd have to watch. Nat was jovial, with a calculated gaiety, but his sense of humor was not hers. She muttered, "Oh, it's not for me, it's for

179

Hadassah." Nat grunted, eyes closed, half sunk in sleep.

She had embarked on a journey, and she would have to chart her way with care. All was so new, so different. Was she a sex maniac as Nat had called her, grinning at her reactions, her unashamed boldness? She had heard so much about the impermanence of early love. One night in the Village, Bunny had fumbled her in a Sheridan Square studio, too drunk to proceed, and had recited something:

> A chi amo
> A chi mi ama
>
> To those I love
> To those who love me.

How fitting to remember that tonight. She leaned over and kissed her sleeping husband, tasting the damp saltiness of his warm skin.

Over the waters of the bay, the yacht party still going strong, came the strains of a popular music that she tried to recall by title, failed, and fell into a dreamless sleep.

BOOK THREE

MACCABEES

19

There were massacres in 1927 and 1928 at the kibbutzim in Palestine, Eretz Israel, by Arab gangs of the Grand Mufti, the British standing by "taking no sides," so that certain Zionists began to seek defense weapons. Some sort of protection had to be set up for the thousands of defenseless Jews on the communal farms, Wadi Hawaith, Hadar Hacarmel and other places, guns given to the *halutzim*, the young pioneers. The Balfour Declaration of 1917 for a Jewish homeland remained a dream.

In Jaffa, Haifa, and Jerusalem, the British had brought in the Royal Irish Constabulary, the notorious murderous Black and Tans, who preferred the Arabs to "the damn sheenies." Killing Jewish rebels was no different than killing Irish rebels.

So Jews traveling widely as citrus salesmen, buyers of textiles, agents for machinery parts, even as students of archaeology, fanned out into European and the Middle East nations to buy guns, ammunition, material for making bombs; costly raids on British police stations and army camps did not provide enough weapons.

One such agent, Paul Silverthorn, was passing as a collector of ancient manuscripts and documents, meeting dealers in French-held Syria, British-mandated Transjordan, Italian Somaliland. He was shipping heavy crates labeled artifacts or ore samples, after some bribes paid to customs officers "not to disturb the delicate materials."

In Persia one morning Paul came out of the Chaikhane Hotel on Khankani Street at ten o'clock, into the blazing, bone-white sunlight of the Persian Gulf. He was feeling rocky, numb, his mind fuddled but rather satisfied with the last two days and nights on shore buying up old World War rifles. Some fever was beating, battering between his ears like a bilge pump in need of repacking. He must have picked up a germ in Basra.

He scratched his hot, tormented ribs. God, the heat was dreadful as he stood in his crumpled white suit (stained with kebab and yogurt and Lord-knows-what), leaning against a stall of a merchant offering him rugs, beaten brass trays, a small cup of thick black sirupy coffee.

"Effendi, goods stolen from Emir Abdel Hadi Husseini's Palace, a tenth-century Kashan rug from a sacred mosque in Mecca. Ten thousand rials or fifty pounds."

"No thanks." Paul sipped the coffee in its small cup, a black muck, the grounds tacky in his mouth.

"For you, Effendi, I throw in this Isfahan silver dish, with a message of the Koran—Mohammed, forgive me—engraved in gold. Eight thousand rials. Both."

"No. Thanks for the coffee."

He moved away to the merchant's farewell and added muffled oath. Paul headed toward the docks of Sandar, moving warily in the humid heat past the silver oil tanks, orange and red pipes, the odor of gases, the skirted men carrying loads, natives in western dress, London ties and jackets buttoned for all the heat. The Persian Gulf was on fire, the sun reflecting its surfaces like a demon mirror; the air had a kind of ferocious insolence. Old chalky buildings stood defenseless with black gaping holes for doors and windows, prosperous structures, he thought for a busy Persian oil port.

He wondered if his fever was malaria.

Two veiled women in ankle-length *chador* and black veils passed him in a hurry, carrying live hens. One had a tattooed circle on her nut-brown brow. Lord, he thought, what is this drum beat in my head? He had only a vague memory of deals in crates of "ore samples" while eating quinces stuffed with lamb.

He had to see if the crates were on board the oil tanker *Morandi*. The captain had been well bribed . . . How glad he was to be done with the deals in shops, cafes, randy-smelling cathouses, musks and armpits, saffron and that goddamn mutton.

Paul was in sight of the harbor of Sandar-ye Zenyan; aware of the smell of sump spill, prime Persian crude, the snake of the manifold pipelines going into the harbor out to the dark blue shape of *Morandi*, taking on tons of oil, sucking it like a baby. The fever sang: "Mum's tit; what a baby, what a tit."

Paul's bloodshot eyes took her in—*Morandi*, dirty, rusty, under the yellow company-lettered flag *Oilco*. Here she was—his home till Haifa, a finicky bitch with five hundred rifles and fifty boxes of ammunition hidden below.

"Ah, my beauty," he said aloud, balancing himself, feet apart.

He had already made arrangements to land his cargo in Palestine; senior British police officers understood how to honor bribes.

Paul retched up a taste of acid and lamb, staggered; a dark hand steadied him. "Our passenger, he been having the good time," said Sieko Mihran, Seaman First Class in charge of the crew of *Morandi*. A dark, hefty Pakistani, one gold tooth, hair turning gray, his

185

impassive head tilted to one side when addressing a white man. Standing next to him in a violet-green sari was his wife, Gemila, a gem set in one side of her shapely nose. She was carrying several wrapped packages—catch a Pakistani male carrying his wife's bundles! Gemila was stewardess on board the tanker. She rarely spoke much except when in their quarters. There it was reported she ruled Sieko Mihran with a sharp tongue.

"How much longer to load?" Paul asked, grateful for the seaman's arm. He felt incoherent with fever.

Sieko shaded his eyes with his free hand and looked out at *Morandi*, set like a paper toy in the immense gulf. It was clear Sieko admired her. "She half loaded now, starting to settle to sailing draft, sar, by the plimsoll line soon."

"One more day," said Gemila. "Ice machine need fixing."

The three of them walked down past camels defecating, cars in dust clouds, a dog being kicked by a street peddler cooking some unsavory, unsanitary dish of *Abgoosht* over a small charcoal fire. To Paul, all this atmosphere, even in his condition, was the romantic east of Medes and Persians, Omar Khayyam, the Gardens of Shiraz he had read of in the hospital when a wounded RAF flier.

At the mesh wire wall of Pier C, bow-legged soldiers examined their papers and waved them onto the oil-stained dock. Paul could hear the oil rushing into the orange arteries of the manifolds loading the tankers, could smell the muck and spill under the dock and the soiled blue-black water. The oil in the water made patterns as it moved in swirling circles, looking, Paul thought, like the colored end papers one found in old volumes of Victorian novels his grandfather Alex collected. Who had inherited them in that old house?

186

One of the launches of *Morandi* was bobbing slightly in a swell of the gulf. The launch's gray sides showed a line of oil, like the stain on the moustache of a man he remembered drinking Guinness in the Crown and Bell in Knightsbridge during the war.

Six of the crew already were in the launch with their paper-wrapped bundles bought in the bazaars of Sandar-ye Zenyan: a teak elephant, some lengths of a garish cloth escaping from a badly done-up package, a colored picture of some belly dancer gyrating her navel.

They were Indian, Chinese, Pakistanis, Goanese; two were blacks from Madagascar, talking Swahili and laughing loudly.

Tankers were usually under Liberian registry, a flag of convenience, taken on to escape full survey, inspection, and taxes of the major nations.

The launch was about to cast off the mooring lines. The glare on the water was blinding; Paul felt he would faint. An officer appeared, very slim and neat in pressed whites, an officer's cap set at a rakish angle over blond hair a bit too long. He leaped briskly into the launch.

"Half a mo. Hello, Paulie." He had a voice of amused authority. He sat down next to Paul.

"You look like the cat's dinner, old man. Been lifting the booze and the veils of the ladies?"

"Cut the 'old man,' Ed. I'm running a fever."

Blond, blue-eyed Eddy Miller was actually a London Jew passing as a Church of England Christian but in fact an agent for the Hebrew Defense League's weapons-seeking section.

Eddy leaned toward Paul as the launch churned its way toward the ship. There was a suggestion of a breeze when the boat was in motion, but the air was warm and smelled of oil spill. Eddy never showed discomfort,

187

never had heat rash. His mind was full of details of chemicals, the rate of gas pressures for making bombs. He had all sorts of books in his cabin, could tell a Greek from a Roman hunk of stone, and was mad over statues with noses missing. He spent a lot of time visiting museums and churches. Eddy never asked where the knocking shops were while in port, never bought any dirty postal cards or showed interest in the tarts, didn't like to hear Third Officer Tott at mess tell one of his saucy stories that kept the officers of *Morandi* amused.

"Felt the heat today," Eddy said as they approached the dark blue side of *Morandi*, a long whale of steel high out of the water.

"Steady," said Eddy, helping Paul to his feet, and whispered in Hebrew, "Cargo all on board. Cases safe."

Paul felt he didn't care anymore. All he wanted was to escape from the burning daylight. The launch nuzzled against the tanker. He felt if only he could get up the portable steel steps now in place, get to his cabin, take a shower, have some hair of the dog (three fingers of the Pinch Bottle Scotch in his baggage), he'd cork off for a few hours before the Blue Peter went up to announce sailing. Carlos, the Genoese second assistant engineer, could be trusted to see the engines were properly primed and ready to make steam in the pressure boilers he cherished and petted, loved and cared for. To get then to Haifa—and the guns through the British harbor police.

The trip up to the deck was difficult. Eddy assisted Paul and Sieko aided from behind, the rest of the crew waiting in the launch to follow at a respectful distance. On deck two of the crew stood in fire-fighting gear, hooded, gloved, prepared as always when loading with fire hoses and foam containers.

The two red-orange manifold pipelines attached to the

ship stirred like muscled serpents. The smell of gas assaulted Paul's nostrils and this with his fever and the heat still rising—104° F, said a deck reading—made his head spin. It was as if rags were being stuffed into his nostrils, mouth, and ears. He stumbled on the canvas covers on deck, covers to keep oily shoes from soiling the deck. Every surface was covered with a film of fine sand blown from the desert lying just out of sight, while on the horizon, fires on the offshore drilling platforms were burning off surplus gas.

Second Officer Ludwig Snell was supervising the transfer of the oil from the pipes into the tank sections below. Snell, a Swiss, who once had taken theological instruction, was middle-aged and tall but with a beer belly that looked out of place for one so strict who was sure of the omnipotence of Almighty God. He looked up from studying the meter that indicated the proper trim of the ship, how the various separate tanks were balancing the cargo—this to make sure there would be no danger of the hull bending and cracking if the fore and aft tanks filled too quickly and the center tanks too slowly.

"*Morgan,* Herr Silverthorn. How is the *kopf?*"

"Just holding together."

Paul made his way to his cabin. He had made two other trips on *Morandi.* Tankers have no quarters below deck. All living was done on an island near the rear of the hull. In his cabin, smelling of hair tonic and stale linen, he managed to get the malaria pills down. He showered, taking it cold at the end, and got naked into the bed screwed to the floor. Fever still knocked in his veins.

Sleep didn't come quickly for all his fatigue. He began in his mind to go over all the deals of the last week—the secret meetings, the depleting of his money belt of its gold coins and bills.

The last image he had was of his Uncle Sidney making a motion picture of the events of the last month in Paul's life and crying out, "It's too fantastic, it's not real . . ."

20

The smuggling of arms was not new to Eddy Miller. He had a mysterious role during the war with the British M-16, then had been a member of Vladimir Jabotinsky's Betar party, a Jewish guerrilla unit in Palestine. His blond hair and blue eyes made him a natural infiltrator in the enemy camp.

As the tanker *Morandi* moved its clumsy bulk at nine knots down the Persian Gulf, he stood with Paul at the starboard railing watching the fruit-colored water streaked with foam hiss pass them.

"The hard part, to begin with, will be to get this tub out of the gulf through the narrow passage opposite Jask and into the Gulf of Oman."

"Lots of tankers do it."

"Our captain is a fat Dutchman who drinks and he comes cheap; that's why he's captain. Not a bad sort, Captain Meyerbeck, for our purpose. He's not curious as to what we have in those crates below, not since I slipped him a few fifties."

Paul felt the cadence of ship engines and the sea. "I'll breathe better when we deliver the crates at Haifa."

Eddy Miller spat into the sea, looked up at the Blue Peter hoisted at sailing. "Plans may change, often do. The cruiser HMS *Euryalus* and destroyer HMS *Brissenden* are patroling off Haifa and Jaffa, stopping ships for a search. How much gelignite you have on board?"

"Two hundred sticks besides the rifles."

"*Shema Yisroel*. If they fire a shot across our bows and by kindly mistake hit us"—he lifted up his arms high—"*Boom!*"

"You're goddamn cheerful this morning, Eddy."

"Had a good breakfast, my digestive system is functioning. Keep your pecker up, Paul. Our clandestine radio from Tel Aviv will contact us by the time we're through the canal at Port Said."

"What good will that do us?"

"Trust, Paul trust the organization. We'll get the weapons to the kibbutzim. Tell me about your uncle, the cinema maker. I mean, you ever get into the knickers of those movies stars?"

"I've not been out to the West Coast. But for you I'll ask my uncle S.S. I'm meeting him in Paris at the end of the month. How can you feel a lech at a time like this?"

"Easy. I like a small-boned redhead, this high and this shapely." He made a cupped chest gesture. "Uncle S.S. has a harem, doesn't he? Quiff at beck and call?"

"Of course not. Right now he's trying to survive. Sound films are all the rage and he's making talking singing pictures in an effort to stay afloat. It's a business, not a whorehouse."

"Not all tits and tickle, eh? Too bad, you shatter my dreams, boychic."

"S.S. is in Paris trying to dump all his silent films to some syndicate. What's bad for us is he's been a big help with money to buy arms. Right now if we can get a bundle there's a hundred Vickers machine guns with a thousand drums of ammo for sale in Djibouti."

"God will provide, Paul. Jehovah doesn't spend all his time floating on the ceiling of the Sistine Chapel. Come on, it's time for lunch. All these projects are a challenge—and the worry is worse than the actual delivery."

"I'll skip lunch. The heat has got me."

"Wait till we get into the Red Sea. Then you'll feel the devil's bad breath."

Paul wondered why Eddy Miller always appeared so cheerful. Perhaps it was the role he played, the jolly English ship's officer hiding the agent of the Hebrew defense group; working outside the Jewish Agency that still had faith in British promises and depended on English soldiers and police to protect the Jewish towns and settlements. As for those Jews supporting arms smuggling, if arrested they were not only given a stiff sentence to Acre Prison, but also twenty-five strokes of the cane.

For all his jitters Paul felt that at least Captain Meyerbeck was no problem. No disciplinarian, a great feeder who served a round of Holland gin at mess every evening. The captain wore faded red bedroom slippers on the bridge, listened to Bach and Mozart for hours on his gramophone in his cabin, most likely made out with dark girls when in port.

"The fat Dutchman knows tankers and harbors," Eddy said.

You felt safe with him. He knew how to get the ship past the Strait of Hormuz, not easy with the bulk and bad habits of tankers. Meyerbeck saw to the safety of the balancing of the tanker's cargo, the danger of fires, explosions. ("They'll never make them safe, Silverthorn; it's not natural to carry so much in such gross-size ships. *Ja*, but the good Gott so far has protected this Dutchman. Join me in a schnapps.")

Off Aden, Captain Meyerbeck fell across the table just as the waiter had brought out the ritual gin in the stone bottle, fell like a land mass across the roast beef and the Yorkshire pudding, a touch of the DTs and so he left most of the running of the tanker to his officers.

In the hot box of his narrow cabin, naked, Paul lay sweating on warm sheets. Had he found what he had been searching for? He thought back to when he was a goofy teenager flying Camels for the RAF in the war, the RAF ace whose reward was a shot-up hip; the years in Paris spent with the other loafers and dreamers; love affairs that got nowhere; then the offer from Aaron Bendelbinder and his uncle S.S. to do something for the Jews, taken on for fun and cash then infecting him like a virus.

He had no hopes of finding in his past, his childhood, something secure, something that would retain the wonder and awe of what he had dreamed. The few children he had known as a boy had seemed remarkable and clever, socially fit, well endowed; they had all been—what?—a disappointment. They had become dull, beaten and cowed by maturity. Or raw and loud, still *dross*. He saw he could only exist on the fringe of society. There were only two entities, the artist and the world. Between the two there would always be, at best, an armed truce.

He saw the struggle of the intellect against easy emotions, against popular concepts of the moment. He was aware, more so of late, that he was racing against time, but if he studied the past he did not worship it. The past he regarded as a calm that had made its inner shell beautiful before it died, but it *was* dead. The love of African carvings, the robbing of Indian graves was not enough. He was embarked on something more human and vital—to recover a homeland.

He no longer hunted a truth beyond the reach of doubt. He was beginning to suspect that truth and perfection were changing things and never to be cemented down. Art itself could be a waste of time, for perfection

194

existed (he knew now) on the inside, in the conception, *never* in the work itself.

Lord, it was hot, and the more water he drank the thirstier he became.

A day later they were seated on deck chairs in the deep blue shadow of the bridge, chewing on dried dates. The sea was calm; there was a personal affability between it and the ship.

"It ever strike you," asked Eddy, spitting out a date stone, "as to the illogic of the logic we're acting on?"

"I gave that up, that kind of thinking, long ago," said Paul. "It's in a way arrogant and presumptuous to think you know, can tell the logic from illogic."

"Look at us. You flew with the RAF, I worked in British Intelligence. Now we're preparing to kill them if they stand in the way of the establishment of a Jewish homeland."

"Perhaps they were just as wrong when we were on their side, perhaps the World War could have been avoided. Whose fault was it, who cares now?" Paul wiped his fingers on the deck. "Someone once said, 'We all boil at different temperatures.' They boil differently than we do. Look at their mystic feeling about Arabs."

"Oh that, Paul; that's because certain classes of the androgynous English love buggery. The Arab makes that game part of his life. From Burton to Lawrence, the lure of the asshole has often dominated English foreign policy. It's not, as some think, heightened political perceptions but lowered pants that determines right and wrong for them. Of course it's only a certain class of Englishman I'm talking about, usually the policy makers, some of the church, army, and navy. How does one idealize one's desires, one's actions? I've had that problem. I was raised on Judeo-Christian absolutes—my fa-

195

ther was an attorney converted to the Church of England. As a young man of no real faith at Oxford, I wallowed in the luxury of stylized despair. I married twice, was a woolen importer. But I didn't fit into an office, bridge parties, the bowler hat, furled umbrella, weekends at Bath, the Cricket Club. That's how I got to M-16; I found the work feline, intensely evocative. Of course there are things I did for the good of the section one didn't talk about—betrayal of a double agent to torture, selling out a chap from the other side I had grown rather to like."

Paul looked off to the tawny red horizon. "How did you come to side with the Hebrew defense organizations?"

"A lot of things—the final straw was seeing British police standing by while some Jewish old men and women were being stoned. Two died, by the Grand Mufti's Arabs. Add the delays in the putting the Balfour Declaration of 1917 into force."

"You think there will be a Jewish homeland?"

Eddy stood up. "Chum, never ask the end, only the way."

It was certainly the hinges of Hell in the Red Sea— "The furnace of the world," Botts the chief engineer called it when he came up from his engine room to cool off his lungs and found the air just as broiling on deck.

"No matter how many bloody bottles of iced beer I drink, me body feels 'orrible. Next time it's a whaling ship I'm signing on with."

Eddy pointed out Jidda and as they came into Suez opposite Sinai and waited their turn to enter the canal he asked, "Paul, how's the damn gelignite standing the heat?"

"How the hell should I know? I'm not going down to check."

"Big stink if it blows up in the Canal. International

scandal, cut Europe and Asia apart. Ha. Marvelous show if it did. Only we'd miss it, what? Go up with it."

"Not a very funny thought, Eddy. I think there might be a future in growing old."

"Do you? Amazing."

The canal was a disappointment to Paul—no great theatrical cut in the earth's surface, just a fetal-colored path of water between sand dunes, a few men on camels in the sterile desolation reeds here and there, the rusting carcass of some discarded craft. Ahead and behind *Morandi* the scribble of smoke from other ships moving slowly.

It was dusk, and their mouths were gritty with sand when they came to Port Said. Eddie knocked on Paul's cabin door, entered. Paul lay bathed in sweat, naked, under the feeble, snarling efforts of a fan to bring some mockery of a cooling breeze into the tiny cabin. He hiccoughed, mopped his neck.

"Up, up," said Eddy, "I've been in the radio room. Just had a message in code from clandestine Solly in Haifa."

"Huh?" Paul was heat-fogged. He could hardly make sense of what Eddy was saying.

"Paul, some sonofabitch of a dealer you bought rifles from has tipped off the British for the reward. They know we've something illegal on board."

Paul sat up, gasping in the foul warm air. "Oh God. Can we toss it overboard?"

"Don't be a bloody fool. They're not going to infuriate the Egyptians by a search here. The British destroyers will lay for us someplace off Jaffa. So we're transferring the goods as soon as we clear port."

"How, damn it?" Paul struggled into his pants. "Getting the stuff out of the locker in this heat, it's . . ."

"Murderous," Eddy grinned. "I've got four of the crew to help." He looked at his wristwatch. "We'll be met at about four o'clock in the morning by six fast motorboats. They'll signal us with yellow and green lights at minute intervals. Want a drink?"

"I'll move the stuff sober."

"Better have a drink. Can you handle a Luger?"

"I handled twin Vicker machine guns in the war."

"But if it calls for just pulling the trigger?"

"You press a trigger, not pull."

Two hours out of Port Said, Paul stood on the deck of the slowly moving tanker. Off to the right some place in darkness and heat was the coast of Palestine, a tormented land locked in history, in turmoil; Bar-Cochba had revolted there against the Romans in the past and the Seljug Turks had been there to slash and rape for Allah; where too many races had tried to annihilate the Hebrew tribesmen for thousands of years.

The breeze was searing, and the heavy ugly snout of a Luger stuck in his belt seemed a stupid return to playing cowboys and Indians. He hoped the safety catch was on or he'd shoot his balls off if he had to pull it out. He had no sense of the adventure that seemed to animate Eddy Miller. Eddy was cheerfully helping four of the crew on deck arrange the crates near the rail where a rope ladder lay coiled ready to be tossed over the side.

"No worry, Paul, these four *havarum* are our men. I didn't tell you before. Why give away a secret? The captain, don't worry, cheerfully full of gin. Everyone else has no weapons so they'll be good boys. See anything?"

Paul was trying to focus in the black velvet backdrop of the night.

"Over to starboard; they'll be coming from that direction."

Eddy picked up a machine gun from the deck. "They call this Thompson submachine gun a Chicago chopper.

Very popular with the Capone boys. Marvelous, isn't it? Light and drum-loaded."

"Marvelous," said Paul. The night seemed thick as smoke; then he saw a pinpoint of light. Couldn't be sure of its color.

"Eddy, I think . . ."

"Saw it." Eddy spoke in Hebrew to the crew members. They nodded, tightened the ropes around the crates.

Paul cried out. "Yellow, green, yellow, green, green, yellow."

Eddy, now brisk and alert, told the crew to put on life jackets. Then he prayed: *"Sh'ma Yisroel. Adonai Elohena Adonai Echad."*

The color spots were coming closer in a kind of loose crescent.

"All right," Eddy called out, night glasses to his eyes. "The damn explosives go over first. Lower them with care. Then the rifles."

From above the bridge in the radio room a figure gestured from a window. Eddy said, "Carry on. I'll see what Sparks is in an uproar about."

On the bridge the second officer ignored them; Paul and the crew watched as the dots of light, the colors of jelly, grew closer, brighter. Soon they could hear the roar of motors.

Eddy came back smiling, showing his teeth. Sparks had been intercepting messages in British naval code: "HMS *Euryalus* identified herself—she is someplace off to our left. Sounds far enough away, Sparks thinks, to miss us."

He was waving a flashlight with a green lens as the first of the motorboats came bumping alongside. An answering green flash came up to them and Eddy motioned for the first crate to be lowered over the side.

"Easy, so easy. That's the explosives. Paul, check the cables on the rifle cases."

Later, Paul tried to recall the events of that night in his journal and failed. He seemed to move about in a kind of fast-shifting dream of jostling, disarrayed images—crates going over the side, more motorboats alongside, soft cries in the night, hulls bumping into the rusted side of the *Morandi*, like sharks, he thought, attacking a whale. He recalled one crate breaking loose and falling into a motorboat; for one fearful second he thought it was the explosives and they were all going to be splattered into the Mediterranean. But it was just cartridges.

He also had an impression of himself moving down the snaking, twisting ladder and someone steadying him and speaking in Hebrew. Then the sound of the engine racing, a stink of petrol, and he was leaving the side of the tanker and there she was, a heaving bulk in darkness illuminated by deck lights, a glow from the indifferent bridge. Eddy by his side, fine white teeth showing, was tense with enjoyed excitement. "We leave anything?"

"Nothing. My luggage."

"Hard cheese."

The motor boat roared off, throwing up a fan of spray on either side. Soon they were alone; the other motorboats had all scattered for safety.

Paul took a nip from a flask handed to him by one of the motorboat crew, a slim lad with thick scholar's glasses—not at all the rough type, Paul thought, needed for such an expedition; more of a Talmudic student.

Eddy suddenly held up a hand. "Hear anything?"

Paul heard nothing. Then on what could be the horizon the searching ray of two more lights creeping along the top of the water.

The Talmudic student said, "Must be the *Euryalus*, all those lights."

"Hard right," said Eddy. "We don't want to dump this load. Not after we got it this far."

The motorboat turned in a fast arc, spume tossing, headed east.

"We hug the coast; she's a damn big British cruiser and can't follow us in without running aground."

The Talmudic student pointed ahead to another searchlight probing the night. "Must be the destroyer *Brussenden*."

Paul said, "They've got us bracketed."

"We could turn back," said the Talmudic student.

"And dump the cargo?" said Paul. "I'm for going in between them, making a run for it. Eddy? Are you game?"

"Sure. Give it the old school try."

The next half hour was even more a series of tattered images to Paul than what had gone before. The searchlights kept hunting through the Stygian dark; soon the motorboat was in the glare and one great lance of light caught them. The motorboat almost tipped on its side as the wheel was spun to get away from the stab of light. Again it caught them. Paul was aware of gusts of wind, and suddenly knew they were under heavy machine gun fire, and then came the *pom pom* of a canon.

"Jesus Christ," said Eddy, "heavy stuff!"

It seemed hopeless. The light held them as if at spear-point, and only for moments could they avoid it by changing course. They heard the thud-thud of the motorboat being struck by gunfire. Paul didn't dare look to see if it had come near the explosives. He felt a strong aversion to dying even if life was deceitful and brutish.

They seemed to be turning in circles. The Talmudic

201

student was firing a machine gun at the triangular shape far to the left of them.

Paul couldn't make out the flaming orange flashes from the destroyer trying to blast them out of the water.

In one more fast turn of the wheel Paul fell and struck his head on the edge of a crate; a purple fruit seemed to explode behind his eyes . . .

At first he heard dissimilar sounds clashing, became aware of the racing motor, of the constellations indifferent to human concern—a sky filled with stars on black velvet. All was under darkness. Paul lifted himself up. The Talmudic student was bandaging the arm of a silent man at the tiller, red showing through the strip of white cloth.

Paul asked, "We clear?"

The student nodded.

"All right?"

The Talmudic student pointed to the rear of the boat. Lying on the splintered deck was Eddy Miller, smiling, a neat hole drilled into his brow between his eyes.

21

Contrary to the newspaper reports, S.S. had come to Paris neither to sign up foreign actors for Silverthorn World Pictures nor to attend the races at Longchamps. The sound revolution in motion pictures had caused turmoil and panic in Hollywood. The success of Warner Brothers' Vitaphone sound projection had tumbled the industry's hierarchical order; first by a series of filmed vaudeville acts and the use of popular singers, then by putting a soundtrack with John Barrymore's *Don Juan*, and (the *coup de grace*) presenting Al Jolson in *The Jazz Singer*, which had songs and a mere two and a half minutes of banal dialogue between a truculent Jolson, who sought absolution for deserting the shul for the stage, and his screen mother. It had sent the major studios into a rush to acquire a sound system. S.S. was forced to turn to singing, dancing, and finally, talking movies.

As S.S. expressed it to Lou Zucker that morning over breakfast in the Regency suite at the George V, "Damn it, Lou, those goddam Warner brothers have created a chaos that can ruin us all. It cost twenty-five thousand dollars just to wire a theatre, and the damn pictures don't move now, they go yack-yack-yack."

Lou buttered a croissant. "I know. Don't get your

balls in an uproar. Try these rolls, they aren't bad. You've giving a press talk at the American Club this afternoon. Sock it to them. That SWP has got twelve features in the works, *all* talking, and you're going to pay Bernard Shaw a million bucks for two of his plays."

S.S. smiled grimly. "He turned us down."

"Who's to know? Look, S.S., we've ten silent pics, dogs that we can't get our negative costs out of at home."

"I'm shooting five-minute inserts of some dramatic stuff to cut in. It will raise the nut, but with lousy music added, maybe they'll work out. But I've got to dump our vaults over here. Ten years of pictures, all silents." S.S. sipped his black coffee and grimaced. He was getting too plump in the middle, his blood pressure was rising: Doctor Printzmedel suspected an inflamed gall bladder. S.S. was also losing hair and needed glasses for reading small print. He resented signs of mortality, loved the essence of life. In his middle forties, S.S. felt in his prime ("doctors are always trying to find something cockeyed to earn their specialist fees").

"Lou, if we didn't get hold of Phonofilm sound we'd be bankrupt . . . We can turn it around. Look at Warner Brothers—stock was selling for thirteen before they found that damn Vitaphone sound gimmick. After their first relese of that cockamamy vaudeville it went to sixty-two. That's how fast things can change. No warning. The customers act like they never heard people speak before. If we can dump some of the backlog to those India show people and Japanese distributors we could come up roses."

Lou wiped his mouth with a crisp napkin, and lit a cigarette.

"The French, I hear, bury their money under the fireplace. Not a sou for us here."

"They aren't even thankful we saved their fucking

bacon in 1917. Anything in their movies we can pick up?"

Lou took out a small notebook. "Nothing I've seen you could show even in a college. This fellow Renoir had a movie *Nana*. Maybe you should look at it. It's about a classy French whore. Only it's in costume."

"The painter is making movies?"

"It's his son. Now this Maurice Chevalier, you liked him at the Folies Bergére. He might make it as a French loverboy in pictures."

"Paramount's signed him. Zucker moves fast."

"Then this Rene Clair, he's got this picture."—Lou read carefully from his notebook—"*Un Chapeau de Paille d'Italie* . . . means 'The Italian Straw Hat'. I'll arrange a running for you."

"Sounds like a dog, but I'll look. Let's hope the Japanese show interest and—"

The door to the suite banged open and Harry Silverthorn and Alice Hansen came in. Harry at ten was tall, a bit too thin, but cheerful, a polite, assertive boy with a persistent look of curiosity and not at all in awe of his father.

"We went down by the Place de la Concorde, Pop, and this man he said they used to cut off people's heads there all day. And Alice and me went to this department store like Macy's, the Galeries Lafayette, and we rode the Metro. Somebody pinched Alice's behind."

"The bastards all pinch here," said Alice Hansen. She was a very beautiful Nordic blond with an innocent stare which, according to S.S., hid a very astute young lady of twenty-six. She had been a dancer, an actress, an assistant in the press department to Lou Zucker, and gave off to S.S. an honest awareness, an enervating warmth. On this trip she was S.S.'s traveling secretary, although Lou called her "the bed rabbit."

Alice was sharing S.S.'s bed at those times when his

problems overfilled his mind and he needed a slackening of pressures by some intimate physical contact. There had been little of that so far, as S.S. was too involved with the studio's future and the hunt for cash or credits.

Alice came from a dismal, overworked Swenski family on a Nebraska farm; she had six brothers and five sisters. She had been using her sexual charm since fifteen when she ran away with a traveling hoochie show. She retained a warm, confiding nature, sometimes obstinate but always reassuring. She was grateful to S.S. for taking her on this marvelous trip. Her affection for him was honest, if not deep. She had hopes of writing successful screenplays and retiring from the sexual ploys, with a few dogs, devoting more time to her golf game. Alice played weekends on the greens of the Zionhigh, the Jewish country club, while S.S. was working or with his family.

"S.S.," said Alice, "you wouldn't believe the way the taxis drive in Paris. I thought we'd go ass-over-teakettle outside Le Bon Marche."

"Lou, hire a private limo for them and a really damn good driver," said S.S.

Harry reached for Lou's cigarette case, and his father said, "Lay off that. You're going to a good school in Switzerland, so no smoking. Alice, I'll be busy all day. We'll have dinner at what's the place?"

"Pop, do I have to go to a Swiss school?"

Lou looked into his notebook. "Tour d'Argent. Specialities of the joint, soupe a l'oignon and bouillabaisse."

"Not for my stomach these days. I'll have breast of chicken. They have plain Jewish boiled chicken, don't they?" He winked at Harry, who said, "Every place they have chicken. Can I have the *specialité de la maison* tonight?"

"We'll see what it is. I have to get a haircut. Send

206

down for the barber. Oh, hell, I have a lunch date with my nephew, don't I?"

Alive picked up the phone. "You'll have time for the barber, S.S. It's getting cute and curly in back."

Harry wandered around the suite. He found a basket of fruit on the gilt piano, took up an apple, and bit into it. His bright, tumultous nature demanded continual change and excitement. He stood at a window looking down at the traffic—taxis darting in and out, honking their odd imperious horns, an old man weak in the knees walking two dogs making their rounds of lamp posts and tree trunks; a hotel doorman arguing with a man in blue denims pushing a small cart, a policeman on a bicycle saluting a girl in a very short dress carrying a hat box.

While sometimes appalled by his father's temerity, Harry also admired him; for Sidney Silverthorn, when not worried, took an exhilarating joy in his children. Harry was aware of S.S.'s hedonism, that his mother, ignoring obsequious gossip, collected milk glass, played auction bridge, and preferred to be in Palm Springs most of the time rather than in the big new house in Bel Air with its five servants and large dinner parties. There was some excrutiating conflict between his mother and father; he tried to keep aloof from that situation. He felt the world was a fine place full of wondrous things, that there were fascinating people in it and that he was destined for some great deed. A general, a scientific genius, a dancer like Fred Astaire. He could be rueful when he hurt someone, sentimental when he read Robert Louis Stevenson, the historical novels of Conan Doyle, Twain's *Huckleberry Finn.*

Harry turned from the window and deposited the apple core in an ashtray.

"We saw this kid pee right in the street in front of everybody. Alice says the French do it any place."

207

"Only the peasants, darling," said Alice, hugging him to her. Alice was very strict about good manners and social protocol. She always suspected a dinner hostess who didn't produce fish forks. The more Alice rose in the world the more she found much that was coarsening. For instance, when tired, S.S. often slept in his underwear.

People sitting on the terrace of Le Dome seemed to S.S. to have aged without ripening. He had heard the characters in Hemingway and Fitzgerald sat there. Elliot Paul, who had sold S.S. a story, had told him, "Anybody who is anybody from America can be seen there."

As he waited for his nephew Paul, S.S. looked about him, sipping his wine. A mangy-looking group: two dark men with wet mouths who looked like rug peddlers; a girl with pimples and a cough; a man in a bowler hat, a Charlie Chaplin cane between his legs, reading *Le Petit Journal*, a woman with bobbed white-gray hair and a long cigarette holder, her chin propped up by a hand displaying rings (and dirty fingernails), a shivery white poodle at her feet.

She waved at S.S., a mixture of affection and condescension. "Hello, you old bastard, how's everything?"

"Not bad, Bee."

The old butch was with some USA news syndicate in Paris, and had been out to the studio in California a few months back.

"That last picture," she held her nose, "*de mal en pis.*"

He winked; S.S.'s winks were famous. He could answer almost any statement, Ira Silverthorn insisted, by a wink.

Paul came hurrying along, nearly knocking down an old woman peddling flowers out of a basket. He was wearing a too baggy suit and a wide-brimmed gray hat. "Hello, Uncle Sid. Want to sit inside someplace?"

"No, this will do. Jesus, you look like a cat's ghost. Terrible."

Paul sat down, admired S.S. resplendent in brown and a Homberg.

"You look fine. How's everybody? Harry, Nora, the little girl?"

"Everybody's fine . . . Come out to California and we'll feed you up, get you some interesting studio work. Want to be a movie director?" He motioned to a waiter. "What will you have, Paul?"

"A Fundedor."

"Hey, Hemingway drinks that."

"I'm sorry. I like it. Nope, I don't want to be a director. Right now I want enough of your loot to buy seventy-five Vickers machine guns—heavy stuff."

S.S. looked around, worried at the wisdom of such talk here. "I don't want to hear—"

"Uncle Sid, two weeks ago the British Navy was trying to blow me apart, and a very wonderful guy was killed. But we got the stuff to the settlements."

"I heard."

"It's a drop in the well. The Arabs are going to pogrom the settlements unless the world wakes up. Think of it as Indians attacking a wagon train of pioneers."

"That's history."

"Palestine Jews are chopped liver? as Malka Bendelbinder used to say."

"You want money? I've my own problems. Talking pictures. We're just starting to make masterworks in silent films, the Russians, the Germans, Griffith, Chaplin, Doug, Mary, and then those fucking Warner Brothers . . . how much?"

"Ten thousand dollars. I have to have it soon.

There's an Italian Jew in Rome who can get the guns. The British have them warehoused in Cairo."

"You want ten grand, just like that?"

Paul drank his brandy. The girl with the cough was being greeted and kissed passionately by a huge Negro in a fez carrying a horn in a dark bag under his arm.

"How do you like that?" asked S.S. "In public, too."

"He was in Jim Europe's jazz band. He's playing at Bricktop's Club, the real Dixieland."

"Never mind Dixie. I'm working on deals to sell out European rights on some pictures. You can help me, represent me in Rome. Contact Tiber Films, Capri Productions. You sell them a dozen old films and I'll pay you ten per cent for your damn machine guns."

Out of cigarettes, Paul took a cigar from his uncle. "I'm no salesman."

S.S. flipped a gold lighter to flame. "Fifteen per cent. It's my way of helping your people in Palestine."

Paul inhaled, expelled smoke. "*Your* people too."

"I'm not turning my face to the wall, am I? Say Tiber or Capri buys ten films for ten thousand dollars each. There's your ten g's. Hell, if I wasn't rushed, I'd flip down to Rome myself."

Paul motioned the waiter for another drink. The woman with the ring and the long cigarette holder yanked the poodle to its feet and passed by S.S.'s table. "I have this true story, Mr. Silverthorn, about the real Mata Hari. It's literature and . . ."

"We haven't come around to literature yet. But send it to my story editor. You're not ashamed, I see, to write for the movies."

"*Il aunt de l'argent.*"

The poodle whined and was dragged off. S.S. said, "I'd hate to find out her story is a good one."

"Someone here has already made a movie of it."

S.S. winked. "I know. Jesus, some day I'll find an actress who can really play the pants off it . . . Right now, Paul, I'm rushing around in four directions at once like a Passover chicken with its throat cut. Don't think I don't feel for the poor Jews in Palestine. But to be practical, with all those Turks, Arabs, British Tommies . . ."

"This friend of mine that was killed bringing in the last shipment said, 'Never ask the end, just the way."

S.S. looked at his nephew and sighed.

"How would five thousand do? You've caught me offguard, Paul. We'll call it an advance of commission on those films you're going to sell for SWP. I'll have Lou ship you the reels care of American Express in Rome."

"I'll do what I can. And I'll take your check."

"Goddamn right you will. Now I have to run along." He put down some franc notes. "Have dinner with us before you leave. Say Wednesday? Lou says Lasserre's is not bad."

"Not bad."

When S.S. had gone off Paul decided not to have another brandy. You had to admire S.S.; a man dedicated to what he loved.

22

FROM PAUL SILVERTHORN'S JOURNALS

Going back to writing in my journal (I didn't make any notes during the gun running—the British finding it would have you shot against a stone wall some dawn—a last cigarette and a refusal of blindfold).

Getting the five thousand from S.S. wasn't easy. I wish I cared more about his damn studio's survival or his films which I find banal.

S.S. is ridiculously inept at doing a favor graciously. He asked me to take Teddy Binder to lunch, said he'd pick up the tab. I said I didn't mind paying for the lunch; I still had a small trust fund my grandfather Alex had left me, and the way S.S. paid for everything, lunches and dinners with that big flourish, made me feel like a bum with his nose against the window of Delmonico's.

Teddy and I met Harry and Alice for lunch at the Brasserie Flo and Harry insisted on *canard aux olives*. Alice was very charming in fluffy gray and pale green organdy, a little cloche hat to match. But I didn't envy S.S. his bed partner. These cool, collected Nordic blonds suggest a sense of frost somehow covering their pale, sensual fire. Maybe I was thinking of Joyce Davis in Rome (mysterious, impulsive, coils of ink-black hair); she is a post-Cubist painter and the Hebrew defense groups' Italian contact, reminds me of Walter Scott's Rebecca in *Ivanhoe*.

I touched Teddy for five hundred for the cause, I've become a consummate beggar. When I see the look of cold impassivity I often get, I feel I'm becoming a bore on the subject.

But Teddy said if I needed more to look him up at the Hassler Villa Medici in Rome.

Even though Gertrude Stein assured me, "Paris is where the twentieth century is," I felt I had been there too long. From 1920 on it had been a haven for my post-war brooding, my hopes of producing an avant garde magazine. But that was all behind me; the grand parties at the Lotti on rue de Castiglione, taking American visitors to Le March aux Pirces to pick over junk as bargains, being lonely and being happy.

One green, silvery morning, I went down to the American Express, got my money in order, whistling "Am I Blue," got on the right train, sat in a second-class compartment. I ate a blue trout in the dining car, sipped a cognac. You are drinking too much, chum, I said to the reflection in the window glass, beyond which pregnant French cows were processing next spring's veal. You are a rummy. You can't stop. Shit, I can stop any time I want. At dinner I only had one ball of brandy.

I travel light: a tweed-belted jacket which holds passport, papers, addresses, introductions I shall not present, half my money. In my pants pocket a worn wallet with the other half of my assets. Addresses of (safe) people in Rome, Paris, London. I also carry matches, a pocket comb, two old Dunhill pipes, a tobacco pouch, a key chain with keys for lost doors and luggage I don't ever lock. This fountain pen—once my grandfather's—

I write with, which, God and Waterman willing, should last a lifetime.

In Rome I first stayed at a little fleabag behind the Piazza Navona called Hotel Fausta where black money market promoters hang out and women with good legs and bad faces sit in the lobby fingering shabby furs. I called Banolo Levi, the Italian Jew who could get the machine guns, and I told him I had half the money and he said half a *tocus* is no deal. He was going to Milano and gave me a number to call him there when I had the entire sum. I talked to several little spinning men, all sweat and high voices, at Tiber and Capri Films, and showed them the movies S.S. had sent ahead. They said yes, yes, in a week, a fortnight, they could buy maybe eight, maybe all. Keep calling them.

So I waited. Called Joyce Davis but she was away sketching, some old woman's voice told me, in Sorrento.

I waited, drifted, avoided museums, churches, galleries; after years of talk about art in Paris, one day you discover that looking at pictures can be cured. It is not the pictures that displease, it's all the art dealers, critics, art histories, collectors. When you've seen them operate the pictures begin to fade out. In Italy the paintings are very dark mostly, so it is easy to avoid them.

Capri Films made an offer next day on six pictures. I phoned S.S. He said, "Say no and offer to take off five per cent. They'll say no. So wait . . ."

I called Milano, told Banolo I was close to getting the whole ten thousand together. He said he'd take two per cent off if I closed the deal in two weeks. If not, he had another prospect.

Next day I asked for Joyce at the American Express on the Piazza di Spagna. The clerk said there was no

215

address. I decided to try Thomas Cook on the Via Veneto.

I was right. At Thomas Cook there was an address for Joyce Davis. I could leave a note and some lira to forward it. They didn't give out addresses. Very proper, I agreed.

Four days later after my visit to Thomas Cook, the desk clerk at my Fausta Hotel handed me an envelope with a note inside: *L'chaim! Sorry you couldn't find me. Holed up now at Via Margutta 104. Not near a phone. J.D.*

Via Margutta 104 is one of those romantic-to-look-at, miserable-to-live-in buildings of stone, rubble, clay and rotting supporting timbers that could have withstood several prolonged sieges. I entered through large splintered gates. Inside was an open shed where some sculptor had begun a statue of a male torso from a flawed bit of marble. The half-dozen doors I passed going up on the outside staircase gave off the odor of turpentine and linseed oil. Joyce's name and a Star of David were chalked on a faded red door. A scrawled note had been thumbtacked under the C3: *Don't knock, walk through, turn right past hammock.*

I opened the door and found myself in a roofed passage in which stood a beheaded sewing machine, a dismantled motorbike, a frame used for stretching lace curtains. A row of red painted pots held dead plants. Past them was a square courtyard with blooming yellow trumpet and bougainvillaea vines and under it a hammock with someone in it—a dark-haired, white-skinned girl in a man's shirt, barelegged under a peasant skirt. She was sitting in the hammock shelling pea pods into a pot set between her clean unshod feet. Here was Joyce, warm, sweating, the soles of her bare feet soiled by the dusty stone flagstones.

She jumped up and hugged me. "Paul!"

I just said, "Joyce."

"So bad about Eddy."

I said yes, it was very bad and she looked good.

"Sit down."

I sat down on a backless kitchen chair facing her. Her very large fine eyes were just a little mismatched, spoiling, some may say, the symmetry of the face, if you're nuts over symmetry.

"Scholmo, he'll be glad to see you. He's sleeping now."

She laughed, lay back in the hammock, naked legs smooth as an eggshell; a real woman, not a pose or a tease. You knew she ate, crapped, peed, menstruated, hiccupped, was marvelous in bed.

She and Scholmo had worked together for a year in the underground. He was living with her as a cover. They weren't lovers. Scholmo had a wife and three children in Jaffa. The British were hunting him for blowing up a police station where they beat up Jews.

We opened the bottle of Strega I brought and drank and talked. Then Scholmo came in his thin torso bare, wearing a pair of baggy soiled cotton trousers of washed-out blue, his feet stuffed into sandals. He had a short shaggy beard; the dark crepe flesh under his eyes gave an unhealthy look. He was too old for underground work.

"You made it," he said. "You got the guns in." He put his arms around me and hugged me. He smelled of unaired bedding, sour wine.

Scholmo picked up the bottle of Strega. "Glasses, glasses." Scholmo was irritable, as he would be with a hangover. "I'm a little shaky. Been here six months. I've got to get us back to Palestine."

Joyce said, "It's suicide."

"Yes," I said, "your picture is on posters every place."

217

We sat in the courtyard while the sun sank into an Etruscan gloom, and little lizards came out to taste the shells of the peas. Some place nearby a couple were quarreling. A child ran past the wall of the court with a fish-and-onion pizza by the smell of it. A gramophone played "A Mare Chiaro." It was like a genre painting and we three Jews far from our homes just sat as if posing.

It was getting to be dusk, the bottle finished, when we left for a pasta place, an artists' hangout in a cellar. The food was strong with garlic and olive oil. Scholmo drank grappa and Joyce and I had a mild white wine. As we ate, a man with a ludicrous face, all warts and hair, played a squeeze box and sang those sentimental songs about Torna a Sorriento and the Bay of Naples; they sounded just right with the pasta and the fried fish.

Scholmo went off to a cinema with a poet from the restaurant; Joyce and I went back to Via Margutta 104 and made love. It was delirious and marvelous.

We had been lovers for two years, ever since she came to Rome to serve as a weapons drop for the Hebrew defense groups. She proved resourceful and audacious. Her correct name was Judith dePoll; her ancestors, Sephardic Jews, had been expelled from Spain by Ferdinand and Isabella. By the beginning of the nineteenth century, the dePolls had settled in England and prospered and, as Joyce said, "become as dull as those petite bourgeoisie Gentiles they envied."

Among four sisters, Joyce was the rebel daughter, studying art at the Slade School, then during a summer spent on a kibbutz near Kailok, becoming aware of the Zionists' endeavors, joining those trying to get the British to put the Balfour Declaration into force. She was a girl, still only twenty-two, but capable and discreet, and I needed at this time her serenity.

* * *

On a Friday Teddy Binder showed up at the Hassler. With him was Alice Hansen, whom S.S. had sent along to help with the film deal (I knew better—S.S. wanted her out of his hair for a while). They looked very chummy—as when Joyce and I had lunch with them at Les Deux Magots. Alice, a vision in pale yellow, her scarf fluttering as in a Sung scroll; Teddy looking very pleased with himself, the tranquility of a fulfilled mate.

Full of food and drink, I felt more hope than I had for the past week. Alice visited the Italian film producers, and amazingly enough, got them to raise their offer, but it still was not enough.

We became a foursome. Joyce knew Rome, and Alice and Teddy were like any tourists wanting to grab it all in. Teddy put up the money for a ticket to ship Scholmo off to Mexico with a promise to speed his wife and children after him. Late at night, alone in our robes, Joyce and I talked.

I poured the last of the coffee into her cup. Her arms, extending from the sleazy robe, were round, white, strong.

She slung herself back in the chair, hair wild, eyes closed, naked legs crossed (the soles were pink and clean now). Her bone structure kept her from the over-roundness of a Botticelli Venus, but I could picture her stepping out of a seashell, her feet in a bed of clam sauce, grated onions, lemon juice.

"Know what I want, Paul? A fine dull life, like my sisters. A striped cat to put out at night. Two kids, girl, boy, in that order. I've a wide pelvis, will deliver easy. A garden with old-fashioned flowers—pinks, moss roses, hollyhocks—a tree with noisy birds in it, a child crying at the pleasure of burying its face in your lap. Why don't you shut me up?"

"Why should I?"

"You understand why I go to bed with you? It isn't just sex?"

"Perfectly."

Teddy and Alice were good company. We spent afternoons savoring the shops, gazing over the *campagna*, quoting Stendhal ("The charm of Italy is like being in love"). We would walk past the shops on the Corso, looking at leatherwork, plaster saints that glowed in the dark, rosaries, editions of Dante, fake Greek and Roman fragments. The Fontana di Trevi wasn't flowing—there was always something wrong with plumbing in Rome—and the giant statues of Neptune led by the Tritons looked like scaly lepers, their dried bodies stained yellow, the bottom of the fountain green with scum and floored with discarded cigarette packages. Two dirty kids were slipping around inside the basin, hunting the coins the tourists had thrown in to make a wish.

The terraced gardens of the baroque balustraded houses had palm trees, hanging vines and oleanders in pots. From a certain spot you could see a panorama of cypresses and olives.

There was a studio vacant nearby, and Teddy got the idea of him and Alice moving in ("Alice wants to try watercolors and I can rent a piano and work on my music").

A huge canvas took up one entire wall of Joyce's studio. It was a work in progress, her unfinished masterpiece—a near abstract, "The Death of Rome." She had caught a great black hearse of polished ebony, drawn by eight dark horses in soot-colored plumes and nets, a hundred-man band, church procession with a cardinal in red gloves and hat wedged among monks and holy orders, hooded carriers of flowers, containers of relics. It would be a remarkable painting if ever finished.

We would make love in the wide brass bed under the huge canvas.

We'd breakfast all four of us on the balcony on *panini*, butter, *caffe nero*, Joyce's marmalade which her mother in England sent her with advice. Joyce would lick the marmalade spoon and cross her legs and I would look at the fine tendons of her ankles, ignoring the murmur of the world over the wall.

We didn't make much of lunch—a bit of ham, a glass of wine. At dinner, we talked tired subjects: art, money, love, fame, God, birth, death. Late at night we'd pass the French College of the Sacred Spear and Holy Nails, a noted nest of pederasts; hear the priests' and novices' singing: "Hallowed be Thy Name . . . Lead us not into temptation."

We'd sleep a full, heavy slumber, feeling life run over us lightly. In the middle of pleasure I'd look down on Joyce and taste bile; every bed is waiting to be a deathbed.

No one who fought in the Great War came out of it as sane as he went in. More or less all of us were touched by a world malaise that didn't go away.

Fall brought cold, fruit-green rains, Roman pine trees whipping in the wind, the fountains clogged with dead leaves. Autumn in Rome was the saddest month—bleak, icy rains, poor heat from little charcoal stoves, the breath we left as we walked along floating like vapor; nights we clung together in our bed sharing body warmth and looking at each other with that pathological dread of solitude.

There is something of a sadness about living with women when it is not in one's own home, when marriage is not part of it, when there is no guilt to say this is not holy, not legal. Then comes the thought, like the sound of one's own heart drumming in a nightmare: better marry and live properly by holy writ, by civil decree. But reflected in the morning coffee are the images of all our friends who failed, the people whose marriages have turned wrong. So we go on hoping for us this will suffice.

In the morning our rooms smelled of the ever-present charcoal gas, cold walls sweating. We would pile on more clothes: jacket on sweater, coat on jacket, muffler on coat, like a mockery of a store dummy. The stones of Rome rang like bells, and the damn bells rang as always from nearly five hundred churches, calling the coughing, hawking faithful to morning Mass, and again ringing at noon, in the afternoon and for the last prayer of the day, the clang of bronze in the saddest hour.

It was soon clear Alice wasn't doing any better than I had with the Italian film people. S.S. would have to take about half of what he had expected. On the phone he sounded tired when I explained it. He asked about Alice, seemed unconcerned about her affair with Teddy—"She'll be back on the coast before spring. The little lady knows what she really wants."

That night, lying by the side of a sleeping Joyce, her arm around me, I cried out, "Tony! Tony Ringel!"

She came awake with a start. "You *mashugah*?"

"Tony, Tony! He flew in the RAF with me. He's rich. Biggest junk dealer in the Midwest. He's staying at Monte. I'll give him a call."

"In the morning."

Tony was out when I called his hotel in Monte at nine the next morning, but I got him at noon. He sounded pleased to hear me; I was sweating.

"Jesus! Paul, I thought you were knocked off in the war. Gone west, we used to say."

222

"I got shot down in a dogfight—a bum hip. How are you?"

"Kicking up a fuss, having fun."

"Can I see you, Tony? I want to talk something over."

"Need some dinero?" The indelicate directness of one suspecting a touch.

"No, not for me . . . I can drive up to Monte."

"Look, I'm on my way to Rome. We'll paint the burg red for old times sake."

I gave him directions and hoped he wouldn't turn out a shit like so many of the old war buddies. In an optimistic mood I wired Levi I'd have the money in a day or two.

On a rainy day, in a fog, Tony arrived in a Duesenberg as long as a tapeworm. He told us it had been made for an actor, Valentino, but he had grabbed it off. He looked just as dark and handsome, as rabbinical and sensual as when he was with the RAF. He wore a tweed suit of loose-belted English cut, shoes from Bond Street of a pebbled leather that looked like fruit peel, silk shirt with a wide gold collar-bar, regimental tie, and a floppy gray actor's hat with the brim down on one side.

The kids in the neighborhood came out in the rain to spit on the Duesenberg. Tony threw coins among them, told them in Italian to keep an eye on it.

In the studio Tony clapped his hands together. "I feel a drink is called for, seeing the old RFC face again."

His big dark eyes looked at the unfinished "Death of Rome."

"*That's* a painting!"

"Yes," said Joyce.

I poured some strega and we drank.

Later I went down to the street with him, the rain falling with a steady purr, gleaming off his car's silver hood. We stood close together in the archway over the outer courtyard, puffing out vapor.

"So what's the big thing you want to talk about?"

"Money, your money." A thick yellow fog was moving out over the Tiber.

"It figured." I could see he was waiting for a cliché hard-luck yarn.

"I want to buy weapons for the Jewish settlers in Palestine. The Arabs are planning to massacre them."

"Guns." He said it blankly.

"Old British war stuff stolen from a Cairo warehouse. I have about six thousand dollars. A film deal went sour so I need at least four more for those guns."

He looked at me, shook his head. "You're too trusting."

"We've dealt with the seller—a Jew named Baldo Levi—before."

"Let's meet this Levi. I'm a good judge of unethical chicaneries."

"He's in Milano. I'll call him and set up a meeting. Tony, it's all worth it. It's saving people's lives."

He looked me over, tilted back his hat with a forefinger. "How do I know this isn't some kind of con you and the beautiful Miss Davis are pulling?"

"Fuck you," I said and turned away, feeling wet, cold, sick, the collapse of a desperate urgency. Tony stopped me, took my arm.

"Come on, give me credit to think of all the angles. Okay, okay, I'm in. You contact this Heeb middle man and tomorrow we convert everything to clean American money. Tonight it's Capriccio's for dinner. You wouldn't want to make a deal for the beautiful Miss Davis?"

I said no, and he saw I wasn't taking it as a joke. The

very rich have a price tag for everything and usually they are right. But at dinner he could see how things stood between me and Joyce.

I had tried twice to get Levi in Milano and it wasn't until a day later, eleven at night, on the pasta joint's phone that I made contact.

"Baldo, I've got it all, the whole ten."

"I don't believe you, Silverthorn. You cry wolf a lot."

"Come down to Rome, pick it up."

"And find nothing? Listen, *shemendrick,* I have some people buying. You be here say by Friday with the sum agreed on and you have the stuff."

"All right. Friday."

"If not, kiss it goodbye, boychic."

"You bastard, keep to your bargain. I'll be there with the money."

"I'll be at the Lord Internazionale Hotel on the via Galvani. Room 307. I'm registered as Charles Owen."

I said, "You're a good Jew, Baldo, a credit to the Chosen People."

He must have caught the sarcasm in my voice, for he said, "*Lig-em-dred*—which translates roughly as 'go to hell'."

Joyce suggested I fly to Milano but Tony said no planes would fly in this thick, blind weather.

"Forget the angst and agony. I'll drive you in the Duesenberg."

"There's the train," Joyce said.

Tony laughed, kissed her cheek. "Honey, no matter what Musso the Fat Boy says, not *all* the trains run on time in Italy, and Paul says if the dough isn't there on the line in two days we lose the stuff."

That was Tony, flamboyant but plausible. He drove off to the Excelsior where he was staying and I and Joyce got into bed and said a lot of wonderful, foolish things to each other, made love, my whole body wondering, was this the last time, would I ever return, would I be alive in a few days? With your naked love in your arms and a parting to face in the morning, a lot of tragic throughts seep into you.

The dawn was foggy. Tony was driving and singing "Pony Boy," and I was sitting and holding on and pumping a plunger set in the side of the car to get the gas pressure up. Tony had added this gadget for additional horsepower.

It was a slow trip—Tony was having trouble seeing, and the roads were torn up or in very bad repair. When we saw the silver ribbon of the Arno flowing past, it was a velvet dusk and we roared into Florence, smoking badly; we had run short of oil and were ass-sprung, worn, and dusty. The Hotel Excelsior doubted we wanted to stay there, but we insisted. We took off the next morning in threatening weather to follow the Arno down to Pisa. The leaning tower was hidden by fog as we turned north to Carrara. It began to drizzle when we came to LaSpezia, and I was for staying there for the night. The clouds were black over the Gulf of Genoa. Tony said, "We'll eat and tool on. The dawn patrol flies rain or shine!"

The eating place smelled of the wet earth; rain, grapes and olive oil brought out images of times past. It comes back, meeting Tony, with distortions—memory is a crystal lens that distorts all objects. Tony rubbed me in spots—I hadn't cauterized my memories as well as I had hoped I had.

I had an omelet of duck eggs in pomidoro I would rather forget about. Tony tried some pasta and edible fungi and brandy, and then we went on along the Riviera dei Fliori. It was raining hard now; the interior was damp and the rear left tire was fraying. Also we

226

had been buying local gas and that seemed to do the car no good. Near dark we discovered for the first time the car headlights had died. We stopped under a ruined tower advertising a popular cow drench for farmers.

"We better find shelter."

Tony smiled and wiped rain off his face. "It's men like you who stayed home when George Washington said come visit the winter sports at Valley Forge."

We blew the frayed tire as we ran across some trolley-car tracks on the outskirts of Genoa, but we limped on. We nearly made it, but we ran into a ditch and snapped an axle. Tony and I climbed out of the tilted car. We stopped a boy on a bike and asked for the hotel and the boy pointed and pedaled off as if he had seen the devil. We were pretty messed up, crumpled, wet, wrinkled.

I said, "Never give up."

He said, "We've sacrificed the car."

We got to the hotel. The rest of that evening was rather anticlimactic. We found "Charles Owen" in his room having his nails done by a manicurist with a big rump and red hair. I introduced Tony, and Baldo dismissed the girl with a fatherly kiss. He said, *"Nu?"*

Tony looked around suspiciously. There was a door to another room slightly ajar. Both of us knew there was someone there. Baldo wasn't going to accept all that money alone. I didn't blame him.

Tony opened the dispatch case we had been carrying and there laid out in order were flat packets of American fifty-dollar bills.

"Count it," Tony said, as if it were a privilege granted. "You can keep the case."

Baldo counted swiftly, the way a bank teller does. Then we all had a quick brandy. It was cold and damp even in the room.

Tony asked, "I don't suppose you give receipts. Just

227

know, Mr. Owen or Mr. Levi, if there is anything queer about this pitch you're a dead Yiddle." He waved toward the door to the next room. "You can have a dozen strong-arm boys protecting you. I am a friend of Al Capone's, no crap, and if I whistle he'll send over a dozen of his best *momzers* if those guns don't show."

I could see Tony was delighted with pulp magazine dialogue.

Baldo made an amused gesture to the slightly opened door and shut it. He seemed not at all impressed, this little hammered-down runt with the gold flecked teeth.

"Mr. Ringel, with you it's a pleasure to do business. I know who you are, and believe me, I believe you about Al and his *momzers*. You've got no fear of this not being kosher. In four days, a Greek freighter, the *Pyngos*, under the flag of Panama, will sail out of Alexandria for Cyprus. You can intercept her any place along that route. The captain will listen to reason about a change of course."

"And what," Tony asked, "will that cost us?"

Baldo Levi showed his gold bridgework in a grimace. "Not a penny. It's my personal gift to the Jewish Homeland."

That sentimental out-of-character gesture sort of spoiled it for us. We had been demeaning the litle swine as a greedy bastard. We had one more drink and left.

23

Take pleasure in the smell of apples, the Rabbi of the Belz Hasiage Court had said. Was there warning, Aaron Bendelbinder wondered, was it anyone's fault we took such pleasure in property? Herbert Hoover had been inaugurated as the 31st president, and the *Forward*, Aaron's Yiddish newspaper, had noted that Trotsky had been sent into exile by the Soviets, and Arabs had attacked Jews worshipping at the Wailing Wall.

Malka, who had taken up mah jong and collecting for the Milk Fund for hungry black babies, advised him, "Stop reading the papers. Good news they don't want. Bad news our friends bring us."

"A man has to keep up with events."

Aaron was deep in his seventies and not as phlegmatic as he had hoped. "I can see the eighties," he'd say. "Snow on top of what's left of my hair."

His limbs were stiffer and he walked in the park with a cane. He carried a pocket of broken bits of bread for the birds, crusts for the squirrels. "Eat, God's creatures, and fear cats and taxis."

The Great Bargain Stores he had created so long ago were run now by a board of directors who favored the stockholders, not the customers. Aaron felt that a corporation with 704 stores was overextended, and that the long-term leases were too costly: "Today no neighborhood lasts twenty years." But go argue with the yearly report. Business had never been better, and twenty more stores were opening. Such places: Broken Arrow, Eagle Rock, Muttberg, Fluteville. Where were the enthusiasms of yesterday? Better to read the postal cards from their grandson Teddy in Europe, which Malka put on the music room mirror near the Knabe piano that no one played, by the sheet music of the year's hit songs: Teddy's "Wonder Why You Wiggle," his rivals' "Stardust" and "Moanin' Low."

The first shock was not Hitler appointing Himmler *Reichsfuhrer* of the S.S. or that public servants were guilty in the Teapot Dome scandal, but that something was very, very wrong in Florida. An incoherent mess was coming into focus on the west coast near Punta Gorda; Seaside and Marlin Point had failed, causing a bank to close its doors.

Nat and Laura came to New York, both looking very well, Malka thought. Laura was a bit too thin, but then Malka thought all the flappers were too thin in their rolled stocking and shapeless androgynous dresses.

Sitting in the parlor, Nat admitted things were getting tight in Florida but nothing as bad as near Punta Gorda. He explained to Aaron, smoking his pipe and listening attentively, "It's just washing out the fly-by-nights, the con men."

"Taking down a bank with them? That's bad, when a bank can't pay its depositors."

Nat agreed. "It was a hole-in-the-wall bank, promoted by some red-necked backwoods characters. Miami is solid. So are Coral Gables and Diamond Coves. We've paved the streets, are putting in water mains, electric lines. Sales are leveling off nicely. No more speculators are buying in the morning to sell before sundown. No sir."

Nat sat back in the chair with a satisfied grin, a cake plate and tea cup (it had been years since Malka hd

230

served tea in a glass) on his lap. From the piano in the next room came racing notes as Laura played "Crazy Rhythm" for her mother-in-law.

Aaron removed the stem from his pipe and blew it. He loved this strange son of his, wondered about him, never understood him. "You're still showing red ink?"

"We may, but next year will be a bonanza. After all, the expensive improvements are done. From now in it's a gravy run."

Aaron was thoughtful; oh, my loving son, words come so easy. "You're in town for a good time, go see Eddie Cantor in *Whoopee*."

Patience, Nat thought, don't rush the old boy.

"There's some items to talk over with the bank. We want an extension on our loans to finish the yacht basin. You attract big boat owners if you have a yacht club— the crème de la crème of estate buyers."

Aaron had reassembled his pipe and held a match to its bowl. He puffed; why should I let him suffer? "Nat, you're in good trouble?"

"Aw come on, Pa." He stood up. "It gets a little tight when you're expanding, but . . ."

"Pull in your horns, Nat. Something is cockeyed in the whole country. I don't like the market. Nothing is worth what it's selling for. Are there assets behind the ticker prices? This *klotz* Hoover, he just sits in his high collar, doesn't shake a finger at what's going on. So you're a card player. Lay out your hand on the table."

"I need five hundred thousand dollars to pay off contractors. If you put up some of your Great Bargain shares for collateral this one more time, it's clear sailing when the fall land sales go over the top."

"You have most of my shares tied up now. But I put something together I was holding for the grandchildren. What about Sidney Silverthorn's movie company? Talk was of it coming in with your interests."

231

"Didn't work out. We traded some stock and last month he sold out whatever he had in Diamond Coves. Movies! Now there's a leaking boat."

"He's doing fine. Got a postal card when he was at the Olympic Games in Amsterdam. Talking pictures, everybody is going crazy for them. Mama and me saw *Singing in the Rain*. Very nice, catchy tunes."

"A fad. Look, Pa. I'll be in the clear by spring. Your shares in Diamond Coves will be worth double, triple, what they are today."

Malka came in, followed by Laura. "Enough talking. We're going to dinner at the Waldorf. Laura has never been there."

"Teddy's music publisher is getting us tickets, down front, for the Gershwin show. Too bad Teddy doesn't have a show this year instead of *shmizing* around Europe with that—" She looked at Laura. "Never mind. Aaron, get dressed."

Nat took his wife's hand, "Look, folks. I have to meet some people. So go on without me."

Laura gave him a mock blow on the chin. "No, you don't, mister. This is a fun trip and I'm damn self-indulgent today. I came to see shows, eat something by a chef who doesn't fry fish, and dance the Black Bottom." She put her arms around Nat's neck. "That's the message, loud and clear."

"I know, sweetie. But it's Monte Spinelli, and he's leaving at midnight for Chicago on the *Limited*. Tell you what, folks. I'll meet you at the theatre. Sign the tab at the Waldorf for me, sweetie."

"You foxy bastard. Pardon me, folks."

"Leave a ticket for me at the box office. I am sorry, but . . ."

Laura shrugged. She was too pleased to be in New York to protest too much, and Nat usually had his way. She was aware Nat was in trouble, and that one didn't rile either of the Spinelli brothers. Nat had to keep them pleased, absurd and obnoxious as they were.

A week later the great east coast multimillion dollar development, Palmcrest, declared itself bankrupt, followed by a collapse of the Florida land boom. Some few developments managed to hold on, mostly those that had Palm Beach money behind them and hadn't expanded wildly and those that were the delight of the Detroit auto magnates tanning in the winter sun.

Diamond Coves declined at a quickening pace; most of those who had built mortgaged homes let the banks take over. The buyers of lots unloaded or tried to unload to the original fishermen and their families. The original crab inlet lost its cars, the silk shirts wore out. The locals came out of the backwoods scrub, the outskirts of villages where trailers or shacks had housed them. They were scavengering the unfished town square of Diamond Coves, tearing out walls, cutting out plumbing from deserted buildings, tearing down billboards for firewood, clapboard, and timbers, repairing shabby fishing boats. Some were soon making moonshine in the thickets; all squatters, going barefooted, accepting the end of a cycle that had returned them to their beginnings.

Several banks took over most of the land. A wrecking company hauled off what buildings survived, leveled the remains of others to recover bricks, lengths of galvanized pipes, bathroom interiors. The tree frogs came back to bark their mating call, the biting insects found new puddles to breed in. Vines, fetterbush, weeds, and wild phlox had been watching, waiting to begin to grow again. Grass forced its way through the hard blacktop surfaces of Broadway, Grand Avenue, Ponce de Leon Drive. And what remained of the sports

233

centers was a cracked swimming pool and seventy-four lost golf balls.

The only place the banks had not foreclosed on was a section of the far end of the inlet deep in Oneika mandarin trees and gallberries, which the Spinellis had marked out for their own group of villas that were never built. Here at night fast motorboats came and went; trucks carried off crates of whiskey, on a newly built road of crushed oyster shell, protected by some of the sheriff's men and a federal enforcement agent who knew his worth. Creditors seeking Nat Bendell could not locate him or his wife.

The maker of intrigues and jealousies whom Sidney Silverthorn most feared was William Fox, whose film company had gobbled up many of the sound systems that Warners did not control. S.S. had made a sort of truce with Fox, who controlled the DeForest and Case-Sponable sound systems, which he projected under the covering title of Movietone. S.S. had exchanged some of his SWP stock to be permitted to use the systems. What worried him was that William Fox was a lone wolf with the greedy-eyed fierceness of that animal. He was one of the Big Five that made motion pictures. He was mean, treacherous, and cunning (his enemies said) and wanted more and more of the new world of the talking film.

"He worries me," S.S. told Ira Silverthorn as they sat having lunch in his office. "He's smart enough to see that with the cost of equipment for a theatre for sound, maybe thirty thousand, the big theatre chains are on the inside. He's sniffing around the David Lowitz chain."

"He's trying to take over Lowitz?" Ira whistled, a spoon of noodle soup held halfway to his his mouth. "That's some swallow, over fifteen hundred first-run theatres. Sid, he'll put his pictures in first and—"

"And be king of the hill. He's also working on Warners, exchanging patents he controls, to get the use of their Allied Vito Electric amplifying system. Oh, William Fox, he's full of chicanery."

"What's to do?"

"Find out, Ira, where he's getting the big money backing to buy into Lowitz."

A waitress served a plate of prunes to S.S. He shook his head sadly. "Nobody prepares prunes the way our old mammy cook did in Boston when I was growing up. Each prune fat as a harem beauty, perfect, not overcooked or raw."

"Nothing is as good as it was," said Ira, smiling seraphically. "Didn't you notice that, Sid? It means we're getting old."

"Not me. All that I notice is that when I was young, fast women took little steps; now they gallop."

"All right, not old, just older. But when there is a kind of Chekhovian sense that it was once better, watch out. What do you hear from Harry in Switzerland?"

"I get postal cards of mountains. He writes he's played hockey. Nothing about his studies. Learned all the words to the 'Ballad of Abdul-A-Bul Amir and Ivan Skivishky Skivar'."

"You're not trying to create a Renaissance prince?"

"Why the hell not? He's as smart as any of the Vanderbilts, maybe smarter. Looks as good as the Rockefellers. I want him to be more than just the grandson of an immigrant who was driven out of Russia because he was a *Zhid*."

The desk intercom buzzed. S.S. pressed a lever. "Yes? . . . Who? . . . No, not now. I'm in conference. I'll call back."

He winked at Ira, who was putting a fork into a wedge of apple pie topped by a square of yellow cheese. "Who do you think?"

"By the quality of your wink, Sid, I'd say a woman."

"Alice, She's at the Beverly Hills Hotel. Let her stew a little bit."

"You don't mind the Teddy Binder caper?"

"Why should I mind? I don't own her. I admire Alice. But in Paris she was a problem when I had to move and deal and she wanted Maxim's and a lot of loving."

"You're a reasonable, unromantic cocksman."

"I put first things first. The studio, my family, then a little pleasuring, fine. But nothing that endangers numbers one and two. Alice, she understands me. I understand her. She's decent, she's bright."

He removed a prune pit from his mouth. "See if you can find out who's really backing Fox. It's somebody big. David Lowitz and his theatres can make a giant out of any studio he combines with."

"I liked it better when you were smaller, more select."

"You grow or you die. A law of nature."

In the next two days, Ira, aided by Lou Zucker and the Wall Street firm of Lazar-Wolf, who underwrote SWP stock issues, discovered that Allied Vito Electric, owner of many sound patents, was seriously considering loaning twenty million to William Fox to buy control of Lowitz Theatres. AVE had not made any move to go to the others of the Big Five—that was clear to S.S. He was running a film in his private projection room at home when Ira phoned him the news; some quick action had to be taken. He said to Lou Zucker making pencil marks in his little notebook, "I want to talk this over with Zucker Lasky, Carl, L.B., Doug, and Mary. Set up a lunch, a dinner, something, and soon."

"You think Fox can be stopped?"

"We'll find out. AVE isn't putting all that money in

someone's hand just to get hold of some sound patents Fox claims he owns."

"Some poet once wrote, 'A man's reach should exceed his grasp'."

"Only if he can lift it off the floor."

Watching a desert scene of an attack on a Foreign Legion outpost, S.S. adjusted the sound button at his elbow. Soon he was deeply analyzing the scenes of the motion picture, deciding to get a better pinging sound of rifle fire, cut quicker to a horse and rider falling. In the harem scene he winced at the costume of the female star. "Lou, for Chrissakes, she looks like a Minksy twat in that crummy harem rig. Have the whole scene reshot. I want something exotic, even erotic, without being vulgar. That camel train was beautiful, beautiful."

He sank back in his seat and Lou Zucker thought, S.S. is off now, emerged in his dream world, his true world, smelling of a hot projection machine and splicing glue.

His vision of things was here made tangible, a fabulous universe he created in spite of the agony of dealing with banks, stock market manipulations, enemies, false friends, actors, directors who lack his grandiose genius. Yes, Lou Zucker thought, it's a kind of genius he's got. For the next half hour he's not with me, not with the world outside. He's making it like he would with a woman; not with Alice, but with his version of Nefertiti.

BOOK FOUR

ISAIAH

24

The earth rotated, rushing through the European night, wobbling a bit on its axis, as Harry Silverthorn learned in class that day; rushed to meet the sun moving over Asia, the Persian Gulf, the Horn of Africa. Harry slept a satisfying sleep, his black eye twitching a the younger students. A most satisfactory victory, and bloodied Jules Balbac, who had been bullying some of the younger students. A most satisifactory victory, and Harry was less homesick than he had been . . . Over Saudi Arabia there were pink hints of a coming day, and the world rolled on, indifferent to the human condition on its surface.

The settlement of Hebron lay in the thick dark blueness of the fading night; the watchmen in the fields were relaxed. It was late August and in the community hall the oldest pioneer and two women were preparing for *Sukos*, the autumn Feast of the Tabernacle in the month of Tisri. There would be the rite of the palm branch and the *esrob* (the citron). It had been a hard summer—much poor land cultivated, guards posted to keep down the pilfering from the surrounding Arab villages.

Paul and Joyce were staying overnight in the settlement. The arms bought through Baldo Levi were safely hidden in caves near the Dead Sea. The problem was how to distribute them. The British were seizing all weapons found in the kibbutzim. Paul was discussing with Moses, the Hebron defense man, where some machine guns could be hidden from the English, who were known to dig up foundations and go down wells to ferret out weapons.

There was a restlessness as the night came to an end. A wind sent loose weeds along the roads, a starving dog messed about a garbage pit, the cows in their sheds stirred, their udders awaiting a morning milking. A rooster on his perch among his fat-rumped harem prepared to announce the coming of the dawn. In a pen by the water tower the settlement's bull snorted at the first bites of the blue-bottle flies.

In the settlement office, a sleepy, dark little man scratched his ribs, waiting for the coffee to boil on the little spirit lamp. It smelled wonderful. The dark little man, Smul Zalman, was going over a list of supplies he was to bring back in the settlement's Model-T truck from Tel Aviv. He scratched his head—he was still not adept at reading Hebrew. Still, he had hopes of becoming a competent student of the language. The phone on the desk beside him rang feebly.

"Yes," he said in Yiddish.

A flood of fervent Hebrew came through. Zalman asked, "Do you speak Yiddish?"

He was called a blockhead and a Litvak. Yiddish was shouted at him. "Arab mobs are attacking the kibbutzim. Already fifty dead. Warn the defense force."

"What defense force? A few pistols, a shotgun . . . This is a joke?"

"Curse you! Listen, you'll be under attack. The Grand Mufti's calling for a holy war to kill every Jew. You must—"

The phone went dead. The wire had been cut.

Zalman stared at the walls hung with farm tools, a

still alive, lay in a pool of water by the punctured water tower. Nearby two horses were dead, already foully smelling in the heat.

Most in the grove stood silently, watching the approach of the uniformed men.

The officer, his weathered face brick-red, looked tired. He removed his swagger stick from under his arm and pointed around him. "You people have really had it."

"Why didn't you come sooner!" shouted Moses, his fists high; he seemed delirious with rage and shock.

The officer nodded. "There have been attacks all over the districts and we've limited patrols."

Moses did a dance of rage, breaking free of Paul's grasp.

"You deprived us of means of appealing for help and defense, betrayed us by empty promises! You did, goddamn you!"

"Appeals, decisions, that's the commissioner's job, not the army's. This is dreadful . . . Elkins, get on the phone, we need aid for the hurt."

"Right, sar."

"The phone wire is cut," said Joyce.

"Elkins, find the cut, splice it. First put that bull out of his misery."

Moses shouted, "You gave the murderers and robbers the opportunities!"

"We'll have some police up soon to search the villages. We still have courts of justice."

Joyce said, "Justice? The Arabs were yelling the government is with us."

"So we've heard elsewhere. It's nonsense, I assure you."

"You refused us enough weapons." Paul was aware for the first time of his bare dirty feet set by the side of the polished boots of the officer.

"What you have is illegal; however . . ."

The officer took Paul aside, offered him an opened silver cigarette case. They smoked slowly. "Lieutenant Aston of the Irish Fusiliers. It's bad, very bad. Over a hundred massacred elsewhere, and now here."

"When can we expect aid for the wounded?"

"As soon as Lance Corporal Elkins gets the phone in working order. He's good at that sort of thing." The officer looked around him. "Damn dirty business."

The next morning graves were dug beyond the grove; the sixty-four bodies of the massacred at Hebron were wrapped in sheets and put down into the earth of Palestine.

A cordon of troops stood at attention. A correspondent from Reuters was moving about, asking for names.

The few male survivers stood by in prayer shawls as Max recited a prayer over the raw earth;

"We consecrate this hour to those we loved;
They have gone beyond time to eternity.
As sons and daughters, we recall the loving care bestowed upon us;
As husbands and wives, we remember the ties of love,
And all we shared of sorrow and joy till parted by death;
As mothers and fathers, we remember children precious to us;
As a people we remember all so untimely gone from us."

25

The day in October, 1929, that Sidney Silverthorn was notified by the U.S. Customs Office of Los Angeles that his Tyso 8A Isotta Frashini car with the Castagna body (115 horsepower, Grebel headlights, blue leather interior) had arrived via ship also saw the crash of the stock market that the *Variety* was to headline as WALL STREET LAYS AN EGG.

S.S. was on the phone talking to Clinton Nash of Lazar-Wolf, his stockbroker, chomping on an unlit cigar.

"What kind of fucking call for margin? You always carried me till the market leveled off. It's blue chip stuff. Glass. Food. G.M. Dupont."

"Mr. Silverthorn, this is not just a dip in the market. There are floods of selling orders. So I have orders to call any stock bought on margin. But of course you will cover."

Clinton Nash remained excruciatingly calm.

"Goddamn it, let me talk to Lazar-Wolf."

"I can't do that, Mr. Silverthorn. He's going to a meeting with other brokers and it's—"

S.S. kicked over the wastebasket beside his desk. "Look, you mealy-mouthed flunky, this is S.S. talking. Sam has been our shares underwriter for years. Put Lazar-Wolf on the line. Pronto!"

"I'll see what I can do."

"Do!"

S.S. had no Olympian forebearance with clerks or underlings. He threw the cigar onto an ashtray and turned to Lou Zucker inspecting some tacked-up two-sheet of an SWP picture, *Maid of Manhattan*.

"How do you like them apples? The sonofabitch of a phony Harvard accent asks me to cover margin calls. As if I were some hick who has ten shares of a cider mill."

"The market's been falling all morning and we're three hours behind New York time."

"What the hell does that—hello, Sam, what kind of cockamamy margin calls am I getting from your stooge Nash?"

Samuel Lazar-Wolf grunted across the continent; his usual smooth-as-silk voice tone had an edge to it.

"S.S., it's a damn deluge. Firms are going bust on the street. We have to stop holding the bag. Your portfolio has half a million dollars in various stocks on ten percent margin. We can't cover you. The decline is that fast."

"You'd sell me out?"

"Listen, S.S. . . ."

"You *momzer*, tell me, should I sell and take a loss or cover?"

"Look, I'll level with you. I've just come from a big meeting at House of Morgan of all the big banking houses on the street. Tommy Lamont put it right on the table: 'Your banks hold six billion dollars in reserve, so form a pool of millions, restore confidence in the stock market by buying, buying.' "

S.S. motioned Lou to bend over and listen.

"No shit, Sam? That's the truth?"

"On my mother's grave. S.S., cover the margin call. It's going to be all right. It's Morgan, not Joe Blow, calling the turns."

"Sam, I hope you're right. I'll have my bank make available fifty thousand."

"Make it seventy-five, S.S., to be sure till the market gets its blood transfusion."

Lou pursed his lips, shook his head.

S.S. said, "Christ, Sam, I don't keep that kind of loose cash to draw from. I'll have to tap some box office returns. Sam, listen, don't screw me. Keep me informed. How's SWP stock going?"

"Still taking a beating, like everything so far. S.S., I've three other calls waiting. Keep your pecker up."

S.S. hung up and frowned at Lou Zucker. "Looks bad, Lou. When those goyim at Morgan's huddle it's serious. I'm going to have to dig into the company theatre accounts."

Lou went to a cabinet, poured two glasses of bourbon, handed one to S.S.

"You look like you just been hit by a rock, a big rock."

S.S. turned on the Atwater Kent radio, swallowed his drink. "More like a house falling on me. Get Kolyon on the *Examiner*, and have him tip us off on their wire service reports every half hour."

The radio hissed into life in the middle of "Young Widow Brown."

S.S., his ear to the radio, listening to a wire service report, groaned, "Whitney is buying U.S. Steel at 205. The sonofabitch knows Steel is selling at 193½."

Ira and Lou were sitting across from S.S. Ira said, "It's a grandstand play."

"Who wouldn't get rid of Steel to him at that price?" said Lou.

S.S. held up a hand to hear the radio report: *"Whitney is buying about thirty million dollars worth of stock. We return you now to 'Vic and Sade.'"*

Ira lowered the volume.

"What's Silverthorn World Pictures?"

"Down seven points. Should I buy at this low? Who the hell knows."

"It's a crass presumption, Sid, that it will not go lower. The damn stock market is lust and enticement."

Lou Zucker said, "Sell, S.S."

"You think Morgan and Lamont and Whitney don't know what they're doing? Eh, Ira?"

"I don't own any stocks, so I don't follow the game. But I feel it's a bluff, this pressure buying, and it's *not* going to work."

Later the radio gave final closing prices; U.S. Steel stood at 206 and thirteen million shares had been bought and sold; SWP had regained four points and stood at 33.

S.S. changed his shirt; it was a damp wreck. "Well, let's hope."

Declines began the next morning. The stock ticker had not caught up with yesterday's prices until eight o'clock in the evening. The decline continued, but hopes held. S.S. was at his office daily at seven o'clock in the morning when the Stock Exchange opened in New York. Prices were not holding. Lazar-Wolf called twice for more margin. SWP dropped fourteen points.

Ira said, "Sometimes you feel life is only the ticking of clocks."

"Let's make pictures," S.S. said. He walked out to the sound stages, the cutting rooms, even intruded into the writers' building. Faces on the lot were pale, serious; everyone—producers, directors, actors, extras—seemed to have been in the stock market.

Lou Zucker, over a cheerless lunch, reported that Eddie Cantor had dropped everything. "He's broke. The Marx brothers are poor again. We're not making pictures, not with every ear to a radio."

"How did you do, Lou?" asked Ira.

"Me, ha! At my third margin call I told them to shove it way up. All I got now is a mortgaged house, second-hand Buick, and a membership in the Zionhigh Club whose dues I'll not be able to pay next year."

S.S. winked, gave Lou a lugubrious stare. "We're both treading water. Now to action stations. We'll cut down here; today cancel seven pictures we were to put in production, stop shooting on the three we just started, and begin firing."

"You mean swing the headsman's axe?"

"Chop chop chop." He banged his desk three times.

"Can you keep the studio open?"

"Even if we're just producing the newsreel."

"Where's the money coming from?"

"Money due us on the last six months' releases. We'll stop paying bills, press hard, and bluff."

"We'll have to make token payments. And there's the payroll."

"Ten percent cut for all."

"All?"

"Look, my friends, when times are bad, people want entertainment to get away from their miseries of this damn despair, as the depression goes on."

"You think so, Sid?"

"I'm banking on it. Get some of our writers off their duffs. Have them start knocking out cheap stories for existing sets; comedies, old-fashioned messages of cheer and hope. Pictures we can shoot in a few days, chop together with lots of gay songs. Good times coming. Have faith in the old flag. God loves us and we love God. Show ordinary people struggling to survive, dancing, carrying on, scratching, and making do."

"Schmaltz?" asked Lou Zucker.

"Call it schmaltz; I call it the human spirit to survive, a time to be tender and solicitous."

253

"You don't look it, Sid," said Ira as they walked past the water tower.

Mike, the security guard, came over and touched a finger to his cap. "Pardon, sir. There's something the ground manager wants to show you at the producers' parking lot."

"Why is he bothering me now? All right."

They walked past the box hedges and privet and onto the producers' privileged parking lot. Lou Zucker and two gardeners were admiring a long, pale blue car, its polished trim gleaming.

"The Isotta Frashini," said S.S.

"It's a beaut," said Lou. "It'll knock the eye out of every other producer in town."

Ira said, "All you need are two nice coachmen and Cinderella." He ran a finger over the hood. "Have Zucker, Lasky, Fox got anything like this? No!" Ira opened and shut a door. "Maybe they'll buy it."

"You kidding?" said Lou.

"Damn right he is," said S.S. "Tell you what we're going to do. Get a driver in a posh uniform and we'll all go to lunch at Victor Hugo's and laugh it up loud. That will put a wild hair up the ass of the industry. Lou, get the papers to send photographers there and we'll pose with the car, smoking dollar cigars; movies were never better, we'll say."

"Great, great, S.S. Shows confidence, boffo business. Laugh it up."

"And maybe die," S.S. said, "but if I go down, goddamn it, I'll go down like they never saw anyone go down. We're not the *Titanic* yet."

As the depression grew, films did seem to hold their own. S.S. had been right, Ira agreed; the one luxury people didn't give up was going to the movies. If they went less often, they did continue to go. The cheaply made cheerful pictures SWP and other studios produced, with their messages of hope and cheer, were the only relief from loss, suicides, foreclosures, bread lines, dust bowls. People sang "Time On My Hands," "Walking My Baby Back Home," "Body and Soul."

Sidney Silverthorn worked harder, lost weight. His personal fortune had gone to margin calls until he put up no more and was sold out. His SWP stock stood at 16, and many theatres did not pay the fees for showing the films, or if they did, paid very late. Those that went into receivership would settle with creditors, sometimes at ten to twenty percent.

But to the Big Five's satisfaction, the collapse of the market did solve the attempt to dominate filmmaking. William Fox was in a bad auto accident. He tried to hold his empire together while he recuperated, but the Big Five seized the opportunity to do him in. They put pressure on AVE to withhold the big loan. Fox, bedridden, found he could not get the cash or credit he needed to cover his falling margins. AVE turned its back on him and moved its financial power to back Lowitz Theatres; without that loan Fox Enterprises collapsed. The man was stripped of his corporate identity, and government antitrust suits moved in. As Fox lay helpless in bed, the options he held on Lowitz shares were taken over by AVE and with it the SWP stocks that S.S. had traded to Fox for the use of its sound patents.

One clear California morning, S.S. found himself in his lawyer's inner office, staring with a sense of an abhorrence.

"It's the only thing, S.S.," said Barney Kornblue. "You have to become part of the Lowitz Corporation. I've vehemently fought their lawyers to cut you free. It's no."

S.S. rolled his head, beat on the lawyer's desk. "Damn it, Barney, the tail is wagging the dog. I make

255

the pictures, they only show them. Round-assed office vaudeville bookers, trained dog acts, that's their speed."

"They have the stock you traded to Fox. They've bought up twelve percent of SWP outstanding shares on a falling market."

"Dave Lowitz began with a pushcart. He knows values? He got me at bargain prices."

"They're forming the Lowitz All States Corporation, combining theatres and film production. They can force you out of the studio. I say take their offer."

"Take what? My stock is at 14. What will I trade it for? They crack the whip and I do a cakewalk."

"The new stock will rise. You get a firm six-year contract. As studio head. I've seen to that. The studio name remains Silverthorn World Pictures. SWP is the trademark. You have full charge of what you want to make, who to star, what properties to buy."

"But they okay the costs, the salaries, the prices for plays, books. I need to come to them like a beggar and ask for pennies."

"Millions. It's the biggest film theatre combine in town."

S.S. again banged on the desk.

"Don't break the glass top."

"They have one of their inside boys as my assistant."

"Matt Gower, a good man at your side. Ex-longshoreman."

"He's a Lowitz man."

"He can handle the unions, keep them in line."

S.S. got up, paced the office, noted its blue Chinese rug, the Second Empire desk. Oh, he thought, lawyers always do themselves well on the life blood of their clients.

He inspected a wall of framed Daumier prints picturing shark-headed judges and lawyers. It was his turn to take the screwing. He turned around. "I could start my own company, Barney, all over again. All I want is to make pictures my way. I could set up a new corporation." He winked at Barney Kornblue. "But you're thinking this schumuck S.S. would be a jackass to let his anger at this fucking setup keep him from accepting the offer."

The lawyer laughed, inspecting his manicured fingernails with their colorless polish. "I had no doubts, never did, that Sidney Silverthorn would not let go of SWP no matter under what conditions. It's your favorite tit. Enjoy it."

"I had to take it. They have me cornered."

"Don't make me cry. You get a good fat batch of the new stock issue five points below listings. You get ninety-thousand-a year salary with lots of perks, an option on preferred stock to be issued and also—"

"I don't own that stock. They hold it till I pay it off."

"There's a clause that you will get a percentage as the profits rise. Read the agreement."

"What profits? We're barely breaking even now. We're luring people into the theatres now with raffles, free sets of dishes."

"Your new picture *Fairground Nights* is doing nicely, nicely, *Variety* reports."

S.S. grinned, almost banged the desk top again, then put his hands together. "And why? It's a happy simple picture. Good clean young love, the hero never even takes a feel, rube comedy, and a hymn to country life. And also my idea I sold to the theatres. I get them to give away a live baby!"

The lawyer nearly lost his silver-rimmed glasses from his well-fed nose. "A live baby?"

"That's right, Barney. I had them advertise it in all the towns and villages: TONIGHT A RAFFLE GIVING AWAY A LIVE BABY!"

"Jesus H. Christ!"

"I tell you Monday night, usually a bad night, every theatre was jam-packed. Newspapers, radio stations, went wild, blew their corks. Churches preached against it. Standing room only. It was a bonanza."

"You actually gave away live babies?"

"Yes," said S.S., "fifty of them—live baby pigs!"

"You sonofabitch,' said the lawyer admiringly. "No wonder you ride around in that big anti-Semitic car of yours."

"Just for show. It's window dressing. Nora drives a Chevy. She even offered to let me hock her jewels. No need for that, of course. I just laid off two gardeners and the second chauffeur."

26

The shares of the Great Bargain Stores fell with most of the rest, and an acrimonious controversy began as to how to proceed. Aaron Bendelbinder was in bed with a broken collarbone, his stiff joints having failed in getting him down the front steps of his house. He had been warned to lie still and let the bone knit. But as the bad news kept pouring out of the radio by his bedside he insisted he had to be at the main offices of the corporation on Madison Avenue. He saw some sort of scriptural warning in the events overtaking the stock market.

Malka insisted he stay in bed.

"Stay? The fools on the board have overextended store expansion to over a thousand. The stock is down to ten. Somebody has to take command, knock some common sense into their martini-filled heads."

"Take command? You're just honorary chairman of the board. Control is management, with the heads of the departments."

"They'll sit, wishing it will go away, then panic, I tell you." He struggled to sit up, winced in pain. "I'll be all right, I'll wear a sling." He added, "I know my bones best."

Malka called Doctor Tuckman, who told her, "Mrs. Bendelbinder, it's better he get up than toss and stew in bed. That would do greater harm to his nervous system than letting off steam. But be sure he wears a sling tight across his chest, and have him carry those pain pills. He's the kind who feels there are no diseases, only sick people."

Aaron dressed slowly with his wife's help, moaning and pausing to catch his breath. But at last he was ready, with a black sling, his cane, and a topcoat thrown around his shoulders.

"Have O'Hara bring around the car. And, Malka, you can't come with me."

"I wouldn't think of it. Lean on O'Hara."

"I'm not a leaner."

Malka fought back tears. He looked so frail, his limbs so stiff, his neatly trimmed beard pure white. Somehow she had always seen him as he had been in their youth in Little Gdansk, that muddy village in Poland . . . She thought how blind one's image is of those close to you. This was an old man unsteady on his feet, but his hands didn't shake and the mouth was firm. The old bear, she thought, as she stood at a bay window in the brownstone house, watching O'Hara, the wiry little Irishman who had driven them for ten years, help Aaron into the back of the Cadillac. Aaron would have nothing to do with a Lincoln since Henry Ford had shown his anti-Semitic side by encourgaging the publishing and circulation of the fraudulent *Protocols of the Elders of Zion.*

She went back to the kitchen, having decided to bake some *rogelachs,* the crisp cookies made with cream cheese and sour cream that Aaron liked. When facing a vexing problem or depressed, she would retire to the kitchen and under the frowns of Katcha, the Hungarian cook, proceed with the mixing, the measuring, the baking in the big oven, taking her mind off everything but producing some marvelous-smelling seed cake, honey bread, prune, date, and nut pudding.

Katcha, watching, said, "You're not measuring."

"After fifty years I don't have to measure."

The phone rang and Maudie, the maid, came into the kitchen. "It's the judge, ma'am."

"David!" Malka rubbed her floury hands on her apron and went into the hall to take the call. David Bendelbinder was a State Supreme Court judge in Albany, also a widower, a recluse off the bench. He usually called his parents on Sunday mornings, so it must be important for him to call any other day.

"Hello, Dovidel."

"Mama, the world is standing on its head. No hope in logic."

"Maybe it will look better that way on its head."

"How is Papa taking in this panic and confusion?"

"Like he takes everything; first he gets angry, then he gets to thinking, then he sees if he can do something. He's down at the corporation offices. They don't come ask for his advice. So he's going to them. How are you?"

"In health. I'm holding my own on the bench. The market? I wasn't in it. What I have is in a small business. Let's hope the little businessmen aren't ruined. It's the end for them if they fail. Don't let Papa overdo it. He's no young buck anymore. I know,"—David laughed—"I'm not young myself either."

"David, you hear anything from Nat?" She stood eying herself in the mirror; a stern old lady's face.

"Directly no. My brother wasn't ever much of a letter writer. But there is the grapevine . . . ."

"Grapes?" She was a clever alert woman, proud and aware of much, but some of the jargon still puzzled her.

"A passing along of gossip. Nat is dodging some investigation on his land deals in Florida and his shady partners. He's some place in California. I think he's getting by. He can't write. They might trace him through his letters."

"He's with the hoodlums, those Italians."

"Mama, not all Italians are gangsters. In fact—"

"Never mind. Take care of your chest. Papa will work out something."

David's mythical weak chest was a last maternal hold she had on him.

She hung up, her thoughts on her older son. David had risen to power in the judicial hierarchy, but she suspected he was lonely, a widower who should have married long ago, not carried the image of his dead wife Josie so long with such intensity. Several times it seemed David might marry but some conscientious doubts always came up. It never came to the *choppah*. She hurried back to the kitchen; as Malka knew the cookie dough needed a lot of rolling out, and Katcha's thick fingers did not have the proper skill for that.

The Great Bargain Stores Corporation, registered in Delaware, occupied four floors near the Grand Central—advertising copy writers, fashion and layout artists, buying offices, bookkeeping divisions, a legal department, testing labs, and administration suits, one of which was kept dusted for the founder.

Carter Dennison, general manager, had a suite with a view of the East River, the Brooklyn Bridge, the Chrysler Tower. Carter was middle-aged, a thin, big-headed ectomorph in a piped vest and spats. On his desk were pictures of his wife, two daughters (Junior League), and his dogs. His gold trophy was prominently displayed. He greeted Aaron over-cheerfully. "It's chaos, pure chaos."

Aaron lifted an eyebrow. "Get me the last business reports."

"They're not fully analyzed yet. And with your arm, it . . ."

"It's a collarbone. Let me see the statements, and

262

call in legal, real estate buyer, and department heads. We can't sit on our *tocus* and hope it's all a bad dream."

"No, of course not."

It took Aaron two hours and three pain-killing pills to grasp the actual state of the corporation—desperate, dismal. The stock was way down, three more points by the latest ticker report. In his own office, he sat thinking, then looked up at the half-dozen people seated, facing him. Miss Montross, the head buyer of wearing apparel, slipped in late. The lawyers looked proprietary, the real estate manager chain-smoked Camels. Carter Dennison whispered to the advertising art director, rumored to be a pansy, biting on a fingernail.

Aaron sipped a glass of Poland water, studied their faces: predatory, fragile, pleasant, boisterous, worried.

"Gentlemen, lady, I'm not going to make a speech. Let Hoover do that. I've not lately followed your work, but Carter tells me you're the best. Your way may not have been my old-fashioned way, but never mind, that's no sure formula to business success. But from my beginnings in needles and notions, buttons, this organization grew to where it is now."

Dennison said, "Mr. Bendelbinder, we never forget our founder." He made a slight bow of almost ecclesiastical unction.

"So where is this business today? A jump ahead of receivership."

There were protests, but he held up his hand. He put on his bifocals and picked up a sheet of paper that he had covered with facts and figures.

"I've studied the latest reports. As I told the board last meeting, we are over-extended, asking for self-destruction. We should have closed two hundred and six stores. Oh, not all at once, but one by one. They're losers. And I'd cancel all orders to wholesalers."

263

"But our buildings' leases, Mr. Bendelbinder, if it were not for this market adjustment . . ."

"It's no adjustment—even a lawyer should see that; it's a cleaning out, a purging, like a physic of a sick stomach. All stocks are overpriced, much beyond any assets and earnings. Too many of our stores are in the wrong neighborhoods. Worst of all around eighty of them have expensive long-term leases and rents we pay out are two-three times too high."

"It was, sir, if I may say so, all voted by the board, and with rising market the last two years we had to pay top dollar to get the good sites away from Penny, Woolworth, Kress, Grants."

"I don't put any full blame on any one person. It was all the madness of this bull market, this crazy Wall Street game. So, I'm speaking here to you department heads of what I'm going to recommend to the board. Cutting out the fancy high-cost items, the loss leaders. Now it's staples, not what people can do without. Cut out the costly fashions. People are going to buy less when they lose their jobs, maybe their homes."

"It will never get that bad, sir. The last few days were aberrations."

"Ha!" Aaron felt pain but decided against another pill. He looked over the flushed faces, the smart alecks, the superior types listening to an old Jew blab away. "You don't remember the panic of 1907. I do. It couldn't be brushed aside as an aberration. This one can't be either. Thank you for listening. Carter, call a meeting of the board, all who are in town, for five o'clock."

Aaron sat, his collarbone aching as if the fracture were bathed in acid. He thought, I'm not one of the *Hachmei*, the wise men of Zion. And all my reading in Joseph Karo's *Shulhan Aruch* and lighting the bronze menorah candelabrum is not going to help. If I had

24

The earth rotated, rushing through the European night, wobbling a bit on its axis, as Harry Silverthorn learned in class that day; rushed to meet the sun moving over Asia, the Persian Gulf, the Horn of Africa. Harry slept a satisfying sleep, his black eye twitching a the younger students. A most satisfactory victory, and bloodied Jules Balbac, who had been bullying some of the younger students. A most satisifactory victory, and Harry was less homesick than he had been . . . Over Saudi Arabia there were pink hints of a coming day, and the world rolled on, indifferent to the human condition on its surface.

The settlement of Hebron lay in the thick dark blueness of the fading night; the watchmen in the fields were relaxed. It was late August and in the community hall the oldest pioneer and two women were preparing for *Sukos*, the autumn Feast of the Tabernacle in the month of Tisri. There would be the rite of the palm branch and the *esrob* (the citron). It had been a hard summer—much poor land cultivated, guards posted to keep down the pilfering from the surrounding Arab villages.

Paul and Joyce were staying overnight in the settlement. The arms bought through Baldo Levi were safely hidden in caves near the Dead Sea. The problem was how to distribute them. The British were seizing all weapons found in the kibbutzim. Paul was discussing with Moses, the Hebron defense man, where some machine guns could be hidden from the English, who were known to dig up foundations and go down wells to ferret out weapons.

There was a restlessness as the night came to an end. A wind sent loose weeds along the roads, a starving dog messed about a garbage pit, the cows in their sheds stirred, their udders awaiting a morning milking. A rooster on his perch among his fat-rumped harem prepared to announce the coming of the dawn. In a pen by the water tower the settlement's bull snorted at the first bites of the blue-bottle flies.

In the settlement office, a sleepy, dark little man scratched his ribs, waiting for the coffee to boil on the little spirit lamp. It smelled wonderful. The dark little man, Smul Zalman, was going over a list of supplies he was to bring back in the settlement's Model-T truck from Tel Aviv. He scratched his head—he was still not adept at reading Hebrew. Still, he had hopes of becoming a competent student of the language. The phone on the desk beside him rang feebly.

"Yes," he said in Yiddish.

A flood of fervent Hebrew came through. Zalman asked, "Do you speak Yiddish?"

He was called a blockhead and a Litvak. Yiddish was shouted at him. "Arab mobs are attacking the kibbutzim. Already fifty dead. Warn the defense force."

"What defense force? A few pistols, a shotgun . . . This is a joke?"

"Curse you! Listen, you'll be under attack. The Grand Mufti's calling for a holy war to kill every Jew. You must—"

The phone went dead. The wire had been cut.

Zalman stared at the walls hung with farm tools, a

shelf of bookkeeping records, packets of seeds, a photograph of the original settlers.

"*Gott, Gott!*" he said as he rose from the desk. He died almost at once as a heavy slug from a Mauser went through his head, sending him sprawling across his list of supplies. From three sides of Hebron heavy fire was coming with the first rays of the sun. Shouts in Arabic were heard cursing Jews, praising Allah. An angry shattering of glass, the splintering of wood. Two watchmen were riddled with rifle fire.

Paul and Joyce came awake together in the narrow brass bed.

"Attack!" shouted Joyce, her naked body rising above the thin sheet that covered them. Paul bounded up, his mind still half obscured with sleep. He reached for his shirt, struggled into it, decided never mind with pants or shoes. The small off-white room held beside the bed two chairs, a small table with an old map, a rough pine bookcase, two suitcases, and a portrait of Chaim Weizmann. From the closet Paul grabbed a submachine gun and four reloaded clips, tossed a pistol to Joyce, who was hastily pulling a dress over her nakedness.

"Your pants, Paul—put them on." She remained calm but for a slight quiver of her lips.

Paul was shouting, "Damn the British, all those false promises of seeing to our safety."

"They'll send reinforcements."

"Don't bet on it. They'd like a lot of Jews dead to teach us a lesson."

"Paul, do we die here?"

"Ask me later."

He kissed Joyce and was gone through a window, making his way to the cow barn. On all sides was rifle and pistol fire, and Paul thought he heard the concus-

243

sion of a grenade. His center of gravity seemed lost, he stumbled, his mind cluttered with a fierce rage.

The Arab attackers were well armed and firing at everything that moved; about a dozen members of the settlement were huddling with half-dressed women and children in the cow barn.

Moses, the defense leader, his upper left arm bloody, a Springfield rifle in his hands, was cursing: "Damn it, we've got seven rifles, sixteen pistols . . . and the English wanted us to turn even these in!"

Paul said, "Moses, try to get together who you can in the cow barn. The lower part is concrete."

"They're slaughtering people in their beds."

The massacre went on. Those caught in their beds had their heads blown off regardless of age or sex. Throats were slashed; Arabs danced on the blood that flowed on the floors. The attackers went from house to house shouting, murdering, slaughtering; pilfering a silver ritual cup, a gramophone; cutting off fingers to get at rings, prowling everyplace, destroying, smashing. One attacker, his face heavily marked by smallpox scars, collected ten watches before Paul's shot brought him down as he tried to mount a staircase to a second story.

An old woman cried out, *"Olov Hasholem!"*

"It's hopeless," said Moses, blood dripping from his fingers. "But we'll save what we can here in the barn."

Two of the cows were dying from wounds that had come through the doorway, moaning as if in labor. Two women in only short nightgowns lay dead in a litter of hay. Two children smeared with blood of the women's wounds were weeping, calling "Mama, mama!"

"Where are the English?" asked Max, a rabbinical figure who had left Orthodoxy to become a farmer. "Where are the English?"

"Having tea. Do you remember a prayer?"

244

BOOK FOUR

ISAIAH

"God of compassion Who dwells on high! Take us into the shelter of Your divine Presence, aid us among the holy and pure who shine as the brightness of the heavens."

Paul, who had been firing steady volumes, felt the gun grow hot in his hands. "If, as I think, it's a planned uprising, they're well armed and attacking Jewish settlements all over Palestine. The British will have a hard time of it."

"Keep your head down."

Paul felt a touch on his shoulder. It was Joyce in one of his jackets, bare-legged, holding a howling child by an arm. The cow barn was filled with panicked faces, lamenting voices, shouting men.

"They're killing everything, Paul. Even the chickens. They beat in Reb Finkel's head with a chair. They put Sarah Zimmer on a table and they're raping her. You can hear her screaming."

"I hear, I hear." Trembling, he reloaded the gun.

Destruction went on all through Hebron; when the Arabs came under heavy fire, they moved around it, howling like Indians. The screaming of the woman being raped stopped abruptly; her throat had been cut. It was later discovered the rape had gone on with various individuals assaulting the dead body.

There was a lull as the sun rose higher—scattered shots, the sound of a tractor being moved off, the cackle of chickens, quacking of ducks as their necks were broken before they were carried off, a dying cow gasping its last, the reek of burning bedding, people coughing from the black smoke.

Warily, Paul went to the barn doors and looked out at the desolation.

"They've gone."

"Careful," said Joyce. "We've got to collect the children left alive. Where are the first-aid kits?"

245

"In the office. Don't go near it."

Moses picked four men to scout the settlement. "Everybody else don't move till I give permission."

By noon, sixty-four dead Jews of all ages were laid out like rag bundles in a grove of Hebron. They had been shot, slashed, raped, mutilated, subjected to every form of perversion. Standing numb or weeping were the survivers, who looked at their dead. All at once a great wailing went up.

The rabbinical man Max, in his prayer shawl, was reciting:

"Mortal man returns to the earth of which he was
    made.
The days of our years are but three-score and ten.
Man is born into trouble as the sparks fly upward;
He withers as the flower, he is cut down as the grass.
May I learn to number my days,
May I get me a heart of wisdom.
The rich man cannot glory in his riches,
Not the wise man glory in his wisdom.
Let him that glories glory
Understand who he is, whence he
Has come, and where he is to go."

The tragedy was becoming clear with an accelerating intensity. Joyce, who was comforting weeping children, their faces tear- and dirt-stained, pointed and called to Paul, "Look."

From the north up through a wadi was a dust column on the road; some men went for their weapons.

Paul held up an arm. "It's a British armored car."

It came slowly, carefully, as if putting one foot before the other. It stopped short of the settlement and two Tommies and an officer came forward. Some of the small fires were still burning. A bull, castrated but

246

still alive, lay in a pool of water by the punctured water tower. Nearby two horses were dead, already foully smelling in the heat.

Most in the grove stood silently, watching the approach of the uniformed men.

The officer, his weathered face brick-red, looked tired. He removed his swagger stick from under his arm and pointed around him. "You people have really had it."

"Why didn't you come sooner!" shouted Moses, his fists high; he seemed delirious with rage and shock.

The officer nodded. "There have been attacks all over the districts and we've limited patrols."

Moses did a dance of rage, breaking free of Paul's grasp.

"You deprived us of means of appealing for help and defense, betrayed us by empty promises! You did, goddamn you!"

"Appeals, decisions, that's the commissioner's job, not the army's. This is dreadful . . . Elkins, get on the phone, we need aid for the hurt."

"Right, sar."

"The phone wire is cut," said Joyce.

"Elkins, find the cut, splice it. First put that bull out of his misery."

Moses shouted, "You gave the murderers and robbers the opportunities!"

"We'll have some police up soon to search the villages. We still have courts of justice."

Joyce said, "Justice? The Arabs were yelling the government is with us."

"So we've heard elsewhere. It's nonsense, I assure you."

"You refused us enough weapons." Paul was aware for the first time of his bare dirty feet set by the side of the polished boots of the officer.

"What you have is illegal; however . . ."

The officer took Paul aside, offered him an opened silver cigarette case. They smoked slowly. "Lieutenant Aston of the Irish Fusiliers. It's bad, very bad. Over a hundred massacred elsewhere, and now here."

"When can we expect aid for the wounded?"

"As soon as Lance Corporal Elkins gets the phone in working order. He's good at that sort of thing." The officer looked around him. "Damn dirty business."

The next morning graves were dug beyond the grove; the sixty-four bodies of the massacred at Hebron were wrapped in sheets and put down into the earth of Palestine.

A cordon of troops stood at attention. A correspondent from Reuters was moving about, asking for names.

The few male survivers stood by in prayer shawls as Max recited a prayer over the raw earth;

"We consecrate this hour to those we loved;
They have gone beyond time to eternity.
As sons and daughters, we recall the loving care bestowed upon us;
As husbands and wives, we remember the ties of love,
And all we shared of sorrow and joy till parted by death;
As mothers and fathers, we remember children precious to us;
As a people we remember all so untimely gone from us."

25

The day in October, 1929, that Sidney Silverthorn
was notified by the U.S. Customs Office of Los Angeles that his Tyso 8A Isotta Frashini car with the Castagna body (115 horsepower, Grebel headlights, blue
leather interior) had arrived via ship also saw the crash
of the stock market that the *Variety* was to headline as
WALL STREET LAYS AN EGG.

S.S. was on the phone talking to Clinton Nash of
Lazar-Wolf, his stockbroker, chomping on an unlit cigar.

"What kind of fucking call for margin? You always
carried me till the market leveled off. It's blue chip
stuff. Glass. Food. G.M. Dupont."

"Mr. Silverthorn, this is not just a dip in the market.
There are floods of selling orders. So I have orders to
call any stock bought on margin. But of course you will
cover."

Clinton Nash remained excruciatingly calm.

"Goddamn it, let me talk to Lazar-Wolf."

"I can't do that, Mr. Silverthorn. He's going to a
meeting with other brokers and it's—"

S.S. kicked over the wastebasket beside his desk.
"Look, you mealy-mouthed flunky, this is S.S. talking.
Sam has been our shares underwriter for years. Put
Lazar-Wolf on the line. Pronto!"

"I'll see what I can do."

"Do!"

S.S. had no Olympian forebearance with clerks or underlings. He threw the cigar onto an ashtray and turned to Lou Zucker inspecting some tacked-up two-sheet of an SWP picture, *Maid of Manhattan.*

"How do you like them apples? The sonofabitch of a phony Harvard accent asks me to cover margin calls. As if I were some hick who has ten shares of a cider mill."

"The market's been falling all morning and we're three hours behind New York time."

"What the hell does that—hello, Sam, what kind of cockamamy margin calls am I getting from your stooge Nash?"

Samuel Lazar-Wolf grunted across the continent; his usual smooth-as-silk voice tone had an edge to it.

"S.S., it's a damn deluge. Firms are going bust on the street. We have to stop holding the bag. Your portfolio has half a million dollars in various stocks on ten percent margin. We can't cover you. The decline is that fast."

"You'd sell me out?"

"Listen, S.S. . . ."

"You *momzer*, tell me, should I sell and take a loss or cover?"

"Look, I'll level with you. I've just come from a big meeting at House of Morgan of all the big banking houses on the street. Tommy Lamont put it right on the table: 'Your banks hold six billion dollars in reserve, so form a pool of millions, restore confidence in the stock market by buying, buying.' "

S.S. motioned Lou to bend over and listen.

"No shit, Sam? That's the truth?"

"On my mother's grave. S.S., cover the margin call. It's going to be all right. It's Morgan, not Joe Blow, calling the turns."

"Sam, I hope you're right. I'll have my bank make available fifty thousand."

"Make it seventy-five, S.S., to be sure till the market gets its blood transfusion."

Lou pursed his lips, shook his head.

S.S. said, "Christ, Sam, I don't keep that kind of loose cash to draw from. I'll have to tap some box office returns. Sam, listen, don't screw me. Keep me informed. How's SWP stock going?"

"Still taking a beating, like everything so far. S.S., I've three other calls waiting. Keep your pecker up."

S.S. hung up and frowned at Lou Zucker. "Looks bad, Lou. When those goyim at Morgan's huddle it's serious. I'm going to have to dig into the company theatre accounts."

Lou went to a cabinet, poured two glasses of bourbon, handed one to S.S.

"You look like you just been hit by a rock, a big rock."

S.S. turned on the Atwater Kent radio, swallowed his drink. "More like a house falling on me. Get Kolyon on the *Examiner*, and have him tip us off on their wire service reports every half hour."

The radio hissed into life in the middle of "Young Widow Brown."

S.S., his ear to the radio, listening to a wire service report, groaned, "Whitney is buying U.S. Steel at 205. The sonofabitch knows Steel is selling at 193½."

Ira and Lou were sitting across from S.S. Ira said, "It's a grandstand play."

"Who wouldn't get rid of Steel to him at that price?" said Lou.

S.S. held up a hand to hear the radio report: *"Whitney is buying about thirty million dollars worth of stock. We return you now to 'Vic and Sade.'"*

Ira lowered the volume.

"What's Silverthorn World Pictures?"

"Down seven points. Should I buy at this low? Who the hell knows."

"It's a crass presumption, Sid, that it will not go lower. The damn stock market is lust and enticement."

Lou Zucker said, "Sell, S.S."

"You think Morgan and Lamont and Whitney don't know what they're doing? Eh, Ira?"

"I don't own any stocks, so I don't follow the game. But I feel it's a bluff, this pressure buying, and it's *not* going to work."

Later the radio gave final closing prices; U.S. Steel stood at 206 and thirteen million shares had been bought and sold; SWP had regained four points and stood at 33.

S.S. changed his shirt; it was a damp wreck. "Well, let's hope."

Declines began the next morning. The stock ticker had not caught up with yesterday's prices until eight o'clock in the evening. The decline continued, but hopes held. S.S. was at his office daily at seven o'clock in the morning when the Stock Exchange opened in New York. Prices were not holding. Lazar-Wolf called twice for more margin. SWP dropped fourteen points.

Ira said, "Sometimes you feel life is only the ticking of clocks."

"Let's make pictures," S.S. said. He walked out to the sound stages, the cutting rooms, even intruded into the writers' building. Faces on the lot were pale, serious; everyone—producers, directors, actors, extras—seemed to have been in the stock market.

Lou Zucker, over a cheerless lunch, reported that Eddie Cantor had dropped everything. "He's broke. The Marx brothers are poor again. We're not making pictures, not with every ear to a radio."

"How did you do, Lou?" asked Ira.

"Me, ha! At my third margin call I told them to shove it way up. All I got now is a mortgaged house, second-hand Buick, and a membership in the Zionhigh Club whose dues I'll not be able to pay next year."

S.S. winked, gave Lou a lugubrious stare. "We're both treading water. Now to action stations. We'll cut down here; today cancel seven pictures we were to put in production, stop shooting on the three we just started, and begin firing."

"You mean swing the headsman's axe?"

"Chop chop chop." He banged his desk three times.

"Can you keep the studio open?"

"Even if we're just producing the newsreel."

"Where's the money coming from?"

"Money due us on the last six months' releases. We'll stop paying bills, press hard, and bluff."

"We'll have to make token payments. And there's the payroll."

"Ten percent cut for all."

"All?"

"Look, my friends, when times are bad, people want entertainment to get away from their miseries of this damn despair, as the depression goes on."

"You think so, Sid?"

"I'm banking on it. Get some of our writers off their duffs. Have them start knocking out cheap stories for existing sets; comedies, old-fashioned messages of cheer and hope. Pictures we can shoot in a few days, chop together with lots of gay songs. Good times coming. Have faith in the old flag. God loves us and we love God. Show ordinary people struggling to survive, dancing, carrying on, scratching, and making do."

"Schmaltz?" asked Lou Zucker.

"Call it schmaltz; I call it the human spirit to survive, a time to be tender and solicitous."

"You don't look it, Sid," said Ira as they walked past the water tower.

Mike, the security guard, came over and touched a finger to his cap. "Pardon, sir. There's something the ground manager wants to show you at the producers' parking lot."

"Why is he bothering me now? All right."

They walked past the box hedges and privet and onto the producers' privileged parking lot. Lou Zucker and two gardeners were admiring a long, pale blue car, its polished trim gleaming.

"The Isotta Frashini," said S.S.

"It's a beaut," said Lou. "It'll knock the eye out of every other producer in town."

Ira said, "All you need are two nice coachmen and Cinderella." He ran a finger over the hood. "Have Zucker, Lasky, Fox got anything like this? No!" Ira opened and shut a door. "Maybe they'll buy it."

"You kidding?" said Lou.

"Damn right he is," said S.S. "Tell you what we're going to do. Get a driver in a posh uniform and we'll all go to lunch at Victor Hugo's and laugh it up loud. That will put a wild hair up the ass of the industry. Lou, get the papers to send photographers there and we'll pose with the car, smoking dollar cigars; movies were never better, we'll say."

"Great, great, S.S. Shows confidence, boffo business. Laugh it up."

"And maybe die," S.S. said, "but if I go down, goddamn it, I'll go down like they never saw anyone go down. We're not the *Titanic* yet."

As the depression grew, films did seem to hold their own. S.S. had been right, Ira agreed; the one luxury people didn't give up was going to the movies. If they went less often, they did continue to go. The cheaply made cheerful pictures SWP and other studios pro-

254

duced, with their messages of hope and cheer, were the only relief from loss, suicides, foreclosures, bread lines, dust bowls. People sang "Time On My Hands," "Walking My Baby Back Home," "Body and Soul."

Sidney Silverthorn worked harder, lost weight. His personal fortune had gone to margin calls until he put up no more and was sold out. His SWP stock stood at 16, and many theatres did not pay the fees for showing the films, or if they did, paid very late. Those that went into receivership would settle with creditors, sometimes at ten to twenty percent.

But to the Big Five's satisfaction, the collapse of the market did solve the attempt to dominate filmmaking. William Fox was in a bad auto accident. He tried to hold his empire together while he recuperated, but the Big Five seized the opportunity to do him in. They put pressure on AVE to withhold the big loan. Fox, bedridden, found he could not get the cash or credit he needed to cover his falling margins. AVE turned its back on him and moved its financial power to back Lowitz Theatres; without that loan Fox Enterprises collapsed. The man was stripped of his corporate identity, and government antitrust suits moved in. As Fox lay helpless in bed, the options he held on Lowitz shares were taken over by AVE and with it the SWP stocks that S.S. had traded to Fox for the use of its sound patents.

One clear California morning, S.S. found himself in his lawyer's inner office, staring with a sense of an abhorrence.

"It's the only thing, S.S.," said Barney Kornblue. "You have to become part of the Lowitz Corporation. I've vehemently fought their lawyers to cut you free. It's no."

S.S. rolled his head, beat on the lawyer's desk. "Damn it, Barney, the tail is wagging the dog. I make the pictures, they only show them. Round-assed office vaudeville bookers, trained dog acts, that's their speed."

"They have the stock you traded to Fox. They've bought up twelve percent of SWP outstanding shares on a falling market."

"Dave Lowitz began with a pushcart. He knows values? He got me at bargain prices."

"They're forming the Lowitz All States Corporation, combining theatres and film production. They can force you out of the studio. I say take their offer."

"Take what? My stock is at 14. What will I trade it for? They crack the whip and I do a cakewalk."

"The new stock will rise. You get a firm six-year contract. As studio head. I've seen to that. The studio name remains Silverthorn World Pictures. SWP is the trademark. You have full charge of what you want to make, who to star, what properties to buy."

"But they okay the costs, the salaries, the prices for plays, books. I need to come to them like a beggar and ask for pennies."

"Millions. It's the biggest film theatre combine in town."

S.S. again banged on the desk.

"Don't break the glass top."

"They have one of their inside boys as my assistant."

"Matt Gower, a good man at your side. Ex-longshoreman."

"He's a Lowitz man."

"He can handle the unions, keep them in line."

S.S. got up, paced the office, noted its blue Chinese rug, the Second Empire desk. Oh, he thought, lawyers always do themselves well on the life blood of their clients.

He inspected a wall of framed Daumier prints picturing shark-headed judges and lawyers. It was his turn to take the screwing. He turned around. "I could start my own company, Barney, all over again. All I want is to make pictures my way. I could set up a new corporation." He winked at Barney Kornblue. "But you're thinking this schumuck S.S. would be a jackass to let his anger at this fucking setup keep him from accepting the offer."

The lawyer laughed, inspecting his manicured fingernails with their colorless polish. "I had no doubts, never did, that Sidney Silverthorn would not let go of SWP no matter under what conditions. It's your favorite tit. Enjoy it."

"I had to take it. They have me cornered."

"Don't make me cry. You get a good fat batch of the new stock issue five points below listings. You get ninety-thousand-a year salary with lots of perks, an option on preferred stock to be issued and also—"

"I don't own that stock. They hold it till I pay it off."

"There's a clause that you will get a percentage as the profits rise. Read the agreement."

"What profits? We're barely breaking even now. We're luring people into the theatres now with raffles, free sets of dishes."

"Your new picture *Fairground Nights* is doing nicely, nicely, *Variety* reports."

S.S. grinned, almost banged the desk top again, then put his hands together. "And why? It's a happy simple picture. Good clean young love, the hero never even takes a feel, rube comedy, and a hymn to country life. And also my idea I sold to the theatres. I get them to give away a live baby!"

The lawyer nearly lost his silver-rimmed glasses from his well-fed nose. "A live baby?"

"That's right, Barney. I had them advertise it in all the towns and villages: TONIGHT A RAFFLE GIVING AWAY A LIVE BABY!"

"Jesus H. Christ!"

"I tell you Monday night, usually a bad night, every theatre was jam-packed. Newspapers, radio stations, went wild, blew their corks. Churches preached against it. Standing room only. It was a bonanza."

"You actually gave away live babies?"

"Yes," said S.S., "fifty of them—live baby pigs!"

"You sonofabitch,' said the lawyer admiringly. "No wonder you ride around in that big anti-Semitic car of yours."

"Just for show. It's window dressing. Nora drives a Chevy. She even offered to let me hock her jewels. No need for that, of course. I just laid off two gardeners and the second chauffeur."

26

The shares of the Great Bargain Stores fell with most of the rest, and an acrimonious controversy began as to how to proceed. Aaron Bendelbinder was in bed with a broken collarbone, his stiff joints having failed in getting him down the front steps of his house. He had been warned to lie still and let the bone knit. But as the bad news kept pouring out of the radio by his bedside he insisted he had to be at the main offices of the corporation on Madison Avenue. He saw some sort of scriptural warning in the events overtaking the stock market.

Malka insisted he stay in bed.

"Stay? The fools on the board have overextended store expansion to over a thousand. The stock is down to ten. Somebody has to take command, knock some common sense into their martini-filled heads."

"Take command? You're just honorary chairman of the board. Control is management, with the heads of the departments."

"They'll sit, wishing it will go away, then panic, I tell you." He struggled to sit up, winced in pain. "I'll be all right, I'll wear a sling." He added, "I know my bones best."

Malka called Doctor Tuckman, who told her, "Mrs. Bendelbinder, it's better he get up than toss and stew in bed. That would do greater harm to his nervous system than letting off steam. But be sure he wears a sling tight across his chest, and have him carry those pain pills. He's the kind who feels there are no diseases, only sick people."

Aaron dressed slowly with his wife's help, moaning and pausing to catch his breath. But at last he was ready, with a black sling, his cane, and a topcoat thrown around his shoulders.

"Have O'Hara bring around the car. And, Malka, you can't come with me."

"I wouldn't think of it. Lean on O'Hara."

"I'm not a leaner."

Malka fought back tears. He looked so frail, his limbs so stiff, his neatly trimmed beard pure white. Somehow she had always seen him as he had been in their youth in Little Gdansk, that muddy village in Poland . . . She thought how blind one's image is of those close to you. This was an old man unsteady on his feet, but his hands didn't shake and the mouth was firm. The old bear, she thought, as she stood at a bay window in the brownstone house, watching O'Hara, the wiry little Irishman who had driven them for ten years, help Aaron into the back of the Cadillac. Aaron would have nothing to do with a Lincoln since Henry Ford had shown his anti-Semitic side by encourgaging the publishing and circulation of the fraudulent *Protocols of the Elders of Zion.*

She went back to the kitchen, having decided to bake some *rogelachs,* the crisp cookies made with cream cheese and sour cream that Aaron liked. When facing a vexing problem or depressed, she would retire to the kitchen and under the frowns of Katcha, the Hungarian cook, proceed with the mixing, the measuring, the baking in the big oven, taking her mind off everything but producing some marvelous-smelling seed cake, honey bread, prune, date, and nut pudding.

Katcha, watching, said, "You're not measuring."

"After fifty years I don't have to measure."

The phone rang and Maudie, the maid, came into the kitchen. "It's the judge, ma'am."

"David!" Malka rubbed her floury hands on her apron and went into the hall to take the call. David Bendelbinder was a State Supreme Court judge in Albany, also a widower, a recluse off the bench. He usually called his parents on Sunday mornings, so it must be important for him to call any other day.

"Hello, Dovidel."

"Mama, the world is standing on its head. No hope in logic."

"Maybe it will look better that way on its head."

"How is Papa taking in this panic and confusion?"

"Like he takes everything; first he gets angry, then he gets to thinking, then he sees if he can do something. He's down at the corporation offices. They don't come ask for his advice. So he's going to them. How are you?"

"In health. I'm holding my own on the bench. The market? I wasn't in it. What I have is in a small business. Let's hope the little businessmen aren't ruined. It's the end for them if they fail. Don't let Papa overdo it. He's no young buck anymore. I know,"—David laughed—"I'm not young myself either."

"David, you hear anything from Nat?" She stood eying herself in the mirror; a stern old lady's face.

"Directly no. My brother wasn't ever much of a letter writer. But there is the grapevine . . . ."

"Grapes?" She was a clever alert woman, proud and aware of much, but some of the jargon still puzzled her.

"A passing along of gossip. Nat is dodging some investigation on his land deals in Florida and his shady partners. He's some place in California. I think he's getting by. He can't write. They might trace him through his letters."

261

"He's with the hoodlums, those Italians."

"Mama, not all Italians are gangsters. In fact——"

"Never mind. Take care of your chest. Papa will work out something."

David's mythical weak chest was a last maternal hold she had on him.

She hung up, her thoughts on her older son. David had risen to power in the judicial hierarchy, but she suspected he was lonely, a widower who should have married long ago, not carried the image of his dead wife Josie so long with such intensity. Several times it seemed David might marry but some conscientious doubts always came up. It never came to the *choppah*. She hurried back to the kitchen; as Malka knew the cookie dough needed a lot of rolling out, and Katcha's thick fingers did not have the proper skill for that.

The Great Bargain Stores Corporation, registered in Delaware, occupied four floors near the Grand Central—advertising copy writers, fashion and layout artists, buying offices, bookkeeping divisions, a legal department, testing labs, and administration suits, one of which was kept dusted for the founder.

Carter Dennison, general manager, had a suite with a view of the East River, the Brooklyn Bridge, the Chrysler Tower. Carter was middle-aged, a thin, big-headed ectomorph in a piped vest and spats. On his desk were pictures of his wife, two daughters (Junior League), and his dogs. His gold trophy was prominently displayed. He greeted Aaron over-cheerfully. "It's chaos, pure chaos."

Aaron lifted an eyebrow. "Get me the last business reports."

"They're not fully analyzed yet. And with your arm, it . . ."

"It's a collarbone. Let me see the statements, and

call in legal, real estate buyer, and department heads. We can't sit on our *tocus* and hope it's all a bad dream."

"No, of course not."

It took Aaron two hours and three pain-killing pills to grasp the actual state of the corporation—desperate, dismal. The stock was way down, three more points by the latest ticker report. In his own office, he sat thinking, then looked up at the half-dozen people seated, facing him. Miss Montross, the head buyer of wearing apparel, slipped in late. The lawyers looked proprietary, the real estate manager chain-smoked Camels. Carter Dennison whispered to the advertising art director, rumored to be a pansy, biting on a fingernail.

Aaron sipped a glass of Poland water, studied their faces: predatory, fragile, pleasant, boisterous, worried.

"Gentlemen, lady, I'm not going to make a speech. Let Hoover do that. I've not lately followed your work, but Carter tells me you're the best. Your way may not have been my old-fashioned way, but never mind, that's no sure formula to business success. But from my beginnings in needles and notions, buttons, this organization grew to where it is now."

Dennison said, "Mr. Bendelbinder, we never forget our founder." He made a slight bow of almost ecclesiastical unction.

"So where is this business today? A jump ahead of receivership."

There were protests, but he held up his hand. He put on his bifocals and picked up a sheet of paper that he had covered with facts and figures.

"I've studied the latest reports. As I told the board last meeting, we are over-extended, asking for self-destruction. We should have closed two hundred and six stores. Oh, not all at once, but one by one. They're losers. And I'd cancel all orders to wholesalers."

"But our buildings' leases, Mr. Bendelbinder, if it were not for this market adjustment . . ."

"It's no adjustment—even a lawyer should see that; it's a cleaning out, a purging, like a physic of a sick stomach. All stocks are overpriced, much beyond any assets and earnings. Too many of our stores are in the wrong neighborhoods. Worst of all around eighty of them have expensive long-term leases and rents we pay out are two-three times too high."

"It was, sir, if I may say so, all voted by the board, and with rising market the last two years we had to pay top dollar to get the good sites away from Penny, Woolworth, Kress, Grants."

"I don't put any full blame on any one person. It was all the madness of this bull market, this crazy Wall Street game. So, I'm speaking here to you department heads of what I'm going to recommend to the board. Cutting out the fancy high-cost items, the loss leaders. Now it's staples, not what people can do without. Cut out the costly fashions. People are going to buy less when they lose their jobs, maybe their homes."

"It will never get that bad, sir. The last few days were aberrations."

"Ha!" Aaron felt pain but decided against another pill. He looked over the flushed faces, the smart alecks, the superior types listening to an old Jew blab away. "You don't remember the panic of 1907. I do. It couldn't be brushed aside as an aberration. This one can't be either. Thank you for listening. Carter, call a meeting of the board, all who are in town, for five o'clock."

Aaron sat, his collarbone aching as if the fracture were bathed in acid. He thought, I'm not one of the *Hachmei*, the wise men of Zion. And all my reading in Joseph Karo's *Shulhan Aruch* and lighting the bronze menorah candelabrum is not going to help. If I had

264

strong, loyal sons with me—but David is a dry-as-dust seer of trivia, torts, and briefs, an honest judge imbedded in a corrupt political system. And Nachum, Nat, a gambler, face it, a gangster, a companion of bootleggers, and worse. Did I hold back in bargaining with God . . . .?

He dozed off, awakened in feverish pain with Carter Dennison telling him six of the board were waiting.

An impressive lot. Bland, successful manipulators of corporation games. Suave, well-fed, some with waistcoats showing, the little ceramic pigs of some college society. Ivy League faces, well-shaved chops, cunning, careful, clever. Aaron waved down the hand clapping and repeated most of what he had earlier told the heads of the departments. Willard Holmes said the board would certainly study the suggestions of the honorary chairman. The stock had fallen two more points before the close of the day's trading.

Aaron was driven home by O'Hara, his forehead damp, fever riding his body. He was put to bed and Doctor Tuckman said, "Not wise, not wise at all," and ordered him to stay in bed.

Malka came in with tea in a glass (Aaron still refused it in a cup) and fresh-baked cookies. He sipped, ate a cookie, and slept facing the wall. He dreamed of Elijah the Prophet in a frock coat and a floorwalker's flower in his lapel. Elijah came to him and asked, "If God created the world, who created God? The sanctity, you forget, of our fragile transient existence is imbedded in the Torah and *not* on Wall Street."

Aaron tried to answer but fear filled his throat and in his fever he dreamed no more.

Monday the panic in the Stock Exchange in the nation resumed. Volume of sales topped nine million shares, the Dow dropped a record 38 points, thirteen percent of the total market value; Black Tuesday found no bottom in the continuous decline. The trading in some stocks stopped, among them the Great Bargain Stores; the Dow plunged thirty-one points. In five days, all the gains of the previous Morgan-boosted attacks were wiped out.

The board of directors of the Great Bargain Stores had paid no attention to Aaron's advice. They neither canceled nor cut manufacturers' orders, and proceeded with plans to open the new stores. As Carter Dennison put it to a reporter from the *Wall Street Journal*: "We have faith in the system. Institutions are much less likely to panic than individuals."

Three weeks later, the Great Bargain Stores went into receivership. Aaron took it sadly but calmly. It had been predicted; investors had lost more than seventy-five billion in the stock market's collapse.

Malka, bringing his bowl of cold borscht with a hot potato, a favorite of his, asked, "So who receives in a receivership?"

"Lawyers, like sharks eating a dead whale, creditors, tax people. A *magillah*."

"We'll come through."

Aaron sipped the red soup. "Everything is gone, Malka. The stock may never have any value, not even as settlement of five cents on the dollar. The banks hold most of it, you remember, as collateral for Nat's Florida paradise. There's the life insurance, but as the corporation paid for it, who knows."

She put her arm around him, avoiding pressure on the healing collarbone. "Aaron, it's been a long journey together and a good one. We've had our tragedies. Yes, a grandson died in France in 1919, Josie, David's wife, in that factory fire. But look, we're here, even if we've become old. That's something. We had the good years. So we'll enjoy what's left, now it's left. There's some infallible purpose to life, I'm sure."

"I'm not going to cry over events," said Aaron, "not in your borscht. I can't carry a pack anymore, but at a time like this the poor, the ruined, will need bargains. There are plenty of little stores to rent and. . . ."

"Oh, you're an old *narr*. We have enough for a living. You forget you gave me some shares in what you called steel, glass, cornflakes, soap . . ."

"They're not worth much anymore . . . peanuts."

She wiped his chin with a crisp napkin. "Sidney's sister Rose, Paul's mother—you thought her crazy, her playing the market. A regular Hetty Green, you called her."

"She looks it these days. A gambler like Nat, in commodities, bearer bonds, shares. She, too, got burned?"

"No. Rose, she saw six months ago something was wrong. And so when I visited in Boston for Passover she got me to sell out, put the money in the New England National Trust and Bank."

"What?" Aaron dropped his spoon into the soup dish.

"I was afraid to tell you. I felt that day maybe I had too much wine and knew you had warned me women don't make good stockbrokers."

Aaron laughed, "Neither do men, I found out."

"It isn't a pot of money, not millions like you said we had, but a few thousand at a safe four and a half percent. We'll manage. We'll sell this house. I hate climbing stairs—also the cars, the summer place in Pittsfield. Too bad I didn't like jewels. Schnorrers we're not."

Aaron looked at his wife and she suspected he did drop some tears.

27

FROM PAUL SILVERTHORN'S JOURNALS

That the British punished a few Arabs for the massacre at Hebron, even hanged two (most likely the wrong ones) was not important. What was paramount was to get the top man who had supplied the weapons the Arabs used. The defense organization, now led by the leader called Moses, got their first clue from my contact with Baldo Levi. He, knowing his way around in the underworld of arms trafficking, came up with the name of Mohammed Ali Joudar, a native of Aleppo in Syria and a notorious dealer in drugs, weapons and stolen artifacts.

Using a letterhead Moses had printed—CARL HORNER, ANTIQUES—I wrote to Joudar in Aleppo that I was interested in Islamic artifacts of the tenth and eleventh century, particularly certain lustre pottery with decor of birds and horsemen, and that I would be at the King David Hotel for the next two weeks. I wondered what I had let myself in for.

A week later I noticed I was being followed as I moved among the antique dealers in Jerusalem. As a dealer in Middle Eastern art I was becoming more and more uncomfortable.

I returned from a dinner of Greek food at the Triana on Carlebach Street after talking by phone to Joyce in

Haifa, when this little man who looked like a French halfbreed came up to me. His features had a beige color. He said he had heard I was interested in certain ancient pottery. I said I didn't deal with freelance dealers but only with those known in the field. He smiled and pulled from a briefcase a small plate of a bird with blue and yellow wings, the real thing. I invited him to the bar and in a corner explained I was interested, but only in barter. I explained (as Moses had coached me) I had some merchandise I had gotten in another trade-off of some Shah Abbas tiles I didn't want and that I was willing to let it go at bargain price.

Sipping "fruit juice" (Scotch), he cast about him a cursory glance and asked what the stuff was. I said I couldn't talk of it there; British agents were all around us. He showed me the letter I had written to Joudar (no, he wasn't Joudar, just a poor relative), and I invited him to my room, which was cluttered with artifacts. The whole project didn't strike me as real until that moment.

He noticed my luggage with the proper labels. "So what is this merchandise?"

I went to the bathroom and out of the toilet tank took a hand grenade, which Moses had provided. "Very modern artifact," I said. Then I told him I was leaving soon and would deal only with Joudar, for I wanted a thousand dollars in gold.

I let him take the grenade as a sample. Two days later the halfbreed phoned and said Joudar would meet me outside the Mosque of Omar at ten in the morning the next day. Joudar never showed. That was that, I thought. Something had gone wrong and I was secretly pleased.

Joyce was in Jaffa teaching smuggled-in children and I wanted to join her and go back to Italy where there seemed to be a better atmosphere for these things. I was being drawn deeper and deeper into creating a homeland, taking risks, that I didn't care for.

A week after the meeting that was not kept I had a call from someone who said he was Joudar. To prove it he gave me the serial number of the grenade. I said I wasn't interested, that I was making contacts with someone else to dispose of the grenades. He said he would pay in gold and not to trust anyone else, as no one else could pay for such a large amount of grenades. I told him to call in the morning and I'd tell him where to meet me.

When he called in the morning I told him I would meet him alone at two o'clock at a large, abandoned wool warehouse on a hill, and to bring the gold.

Moses wanted to plant some men in the place but I said no. Joudar would now be watching the hill. Anyway with Arab villagers around they'd report any men at the warehouse.

Moses sighed. "Do it your way then. But we'll be at the Kafa crossroads ten miles away."

The old zing came back to me, of the crazy, foolhardy days of war in the air. But I was older, and while I could handle weapons, I wondered how this adventure would turn out. It wasn't that I was being heroic; it was that I found myself in a situation that pride, and Moses' faith in me, didn't let me withdraw from.

In the RAF we had braced ourselves with a mixture of milk and brandy, but I decided to go through this thing without that kind of help.

Deep down I do not know really how I felt, for I forced myself to think of other things. Joyce, would I ever see her again? My Uncle Sidney, the good and bad years?

At 1:30 I was at the old warehouse in the main room facing the big double doors, standing by the staircase leading to the loft. I was fairly calm, smoking a rank cigar. I knew I had been observed. I was sure of that. I hadn't brought a weapon, but Moses had planted some a week before.

I finished my smoking and felt tense. I grinned, driving off ideas I didn't want. I would have liked to light another cigar but needed a direct view for what was to come, and handling a cigar and a gun was enough to lose a needed second. I walked to the water barrel standing by the old wool shed, and brought up an oiled goatskin water carrier, which had not been visible in the dirty water. I untied the neck of the skin and took out a Colt .45 and a container of shells. I put the cartridges into my right-hand pocket. I released the cylinger of the .45, spun it, and saw the six bullets in place, fingered the trigger and the filed-down hammer. I unbuttoned my shirt, pushed the pistol in next to my skin, butt almost protruding. I felt the comfort of a man armed.

Steep stairs led to the second story, where a 12-gauge shotgun was hidden in the opening to the rope lift. I started for the stairs but heard a car motor on the flinty road. I turned and stood facing the opening, thumbs pushed in under my belt.

Two men got out, approached the open doors, dust on boots and dark hats. One was a lean Arab with a face showing old worn-down scars; the older man was Joudar, I was sure.

The lean man held a Luger in his left hand. I thought, the way he holds it he's good with it.

I said, "You were to come alone, unarmed."

He smiled, showing strong teeth. "Just my bodyguard."

"With the gun toter there, no deal."

With a hardly accented English: "So you have grenades?"

"I have them nearby." I pulled out a list. "Here's the original inventory. You have the gold?"

"When I promise, I promise."

The younger fellow took a step forward to reach for the list. Joudar struck him with the back of his hand on the chest and spoke crisply in Arabic.

Holding the inventory list lightly in my left hand, I raised my arm in an offer. Joudar came forward slowly. I saw it was no good. The other held the Luger very steady. I threw the list down on the dirt floor. I said, "You changed the rules."

Joudar almost bent for it himself, then nodded to the man with the Luger. We watched the Arab bend over to pick it up. It was like a tight poker game. One had to make his play just right.

The man bent, the Luger pointed at my chest, his eyes lowered to locate the list. I made my move, fast—with a deliberate easy gesture.

In France I had been taught for quick results to shoot without aiming. And I'd had practice since. Just push the pistol toward the target, with the same motion press on the trigger. The Luger man, his eyes on the list, screamed, then dropped. I turned to Joudar. He had a pistol out of a pocket. I squeezed the trigger and the Colt kept pumping slugs—the body seemed to leap under the blows. I looked around. There was the thump of running boots, one pair, from the car. Another of Joudar's men. What a careful, prepared man he was. No trusting dolt like myself.

I took two steps toward the doors. A blast came from behind me and something very hard and hot hit my right arm just above the elbow. I turned without thinking and fired again and again into Joudar. His body had fallen on its face in the straw dust after getting off that one last shot, his pistol fallen from his fingers.

My pistol, now empty, fell from my numb wet fingers. It was a flesh wound. No dark blood. Just the bright red. It had thrown off my muscle control and I had also emptied my pistol without thinking. No time to reload. I jumped for the stairs as splinters of wood exploded around me. The man was firing wildly, thrown off by seeing two dead men on the floor.

I was working by instinct now, blood pumping in my body. I reached the second story's rope-lift opening in the outer wall and put my left hand through it, staring at the right arm, shiny with blood. I groped and felt the butt of the shotgun. I pulled on it clumsily and it came up. The stairs creaked. I prayed that the shells loaded with a 12-gauge deer shot were in place.

The man had seen my Colt on the ground, empty; it must have given me the couple of extra seconds. The problem was how to hold and aim the shotgun. The right arm was losing feeling fast and I couldn't trust the trigger finger. I'd have to use the left hand. My eyes were blinded by sweat and I blinked to clear them.

Moving back away from the front wall, I knelt down by a large storage door. The man appeared on the steps—a head, a red face under an Arab headdress. My shotgun slid across the bloody arm. I could feel the pain. I cocked it. The man heard and rushed the last steps, firing a bit too soon, but I was hit. I pressed the right trigger.

The shotgun blast made a dreadful sound. The man had taken the spread-barrel load in the head and throat at four feet. He fell. I had been hit on the inner thigh. I went to the head of the stairs and looked at my soggy pants leg. Very dark blood. I had to stop it. I tried to pull off my belt. The buckle opened, but I couldn't pull it out of its loop with my bad right arm.

I panted and sank down to my knees by the dead man and groaned. I got the belt off awkwardly with my left hand and tied it above the leg's gush. I needed a stick to tighten the tourniquet. My fingers found the man's pistol and inserted the warm barrel between belt and wet pants leg. I twisted the barrel, tightening the belt. I felt a spreading stab of pain. The light blurred. Images drifted by with a darkening obtuseness.

Moses found me half an hour later. I was in bad shape. He got me to a settlement doctor, who bandaged me up. And I left that night for Haifa and Joyce and Italy.

The British had a five-hundred-pound reward out for me in two days' time.

On the ship, Joyce frowned at me. "You're too old for this sort of thing." I had to agree.

28

Now there is a flood, a new exodus in the perversities of human history; so thought Sidney Silverthorn of Silverthorn World Pictures as he studied the list of names and addresses on his desk to process entry visas for German Jews—writers, directors, costume designers, cameramen, all desiring to flee, seeking shelter in America now that Hitler was Chancellor and the ruins of the Reichstag fire were still being raked.

Already in 1934 they were arriving, the look of fright still in their faces. Jews who hadn't thought of themselves particularly as Jews, condemned as degenerate non-Aryans by the shape of a grandmother's nose. A few were not saved by an early conversion to the Roman Catholic Church, once proud Germans and Austrians, now just Jews, running, with few possessions; fugitives from violence, beatings, arrests, barred from their proud professions; professors removed from classes, department store owners whose smashed windows bore the swastika and the painted word JUDEN! Left behind were most of their furniture, paintings, their factories and warehouses. These first refugees were agonizing to get U.S. visas. Those with relatives or sponsors in America came, baffled and bewildered, moving across the continent to St. Louis to Chicago to Los Angeles in a reversal of fortune.

They were the first of a gathering tide—those who

could manage to escape. Many, as S.S. discovered, were to enter a shul for the first time, to wonder, wear the prayer shawl, finger Hebrew prayer books they could not read. They were mainly Jews without Yiddish now, hoping to enter into the life, the habits of these American sponsors—the second and third generations of immigrants—who seemed to them often as strange and outlandish as the Indians they knew from American films. They were still feeling the pain of transition.

ORT, Hadassah, VJA, and other services in Los Angeles found themselves trying to settle, find a living for these once-proud *Deutsche Yehudim*.

"More German than the Kaiser," was the way Ira Silverthorn put it, lunching with S.S. at the Zionhigh Club. "These once well-heeled ones can somehow get out, but what of the millions and millions of Jews— shopkeepers, students, farmers, tailors—who can't? We must see they get sponsors. They're doomed, Sid, and there will be others soon from Poland and Russia, Austria, Romania, more and more . . ."

"Please, Ira, don't spoil my boiled chicken. I don't think it's as bad as you gloom-chasers think. Hitler, the mangy sonofabitch, has Germany by the balls. The Jews are his propaganda gimmick. He'll level off, drill all his Germans, kick their asses, and they'll kiss his toes."

Ira looked at the wedge of cheesecake the waiter set before him. "Sid, Americans, Jews and others, don't understand Hitler. He isn't Chaplin clowning. He may be nuts but a crazy man of genius. Look how he sways the Germans. They have orgasms when he passes, when he speaks of 'tomorrow the world! Abolish the Jews!' He's going to murder millions of Jews."

"Ira, eat your cheesecake . . . waiter, get me a slice. I'm up to my ass at the studio. Hungarian playwrights with first acts, no second acts, just *first* acts.

278

But I hire them. It's pitiful, their letters of appeal, and where else to go? That *momzer* Oswald Mosley and his London Fascists meeting to toss them out of England. How can the English allow that kind of talk with Hitler and Mussolini meeting in Venice?"

"The British will go down if they have to with cries of free speech. Maybe now they'll open up Palestine as the homeland."

"Once the panic is over in Europe somehow things will fumble through. There is talk of not playing our pictures, but there is always someone to deal with."

However, the turmoil, horror, and shouting in the Third Reich didn't settle down; clearly *Mein Kampf*, Ira insisted, was a blueprint.

Los Angeles was to get radical playwrights, novelists, painters—Chagall Lischitz, Man Ray, Max Reinhardt and his family, even some minor Rothschilds. There were actors in pointed suede-topped shoes trying to convert their language from German to at least a guttral English.

As Ira put it the night Max Baer won the world heavyweight championship, "We'll awake some morning to find a German family: Herr Papa in a fur-collared coat, the kids in leather pants, Mama with bundles, but still traces of grand dame, good luggage, with all they could carry—and right on our doorsteps. I've six families on the little place I own in San Fernando Valley."

"We have a new Jewish world heavyweight champion."

"I have a professor of Oriental art using a hoe, two newspaper editors, feeding chickens and collecting eggs. And I think one is a lager brewer."

"Okay, they're different than the immigrants of the turn of the century, Ira. Those were the poor, the pogrommed, the ignorant, but loyal to the Torah. These middle- and upper-class ones are not much interested in Judaism. Their suffereing is sudden, not like the early Ellis Island steerage people who had suffered generations of murder, cruelty, second-class citizenship. It's like waking up in the morning and being thrown naked into the street."

"You'll just have to hire more Hungarian playwrights and hundreds of people who knew Max Reinhardt."

S.S. did what the studio could for the early refugees, but SWP was now part of the huge Lowitz Corporation of theatres, vaudeville circuit, and radio stations—a dominating entertainment combine. S.S. had done wonders as the studio head, and by 1934, SWP pictures were among the major winners at the box offices. The depression was still at its worse—even if Franklin Delano Roosevelt had been elected and had a New Deal in progress. Hundreds of thousands lived in shacks called Hoovervilles.

The SWP product was glossy, full of happy family life, stories of secretaries who marry their rich bosses; evil was always punished. The Hays Office, guardian of moral values, dictated what could be shown ("No naked inner thighs, not even married couples in one bed together; kisses timed by a stop watch; for lovers on a sofa at least one foot always on the ground"). In the popular gangster films, the crime boss or hoodlum hero always ended up executed or imprisoned by law and order. But the gangster as movie subject matter, S.S. saw, had to change.

"Clearly," he told a staff meeting, "when the Twenty-First Amendment to the U.S. Constitution repealed the Volstead Prohibition Act, the age of the mobster, the crime empires, were over."

His story editor said, "We'll make G-men pics."

"Maybe. Gangster films were good while Prohibition lasted. But it's going to be a more settled country. We must find good happy stories with some schmaltz, and noble themes. I don't want corn or the old hokum."

"Of course, S.S." said Ernest Benson, who had a college degree in the arts and had read Proust and felt he had cheapened his values working for the vulgar studios. "I have this snazzy idea, S.S. You'll like it. A typical American family, small town, father the mayor or water commissioner, mother the typical housewife. Young daughter on her first box of Kotex, a jazzy baby, a Charleston winner, necking and petting, but under it all a basic Christian virgin—sort of F. Scott Fitzgerald *Saturday Evening Post* type, solid stock. Kid brother rebuilding a flivver, shy of girls, but plays the trap drums in high school band . . . Penrod and Harold Teen, see? Maybe a Nigra maid for comedy, sassy but lovable."

S.S. said, "Christ, Ernie, I don't believe a word of it. Give it more values of the depression. Damn it, the Dust Bowl has blown away, millions of Okies in overalls and sun bonnets are on the road in their jalopies. I want more than a father who's an Elk and a comic-strip kid brother beating his meat. Let me see some story treatments with a runaway kid on the road. No broken families but hard-going and clean, you understand? No fucking art theatre gloom. Hope, *hope.*"

"Hope is the thing with feathers."

S.S. looked up, a cigar at an angle in his mouth. "What the hell does that mean, Ernie?"

"It's from a poem by Emily Dickinson."

"I hope she's not on our writing staff. I want you at the Chinese Theatre premiere tonight. Bring some writers—Faith Baldwin, Zane Grey."

"I hear *Man Hunger* is a great pictures. Giles Redmond is a quality director."

"His pictures return their cost. Get me those story treatments."

S.S. wasn't too proud of the pictures that the world depression had forced him to make. He wanted to do a film about the Battle of Gettysburg, not just the fighting but the human values. However, the Lowitz people had said, "no, not the Civil War, a money loser" (and so S.S. never did bid later for *Gone With the Wind*.)

Would he ever dare suggest a movie about Chaim Solomon? You could get a nun and a happy, sports-loving priest into a movie, but New York didn't approve of bearded rabbis or Jews playing Jews in films.

S.S. was very fond of Giles Redmond, a Canadian with a mysterious past but clearly an educated person, a gentleman. He had appeared at the studio claiming to be an actor from England; perhaps so. He fitted neatly into the roles of the smooth, black-haired seducer, the suave international sportsman, sat on a polo pony well. He wore his evening clothes and top hat as if born to the gentry and Bond Street tailoring. He had soon asked to be permitted to direct pictures and his first two films, *Foolish Moment* and *Dancing Wives*, had been box office successes. Tonight there was to be a major premiere of his newest film, *Man Hunger*. It was a costly film, had a color segment, during which Helen Morgan sang Teddy Binder's torch song, "Wailing Blues."

He would have to talk to Giles about his personal life; if any scandal broke, the Hays Office would scream, the Legion of Decency would picket. Giles was admittedly "a handsome middle-aged playboy," as Louella Parsons wrote in her column, a sought-after escort and lover. Certain disreputable local publications had hinted that he attended opium-smoking parties. His current favorite companion was Alice Hansen, the talent agent, though "a budding new romance" with Violet Browning was gossiped about. Violet was the studio's new young star playing demure maidens, shy country girls, sensitive virgins just coming to an awareness of life. Alice could, S.S. decided, take care of herself; as a talent agent she had at last found her suitable niche. She lived a gracious, exuberant life in her Holmby Hills home with its blond-oak moderne and Jugendstil furnishings, her Malamute dogs and tiled Roman bath.

S.S. himself had no intentions to test Violet's purity himself. He was thinking of the studio; his own natural desires he kept under control. His relationship with Nora had settled into an acceptance—he went his way; she was socially prominent—the *Los Angeles Times* often pictured her at some charity affair.

S.S. tried to live stripped of pretense, but knew he had not yet achieved that state. Flattery was good to hear even if he knew it was insincere ("I eat it with a spoon"). He was generous and warm with people he liked and yet could be fiercely cruel toward an actor or director who stepped out of line. Those who appeared snide or lacked respect could no longer get work in the industry; S.S. passed the word along. When asked at a party by a *Variety* reporter if there was a blacklist, S.S., who had drunk two brandies, had answered, "No, of course not. We do it by phone."

He had long since forgiven his father; all those years he had resented Alex interfering—that marriage he had prevented with S.S.'s first love.

Ira had told him of a story by a Greek philosopher, "A son enraged and angry was dragging his father through the family orchard by an arm and the father cried as he was being dragged, 'Stop, I didn't drag my father past the second row of trees.'"

S.S. wondered how his children saw him as a father. The girl Sari was at Marymount, a good private school, and Harry—Harry the rebel, in Switzerland; at sixteen, he was threatening to run away from school and join his Uncle Paul in Italy on some cockeyed adventure.

S.S. had joined a reform temple on Wilshire Boulevard and on High Holidays stood and recited, "Grant peace, goodness, blessing, grace, kindness, and mercy. This is my God and I will praise Him, the God of my father, and I will exalt Him."

He had hoped as he matured that life would be easier. But new fears had come, distracting ideas that plagued the nights. So he would wake and walk out on the balcony of his Bel Air home and look down at the sleeping city under a sky dusted with stars. He wondered not what it all meant; he knew very well what his world meant. It was what his world didn't understand that bothered him; the failure of qualities of reason, of order and authority. What if Ira was right?—he was a lucid man and seemed to grasp fundamental truths. Would the Jews again be the world's helpless victims? Wasn't it time for the Christian world to begin to listen to their Jesus, that all men are brothers? Must we, he thought, always be packed and ready to run, always to be the victim of fanatics, the prey of madmen? Why the damn label "the Chosen People," who were resented as if they were the keepers of the morality of the world? How odd of God to choose the Jews, and if God had retired for an eon or so, what a ghastly deed he had created.

Sleep came to S.S. only after two pills, a heavy sigh. But often the dreams were worse than sleeplessness; the drumming of one's heart in a nightmare, awakening in a bile-tasting daze, to face an aggressive day.

29

As he had for many years, Ira Silverthorn lived a casual life in the back of a termite-drilled cottage on La Brea, just below Sunset Boulevard. His old real estate sign still hung, a bit aslant, over the front door. But he did little such business now, being a sort of technical adviser to SWP Studios on historic details in western films, frontier wars, the proper war paint on Indian extras, how a river crossing with oxen was made, the correct dress for homesteaders, cowboys, dancehall girls.

Ira, a well-adjusted widower, lived alone; his two children had long since grown up, married, made lives of their own in distant places. He heard from them rarely. He relished his solitary life, feeling that a kind of wisdom comes when one discovers there is no permanence and one can live with most changes. Once a week he played poker or pinochle at the Zionhigh Club, enjoyed the excellence of life as a taciturn bystander. A tall, hulking figure with his Buffalo Bill moustache and beard, he took the world as it was. As he told S.S. when his friend seemed trapped in some studio crisis, "Who of us knows the sleep of the just? Not most old geezers."

Ira read a great deal—pre-Bolshevik, Russian novelists, French writers up to the time of Balzac and Zola, and Dreiser and Mark Twain. He had with some difficulty taught himself Hebrew and read *The Orchard of the Pomegranates*, the *Zohan*, the texts of the Hasidim and the Cabala. On his trips to Fairfax Avenue to buy smoked whitefish and corn-rye bread, he would drop in at the store-front shul of Rabbi Esserick to discuss the text of the Pentatuch, Rashi's commentaries, clean-shaven Beverly Hills rabbis, and *is* parsley an aphrodisiac? "Everything Silverthorn is given on loan and a net is spread for the living."

Ira lived with a self-effacing adroitness with a boot in both camps—the Orthodox fervor of the poor struggling Jews on Fairfax Avenue, and the world of films and radio, sharing a fat *matzes* herring with Rabbi Esserick in the back of the store-front shul or attending an opening of a motion picture at the Chinese Theatre on Sunset Boulevard, where sapphires and chinchilla were exposed to the glare of huge spotlights stabbing the California sky.

He awakened this morning aware he had promised Sid he would attend the new Giles Redmond film *Man Hunger* that evening. He scratched his ribs, recited a short prayer: "And all life will give thanks to thee, Seleh," then stood in his underwear, looking out of a dusty window at the garden where he fought insects and dogs to raise Big Boy tomatoes, lettuce, and carrots.

He twirled his moustache, combed his wedge of beard with his fingers, and in an old but loved blue robe prepared breakfast: stewed prunes and figs, three eggs fried a bit on the runny side, two thick slabs of rye bread unbuttered, a pot of coffee drunk with condensed milk added cowboy style. Visitors and guests called this concoction "battery acid."

Ira rarely read the local newspapers ("I know the perfidiousness of mankind") but as he savored his breakfast, he listened to the small RCA radio that was part static, part speech.

286

Hitler was howling again; Hindenburg (the old fart) had died; Chruchill warned Parliament of the German air menace; a man named Beebe was still going down over 3000 feet in a steel ball on a string in the ocean off Bermuda. There had been locally the discovery of the limbless torso of a young woman in a litter container in Griffith Park.

Limpid, lachrymose music came on. He turned off the radio and had a good three fingers of Old Crow bourbon. At the Zionhigh Club they were turning to Scotch as a social status drink, but the hell with that.

He washed his armpits and crotch in warm soapy water; he bathed only twice a week so as not to remove needed protective oils from one's hide and let in germs for an easy victory. He dressed in half boots, black twill pants with a heavy belt and an Indian silver buckle, pants with Mexican embroidered pockets, a tan jacket. He briskly brushed back his gray hair and donned his brown, well-creased Stetson. It was not for show but for comfort that he dressed as he did. The only change he made for formal events was to wear a black jacket, un-belted. In his middle sixties, Ira now stooped a bit and needed glasses for reading, but otherwise with teeth and hair, he still felt he retained most of the vitality of his youth.

The phone rang on the rolltop desk in the parlor. Tasting the bourbon in his gullet, he went to answer it. It was Lou Zucker handling the publicity for the night's opening of *Man Hunger*.

"How's it going, Lou?"

"Looks fine, got stands set up for the fans. Six big bastards of searchlights."

"What the hell is this use of lights for all openings? Even a butcher shop on Melrose has lights for a grand bargain in roast beef."

"Never question a tradition, Ira. Look, S.S. wants to

287

take a few people, say half a dozen, out to the *Good Luck*. You know how this thing works. So, do a favor, have a boat taxi standing by at the Long Beach pier at midnight. Say, is there any chance of a raid?"

"Safe as a mother's tittie. The ship is beyond the three-mile limit. Besides, money has changed hands. They have a great chef on board. I may come for the *blanquette de veau,* the *poulet saute chasseur.*"

Lou laughed. "You moocher. Studio publicity will pay for the food but not your roulette losses."

By sunset, lines already were forming outside Grauman's Chinese Theater "more Fu Manchu than T'ang," as Lou Zucker put it; those strange people, fan clubs with autograph books, solitary perverts, housewives, worshippers of screen personalities. SWP had ballyhooed the new movie for months and now followed the pattern: lights, crowds, a continual line of sleek cars (but for a cowboy actor who arrived in a dusty Rolls Royce, long horns over the hood) discharging the celebrities.

Stars and film personalities praised a picture they had not yet seen. A continuous cheering came from the stands along with the odor of popcorn, face powder, and urine.

Giles Redmond, escorting Alice Hanson, was wearing an opera cape with red silk lining, his handsome middle-aged features with the usual seductive look. Alice, who had filled out over the years, was resilient as ever in a pale gold gown worn with a short silver fox cape.

They uttered into the radio microphone a hope of greatness for the film and a thanks to the stars and that entrepreneur and pioneer, S.S. Giles didn't speak the heightened stage English of most actors from Great Britain in Hollywood. His was a pleasant, educated voice.

288

"I do hope it's a success. If not, I hope S.S. doesn't ride me out of town on a rail in tar and feathers . . ."

S.S. escorted Violet Browning, who, with her flaxen hair, big soulful eyes, bee-blown lips, was low-voiced and shy: "Oh I do hope it's all we worked so hard on. Thank you."

Mrs. Silverthorn never went to openings.

Ira used a side exit and sat in the rear of the theatre.

No print exists today of *Man Hunger*, just two dozen stills; as with so many early movies, the can of films were eventually destroyed to recover some of the silver used, or the reels may have just turned to dust.

The *Good Luck* had begun as a Japanese freighter and passenger ship, as the *Haki Maru*. After a fire at sea she had been sold to a Chinese firm of wreckers and scrap iron dealers in Hong Kong, but Monte Spinelli had rescued her from the cutting torch and refitted her as a gambling ship. She swung now off the American continent just beyond the three-mile limit, painted white and red, long strings of various colored lights hanging from the bridge and funnel and cargo masts. A band on board was playing "Stars Fell on Alabama." Burly, muscular attendants with a thick ear or a boneless nose stood by the gangway as parties arrived in motorboat taxis. The smell of brine dominated the wet night air.

S.S.'s party was loud and happy, having drunk champagne after the gala opening of the new film. It had gone well. Backstage the press had asked foolish or too probing questions, gotten bland answers. Giles Redmond and Violet Browning had distributed the credit to all, down to the prop man. S.S. had said little, only that Violet was their most popular star of the future and more of her films were being prepared for release, that certainly her and SWP's future looked brighter than the stars in heaven. He was always flowery with reporters. They could, he was aware, sting with scorpion tails.

They came on board, Ira last, refusing an offered hand as the ship rolled slightly, a tart breeze snapping flags against the stubby cargo masts. The sound of voices, the patter of the wheel man at the roulette table mixed with the band music, creating an atmosphere of evanescent, daring pleasure.

Violet giggled. "Can I shoot the dice?"

"You shoot craps," said Ira. "You *handle* dice."

The main saloon, much enlarged from its original size, was pale pink and gold, active with two roulette wheels, three dice tables. The cabins were reserved for high-stakes poker and private dice games for big rollers. The dining area, where the band was now into "The Continental," also had a small dancing area.

Alice looked around her, inhaled the cigar smoke, the fumes of liquor, the perfume of the women at the gambling tables. She exclaimed, "Better than fresh air. Somebody, buy me more chips."

Waiters moved about with trays of drinks; long-legged girls in short skirts and net stockings offered cigarettes, cigars, flasks of scent, and were mysteriously slow in producing the right change from the folded bills held between the fingers of their left hands.

S.S. took Giles by the arm. "Let's go find a private poker game. Too crowded in here."

"More geese than swans now live," Giles recited as they walked, "More fools than wise . . ."

S.S., with an apprehensive glance around, stopped Giles by a hand on his arm, as two couples, laughing and staggering a bit, passed them.

"Giles, we got a million-six tied up in two more pictures and future story costs on Violet. Man to man, Giles, stay with Alice. Any scandal, any problem with Violet, and the Hays Office will up our ass with a pitchfork. Also the Legion of Decency and not forgetting the goddamn press."

"My dear man, I am aware of the situation in the industry, what it's been like since the Fatty Arbuckle rape case, and Alma Rubens and that chap Wallie Reid were done in on drugs." He put a finger to his lips. "Discretion is all, what? Now I hope to win a thousand off you tonight at poker. It's my lucky month. I'm an Aries, you know. Solid buoyance in my horoscope."

"Cy has a couple of poker sharks in every game working for the house." Cy Gray ran the *Good Luck* for the Spinellis.

Ira, having bought two hundred dollars' worth of chips for Alice and Violet, went to the stern of the ship where a hard-faced man with a wandering nose stood by a red door.

"Hello, Dom. Cy in?"

"Yeah, sure is, Mr. Silverthorn."

He opened the door and Ira went down a short hallway smelling of bilge, fresh paint, and insect spray; no one had been fully able to get rid of the tropical cockroach.

Ira tapped on another red door and turned the knob. A big, broad-shouldered man sat seated behind the desk smiled, waved a finger. "Hi, Ira. You're not sending me enough of the big spenders."

"There's a depression, Nat."

"Cy Gray. Remember that. Not Nat."

"I keep forgetting. How's Laura?"

"Went East. Her grandmother died, or, as the old biddy woulda said, 'passed on'."

"That's right, Christian Scientists never die. They just bury them. How's *keshaft?*"

He who had been Nat Bendell nodded. "Good, good. If it weren't for the damn payoff to a half dozen grafters and moochers. But this ship gambling is peanuts.

We've got hold of a Chicago horse wire service; we're signing up all the big West Coast bookie rooms to use it."

Ira smiled. "Don't tell me more. I know most of the deficiencies in human beings."

"A little drink?" He pointed to some cut glass decanters.

"As James Joyce once said, in response to a similar offer, 'Sure, now to an Irishman there is no such thing as a *small* whiskey.' For this Jew also."

They sipped their drinks, the music faint but clear; a woman screamed, laughed too loudly, a glass broke.

"Jesus," said Nat, "the way things swing you around, I shoulda been a respectable home owner—me and Laura, Dagwood and Blondie. Instead I have to be the brains of the boys. They had a hold on me. You know we all lost plenty in Florida and it seems best." He laughed, choked, wiped his mouth with a silk handkerchief. "With a Tommy gun at my head and an offer to organize West Coast gambling, I didn't have to think hard *or* long. They got the muscle. But"—he tapped his head—"up here they feel violence is everything, bookkeeping for the birds. Finesse, I tell Monte—he's the smarter brother, the velvet tough guy. You can get what you want. Delay the menace, just keep the fist. Everybody wants the same thing, I say."

"Balzac was sure it's wealth, fame, and power."

Nat agreed. "That's it, short and sweet. Two out of three isn't bad. The fame we can skip. Those damn gangster movies S.S. and Jack Warner make give us too much exposure. That Cagney is something, eh? Jack comes here, gambles from time to time, drops a bundle, makes jokes. How was the movie tonight?"

"I have a good answer when S.S. or any producer asks me. I say, 'you have a movie there, yes sir, a movie.' That, Sid accepts in any way he wants to, and

I'm not committed to a lie. It's always a movie, right?"
Ira stood up. "Give my best to Laura."

"Sure thing. She doesn't like L.A. Says it's the glass asshole of the world."

There was the sound of running feet on the deck, shouting, noise of some object hitting the water.

Nat pursed his lips. "Some drunk most likely taking a header into the sea."

He picked up a wall phone. "Hello, Chris? What the hell's the ruckus? Yeah, all right . . . Him again? Haul him on board, put him in a cabin till he comes round . . ."

He hung up. "One of our regular slobs. Family owns one of the newspapers down here. I got markers of his for twenty very big ones."

There were protests on desk and slurred oaths from the rescued man.

When Ira was gone Nat sat back in his overstuffed chair, closed his eyes. Why was his life always on a high emotional level? He had talked too much, but Ira Silverthorn was all right. Anyway, he thought, I wouldn't be here much longer. I'm more than just a *paisan* for Monte and Benito. There are big organizings going on and Number Uno himself has been in contact with me. I said I run things like they are General Motors, Dupont, RCA. I told Number Uno, just follow their patterns. It's all there for the taking so let's begin moving into hotels, industrial laundries, refineries, grain elevators. Wash the money clean so you can't tell a tainted C note from a wage slave's week's pay. Even pay your income taxes. We knew after the fall of Big Al that's the way to cozy up with the territory.

Nat sensed that as a gambler, a handler of money, he was unique and needed. He felt he had found himself, been handed the chance by circumstance.

How did I become fifty-six years old? he wondered.

I'm like a mountain range that has come out of the sea to dry itself. It's like when I was a boy in Poland when in that muddy village and Papa brought me a copy of a book by Dumas and I dreamed of being Monte Cristo yelling, "The world is mine!" Why not? Aaron and Malka, they'd never understand.

Look what the big shots and their stock exchange, the depression, had done to Papa. Busted the old man. He and Mama, sitting on their duffs in their little house, in Atlantic City, counting dimes, walking the two blocks to the boardwalk, sitting in the sun. Still stiff-necked, proud, but taking a little from him. It isn't a Crackerjack prize to be old and not as frisky as you once were.

Laura is still a good wife; we love each other. She never pointed a finger and said I was not a Horatio Alger hero. She doesn't like it, what she calls the rackets. But better, I told her, a life with me with the Spinellis than a dead Jewboy so goddamn sanctimonious he'd rather be rubbed out than turn against the Ten Commandments. Life is more—it's energy, Ira says, patterned by intelligence. So I skip the smug self-righteousness. Did Rockefeller or J.P. Morgan stick to traditional Christian values, the stuff they learned in Sunday school? Hell no. What whips our behind, drives us on to grab for the brass ring on the merry-go-round is money and power, power and money. Every poor bastard wants the same thing; only society has said no, no, be a good boy, bow to the boss, punch the time clock, don't jaywalk, keep your nose clean, and in forty years the firm will see you get a gold watch and a free park bench . . .

Nat poured himself another drink.

30

The day ended in a restless heat. A wind from the desert, the dreaded Santa Ana, was promised. The rats living in the palm trees on the best streets sensed the change and stayed in their nests among the fronds. The mist that had flowed in from the ocean began to darken as the Japanese gardeners came home from their bean fields. The big red trolleys under singing wires carried loads of tired picnickers to their destinations.

Giles Redmond was about to sit down to dinner in his bungalow. A prominent motion picture director with a new successful film, he admitted cheerfully he was not a D. W. Griffith or a Charlie Chaplin but rather a respected film craftsman, one of the most reliable, producing a stable much-needed product.

This evening he had been working on his income tax return. His income of $55,000 was very good for a depression year. He set aside his tax accounting as his Negro houseman, Jed Baker, announced that dinner was ready.

Jed did not live in, but left after cleaning up after dinner and would return to prepare breakfast about 7:30 in the morning.

Giles, as a middle-aged bachelor, led a free and easy life. He usually was involved with women, mostly actresses from the film industry. At the moment he favored those slim, chestless flappers with bobbed hair, helmet hats, and a long cigarette holder between their well-kept fingers; also starlets in beads that hung around long pre-Raphaelite necks, their faces reflecting a kind of satisfied euphoria.

No servants were found on the premises in the evening unless a party was in progress, the gin flowing, the hand-wound Victrola playing what passed for jazz, Tin Pan Alley rather than the true Storyville.

Giles lived surrounded by film people. June Watts, a buxom blond character actress, lived just a wall away in the adjacent bungalow. Across the courtyard, Lou Zucker, a widower, lived with his aunt Nellie.

With his four-carat diamond ring and his thin platinum watch, Giles seemed a citizen of the successful Hollywood with no interest in any other life style. He admired the Jews who had created the motion picture industry when no one else saw much in it but crude sensation. He disliked the idea of aging and had told Ira Silverthorn, "Old age is a collision, like a bad auto accident that doesn't kill, only injures."

Perhaps, Ira thought, that was why Giles had the reputation of a hunter of young vulnerable flesh. In fact Giles's reputation was exaggerated by the gossip columnists; it enhanced his value as a director of motion pictures.

That evening, the chauffeur-driven car of Alice Hanson drove into the court. When she entered Giles's house, he was talking on the phone; the door was unlocked. Waiting on the coffee table was the ubiquitous cocktail shaker featured in the Giles movies as a symbol of sex and sin.

Alice had come to Giles at his request, as he was very anxious for her as an agent to read a book—*Rosmundy* by Ethel M. Dell—that he wanted S.S. to buy for his next picture. "It's damn good for pictures. Passion and kisses."

Later, Giles escorted her back to her car and returned to his bungalow. Lou and his aunt, just returning from seeing Mae West in *She Done Him Wrong*, waved to him.

The next morning the dutiful Jed Baker appeared at 7:30 to prepare breakfast. He opened the door with his key and discovered the body of Giles Redmond lying on its back, feet pointed toward the door. He turned and yelled and then yelled again.

Sidney Silverthorn was soundly sleeping without the aid of pills, deep in a recurring favorite dream: he was very young and roller skating with a girl named Mary Katherine Corey in a big wooden Boston rink; the organ was playing "The Skaters' Waltz." He and Mary were planning to run away and get married against strong family opposition. The dream usually ended with them skating all alone, skimming over the treetops to the tune of "The Whistler and His Dog." The dream usually ended here, but now it went on and he was at the wheel of Mary's father's car, a chain-driven Simplex monster with red running gear. Rain was falling like a curse from heaven and the car at great speed tried to brake to avoid a huge tree lying across the road and their screams rose . . . S.S. sat up in bed, badly shaken. He didn't want to recall how Mary had died and he had been seriously hurt. The scream was somehow becoming the ringing of the telephone on his night table.

He picked it up to hear Zucker's excited voice: "Hello, S.S. Trouble!"

"The studio's burning!"

"No. Giles Redmond, he's been murdered."

"Christ, Giles murdered! Can we keep it out of the papers?"

297

"Be practical, S.S. We've got to do what little we can to keep the studio out of this."

"Meet me at the studio."

Quickly people gathered and the police and a doctor arrived. The physician noted casually that "death was from natural causes, a hemorrhage of the stomach," a diagnosis made without benefit of an autopsy. Men from the coroner's office arrived and disagreed. Giles, they pointed out, had been shot by an obsolete .38 caliber revolver. The slug had entered the left side at the elbow and lodged in the neck on the right side. The position of the dead man on the rug was also rather odd. He was laid out as if for burial; the shirt, tie, collar, and cuffs were unrumpled.

It was determined that the shot had been fired at close range. His watch, the diamond ring, and $178 in cash were untouched. Nearby on the desk was the unfinished income tax report, a pen, and an open checkbook.

Lou Zucker's aunt Nellie remembered hearing a shattering report some time after eight the night before. She also recalled seeing a figure leaving the bungalow sometime earlier. "It was a man wearing a cap and a muffler around his neck."

She wasn't sure if he had on a topcoat. She also thought it *could* have been a woman wearing men's clothes. Nellie Zucker appeared effusive but serene.

Henry Inch, Giles's driver, said he called the house at 7:55 P.M. and received no answer. At 8:15, he rang the bell and still got no answer, so he put away the car and went home. As he was wearing a cap and raincoat, he may or may not have been the man Nellie Zucker saw. The police set the time of the killing between 7:40 and 8:15 P.M.—the usual unscientific guess.

298

Two pictures of Alice, framed and signed, were found in Giles's bungalow, and there was a locket with her picture in it with the inscription, "To my dearest." It did not appear bizarre or inappropriate to their friendship.

Lou Zucker telephoned Alice and told her Giles had been murdered. Alice rushed over to the bungalow and was very vocal in her demands that certain of her letters and telegrams to Giles Redmond be returned to her. She knew, she added, just where they were kept and wanted them to "prevent terms of affection from being misconstrued."

Later, she denied to S.S. she had gone to the bungalow just to get the letters but rather because the detectives had asked her to show how the furniture and art objects had been arranged when she last saw them.

Given permission to retrieve the letters, she went up to Giles's bedroom and opened the top drawer of his dresser—the letters were missing. It was rumored that someone from the studio where Giles worked had been there already and removed Alice's letters, among others.

It had been Lou Zucker, entering from the alley and through a window, who took them. S.S. had them burned in the studio's trash incinerators.

S.S. sat in his office, staring meditatively at Lou Zucker talking into a phone:

"You bet, sugar, anything we have on this tragic event, you get it first. But it's most likely just some bum who came in through the window. No, not a fact, Louella, just a good guess. Thanks, sugar. I'll give my aunt your regards."

He hung up. "I wish my aunt would shut up. She's enjoying this like a Passover seder."

"Lou, you know what I'm so worried about?"

"Hell, yes, that there's some letter from Violet

299

Browning we didn't find. Alice's don't matter. She's shopworn stuff, and anyway, she's not working for us."

S.S. winked sadly. "You know how much we have tied up in Violet's pictures?"

"Three million and a few thousand, give or take a few. With publicity, half a million more. We'll get theatre pickets. If so we'll never be able to release the two pictures. Our whole product may be boycotted. That cunt-crazy limey!"

"Canadian, S.S. You're fantasizing. Boycotts!"

"Am I? If we can't show her pictures, the studio closes."

Lou whistled, beat his fists together. "What kind of contract do we have with Violet?"

"Seven years. There's a morals clause. But that's no help to us."

The blow fell at 2 o'clock—a police officer rummaging in Giles's library picked up a book and a letter dropped out on which V.B. was embossed. It said, *Dearest, I love you so, I love you. I love you,* ending with several X marks and an extra big X, signed, *Yours always, the wood spirit.*

Violet told the press that she and Giles Redmond had been engaged but had kept it secret. Later that day, in a riding boot in Giles's closet, police found a dozen fervent love letters signed *Vi.* They also found two strands of blond hair on the murdered man's body.

S.S., trying to remain taciturn, ate dinner with Lou and Ira in his office. The national wire services had picked up the story and certain details of Giles Redmond's life in the past were coming out. Beyond the windows, the doleful drone and rattle of a Santa Ana wind savaged the shrubbery.

Lou put some horseradish on his roast beef sandwich. "I've got Violet to clam up. She's moved in with her aunt in Pasadena. The kid's hysterical. She had to be given sedation."

S.S. beat an ivory letter opener on his desk. "You think she killed Giles? Level with me, Lou."

"What, a sweet little thing like that? You blow on her and she'd fall over."

Ira said, "Lizzie Borden was a sweet little thing. She used an axe to chop Papa and Mama."

"What about Alice?" Lou asked. "She's being by-passed for younger stuff. She knew what was up between Violet and Giles."

"What was up!" shouted S.S. "Maybe just an older father figure. A virgin, hardly out of her childhood Look, you know Giles was no depraved monster. A nookie hunter sure, but—"

"Jesus, Sid, you sound like a title writer for Griffith. Face up to it, Giles fucked them; if not, he wasn't interested. How about her Pasadena aunt doing him in? Proud old family, innocent niece defiles solid family. Auntie gets some men's clothes and gets grandpa's World War pistol, does in the dirty seducer of innocence."

"Who's the corny writer now? We made *that* picture. Anyway, respectable old aunts don't kill. More likely some jealous husband did it."

Ira asked, "Who directed the two unreleased pictures?"

"Carlton Adams and Henley."

"That helps your *one* chance. There's a long shot, Sid—To play up poor Giles as a dark Victorian villain, a buster of maidenheads, a bestial mobster stalking the native virgins. Hokum but passable."

"A smoke screen?" asked Lou.

S.S. studied their faces. "God, a long shot, very long shot. Giles, I liked him. He was in many ways fascinating. Damn it, yes, sex crazy, but that's the occupational hazard of this town. You can upholster your car in pubic hair. But no, he was a friend. I can't do it to him."

Ira asked, "How are they taking it, the Lowitz Corporation minds?"

"They may be waiting for me to resign. Well, to hell with that idea. As I told their shyster lawyer, Homer Compton, on the phone, I'm their best bet to hold the studio together and save our production output." He sighed. "I wish I believed it."

31

It was discovered Giles Redmond had been called William Chatterton when he lived in New York City, where he carried on a successful importing business. He had served as a captain with the British Army in the World War, had a reputation for geniality. He seemed settled into a proper upperclass New York clubman's life with a charming wife and a beautiful daughter.

Yet in the autumn of 1920, after a pleasant day at the Vanderbilt Cup Races on Long Island, he sent for his personal things (kept in a hotel room he maintained) and with five hundred dollars drawn from his office account, simply vanished from business, family, and friends. He turned up in Alaska at least three times, but what he was doing there was not discovered. In 1931, he appeared in Hollywood and was accepted in the film business as an actor from England. With the swiftness possible to an aggressive type with charm, he became in a short time a good director.

The search of Giles's home produced two mysterious items—on Giles's body, police found a key ring with several keys on it for which no doors were found, in Giles's bedroom closet was a splendid woman's silk nightgown which the houseman Jed said had been laundered only once or twice. It bore no initials.

There had been a series of burglaries of Giles's bungalow. Jewelry was stolen and Giles's private brand of cigarettes taken. Pawn tickets made out to William du-Bois, his secretary, had been mailed back to Giles so he could redeem the stolen items. Six months before his murder, when he returned from Europe, Giles had accused duBois of forging his name in buying clothes and lingerie for women. duBois vanished and was not to be found.

There was a letter from a former British officer stating that while in London with him after the Armistice at the Elephant and Castle Pub, Giles pointed out a man in an Australian uniform and said, "That man is going to get me if it takes a thousand years to do it. I had him courtmartialed for the theft of army property." Several courtmartialed soldiers who had been heard making threats against Giles were investigated, but in the end that story did not lead Lou Zucker's detectives to the murderer.

In time, more than three hundred people in the nation had confessed in person, by letter, or by phone to the murder of Giles Redmond. There were juicy confessions as far away as Paris and London.

Giles Redmond's murder became a Hollywood legend that grew larger, more fantastic. Opium smoking was added to his vices, mysterious women were always hidden upstairs, blackmail in big numbers was mentioned. The open checkbook suggesting blackmail and the formal laying out of the body by the killer suggested some sort of bizarre cultism.

What was clear was that Giles had a strange, eventful, and not always a rational life.

Ira presented a very plausible theory: "Giles was really killed by someone outside the film industry—a woman who loved him very much. She found out he was involved amorously with other women—Alice, Violet. She was lurking around the bungalow, saw Alice enter, heard the chit chat or more over cocktails—sexy talk; maybe he mocked the love of the listening woman. The angry woman killed Giles, then as a sacrificed betrayed lover, laid him out properly after the deed. Would a man do that? Hardly."

"Somebody killed him, that's all we know," said S.S. "We'll always think Violet or Alice may have pulled the trigger. They ever find the gun?"

"No," said Ira. "Will they find the killer? I'd feel bad about it only he's dead. Nothing can hurt him."

Lou Zucker said, "My aunt asks when we're going to release the other two Violet Browning pictures."

S.S. nodded. "The one in release is doing good business. People right now want to see the suspect. But once the novelty wears off, will they come to the other pictures?"

No one ever knew if people would have come to the other Violet Browning pictures. Lowitz Corporation ordered them *never* to be released after its stock fell nine points in one day.

That order saved S.S. from a head-butting test with the New York office that might have cost him his job as head of the studio. He had extra prints of the pictures in a vault and threatened to show them in Europe if they withdrew the release. For some time he dreamed of Violet (or Alice) approaching him, gun in hand.

Violet Browning retired from the screen, opened a gift shop with her aunt in Pasadena, and decorated some of the floats for the Rose Bowl Day Parade. She never married. No one was ever tried for the murder.

The murder of Giles Redmond irritated Ira Silverthorn like a sore thumb, not just the brutal mystery of it, but the stupendous relish with which the press and public enjoyed it, the coarse but adroit way the newspapers and the radio newscasters worked up public interest. Ira felt that a kind of naked humiliation had been done to the memory of the dead man. Even the abrasive text of the clergy got their comments in. In reaction, he read comic strips, became a fan of Laurel and Hardy, had his teeth fixed.

He released his anger and frustration in letters to S.S.'s son Harry, who was in Europe again. He attended the Swiss school for two years, was expelled for setting off fireworks on a Fourth of July, then came home to attend Rutgers Prep for a year, decided to become a photographer of race and show horses for rich breeders, but that faded out when he developed an allergy to horse hair and hay. After six dull months at Stanford, Harry was back to Europe with cameras and a notebook, planning a book on the toursts' Italy. At nineteen he was tall, presentable, a bit quixotic in two languages.

Ira's long letters to Harry were amusing, witty, never given to sage advice for a young man. But Harry rarely wrote back. So Ira Silverthorn was left with a violent anguish that remained even after interest in the murder had tapered off.

He thought of himself as a solitary, uninvolved observer of life, submerged in his own reveries. His only companions at home were two old wall clocks recovered from junk sellers calling themselves antique shops—a round regulator from a dismantled depot in Glendale and a turn-of-the century item from a country schoolhouse. Ira treated these clocks with care, oiled and polished the golden oak cases. Their ticking in the night he called "the sound of my dreams, sweet breathing."

Actually, although he passed for a widower, Ira Silverthorn did have a wife. It was a fact that not even S.S. knew about. For Ira felt a secret is a private luxury. She was Martha Ornstein, who ran a pungent finesmelling bread concession at Farmers Market. The Farmers Market had once actually been an outlet for farmers bringing their products to town to sell from stalls. But now the place was a Los Angeles feature, several expensive acres of shops and concessions that sold at a cozy markup everything from Amazon parrots to rose hip honey, Indian jewelry, cactus candies. Martha's stand stood between the Original Vienna Sausage Factory and Yolson's Smoked Fish, which sold everything from jellied eels to frozen king crab.

Martha was a handsome woman in her late thirties with curly red-gold hair worn in wild, disordered ringlets. She had a cheerful round face and a marvelous body that she dressed in loose garments based on Isadora Duncan's notion of proper, healthy garb. Martha had known Isadora, Emma Goldman. She came from a Budapest family of Hungarian radicals who had discarded Judaism ritual for socialism, anarchism, Marxism, could quote Liebknecht, Proudhon, Bakunin, Engel.

Martha had left the American Communist Party when Leon Trotsky went into exile. She was attempting to form a Trotskyite opposition party on a West Coast impervious to the idea. She shouted, lost her temper, but could also be tumultuously cheerful, do a little dance she had learned from Isadora. She read the *Daily Worker* (warily) the Yiddish left-wing press, the *New Masses*, and spoke of the revolution "as inevitable as California sunlight."

Ira met her when he went to the market to buy a dozen Kaiser rolls. He found her a delight, and soon they got into a shouting match over Tolstoy's true faith and the massacre of the Kronstadt sailors. He went back to Martha's display of corn and potato bread, graham, grist ground wheat, bran muffins, pumpernickel, bagels, byolies, sour dough, pitas (she didn't sell white bread, which she considered "pure poison").

After the third visit, Martha refused to go to bed

with Ira. "Oh boy, the capriciousness of a putz. Marriage, yes, *stupping* like with a *nafka*. Forget it, Charlie."

"Marriage?" Ira clutched his bag of bagels. "How many times have you been married?"

She rearranged some long phallic French loaves. "Never mind that talk. So in the past maybe Emma Goldman ideas got me into free love. But, Mister Silverthorn, now I want the ring and the city hall paper." She laughed and slapped him cheerfully on the shoulder, hard. "Please don't stand in front of the stall. I got customers, a living to earn."

Martha said she didn't want a ritual Jewish wedding. "No *choppah*, no rabbi with dirty fingernails belching herring and pickled onion in my face."

"No? What?"

"A justice of the peace. Judaism is a dead fossil. Also, I don't give up the bread stand, and it's a weekend marriage. I don't move in with you or clean or wipe your ass, understand?"

Ira said, "Martha, you're the perfect wife, with the sagacity a philosopher wants."

"Go on with you, Silver, don't josh." And she blushed and slapped his shoulder hard. He winced and leaned over and kissed her in front of the waiting customers with their net shopping bags.

It was a marriage that delighted them both. It revived his audacity in sex, and a valid companionship developed with a warm, lively opinionated woman. As for Martha, it was a love affair that gave her someone to adore and housebreak (a bit). She took a sensual delight in their weekends of lovemaking in her apartment on Pico Boulevard. She washed his clothes, cut his toenails, made him mow some of the "facial shrubbery," as she called his moustache and beard. She refused to spend any great time at his cottage.

"If I got too domesticated there, Silver, I'd tear it apart and soak it in lysol, maybe burn it down."

She fed him sturgeon, cream cheese and black olives on rolls, barley soup, a *cholnet* of beans and meat (an epic in heartburn). Martha enjoyed a glass of slivowitz, wept over Molly Picon records of "Yiddel with a Fiddle," while from the rose-colored walls Karl Marx, Trotsky, Boris Tomashavsky, Margaret Sanger looked down and listened. Martha did not take the murder of Giles Redmond seriously.

"A victim of his own bourgeoisie trash. Eisenstein, Strindberg, Stanislavsky, now you're talking. But Hollywood movies are just chains that bind the slaves to their wet dreams."

"You express yourself so tidily, Martha."

"Oh boy, in bed I hope. If you only read Marx."

"I have. No use me pointing out the flaws in his themes, the damaged quality that passes over the essential in man."

"As Lenin said . . ."

"Fuck Lenin."

"I wish I had . . ."

Ira grew to depend on Martha, the gonads and adrenals satisfied. She was so solidly sure of herself, independent, pitied the world's frailties and catastrophes, saw the nations (all but one) living a collective insanity.

One weekend Ira found her sad, somewhat high on slivowitz. She slowly shook her head. "Stalin, it seems, has started big purges. How right Trotsky is not to trust him. Lenin left a will saying *not* Stalin, *not* Stalin, and now he's destroying everything."

"What will he do to the Jews?"

"Never mind the Jews. That's a narrow view. What will he do to the old Bolskeviks, the intellectuals, to Babel, Radek, the poets and writers?"

309

He comforted her in his arms, they drank, ate smoked whitefish, kissed, made love; he consoled her in the big wide bed. Ira was pleased he was there, happy to know he could do something to aid a human being whose pretty political balloon had burst. He himself had no sanctimonious noble causes, indulged in no great righteousness, and also was in no final despair about the world.

In the morning, they lay in a lazy sabbatical free from weekday duties. Over the blintzes and the coffee with chicory Martha said little. He smiled at her and held her hand; she leaned to kiss his wrist.

"Silver, I want we should make a baby."

"At my age?"

"Never mind the age. It stands up, it will do its work."

"But why?"

"If all I marched for is to end in ruin at least let me leave something alive, something"—she gave an insouciant hiccough—"we two shared. Oh, Silver, Silver, be good to a foolish idealist. Let us make a baby. Is that asking too much?"

He said, "Let's be practical. Are you sure?"

She said she was sure. "Let us add just one drop of consciousness to the future."

He wondered if the line was from Sanger or Marx. Later he found it in a short story by H. G. Wells.

32

She stood, a graceful figure unmoving in the ocean breeze, at the boardwalk's railing, aware behind her of the chairs being pushed by the black men at a steady four miles an hour along the wooden road, the passengers half-dazed by the afternoon sun. Laura felt vulnerable, oh so vulnerable, held by a certain vague and fragile sense that one must never go back to the scenes of a childhood. She had come to Atlantic City with Grandma several times in the years of a child's wonder at all things to enjoy the diving horse at the Steel Pier, the free samples of messes on crackers at the Heinz Pier, and the magic show opposite their hotel, The Breakers, where Underwood invented the cast-iron typewriter.

To no longer have those breakfasts in bed, Grandma taking a large Armagnac, and then in her ocelot coat, if their visit was in the fall, and she in her "genuine" squirrel, briskly walking the boardwalk, attending the rigged auctions, the salt-scented air mixed with smells of pigeon droppings, buttered corn on the cob, and salt-water taffy, wrestling the pink ropes of the sweet stuff in open booths.

Now Grandma was "passed over," and Atlantic City was on the decline, the boardwalk splintered, the hotels going shabby, and no more diving horse leaping from the end of the Steel Pier, nor the nets so well filled as once with strange sea creatures and thrashing fish dying in the sunlight.

She took out a cigarette, put her elbows on the railing, and looked out at the mouse-colored sea, the horizon line as if drawn with a warped yardstick.

"Hello, Ma."

Laura felt a tap on her shoulder. She turned in near panic and there was Teddy Binder in straw skimmer, white ice-cream pants, and striped jacket. Teddy, her stepson, one of the heroes of Tin Pan Alley—a producer of popular music, able to achieve an immediacy of likable tunes.

"Teddy!"

"Laura."

Then both together: "What are you . . ."

They laughed. Teddy held a lighter to her cigarette.

"You first."

"Grandma left me four lots here on Arctic Avenue and the estate, lawyers said they had a good offer for them, so . . ."

"Knowing what chiselers and crooks lawyers are with an estate you came to see for yourself."

"And you?"

"We're here trying out my new show, *Come to the Party*. So far it isn't breathing. I'm piddling with the temptation to close it here."

"What's wrong?"

"Has a great first-act curtain, a takeoff on a Noel Coward romp and party at a Long Island weekend. Bolo Newton did some great choreography, but so far the second act is sick. The actors don't feel it . . . However, what are you doing for fun? Nat with you?"

She flung the cigarette away, watched a thin man and fat woman get into a chair and a large big-bellied Negro begin to push.

"Your father, he can't tear himself loose of the Coast."

"The Spinellis." Teddy grabbed for his straw hat as the breeze grew stronger. "With Pop's brains he could be running a business legit. But I guess you know Nat. It's the danger, the planning, the expectancy, doing things other people don't dare."

"He swore several times to break away."

Laura felt less vulnerable talking to her stepson, someone nearer her own age. "Oh he promises, he's good at that. 'Just one month more, sweetie, just till I get the damn gambling ship to balance its books.' 'Sweetie, we got this horse room wire service almost set on the West Coast.' Teddy, he'll never get out. He's irrevocably cemented in there."

"Don't say cement. The mob uses it to do people in. You need a drink, I need a drink. I think, me thinks."

"I hope your lyrics are better than that."

"Come on, booze time. You tell me how things are all haywire with Nat and I'll tell you how the top banana is lousing up my best patter song."

Already over their heads was a star islanded in infinite dusk. Soon they were sitting in a dark bar off the underlit lobby of the Haddan Hall, drinking martinis, two each, listening to a radio have its way with "Smoke Gets In Your Eyes."

"Getting old is real shitty and getting there can be too."

"Yesterday I was with them for lunch, Teddy. They're both really creaky now, but your grandmother Malka, she doesn't let that stop her. As feisty as ever. She doesn't accept they went broke in '29. She still has that intensity, that pride. And still offering the world fruit."

"Nat and me, mostly me, see they get by. But

Grandpa Aaron, he's really stiff. I walked with him to the boardwalk two blocks and it was a task. I almost cried. He's such a damn noble person and when I think of what he and my grandmother went through. My mother knew them in those early days."

Laura ate the olive from the last martini, grinned. "How is the fabulous Sonia?"

"Mama? As kookie as ever. She's a tumler in a Catskill mountain hotel. A hilarity organizer, puts on weekend shows for the cloak and suiters in the Borscht Belt. Does impressions of Sophie Tucker and Fanny Brice with the band, sets up games for the guests without exerting their high blood pressure. Sonia, she's marvelous—had her face and tits lifted. Never say die, that's my Yiddisha mama. How about one more?"

Laura tilted her head to one side and curled up one corner of her mouth. The bar was in shadows like heavy dark dreams, animated Rorschach tests.

Half an hour later they were in bed together in her room at The Breakers. They made love earnestly, letting instincts rule. They lay side by side, thoughtful. The window leaked in the garish color of neon, spelling out pleasure to be had on this sand split on the South Jersey coast.

"Who says it first, Laura? It was *great*."

"Yes it was. But, dear, you mustn't make too much out of screwing your stepmother."

"I'll make what I want of it. If I didn't know things were goofer dust between you and Pop I wouldn't have . . ."

She took his hand and kissed his cheek and he held her close and caressed her naked shoulder, mouthed her breasts. She made moaning sounds with a gentle intensity. But she held him off.

"Teddy, don't get any ideas. I'm going back to Nat. I'll always be there, no matter what."

"Don't be so fucking loyal, Laura. Pop needs no one; he is enough for himself. He's selfish, always was. He ducked out on Sonia. He's had dozens of janes, even ladies like you, and he's treated ladies like broads."

"Look, Teddy, we're not lovers trying each other on like new shoes. You have a second act to rewrite. And I'm selling lots."

He looked at his wrist watch on the night table, then out at the gold-beaten night, "Geez, I'm due in an hour to present insert material. If this show is a turkey, a bomb, or a smash, come with me to London. We're opening a revival of *American Doll* there. I have a flat at the Grovenor, and we can get down to Monte or to Saltzberg for the Mozart and . . ."

"Teddy"—she laid a hand to his mouth—"put away your opium pipe. You know I love you; always have. But I love your father more. Maybe I only love the memory of what he once was, when the Florida land boom was on. For a penetrable kindness when I needed it. Maybe he's just a gangster now, a hoodlum with the Mafia and the racketeers. Oh, Teddy, I've been so miserable." She gripped his naked torso and held on, her tears falling on his chest. "I'm afraid he'll be killed. Those people settle a grievance with a shotgun blast or a slug in the back of the head."

"Laura, Laura, you've been seeing too many Eddie Robinson movies. Whatever Pop is, they need him. He's a better organizer, handles their banking, investing, promoting, settles differences."

Laura wiped her eyes on a corner of a sheet, sniffed, blew her nose, and smiled. "I'll manage, and, dear, don't ever feel guilt about this . . . this was so good . . ."

"Is, *is*. Nat *was*. Once more around the park?"

They made love again and Laura was thinking as they came down from a climax, *no guilt, no guilt, Laura*

315

baby. She dozed off and Teddy dressed to go to the theatre and she muttered in her sleep: "It's all in the family, all in the family."

It had been a hard year in Rome for Paul and Joyce. No plausible explanation of the situation in Palestine seemed possible. The Arab High Committee had been formed to destroy the Jews, to continue attacks on the settlements. Overshadowing it all was Franco and his Moors cutting Christian throats. In July Fascist army officers set up the *Junta de Defense Nacional* in Borgos, and Franco's enemies of the Republic took Badajor, laid seige to Madrid. The government moved to Valencia.

In the fall of 1936, Joyce was pregnant, and Moses, now one of the major leaders of the underground Jewish defense organizations, came to Rome.

He was a man whose sensibilities had been rubbed raw. He sat with Paul under the pots of basil and rosemary in the courtyard, tugging on a newly grown brown beard.

"It's the way and no other way. We've got to help the Republic in Spain; Hitler and Mussolini have proclaimed a Berlin-Rome axis, and that means more trouble for Jews. They're sending weapons, tanks, planes, military advisors to Franco."

"Franco is of Jewish descent, I hear," said Paul.

"Send him roses on Yom Kippur. I'm helping organize an international brigade to fight in Spain."

"Why? Let them cut each other's throats."

Moses looked at Paul with wonder. "Why, you schmuck? Because it's a republic in trouble; if the Fascists win there's one more enemy in Zion against humanity. If the Republic stands, friends *we* helped may some day help *us.*"

"May, may not."

316

Joyce came out of their rooms with a bottle of wine and glasses on a blue tin tray. Her pregnancy was showing a bit under the buttoned cardigan. Paul had insisted on a wedding ("living together for lovers is fine, but producing children calls for a more formal domestic setup").

She set down the tray and looked from one to the other as if searching for layers of subtley. She watched Paul pour the glasses halfway full. "The Palestine wine will be as good as this?"

"*Haliwiy*—let's hope."

Joyce threw back her heavy black mop of hair with a toss of her head. "He's not going, Moise."

"What, where?"

"Spain. He's not a young hothead, and he's going to have a family. So don't spread the old camaraderie crap here."

Paul said, "You're jumping to conclusions, Joyce."

"I'm a good jumper in *that* direction. The Loyalists' modern planes you could put in a cigar box. Franco is getting German and Italian fighters, bombers. So . . ."

"The Soviets will send planes," said Moses. "Also tanks and military commanders. They're breaking out of the zoo of Marxism."

"They'll treat Spain the way they treated Trotsky. Why are you bothering Paul?

Paul said, "We're still involved in the homeland defense, now the Arabs have stated their intentions."

Moses stood up, banged his fist on the wooden tabletop; a glass of wine spilled. "Goddamn it, what's wrong with helping the Republic with their air defense! I didn't ask Paul to actually fly, but to aid setting up ground coordination, repair facilities."

"No," said Joyce, "he's been shot, beaten, chased, had a reward on his head. But all that was for us."

"Who's us?"

317

"Us is me, the baby inside and our marriage. I'm tired of being a kosher Joan of Arc. Think of me, you bastards, carrying a child, the morning sickness, very little money. I'll be living here like a vine cutter or privy cleaner and you heroes in Spain in your smart leather flying jackets will be living it up—all the jolly Hemingways."

Paul signaled Moses not to continue the conversation, with a look of you-know-pregnant-women. But Moses was heated up, his face lobster red, his beard in disorder.

"In America they're sending over an Abraham Lincoln Brigade."

Joyce said, "Then let Roosevelt help with tanks, planes, weapons. He'll get reelected by a landslide vote."

Moses grunted. "Roosevelt was warned by the New York cardinal, if he wanted the American Catholic vote it was to be hands off. *No* help for the Spanish Republic. There will be no arms or weapons from the United States—you can bet on it. The Vatican has spoken. *Deus est qui regit omnia.*"

"But America is a democracy," said Paul. "Damn, they can't let the Spanish Republic die under the murderous Moors, Hitler's degenerates."

"Don't hold your breath till they send aid."

Joyce picked up the spilled glass. "Damn if I'll cook for you two tonight. We'll go out." She went off and Moses cracked his knuckles. "Women."

"Moses, she's pregnant and she's very sick mornings. Women aren't their normal selves during this period. A very singular change. They think only of their young."

Moses shook his leonine head. "We'll talk some more later. I've sent for Tony Ringel. He's been cutting up some old steel bridges in France. Was he a good flier?"

"Everybody in my squadron was a good flier if he survived three missions. Tony was a *great* flier."

"You think he'll go to Spain?"

There was, Paul decided, a tedious fanatical side to Moses—a man lacerated and transformed by causes.

"Moses, it's twenty years since we old crocks flew. The planes of 1936 are not the flaming coffins of 1916–1917. The Camels and Spads were spit-and-muslin kites. We're old men when it comes to flying today's supercharged ships. Only trained young men should be used."

"Training takes time. Hitler has marched his troops into the Rhineland, Mussolini had just proclaimed that midget king of his Emperor of Abyssinia. If Franco's assassination of the Republic spreads into a wider European war, what will England do? If they knuckle under and play footsie with the Germans, the English may pull out of Palestine and the Jewish settlements will be wiped out, for the Arabs will be armed by the Axis. Spain must survive. It's the testing block for whatever minimum of human rights will survive."

"Moses, you lack a sense of balance, like all fanatics."

"Do the millions of Jews lack a sense of balance while being put into concentration camps, being beaten to death, tortured by the Gestapo?"

"All much exaggerated," said Paul. "I admit the German Jews are in a bad spot."

Moses shouted foul words in Hebrew.

Not as easy a task as it sounded, Paul thought, for neither the Talmud nor the Torah had specialized in that field.

BOOK FIVE

JEREMIAH

FROM THE JOURNALS
OF PAUL SILVERTHORN

There is something about a pregnant woman and a civil war that upsets one's rational ideas, one's blind Aristotelian acceptance of logic. How things differ than from what we expect. Joyce seemed to set up a buffer zone between her treasure-laden belly and the rest of the world. So, too, the war in Spain appeared illogical, some barbaric return to the violences of evils of the past. There were executions, the slaughter of intellectuals and radicals by the Fascists in the village bull rings. The reprisals, the horrible destruction by the Moors, actions as murderous as Stalin's Moscow trials, his great purges climaxing in the execution of Marshal Thachevsky.

Meanwhile Moses and Tony Ringel were active in trying to get aid, weapons, men to the Spanish Republic. Franco was on his way to destroy Malaga, Guernica, Gijon. The government had moved to Barcelona with Madrid under seige and had launched its own offensive at Teruel.

Tony was excited about flying in Spain. He didn't see we were no longer the young dashing (half-drunk, half-pissed) aces we were in 1917. He was much taken with Joyce's condition and sent her boxes of dainties ordered from England and Paris. He sent a car for her when she wanted to see *Snow White and the Seven Dwarfs*. We went to visit him at his suite at the Hassler. We had no sooner arrived than Joyce disappeared into the gold and white bathroom to float in the pink-veined marble tub. Tony, who was going through a batch of bills, handed Moses and me each a dreadfully expensive cigar and we sat smoking while he paced the rug.

"Of course we'll fly."

Moses looked at his glowing cigar end, scratched his whiskers. Tony smiled. He always had that charm some people have who are sure they can win others to their way of thinking—a belief in their own infallibility. That's how wars start, and bad love affairs.

"Moses, cheer up."

"It's a ground war."

Moses carefully killed his cigar in a gold-plated ashtray, as if breaking a neck, and stood up, hands in the pockets of a worn blue wool jacket. "It's all damn fine, Tony. Let's *do* not talk."

Tony said in a low voice too much under control, "I'm the stupid sonofabitch who puts up the cash for a plane. I'll fly it."

Tony didn't show any comfort in his victory. I yelled at the bathroom door, "Damn it, Joyce, you've boiled enough. Climb out of there. We're going home."

Tony looked at me and then looked away. "She'll catch cold leaving here all steamed up and overheated, walking in that cold outside. Let me order a car."

"We'll take a taxi . . . Get out of that bath!"

"Stop rushing her. She's getting heavy and she may slip in the tub."

The bathroom door opened and Joyce came out. She was getting heavy around the middle but for all that she was still trim, and in her robe she looked like a Greek goddess. Though she was annoyed at me, she retained a resigned tranquility.

"Stop howling and I'll dress."

In the taxi Joyce was bundled up against the cold

that seeped through the loose doors of the rattletrap machine. Moses just sat and stared at her.

She looked at him over the two mufflers I had wound around her neck and shoulders. "Moses, Paul is not going to Spain."

"Let him decide."

Joyce gave a hollow laugh and hunched down into the mufflers. "Hah! Who knows? You've bewitched him. Look, stop him, he's coming in his pants to go."

I told her to shut up.

Joyce shouted in Italian for the taxi driver to stop. There was a screech of loose brakes, and before we could react she opened the door and ran off through a market area and was lost among the stalls lit by flares. Night was falling in the cold street.

I got out of the taxi and ran toward a group of charcoal braziers where women muffled to the ears were gutting giant bluefish. Moses was at my heels. He gave me a small smile. "All right, *paisan,* we'll go find her."

We told the taxi to wait and went into the market area among obscenely gutted sheep, sides of pork, split-open fish, lobsters, crisp and icy.

Joyce was inside a glass booth on wheels drinking cafe expresso in the steam of cooking sprats, heavy men eating sandwiches and drinking grappa. Joyce sipped the hot brew, poker faced.

"I'm all right now. Sorry I acted like a shit," she said.

We both knew it was not at all right. Outside lost bits of paper were scattering; a dog drifted by avoiding puddles. Rome in bad weather.

Moses went off without even a goodbye.

Joyce didn't get pneumonia or pleurisy as I feared. She began to stain in the middle of the night. The Italian doctor I routed out of a double bed said it was nothing, nothing at all: "She should stay in bed and not get up till I tell her." Tony brought in food from the pasta place. Joyce looked very pale and worried and wonderful in the brass bed, saying she didn't want to be any bother. The staining stopped but her bladder didn't seem to function properly. At the end of the week I insisted we get an English-speaking doctor from the Salvator Mundi International Hospital, which had staff members who believed in germs and clean hands.

Moses had gone off to see to organizing a fresh international brigade.

Doctor Adams was young. "If the staining doesn't come back I don't see anything to fear. But your wife is anemic. I'll prescribe something to build up her red blood corpuscles. Liver should also help, not too well done, *lots* of liver."

"Lots of liver," I said. "What's the fee, doctor?"

"Well . . ."

"A hundred lire?" I said, reaching for my wallet.

The doctor wrote out a prescription and took the money, looking from Joyce to me. "I suppose among creative people, I mean having children . . ."

Sickrooms have always depressed me; truth is, they frighten me. Not just the bare intimations of mortality; bowels, bitter medicine, bed-made odors. So I flee like a coward. I took to walking by myself. To me a Roman winter is mean and yet strong too, like January quarters for horses where their animal strength is held back for spring. A solitary winter day was a total incomprehensible happiness for me. I was alone—I couldn't talk to Tony—I was worried about Joyce.

I walked, saw the leaden ruffled surface of the river, ragged, freezing people burning trash under bridges, wetness running from weathered noses, bodies bundled up, lines of priests, seminary students bent against the wind. The bells sounding as if one ring would shatter bronzelike glass.

326

I must confess I was in a bad state. Joyce had become a stranger. No use being told some pregnant women get this way. And Tony would be leaving soon for Spain; he was sure he could buy old French fighter planes in Algeria. I wanted to escape with him, get out of Rome. But I could not leave Joyce, I could not be that kind of a heel. Or could I?

I headed toward the piazza of St. Peter's, avoiding the pigeons that had fallen frozen from the eaves, past the few pilgrims, their zeal not keeping their toes warm. They were banging their feet against the walk of the Bernini colonnade. The dome of Michaelangelo Buonarroti looked frostbitten; the chipped saints all along the roof seemed to shiver in the cold wind.

Always there was a droning of Latin in the interior of St. Peter's, the basilica and the golden apse looking as vulgar as ever, everything overornate in that unholy presumption that they had captured the only true dogma—too rich, too vain for the simple Jesus.

I didn't linger in the stale old priest smell but went to the Sistine Chapel, where I had made friends with a little monk who controlled a side door. I always slipped him a small flask of grappa or a cake called nun's-thigh; he was a drunkard but very cheerful.

Nothing was settled in my mind. Walking back, the wind sharp and cold down from the Alps, I went past the stalls where they sell the holy junk to tourists and pilgrims, boarded up now; two short Italians, backs to the wind, were carrying on some sly deal, hands inside their worn overcoats as they haggled.

Past me on bicycles wheeled the bearded old priests, smelling of artichokes cooked in oil, toothless old men, varicose veins on their blue cold legs under their robes, carrying the little bag, the bell, the holy unguent, to go build a salad of ash and oil on some dying person's brow.

I passed the cafe where the faggots hang out, flaunting their *culs,* in tight pants, smoking cigarettes in long paper holders, running slim hands over heads of marvelously marcelled hair, whispering to me: *"Venga, venga,* hey Joe, *fottere yo?"*

Joyce was sleeping when I peeked in the bedroom. Seated by our small stove was Harry Silverthorn. He looked fine, healthy and filled-out. No more a kid. I figured he was about seventeen now, and as he stood up, smiling, to take my hand, I thought Sidney his father must have looked like this when young before his hair went and he got a paunch and wrinkles of worry and anger.

"God, Uncle Paul, it's cold in here as Kelsey's nuts."

"You get used to it. Where the hell have you been? Not a letter for months. Last we heard, you were in Malta."

"Been in Sardinia for two months, following the tracks of D. H. Lawrence."

I noticed camera gear in worn cases, a knapsack on the floor. "Still taking pictures?"

"Now it seems tame. How's Aunt Joyce? She was asleep when I got here, so I let myself in."

"She's going to have a baby."

"That so?"

He seemed to blush; perhaps it was only the cold. I added coal to the stove, opened the damper a bit. "How's the book going, the *Tourists' Italy?*"

He waved off the question. "Seems small potatoes with a war in Spain. Look, can you fix me up, get me a visa? I want to photograph real fighting."

"Don't be so goony. S.S. would have me shot. I mean he'd break my ass if I let you go to Spain. Forget it, Harry. War is mean, dirty."

"You had *your* war." He said it as if I had enjoyed a great privilege.

"I had my war . . . you hungry?" I got out some cold fried chicken, half a loaf of bread, a bottle of wine. I put the coffee pot on the stove. "Tuck in."

"I am hungry. Short rations. Took this flea-bitten train down from Milano, as I'm sort of out of cash. S.S.'s office sent an American Express money order, but it's lost. You have any milk?"

I said we didn't trust Italian milk.

Harry ate with relish, a happy look on his face. At his age I'd been a shot-down flier in a London hospital with an overwhelming fear. I'd recovered enough to be sent back to fly.

"Uncle Paul, don't be so damn square. Everybody should have a bit of a war experience. Like hair on your chest."

"Harry, you're full of the bullshit from *Farewell To Arms*. Read Barbusse's *Under Fire*—that's the real McCoy on war. No nurse sex toy laying her golden twat on a silver platter for you and saying, 'was I good?—is there anything you want, I can do'."

"I'll get there somehow."

I heard Joyce stir. I lowered my voice. "Not if I can help it. Where you staying?"

"Just got in. Where's a cheap armpit pension?"

"You can stay in Joyce's studio. There's a cot and she isn't using it just now."

He wiped his mouth with the palm of a hand, nodded. "Just till I get some American Express money orders."

I said, "Just till," and Joyce came in and the two of them got on well as she warmed herself at the stove. Harry used to come to visit us when he was in the Swiss school, but not since he was kicked out over that firecracker business.

Harry was a good house guest, cleaned up after himself, kept Joyce company. She became much more cheerful. They went to see *Snow White and the Seven Dwarfs* again. It was just out and very popular. Tony had given Joyce a small gramophone and Harry and she would play "The Dipsy Doodle" record and "Bei Mir Bist Du Schon"; only Joyce said it should be pronounced "Shane" and not "Schon."

I went to the American Embassy where I had a pal, Barry Orr, and asked them *not* to issue a visa to Harry Silverthorn for Spain. I took him and his camera for long walks. He made a dark room out of a closet. His pictures had merit, I thought.

"Forget Spain. With your skill, Harry, I'd have your father let you make movies, direct pictures."

"Maybe I will do a documentary of the Civil War."

We walked past Alfredo's trattoria, where the gross feeders were at work over filled plates, winding it around forks, shoveling it in, sipping it up from spoons, soaking it up in a good crust of bread, washing it down with white wine, red wine, imported beer, Strega. Their faces sweaty with the effort of eating, they reach for the bread, the sauces, sighing, grunting, belching, farting. Harry was delighted, took pictures, said man is made to eat, to dissolve in acids the tissues, organs, flesh of lesser breeds. He'd press a cold nose to the plate-glass window and in the freezing air watch them tear a whole limb off a chicken (what teeth), watch the waiter debone a trout as if performing a sacred rite. I'd turn on my X-ray eyes, see their glands spurting bile into their gorged stomachs, the acids attacking the fragments among surgeons' scars, the colons twitching, the kidneys washing out the impurities drop by drop, filling the bladders with rich yellow fluid. All the grinding, pressing, coiling, turning; then only a little rest, because in a few hours they must do it all over again. Repack the guts, evacuate, swell the glands.

We moved away to watch some wet-nosed children

330

slide on an icy sidewalk that dips past trees that are black stalks now, kids, Harry observed, who would become Michaelangelos, movie actors, Mafia gangsters returning from Chicago, faggots at the espresso joints, little fat husbands with many bambinos, little girls in white to be confirmed, bearded priests on bicycles, sitting on walnuts, not balls, lacking the grit and guile to advance themselves into a soft Vatican position.

Tony's Alfa Romeo was parked in front of the house. It was too late and too cold for any of the kids to be out crawling over it, working their protection racket. Tony was sitting alone by the little glowing fireplace. He looked as if someone had stunned him with a club, leaving him alive but numb. His eyes prowled over my face.

"Joyce," he said, "she's in the hospital."

"Oh Christ."

"I came back to pack some things for her."

"She's all right?"

"A hell of a husband gallivanting around town."

"Let's get to the hospital."

We named the little girl Shana; at my first sight of her I wasn't too impressed, but they said she would improve and in a few days she turned into a beautiful baby with that intense, innocent stare.

Joyce seemed happy and I said I was happy. But I wasn't. Tony got me to hire a nurse, a large Scotch woman named McDouglas, for Joyce and the baby when they were brought home, and he sent over pots of poplar roses and amaranth. I learned about motherhood; the devotion to the baby, its care, its welfare. Does it eat, does it spit up, why does it cry out—does it have gas in its tummy? And why does its navel look like a melon stem? The perfectability of those *so* tiny fingers and toes.

I set all this down because Joyce was fearful I'd go to

Spain and I was fearful I'd bolt and yet I was attached to my wife and child. Shana was a good baby, no more smelly than most, a good sleeper, a strong crier; Joyce fed her with her ample breasts. Watching the baby suckle I knew it would never be the same between me and Joyce. The old free days of comradeship, living loose, loving easy had been replaced by a new way of living, by a child and a new kind of love, a mother's.

Tony, missing his own children, was as attentive as a mother cat. There was something in him that I lacked, the Jewish father syndrome perhaps, a sense of the domestic.

"Why don't you all go home?" Tony asked me when the baby had a breathing problem suddenly in the middle of the night and we took turns holding her by the legs over a tub of steaming water.

Harry had been with us two months, bored by a baby in the house, fretting over some private dissatisfaction. Then one morning he was gone, along with his camera gear and one of our good suitcases. A note written in that sprawling, still-boyish handwriting:

Paul, gone to Spain, shipping on a Greek freighter to a French port, will take it from there. Best to you all and thanks for all you've done. I am grateful. Kiss Shana's butt for me.

I tried to trace him, seeking the route of the Greek ship *Hermes,* but no one knew her whereabouts. I suspected she was carrying contraband for either the Republic or the Fascists and had put in at some Spanish port.

Tony again insisted that I take Joyce and Shana back to the States. I said Joyce was English and had never been to the States, didn't care to go there. He said I was a selfish bastard and a lousy husband. I answered did he think he'd be a better one. And the way he looked at me and didn't say anything, I suddenly got the whole picture! The sonofabitch was in love with Joyce! A real French farce was taking place under my nose and I wasn't laughing. Everything wears out but domestic clichés.

I put it to Joyce while Shana slept in a basket in the courtyard. Joyce was cleaning carrots, preparing for supper. It felt a renewal of an old scene. It was like I had first seen her in Rome, me just arrived from Palestine, she snapping beans into the pot in her lap. Somehow that day seemed centuries ago. Now there was a kind of hidden rancor between Joyce and myself, the old audacity and verve were tamped down to a vague hostility, a curtain put up between us. Did she feel I would go to Spain after all, desert her and the baby on the spur of the moment? Was I sensing that she and Tony had made some sort of commitment? Worse of all, nothing was clearly defined; neither of us had spoken of this situation that now was coming to a climax. I had to talk it out.

"Joyce, this business with Tony, his interest, his always looking after you. What the devil is going on?"

She looked at me with a kind of derisiveness as if asking *what* are you saying, as if you were supercilious and out of your mind. No anguish, no confusion or guilt visible.

"You're out of your mind, Paul."

"He is fond of you. More. He acts like there's an emotional commitment."

"Fond, yes. More, no. I think this civil war business has addled your senses."

In some ways I had failed Joyce sexually. The conditions of our times, our lives had affected me; my emotions were in a chaotic turmoil and that didn't help my performance in bed. I seemed to have gotten a nearly

333

masochistic pleasure in knowing I was going to fail to pop off, or with no great satisfaction. Then your mind keeps hinting she isn't too interested in all this thrashing about. It's more like a hatha yoga exercise with her than a proper orgasm. Then again, maybe it's all apprehension, my imagination, going cockeyed.

One spring afternoon I was returning from an underground meeting in Naples dealing with a source to get six late-model French fighter planes out of Indo-China. On the taxi ride home, I enjoyed the spring weather when Rome shakes off its winter. In the courtyard, green was showing in the herb pots. I found no one in the studio nor in the rest of the place. Shana's folding crib was not in the patio. In panic I searched the place. Joyce's best things, her handbags, were missing. Left were only two pair of run-down shoes with worn heels, stockings with runs in them hanging over the tin bathtub. And a note written with a clear looping hand on a sheet from a sketch pad:

Paul dear, Tony is taking me and Shana to my people in England. What we'll do from there I don't know yet. There was really a change in us—you, me—after that massacre in the Hebron settlement. Then, me getting pregnant. I can't pinpoint the decline in our relationship. I suppose we changed emotionally, chemically. It was good, very good. Never forget that. What this parting is going to mean from now on I haven't fully figured out. Don't blame Tony. There was a psychological moment between you and me, some inner failure or challenge we couldn't handle. Be lucky in Spain. Joyce.

I couldn't fully figure out cause and effect. This kiss-off, this futility, the loss of so much. I found myself walking down a street, people going about their tasks or business. Why didn't they notice what had happened to me? Surely they must see grief, the despair written on my face. My wife, my child, my best friend. People laughed at the situation on the stage, in the movies; art vulgarizing life.

Sitting in the Comparetti Cafe near the Capitoline Museum where the Greek and Roman statues no longer appeal (how many times can you look at the dying Gaul—all he needs is surgery and iodine—or Cupid and Psyche at foreplay?), I waited, drinking black coffee, nibbling on hothouse grapes that were not too well cleaned of the sawdust they had been packed in. It was warm. I thought I was weathering the shock well; each inside has an outside, I mused (trying not to think of anything too involved), and the outside has streets, cities, fields; besides all that there is the moving of time present, carrying time past in its mouth by a tail and butting its nose into time future—all marked by night and day, and years of no Joyce. Joyce!

I made excuses for her. Dissimilar values, small slobbering habits. She was irritable from trying to live in the male world. Women have a lousy setup in our society.

How to explain the loss, or our first fascination? Perhaps it was a pathological illusion we shared. I remembered her inky hair loose and flowing around her head ("I'm thinking of bobbing it—everybody is"), her relaxed body magnificent under the sheets. She was not in herself anything mystical; she was an evocation of reality, not an idea.

Was. That would be the hard part: to accept *was* instead of *is*.

34

S.S.'s glass-topped desk ("not as large as a skating rink, said Lou Zucker, "but you could bowl on it,") held a silver Queen Anne pen-and-ink set, a red leather blotter and file initialed S.S., two phones, an intercom, an alabaster ashtray, and two silver-framed photographs—one of him, Nora, Harry, and Sari standing on the steps of the Capitol in Washington, also a picture of Harry and Sari, aged five, on their ponies. Otherwise his desk was kept clear but for the two daily trade papers, the *Hollywood Reporter* and *Daily Variety*, set down on the righthand side of his desk.

Lou Zucker looked at his watch, which he pulled from his waistcoat. "Getting that time, S.S."

Lou put down a dark, narrow jeweler's box on the desk. S.S. opened it and took out a string of pearls. He held it high to let the light catch the translucent beauty of the little globes.

"Think she'll like them, Lou?"

"Of course she'll like them."

S.S. looked at the picture of his two children on their ponies. "Imagine, Sari, sixteen. Jesus, the years travel by rocket. I remember Sari as a baby in her first pair of tiny shoes, trying to walk. Sweet sixteen. There will be two parties. Got this swinging band for them in the drawing room, and for the grownups on the terrace something more relaxing. You'll bring your aunt?"

"She wouldn't miss it. To see how the exploiters orgy."

He gazed at the necklace. "You think it's long enough?"

"The Tiffany man said you can add pearls to it from year to year." S.S. wrote a little note, put it with the pearls in the box, and snapped it shut.

The story conference began at 11:30 that morning. Six men and two secretaries were seated around a heavy teak table; the walls of the room were covered with posters of films Silverthorn World Pictures hoped would make them a great deal of money.

S.S. entered, flanked by Lou Zucker and Miss Minton, his chief secretary. He nodded to Sales, the director, film editor, ignored Story, Music, and Costume.

"All right, all right. Let's get to it," S.S. said. "We have to recut *Dames In Danger*. Can't use the word 'dame' in the title—the Hays Office said it's too aphrodisiac, also said no to the sailors' orgy—too much inner thigh and tits."

The new story editor, Gary Reeves, a recruit from the Theatre Guild in New York, picked up a looseleaf notebook. "Mr. Silverthorn—"

"Everybody calls me S.S. No 'Mr.' at SWP."

"Yes, sir, S.S. We're getting static on that picture we're shooting with a background of the war in Spain."

Lou Zucker said, "Oh, balls. It's not a war picture, it's a nice little romance between a crackerjack American reporter and a Spanish dancehall girl who rallies the people to defend their village against the enemy. What's the problem, Reeves?"

"No problem on the set," said the director.

Manton Black, sales head, doodled on the scratchpad before him. "It's that we're telling it from the Republican side. They're the good guys. We're picturing the enemy as the bad guys, killers of men and women and kiddies. Burning towns, bombing from the air without sense. War on civilians."

The director said, "Conflict, that's what makes movies."

S.S. said, "The *New York Times* doesn't lie. It's happening."

Reeves rifled through his notes. "It's been suggested by pious church pressure groups who don't support the Republic and its Stalinists' backing that we don't finish this picture. Chauvinism on both sides."

Manton Black finished a doodle of a shooting star and a cross-eyed nude. "There are millions of Christian moviegoers supporting Franco. Think of the market for this picture. We can lose in Italy, in South America. We can't show the Fascists as shits—pardon me, girls. Always, S.S., we gotta think of who buys the tickets."

S.S. shook his head. "We've put a million-two into the picture. It's in good taste. We cast it handsomely, rented the best uniforms from Western Costume. It's a good clean melodrama."

"No dice, S.S.," said Manton Black. "Two-thirds of our overseas market would be gone. We'll get *all* our pics barred in Italy, Ireland, Brazil, the Argentine. Maybe the Mexicans won't care but they can't even afford toilet paper."

S.S. looked at Reeves. "Mr. Story Editor, we maybe can make this a mythical kingdom. What the hell, the love story is solid. The spectacles look great."

The director said, "We're two days ahead of schedule."

Lou Zucker said, "You've seen the dailies, S.S. Spanish signs all over the place, Spanish costumes, castanets and flamingos—you can't call it 'Prisoner of Zenda Revisited.' The bullfight isn't lawn tennis; scrap a hundred thousand dollars we put into the bull ring stuff? All that Mexican location work?"

The director took a bit of a tobacco plug.

Reeves moved around the table. He was in the enemy camp and now he knew what scurrilous gossip had told him in New York was true: anything goes sour, they look for a whipping boy—duplicity and backstabbing is a way of life. He was new and untried, vulnerable. He said, "The solution is simple. We never identify either side by name or title. Let the public decide which side is the Loyalists, which is the Fascist side." He gazed around the table; all faces were expressionless, looking to S.S.

S.S. said slowly, "Reeves, you got a head on you. Lou, what do you think?"

"Ask the director."

Jasper Conrad, the director, had so far made only a few comments. He was a cagy old vet of films, chewed tobacco, had worked with Ince, Griffith, Lasky, clawed his way into becoming a trusted director of fast-paced action pictures. He had no political viewpoint, disliked dialogue in his pictures. He insisted motion pictures should move. Beyond a sense of grandeur in wild scenery and fast action, he had few ideas.

"Well, S.S., I don't give a shit—sorry girls—who wins in Spain, the commies or the fancy farts—sorry." He spit into the spittoon always set up for him. "Sure, we can just say 'the people' and 'the enemy.' We can cut some crappy talk. Maybe have to retake a few hundred feet where there are flags and insignia."

S.S. sat as in prayer, fingertips on his chin, head down, eyes closed. He lifted his head, opened his eyes. "Fair is fair. I hate to be pressured, but we're just part of the Lowitz Corporation. And, Conrad, it will still be an honest picture. I mean no downbeat brutal stuff, lots of love interest, talk of country, of the grape harvest,

340

the wine. Lots of comedy, soldier stuff. Two guys, rivals over one broad. 'What Price Glory' stuff. Yes, Reeves, good thinking, very good thinking."

Some secret liberal or commie fink in the studio gave a Bronx cheer as they all filed out, most to go for lunch at the racetrack. Thunder, the Silverthorn Stables' bay stallion, won—paid six to one.

As S.S. was waiting for his Rolls Royce to be brought up by the track's valet parking service and people were congratulating him on Thunder winning at such nice odds, he saw Nat Bendell and Laura just a few feet away on his right. He went over to them and exchanged greetings.

"Did you have my horse?" S.S. asked.

Nat, in racing tweeds, a porkpie hat, a huge pair of field glasses in a pale leather case, said, "Did I have him, S.S.? In spades. I had two five-hundred-dollar tickets on him to win. Never mind show and place just to win. Laura, she had a dog."

Laura smiled. "I use the hatpin method of picking a horse. I stick a hole in a program. My pin wasn't very smart."

"She played Seaside. S.S., you gotta get Thunder to the Derby. A shoo-in."

"We'll see, we'll see. Nat, could I have a word? Pardon me, Laura."

Laura nodded, looking over the crowd pouring out to find their cars. It was a Friday. She remembered Malka and Aaron and the Friday night service in Atlantic City she attended—"The Sabbath is a bride, the twilight, the wedding hour."

Malka had written to Nat:

    Aaron is ailing, growing weaker. He is tired and
sits thinking. He so wanted to see Jerusalem, also

341

he would like to see you both, the new generations, he says; I try not to think. In God's hands
we rest our faith. May I go first. Thank you for
the box of oranges—so much tastier, more juice
than the ones from the A&P.

S.S. was talking very low and Nat was listening now
and then shaking his head.

"I know, Nat, the studios have to pay out *smeer*. But
rachmonous, pity. That goddamn chowderhead Benblow—his Laborers and Studio Crafts union is milking
us."

"He's got clout, the goons, S.S. What's the bite?"

"He wants thirty grand—not to call a strike, just as
we're putting out our biggest pictures."

Nat looked over the departing crowd, waved at a city
councilman, at a police court judge, Madame Francis
(the well-known madame), a building contractor. "It's
too big a bundle. I'll talk to some of the people and
we'll hose Benblow down. What if I get it down to say
twelve, fifteen g's?"

"If I have to, I have to, Nat."

"You have to. Big changes in labor, no more gar-
ment district Yid unions. It's all strong-arm *goyem*. The
boys are locked in on the waterfront. You can't move a
fishhead until it's cleared. Auto factories, trucking,
processing, all ponying up. Play it safe so they don't
burn the studio and I'll keep the ante down for you."

"Jesus, at least they have somebody like you, Nat,
with sense to talk things over. Anything personal I can
do . . ."

"Nothing, S.S. After all, it's sort of all in the family,
eh? Oh, we got the horse-room wire service, track results on the nose. You ever want to put a big packet on
a horse and want it laid off so it doesn't get out and
spoil the odds; just say."

"I'll keep it in mind. How are the folks?"

"Papa is sinking, I think. I'll have to go East and cheer him up. He yells I'm a bum, a no-good—that cheers him up." Nat firmed his jaw line. "I wish I were half the man he is. He never sold out, never chiseled or double-timed anyone. Never rooked a soul. And he's still a Jew, I mean the old-fashioned kind, you know, S.S. All the way, not half-assed temple crapouts like the rest of us."

"These are different times, Nat. And don't give up on the old man. Modern medicine can do miracles."

Laura came to their side. "Our car is here."

S.S. said, "Let's have dinner sometime soon. Not tonight. I have to be back at the studio. We're filming a really great war picture."

The siege of Madrid went on with the heavy German and Italian guns doing damage to historic streets. The Russian "advisers" shot any man who failed to hold his position. As Harry Silverthorn found when he arrived at the Madrid headquarters of the Fifth Regiment of the International Brigades, the Soviets were as dangerous to the Loyalists almost as the Carlists from Navarra. They were eliminating many socialists, anarchists, anyone suspected of being a member of the *anarco sundicalismo*.

The H.Q. at Velezquez 63 was active; unswept halls, tangles of wiring, boarded-up windows. A thin dark girl at a desk ignored Harry in his crumpled uniform of blue cloth, his dusty beret. She at last put aside the party paper, *Mundo Obrero*, and said after a glance at his papers, speaking in English:

"You are *Ingles*?"

"*Americano.*" He handed over a green card that had been given him when he joined the International Brigades in Paris.

"It says you are a *cameraman*." She gave him a searching look. "So where are the *cameras*?"

"I had my camera gear stolen when I was on a ship going to France. And here it's impossible to replace what I had."

Several wounded men were walking in through the door with the cracked glass, shouting, "*Salud, camaradas!*"

The girl stood up, shouted, "*Salud, compadres!*" She sat down. "Very sad. Valladolid and Avila have fallen. So, why do you want to see General Em?"

"I knew him in Italy."

"He is very busy."

Harry watched some stretcher cases being carried in. The wounded lay silent, Harry thought, like the meat in a repellent butcher shop on Pismo Beach in California. He took a letter from inside his jacket. "This is from General Em asking me to come here."

The girl said, "All letters should be cleared by a commissar." She turned her head and yelled in agitation, "Pablo!"

A short, stocky boy of fifteen or sixteen who had been seated on a bench rolling a cigarette in a bit of newspaper rose and came over. A tooth was missing; his uniform showed heavy creases.

The girl spoke in Spanish and Pablo nodded and said in broken English, "You foller me, I Americano too, Mehiko City."

"Close enough," said Harry. The girl blinked myopically and waved them off.

General Em's section had guards armed with machine guns. After passing two inspections Harry was shown into what must have been at one time, judging by the mirrors, a private dining room. Behind a table covered with a green cloth sat a wide-shouldered, brown-bearded man in a neat uniform with no insignia. He was staring meditatively at a map spread on the table.

Pablo said, "General, sir, a recruit sent by Paris." A sloppy salute and Pablo turned and went out.

"Well, Harry," said the general, looking up. "Come to see a war?"

"Been trying, Moses."

"Em," said the brown-bearded man. "General Em."

"Sorry. There seems to be some mixup about putting me in with the international brigades."

The phone rang. General Em shouted into it, "No! *El hijo de le gran puta.*" He hung up and turned to Harry.

"You see, it's a prickly situation. The Abraham Lincoln Brigade has suffered big losses near Estremadura. It's made up of earnest, idealistic kids like you who saw too many Gary Cooper movies. We feel you should be with them. Some of the early units are coming apart like a boiled pullet."

"I'd rather be with the International. I've lived in Europe a lot, speak German, French, fair Spanish."

General Em got up, walked to a map tacked to a wall, ran his finger along a red ink line. He was an imposing figure in the well-cut uniform, the heavy black pistol belt holding a cased Luger, the boots shined to a high polish.

The general turned. "Maybe the Cordovo front. Our brigades aren't kids with dreams in their eyes. Lots of workers, Jews driven out by Hitler, German radicals, Italian exiles with years of underground work and street fighting. Brigade Commander Wagner was in the Spanish Foreign Legion."

The building shook, dust fell from a cracked ceiling; thuds of explosives came from the streets.

General Em looked at his wrist watch. "Five o'clock

345

bombers. German Dorniers D17s, big Luftwaffe stuff. Always come before cocktail hours at the Hotel Florida. I'll put you into Wagner's section."

"Thanks, Mo—General."

"How's your uncle?"

"Uncle Paul? He's in Paris. I'm not supposed to say why."

The general gave a short snorting laugh. "He's working out the smuggling of planes and pilots for the Republic. Good idea to keep your mouth shut." He waved off an officer who came in after one knock with a batch of papers. "Not now, Feldmann." He waited till the door was closed. "This is no holy war of heroes. Franco has everything; we have little. Worst of all, the Republic is not united. The Russians rule the roost. They're by the book, Leninism, Stalinism, strangling any group they object to. The French Communists are led by a madman. The anarchists are our best soldiers. They tell the Russos to go fuck themselves."

He looked at his watch again. "I'll have your orders sent to the Chicoles Cafe in an hour. You can get anis there. A good drink. Pablo will go with you. He's helped blow a train at Arevalo, he knows the ropes."

General Em held out his hand. "Good luck, Harry." And as an afterthought, he added softly, "*Ein k'eloh-eynu.*"

The cafe was crowded, the atmosphere thick from tobacco and heated olive oil. There were soldiers, some bandaged, in various uniforms, drinking wine, eating, trying to impress the waitresses or some women in military shirts and caps. From a corner came the whine of a piano-accordion.

A fat soldier with a patch over one eye offered Harry a glass of wine. "*Salud y cojones!*"

"*Salud.*"

346

The wine was tart and strong. The accordion was playing Schumann's "Arabesque."

"Russo?" asked the fat soldier.

"No. Americano."

"Olé! You want to go to the whores? All fine loyal whores." He made an obscene gesture with fist and fingers.

Harry said no, he was going to the front. Harry was served a stew that was called kid; he wondered if it weren't cat. Pablo came in carrying his machine gun over one shoulder.

"So we go soon as get dark. Two squads, guide get us out. Don't eat that. Come eat at the Gran Via."

"It doesn't look like goat."

"Don't ask what is it."

"I won't," said Harry.

They went out arm in arm.

In the next six months, Harry became a front-liner soldier with the Fifth Regiment of the International Brigade. He learned to talk foul, drink what he could find, eat anything he could swallow. He saw death at his side, the entrails of men he had just been talking to dangling on a fence. He walked a lot, sweated in fear under heavy burdens, rode in springless trucks, wandered in the night of an attack, saw dead Falagists, also found civilians Franco had shot in the village squares or bull rings—men, women, any schoolteacher intellectual, unionists, radicals, suspected leftwingers. A priest, Harry was told, gave last rites and stood by as the firing squads chopped down the population. Few prisoners were taken by either side. Moors were carrying ears on strings. *Guardias civiles* got short shift. Harry wondered how swift or cruel his own death would be.

35

Dear Uncle Paul:

No, I'm not wounded. Dreadful weather kept
the German and Italian planes grounded and not
bombing us during our last offensive, but I got a
sore throat and then pneumonia and have two
weeks of touch and go. You can imagine the shortage of drugs and also doctors.

You were right on the nose in Rome about war.
It's all a damn fuckup. I've had my gut full. I
dream it every night. There we were, thousands of
us moving up in trucks along potholed goat trails
in clouds of yellow dust, deploying for the attack.
We had the shit beat out of us at G—, heavy
losses, but we fight.

Mostly German Jews, Marxist workers in exile,
my squad and three others go on over very rough
land, past houses with no roofs, dead dogs in
wells. In thickets you find old dead and on the
ridge new dead. The sun burns off the mist but it
will rain again soon. We feed on rotten anchoas
and cold arroz.

My squad (I don't use their real names—it's
dangerous) has been together now for two
months. Six losses, four replacements. We look

like scarecrows and talk of leave to a big city, a hot bath, clean clothes, and maybe a girl to oblige a soldier. An attack is not as in a movie charge. We move slowly, coming up around dead mules, a stalled .75 gun. There is blasting, shell fire, from a high hill, and down goes Drippy, our squad clown, playing with a short deck since the hell of the last attack, when he was buried for two days under half a church. There is a gush of bright blood, then he folds up like a jackknife and his heels do a fast drum beat in the yellow dust. Soon he dies with the blue, star-shaped shell fragment in his right eye. I step over him, and my chum Cherry-nose makes the sign of the cross and follows in my footsteps. My eyes are dry. Pity is too precious to waste on death. We just hitch at our guns.

The captain chews on his cigar and the hard corners of his mouth grow even harder. He and Drippy ran a taxi stand in Naples. Also, his only sister is now a widow with two little girls.

We bunch up as we think of Drippy's end, but Yellow Trenchcoat, our sarge, who was twenty years a sergeant in the French Foreign Legion, cursing, orders us to spread out. The swearing does us good. We swear back from dry mouths, go on slowly, wondering who is next.

At the edge of the green woods, right beside the two dead white horses, we receive three hand grenades each and clip them on over our growling stomachs. Ahead it's as if all Spain were on fire. The captain lights a new cigar and Yellow Trench-coat's red beard glows as they bend their heads over watches and nod with polite bobbing of heads across the swelling horses. Big Stomach rubs the only steel helmet in the group. He swiped it from a poor dying Italian boy upon whom the hill dogs had been nibbling for days. He smiled when Big Stomach, with delicate mercy, pumped two Luger slugs into his face and then took his steel helmet. Big Stomach chews the corner of a moldy square of gray chocolate and offers me some.

I shake my head and duck as the whine of a German air engine sounds beyond the yellow-rusted cypress trees. From long experience we bounce down in the roadside grass, watch the calm, fast movements of the captain as he and Yellow Trenchcoat point the thin nose of the machine gun skywards. We don't have long to wait.

There is the crunch and zizz of an incendiary bomb as the yellow trees bow in flames. Straight across the sun flash the polished wings of a German airship—big, black, and fast; two strafing guns pour fast-spinning belts of bullets down on us. Our machine guns answer without much hope of a hit. The plane comes lower and I feel the thuds as foreign slugs dig deep little graves in the soil of Spain. Down our whole earth-hugging rows glides the plane and, like a watering can, sprays us in garden formation. We do not answer. Only new troops take the trouble to return the fire with their rifles.

The planes pass. A red-haired boy—some say that he came from Holland—is choking in a deep rut. Pink foam comes from his mouth and his chest is moth-eaten with holes. "Ave Maria Purisima."

To keep from showing my feeling I think of my home in Bel Air, S.S. floating in the swimming pool, Sari and I kicking each other off the diving board and the butler announcing lunch. I imagine a roast turkey, Beef Wellington, shrimp in dill, blueberry pie.

So dies the Hollander as he gurgles like a Turkish water pipe. We can do nothing. His own blood in his lungs is drowning him.

A little brown man cheerfully holds up a red-ribboned paw and trots quickly to the rear. We watch him with a tight pain in our throats and decide that in twenty lucky minutes he will be back in the village. We pray for a light wound and finger our cartridge belts.

We hurry on—and a strange song sings in my ears. A tank gutted by fire blocks our path. We walk around it. The seared torso of its lone crew lies beside it. The dead are thicker now and all lie on their backs and watch the sky. The wounded whimper among the bushes, and far up the road, a horse screams in pawing pain and comes toward us. We split apart and it drags past us, frothing pink and white.

A man retches into the ditch and suddenly the captain yells, "Fix bayonets. Double time, my *gringuita*! We take the hill ahead and hold it until the 75's come up. No stragglers."

Yellow Trenchcoat reloads his Mauser and growls at us, "Keep noggins down, your bayonets in front. If you're hit, stay down."

The cruel coolness of bare steel steadies my hands. I feel silly as beads of sweat run down my sun-stained nose and I wish for water.

I wonder, Uncle Harry, how it was in your war?

A whistle sounds, piping against the full volume of shellings. The hills loom ahead, but I see nothing except heat-hazed shrubbery and high up, the angry spit of machine guns nested with great cunning to flay all who approach. We walk faster now, remembering old deaths and past battles. Soon we are running, and from our rasped throats there is a wordless shouting grunt—half laugh, half snarl—that none of us seems able to repeat later on in calmer moments. My feet push the ground behind me and I keep going, leaning way over, sweating until it burns down my torso from my armpits. My mouth is wide open and I scream—but I hear nothing. Up ahead the office chatter of friendly typewriters sound, and I know I'm walking into machine guns. I keep going, yelling, running—all the others do the same. The crackle of my companions surrounds me. All keep going forward. Why? Because trained line soldiers go forward on orders—without reason.

Two men go down on my right. One throws arms high in cheerleader style and glides down like a ballet dancer finishing a difficult routine. The other is suddenly stopped with a slug that grunts into him, and turning quickly, surprise in his wide blue eyes, he hits the ground with a heavy thud, turns over on his back, and eyes the sky, slack-mouthed. All seem to die on their backs. I make up a game. I hunt for a dead man lying on his face. I see none.

Suddenly I find myself hovering over a machine gun nest tucked into a brown leaf-strewn hole. Three men in coal-pail helmets lie in a small, stale hole, caressing a water-cooled machine gun. Their dirty red fingers coax the belts of bullets into the clattering steel tool and keep up a steady burst against my friends. I flex all over. I am calm now.

I tug a grenade from my belt. The metal ring tastes salty in my mouth as I pull the firing pin and release it. I slowly count to four—then, with a wide, walloping heave, I throw, and grind my whole being into the soft ground until my face is mashed deep in the dusty mold. I smell decay, the sweet stench of shallow graves.

Crimson earth is showering down on me and I wish it would bury me; then I could sleep like the Babes in the Woods. All is over, except the heavy sharpness of smoke.

A scream floats over and I am on my knees peering ahead. The nest of the three gunners is gone. The gun is gone. Only a few pink shreds of flesh are seen and the dirty face, deeply freckled, of a long-armed torso. Legs? There are none—only bloody rags. The Thing lifts itself up on its arms and the red mouth screams at me. I come in fast, bayonet first, and aim at the throat. I gag but push the steel home and down with a professional twist of the wrist. The steel flicks out bright rusted. Life seems simple. Kill or be killed.

I throw the rest of my bombs. Far ahead I see the yellow trenchcoat of my sergeant darting in wild glee among gun barrels. Demons yell around me and I yell back, pour flames down on flushed faces in a shallow trench. They swallow fire and sag down to the ground. Tanks, small ones like mailed nervous whippets, come toward us. We go down gasping and wait as they clank like cheap iron pots. Big Stomach reaches for pint bottles of gasoline and winks. He yells at me and laughs. I grin back and nod. Big Stomach is a card—and an antitank expert, self-taught.

Big Stomach stands up and thumbs short, stubby fingers to a broad, pock-marked nose, wriggling his pinkie with glee. A tank glides toward him. He roars with joy. He is very happy; his mirth is almost beyond control. With perfect calm, he throws three bottles under the tank. The glass flashes in shattered fragments in the sun's rays and

354

then Big Stomach throws a nicely controlled bomb and we all stop and wait.

The tank disappears in a blinding roar of flame. It rears back and plops down and opens like an oyster as the flames engulf it. Two men, banging fire out of their hair, are propelled from the tank, and Big Stomach grins and calmly shoots them down with two expert tosses of his Luger. We hate tanks—we see something unfair in their use. We make no move to stop Big Stomach.

A shell hits very close and I fly through the air. Am I dead?

Blood sings in my ears; my lungs flap air like a fresh-caught trout. I can even feel the bite of sour wine from my last meal. Every little nerve stands on end and begs for attention.

For a dead man I am *very* much alive. The world is a red daze of fire and nothing seems to be in focus. Little brown leaves float lazily down on me as the shears of yellow gunfire clip them in ragged patterns and peel the twigs until the pale green of the underbark shows.

I feel my arms, rub my face, with dainty care; I explore my torso and the soft dimples of my numb stomach. The legs are solid and no red seepage announces any wound. The shell was close, but not close enough. I get up and stagger on toward the fighting. Why, I do not know.

An acrid wind strikes me and the sun draws blinking tears from my eyes that taste salty in the tight corners of my mouth. The top of the hill at last. Cadavers lying about—and I find one at last on his stomach. He doesn't count; a tank has flattened him out.

That night we move around everything—even the soup kitchens—to mass for a counterattack.

"We're just a shell here and nothing covering our arse, so keep your eyes open. Those damned Moors move like Indians."

Yellow Trenchcoat drains the last drop from the pale green bottle and heaves it into a corner. He gives us a short salute, sets fire to a small yellow cigarette stub.

We sit in the barn and under the clear moon play scat with a limp deck of cards that we know by feel. This is just as well, as the faces are only oily blots.

Far down the road a dog barks at the moon. The guttural echos of his howls come back from the grim hills. Someone kicks the dog without kindness and the night is quiet again, except for the heels of the gun mules testing their walls and the singsong of crickets deep in old habits.

We sit—dirty, unshaved soldiers, Jews, Christians, Marxists, inebriated by food, deep in conversation. Overhead the stars are bright and we wonder, over the picked chicken bones and the bottles, why the enemy fliers are missing the chance of a lifetime to give us a few stingers. The cards glide. The night is gay, and we are comfortable.

The kicked dog whines in self-pity; a light wind tosses leaves in a silky rustle over the earth. The burned ribs of the white town are bathed in moonglow and shadows, and dynamic compositions that remind me of the Picasso show I saw in Paris about three thousand years ago.

A week later, leaving our dead unburied, in retreat. I am at M—with lungs full of water and the nurse asks in a whisper, do I want a priest? I say, can she make it a rabbi?, and the poor peasant woman clutches the brass cross around her neck

356

and from the look of horror on her face and the way I laugh I know I am not going to die.

There is a shortage of everything—machine guns, tanks, food, men too, and I shall be back in the fighting soon, I'm sure. It's going badly. I am now one of the old ones in the brigade; it and the others have been cut to fragments.

I keep thinking of home, of Los Angeles, and Mom and Sari and my old man, the great S.S. They show tattered, scratched versions of his movies to us. And I think a lot also of Uncle Ira, imagine him married *and* the father of a baby! Mail is rare, but Aunt Laura wrote. Morale has slipped badly here and there is a lot of the use of the wall and the blindfold by the *maldito malcriadios*. You can get your ass rammed if you recite the wrong slogan . . . General Em met a firing squad after a short trial.

A pal of mine I met here at the hospital base is going acros the border tonight, so I hope this letter gets through to you.

The snotty kid,
H.

36

The depression was finally over, S.S. proclaimed in an interview after the opening of his most costly musical motion picture, *Good Times of 1939*.

"People want to forget the lousy years, want to laugh, enjoy themselves. There's enough trouble in the world what with the Germans and the Soviets signing that nonaggression pact. Imagine Hitler and Stalin lying down together in the same bed. But I have to go home. It's my daughter Sari's engagement party. Just a little celebration, mostly family, friends. The studio publicity department will give you details and pics."

Riding home in the silver-colored Rolls Royce, S.S. felt satisfaction, even if part of the plenitude of his youth was gone. He'd have to take off his paunch, exercise more; maybe fifty pushups mornings, cut down on the cigars. Women? Well, they didn't matter much anymore. Their fascination demanded too much effort and time.

He didn't worry over that as much as the dealings in the stocks of SWP. It had skyrocketed, and he had reaped a fortune, selling off twenty percent of his holdings; he'd buy back when it dropped in price. But what if the *momzers* at Lowitz Corporation and their lawyers and relatives were buying to diminish his control of the studio?

He felt assured. They couldn't replace him; no one else could run the place, produce seventy pictures a year. All production at SWP was under his control; the directors, producers knew who ran the studio, were aware of the successful policy he had perfected for the building of stars. "Names sell pictures, sex bunnies, mysterious sirens, tall leading men who were walking cocks. And the popular homey pictures of the good American life in small towns, picket fences and acne-free teenagers who are thrilled taking a girl out for an ice cream soda and Ma baking apple pies."

S.S. wasn't cynical. He wished life were that pure, simple.

Profits were up and he still got a kick out of a well-made picture; it made him love films the more. He would often recut a picture, order reshooting, replace a star with another star just to prove to his producers he knew what was what, to show that S.S. was top man and ruled by his abilities, not just by bureaucratic procedure. The studio, with a little jockeying, had won fifteen Acadamy Awards in the last four years. He'd have a few himself if he ever took credit as a producer. But he kept his name off all the picture production credits; just the name Silverthorn World Pictures *before* the titles.

He thought of his daughter Sari, of her engagement to Arthur Bogenstein. As Nora had said, "Thank God he's Jewish, from a good family and Orthodox."

Sari, tight little breasts, sophisticated mouth, had gone up to Mills and studied biology, sang in the glee club, joined the Sierra Club. She had though of studying medicine. But ugh! Cutting cadavers. She was a well-built girl with the features Nora had made famous as a European actress before her marriage. There was a radiant, tranquil quality about her, S.S. thought, and wished he knew her better. As an adolescent Sari had liked horses and dogs, not dolls, drove her own car at fourteen. For six months she had studied ballet with Nijinsky's widow and was told she was too tall. This led to a period of austerity and dedication to the cure of homeless city animals. In a secret diary she mooned over Leslie Howard, Robert Taylor. At Mills Sari got good marks. She was amazed to discover in chemisty class that the universe is a vast, rolling mass of organized gases and rocks. It left out too much. God was more than hydrogen. So she attended the Friday night Jewish services in a high school gym nearby. There was also some gratification in having a friend, Stella, a basketball hotshot from Nebraska. But when it came to hugging and kissing she wondered—and when one night camping out in Yosemite on a field trip to study rock formations Stella came into the tent and moved to a little clit-bumipng, Sari withdrew in horror and went to sleep in the camper.

The Friday night services at the high school were directed by Arthur Bogenstein. He was a young Hebrew seminary student about to be graduated as a rabbi—Conservative, not an Orthodox as Nora claimed. He could justify *Ketz hayamin* and Maimonides.

Arthur was too thin, too pale, his features delicate but for a strong nose and long jaw line.

When Sari, showing an interest in *kashrut* (kosher), offered to drive him to San Francisco where he was assisting in a temple, he seemed pleased, then worried. He was not a city boy; his family were farmers, grew tomatoes and melons in the Imperial Valley.

"Miss Silverthorn, I'm twenty-four and I admit I fear young women. They expect one to participate in their world. I'm no prig—and my emotions are human."

"Golly, you a sex maniac, rabbi?"

"Not yet a rabbi. And no, I'm normal and it's disquieting to look at your legs."

"You should see my mother's."

She didn't know if he was square or ironic and she settled on ironic.

Once he accepted her he showed he had a good sense of humor, even if a bit scholarly. Mostly he had a strong belief in his faith.

The third time she drove him to San Francisco they hugged and kissed, and she nuzzled against him and was pleased to discover the expert on Rashi script had an erection. Next day Arthur wrote her a letter:

> Dear Miss S: I do not think we should meet again. I have a great deal to do, a long way to go. I aim to find a small-town temple that needs a young rabbi. My mind myst stay on the Torah and the Talmud rather on the friendship of someone near my own age. Temptations directed by a disquieting mind can be mischievous, distracting. "In the house of the righteous is much treasure but in the avenues of the wicked is trouble."
>
> A. Bogenstein

Sari sensed at once this was no letter of parting but a love letter. She went to a shop that catered to the Orthodox pious on Sutter Street and bought a large and expensive prayer shawl.

"Young lady, a *tallis*," said the old man in the skull cap, "so now to match a set—*tefilim,* the phylacteries, and a royal King Solomon red velvet bag to carry them, with a genuine gold thread in a pair of Lions of Judah."

It cost Sari two months allowance, and the sale of her radio.

She sent the gifts to Arthur with a note:

> Goodbye. Get yourself a little fat wife. Only married rabbis get a good congregation. It is better

we don't meet again. "And if a stranger sojourn with thee in your land, ye shall not vex him."

She got that line from the Book of Leviticus in a copy of the school's edition of *The Bible, Designed to be Read As Living Literature.*

Sari dreamed that night she was in the Garden of Eden and was nude but for her first pair of nylon stockings (the first on the market). Arthur was facing her, also nude and no fig leaf. The Snake, not at all frightening, was singing "Roll Out the Barrel."

She came awake as she and the young rabbi were about to make love. She sighed, tossed around, then had a pleasant little affair with herself, a lovely coming, and slept until her alarm clock gave its shrill warning that it was twenty minutes to her first class, French II.

Arthur was waiting for her as she came out after the class, his rust-colored hair in disorder, his eyes a bit bloodshot and with a kind of baffled stare. Under one arm he carried her gift package badly re-tied.

"Now look, this is a crazy whacked-out thing." He grabbed an arm as she walked on head up, buttocks taut.

"It's not whacked out. It's a prayer shawl and little black holy boxes."

"I can't take these things." He tried to push the package under her arm.

"They're kosher, aren't they? I mean, we don't go in much for this at home and I'm not sure."

"I haven't worn them. They'll take them back."

"Help me, A. Bogenstein, I need faith." She laughed. "What a way to sign your love letter: 'A. Bogenstein'."

"It wasn't . . . Sari, what is to become of us?" His puzzled graimace turned into a sad smile.

"Get married, you dope. To think of a sin is as bad as doing it. It says so in the Book of Judges."

363

"It is?"

"No, I made it up. If I'm to be a rabbi's wife you better instruct me."

"You said I should pick a fat one."

He looked around him at the hurrying students, at a group of girls sucking on ice cream cones on the steps of the library. He dropped the package, it fell open, and he turned red-faced as he Sari bent to recover the sacred items and repack them. He took her to lunch in a dairy-food eating place near the Golden Gate Bridge that smelled of cheese and sour cream and he said never again to put cream in her coffee after a meat meal, and to shun lobster and crab, also her favorite, bacon and tomato sandwiches.

They met several times a week and while they were passionate and exploratory to a thrilling, disquieting point, he said he would feel polluted, a disgrace as a rabbi, if he penetrated her. She said they had better announce their engagement.

"Do you have wet dreams, darling?"

He recited to her as they stood on the step of a Market Street cable car going uphill:

> " 'And, behold, there met he a woman
> with the attire of a harlot, and wily of heart,
> She is clamorous and willful.' "

"Old hat. My father, S.S., used those lines in his movie: *Vamp of the Nile*."

"He sounds like a profane man. I look forward to meeting him."

Actually S.S. took to Arthur at their first meeting, called him Artie, offered him a cigar, which Arthur smoked with relish and decided he must not accept any more—he would become an addict to costly tobacco. He was dedicated to a simple, pious life, he told himself over the Silverthorn prime roast and the potato pancakes the French chef had made for him ("Jew food").

The formal engagement of his only daughter, S.S. dicided, would be in April and the wedding in June. The sooner the better. There was an ache in him thinking of Sari in a bridegroom's bed, but every father had to face it, he admitted, as in *Our Daughter*, a film that had been a disappointment at the box office but expressed what S.S. felt about fathers and daughters.

Lou Zucker had once said to him: "You know, S.S. your thoughts and ideas, you make a picture of them, your feelings. It's your way of taking off your clothes before the camera."

S.S. thought of that remark of Lou's as his Rolls Royce came up to the gate of his Bel Air estate, the pedimented portico, the balustrated wing. The chauffeur pressed the radio control signal on the panel of the car and the gates sprung open as the message reached them. It was a new gadget and S.S. loved gadgets.

As the Rolls Royce rolled up the blue stone drive a radio signal closed the gates behind them. S.S. grinned. There had been a hell of a hassle over those gates.

The Columbia Broadcasting System, in its insolence, complained that the Silverthorn radio gates were on the same wave length as their local broadcasts; they were getting program interference every time the gates were opened and closed. What could be done about that? a vice president had written.

S.S. had answered in ink across the face of the CBS letter:

CBS should change its wave length.

Of course after the FCC got into the act and made threatening gestures, he did have the signal changed. But he had enjoyed the whole episode.

There were florist trucks on the service drive; the caterers (kosher, for Arthur's parents were Orthodox

Hasidics) were moving in trays and covered crates. Trucks were unloading extra chairs and folding tables. The sun with its infallible instinct was setting in the west. He enjoyed coming home from the studio early to stand on the terrace of this French chateau (touched by Teutonic gloss to look over the city. This screwed-up dream city that he loved, that he had seen grown in its own spontaneous, daffy way. He once had interviewed William Faulkner about a screenplay assignment and had been amused by the boozy bastard's remark about Los Angeles: "Los Angeles is the plastic asshole of the world."

S.S. went indoors and saw that tables were being set, cloths unfolded, chairs moved about. There was the scent of cut flowers, that funeral parlor odor he detested. No matter how fresh the flowers, they always seemed to start dying once they were delivered. He went upstairs to his room and latched the door from the inside. Nora, Sari, her school chum house guests, were most likely going through that routine of dressing, undressing, trying on, lamenting, giggling, and horsing around. A hell of a cute idea for a movie.

His valet Waldo was some place downstairs helping open the wine crates. Not that he minded having a valet, and Waldo was not one of the worst; you had to have a valet if you were in a certain studio bracket. Besides, Waldo had once been Ronald Colman's valet; he knew how to shine a shoe properly and could give critical appraisal of a house guest's evening clothes or handle an indiscreet phone call from some drunken woman making incongruous demands.

S.S. slipped out of his shoes, waistcoat, jacket. He had long ago discarded shoes that needed shoelaces. He preferred shoes one could toss off one's feet without bending over to untie.

On his night table were six scripts, a silver thermos, a

gold Waterman fountain pen, and a pad of pale blue paper. Sometimes when the pressure was and he couldn't sleep, an idea would come to him, what star to ire, what story to buy, even an idea of his own for a ilm plot.

He reclined on the big bed, fly unzipped, hands be-ind his head, and thinking of his daughter Sari's party, he slept. He didn't dream logically, just images rushing by, spinning like wings of great birds, brushing him with their feathers. No sense to it, no relationship to anything real, just a haunting flow of patterns.

37

The Japanese lanterns strung all along the drive were glowing congenially as the first guests arrived. Harry and Paul came in a taxi from the airport, Paul complaining of coast-to-coast air travel; it would have to be much improved to rival the Santa Fe *Super Chief*.

Harry looked fit, tanned. He was working as the European editor for SWP Newsreels. The small v-shaped scar on his left cheek, some war injury from Spain, was visible only when he was angry or excited.

"The house, Paul, it's still a goddamn absurdity, but it's home and they have to let me in."

The butler and one of the maids greeted Harry, as Paul put it, "as though he were the young master returned from the Trojan wars."

"Why not?" Harry asked. "Let's find some drink."

He and his uncle found a tray of bottles in S.S.'s den. "I suppose some day half of all this will be mine."

"You can't auction off a family."

Paul was examining a wall of awards and family pictures.

"Harry, you didn't know your grandfather, old Alex. He got to Boston from Russia in 1894, escaping with your father Sidney and my mother Rose and her sister Tissa. It was a mean struggle. Now just look around you. S.S. started it all by believing people would enjoy watching pictures move on a bed sheet."

369

"Well, immigrants weren't welcome on the board of Standard Oil or DuPont or General Motors, so he made movies."

Harry, sipping brandy, examined a yellowed-creased photograph on the wall. "Did my father really look like a dandy: spats, cane, even a head of hair?"

"Sidney was what they called a dude, a sport in those days. Taken when he was knocking out two-reel movies on the rooftops of New York in 1912 and fighting off Thomas Edison's goons trying to smash his cameras."

"Why?"

"Edison claimed all patents, and if anyone built a camera, he'd smash it. S.S. was a brawler in those days. Take on any two men in a saloon."

"Did he really break with grandfather Alex because some girl he was in love with was shot?"

"Jesus, no," said Paul, "that's all cockeyed. Sidney was in love with this Irish girl, Mary Katherine Corey, and they were running away because their families frowned on mixed marriages. Their car was in a smash-up in a storm and the girl was killed. Your father never forgave her family, or his. Not like today's acceptance. I hear the groom is to be a Hasidic rabbi. They used to be considered crazy people, the Hasidim, dancing with joy in their love of God."

S.S. himself came in, a bit of sleep still on his features.

"Just had a catnap. So the flying machine works. Didn't expect you here so soon."

He embraced his son, kissed his cheek, then put an arm around Paul. "Nora and Sari will be plased to see you. We don't have too much family out here. So act like a crowd."

"I didn't bring any present," said Paul. "It was a last-minute idea that I come out with Harry."

"You want to change? The show starts in about an

370

hour and a half. You know the food is all kosher to-night, a hell of a problem. Arty's folks are Hasidim, and would you believe it, farmers?"

He poured himself a brandy.

"I believe it," said Harry. "Paul is trying to sneak a batch of them from Poland into Palestine, past the British blockade."

"Did you get newsreel footage of it?" S.S. looked over his shoulder as he pressed soda into his brandy.

"Yes, Dad, I did. It's not very cheerful. Can I bust in on Sari, Mom?"

"Go right up. They're dressing, have been for hours. Want to direct a feature picture for me?"

Harry smiled. "No thinks." He went out.

S.S. turned to Paul. "I think that crazy little war in Spain has churned up Harry's brains a bit."

"It wasn't a crazy little war. It was a massacre of a million people and here you all sat on your hands and let it happen."

"Please, Paul, don't be petulant, not on my daughter's engagement. I gave for the Loyalist Ambulance Fund, Milk for Spanish refugee children."

"And made that dreaful false movie in which . . ."

S.S. scowled, then smiled. "I don't provoke over that. We lost a bundle on it, so why rub in salt? The Hays Office fucked it up for us. You'll stay here and I'll introduce you to some well-stuffed rich Heebs and you can milk them for the refugee ships."

"Ships that Roosevelt turned back off the coast of Florida. Most of those people drowned."

"Politics, you wouldn't understand, the pressures, the crap you have to swallow to get things done."

"That may be . . ." There was a tap on the door and Nora came in. She looked remote, as usual, but splendid in a tight-fitting pale lemon gown that showed off her ample figure. After greeting, kissing, she said,

371

"Come out, stop drinking. The guests are arriving. Sidney, keep the young people away from the bar."

"A little booze can't hurt them with their crazy dances and songs—'A Tisket, a Tasket' and 'Jeepers Creepers'."

Actually the orchestra at that moment was playing "You Must Have Been a Beautiful Baby."

Nora picked up a house phone, pressed a button. "Sari, come down," she said. "People are here."

Nora smiled and left; Paul as usual felt she wasn't present, more like a spirit.

It was, all agreed, a very festive evening. Lou Zucker had freely used his imagination in a press release about the engagement. "The groom-to-be's parents are stock breeders on their ranch in the Imperial Valley. Arthur is expected to serve at the fashionable Ohrb Sholom Temple on Sunset Boulevard. The nuptials will take place in June." The press release padded the list of guests present—Jews, Gentiles, the Chinese consuls and English nobility (those working as extras in films). It would impress people who read gossip columns.

There was dancing in which the parents of Arthur at first watched, then joined. Isadore and Rifka Bogenstein had been weathered by sun, wind, and hard work on their farm (not a ranch) raising tomatoes and melons. The father's beard was long and gray, his wide-brimmed hat replaced by a yarmulke.

Rifka wept a bit to show her joy. The other Hasidic guests—men, women, and a few children—who claimed to reach God by the heart and not by the mind, danced, drank, and laughed. The men took out large white handkerchiefs and waved them while they danced in a circle in the Silverthorn ballroom while the women clapped hands.

The young people, interested, broke off their own dance steps and joined the chanting circle. The local middle-aged guests drank champagne, the men smoked cigars, a few of the women lit cigarettes. A cameraman from the studio adjusted lights and took motion pictures until one cameraman who had been nipping brandy fell into the fish pond, scattering the foot-long goldfish.

Sari and Arthur held hands, both very happy.

"Your folks, Artie, know how to jive."

"Your father really overdid it. I mean, Sari, the cameramen, it's like he was making a movie."

Sari kissed him as he struggled to move out of mouth range.

"Honey, he *is* making a movie. Pop's life doesn't exist outside of the medium of film. He's going to present us with a two-reel documentary of tonight."

"God forbid, why?"

"And in color. For the wedding he's having a special score written by Irving Berlin."

"You're putting me on, as your friends say."

"Yes, a little, honey. Come on, let's dance."

He said he wasn't much of a dancer but he proved to be a fine stomper and soon others joined—even Lou Zucker and his aunt—and the ballroom became a moving round of dancers, first moving clockwise, then counterclockwise with the Hasidim singing and clapping:

> *"Hava nagila v'nism cha*
> *Luru achim b'lev samayach!"*

> "Let us rejoice and raise the roof,
> Let us sing and kick our heels."

Ira was having a grand time. His wife Martha was delighted to be able to see firsthand the "enemies of society," as she called anyone not a follower of Trotsky; but Martha being good-natured, a lover of people,

373

never let her political views stand in the way of her enjoyment of the pleasures of life.

Ira, his moustache and beard much more cared for and trimmed than before his marriage, was as good a dancer as the dozen Hasidic families the Bogensteins had brought to the engagement party. He left the dancers to get another drink of brandy and stood smiling as he sipped, mopping his neck with a napkin.

"They're wonderful people, the Hasidim," he said to Paul. "Joy, joy. Come on, Paul, let's see you enjoy. Look, there are a few zaftig hot-blooded girls, farm workers by their heft and muscle. You could recruit them for something—love or going to Palestine."

Paul rolled his head; he was drinking too much. "They're troublemakers, these pious people. They love and laugh and don't belong in the twentieth century. They're waiting for the Messiah, not for the British to give us a homeland."

Rabbi Charles Shaphan Pedlock, whom people said would go far in the Jewish society of Southern California, made a short vibrant speech with the proper quotes. The women and girls were taken by his dark good looks and his rolling vowels as he ended with a quote:

" 'What shall we then say to these thing? If God be for us, who can be against us?' "

At a table Ira whispered to Paul, "This rebbe, he never heard of Hitler?"

"Please, no politics, no problems," S.S. said, "not tonight. All that exists is this house and all these happy people."

Ira grabbed Martha. "So, yenta, let's dance!"

Paul sat alone, not as happy as the guests, the families, the prancing Hasidim. His thoughts were on his two-year-old daughter Shana someplace in England with her mother Joyce, living with that sonofabitch Tony Ringel.

"Ah yes," he said to no one. "It begins like this, engaged young bodies having an affinity for each other. Life is beautiful, the future all wine and roses. Then everything changes, all things once solid turn to snowflakes, melt.

> 'Saint Joseph thought the world would melt,
> But liked the way his finger smelt . . .' "

Having delivered this he collapsed across the table, his head in a fruit bowl, completing a still life of apples, pears, and a shape twin to his own head, a splendid Hawaiian pineapple.

The long silver train, having crossed the flat, hot, distorted desert, was climbing north and east toward a rim of mountains pale violet on the far horizon. In Compartment B4 the fine leather luggage had been placed on racks and the two well-dressed people—a man and a woman—were leafing through a magazine as the train slid along on its well-ballasted roadbed.

Laura closed her copy of *Life* and looked over at Nat staring out of the window. The black silk sling holding up his right arm was hardly visible against the dark jacket. He wasn't reading his copy of *Colliers*, just staring at the printed page. Laura knew he wasn't in shock. He was too tough for that; just that he couldn't admit even to himself the true reason for this journey. His father, old Aaron, was ailing, had been moved to David's apartment in New York. David, the dry, serious federal judge, the widower—hard to imagine him the brother of Nat Bendell, who because of his mob connections now carried his arm in a sling.

Nat had been involved in a war in Southern California to control the bookie joints' wire services and the juicy take of millions from track betting. A local hood, Matt Kuhn, had tried to win control of the Southern California bookies. He provided anti-union goon squads, the smuggling in of aliens, taxi cab payoffs, protection in Chinatown; was partners with fences and bail bondsmen; controlled gambling in the suburbs. He ran a horse book with a shoe store as a front on Santa Monica Boulevard near LaBrea. Always present were a few of the sales clerks, hefty fellows with bulges in the left armpit of their double-breasted jackets. Matt would hold court here, tell tall stories of his boxing days, give interviews. The city's press loved him as a news item when events were dull. Matt would retire to a bathroom at least once every half hour to wash his hands. No one dared be openly amused at this compulsive trait. Matt was suspected of at least three personal killings, his gang of at least two dozen. The citizens of Los Angeles usually shrugged it off: "Oh well, they only kill each other."

Nat had had several meetings with Matt Kuhn at a neutral night club, Ciro's. Both sides brought escorts of solid muscle.

Matt had put his cards on the table: "This is my turf. I been here, geez, twenty years. You people come here like you owned the whole world. The answer is don't shove Matt Kuhn. Tell that to your ginnies."

Monte Spinelli sent out muscle to back up Nat . . . You try to run things like a business and some bum thinks he's Dutch Schultz.

Two days later as Nat was in the steam room of the Beverly Health Bath Club having the big Greek slap him around on the table, a man came in in a sports jacket. The man came over to the table and looked down at the naked Nat.

376

"Mister, I gotta message for you from you-know-who."

In a reflex, almost automatic, Nat rolled off the table with a surprising quickness just as the man fired a large hand weapon he casually took from under his belt. Nat felt a stab of fire like a hot iron in his right shoulder as the big Greek with a shout poured a bucket of water over the assassin and then flung the bucket at him. The man fled and Nat saw a dime-sized hole in the tile wall behind him where the slug, after penetrating his upper arm, had imbedded itself.

It was decided by the organization, after the local press made a big thing out of the attempted killing, for Nat to leave town while the muscle men took care of Matt Kuhn.

The wire to Nat from his brother David that their father was sinking provided a cover for his panicked flight with Laura. As Monte Spinelli had told him over the phone from Hot Springs, "Look, Natty boy, it's not your piece of cake. The company will clean house. You're too valuable to us to have any harm come to you. Take a few weeks, see the Broadway shows. Regards to your lady."

Monte never used gangster movie talk. Never said *racket, gat,* or *rubout*.

They had been living on Kings Drive in a three-room apartment overlooking the city. There were extra locks on the door, three exits from the lobby downstairs, and Laura knew Nat had weapons in the place. After the attack in the Health Club, there were usually some men outside in a car or walking about as if counting the yucca plants; the organization had sent them to protect Nat until he would be able to board a train east.

Laura came into the bedroom with a breakfast tray,

put it down, and said, "This time you have to get out."

He winced, sipped coffee with his left hand. "I promised to taper off, didn't I?"

"I want you *fully* out. I don't want to play this for a big emotional scene. Can't I get through to you? Nat, I'm leaving you if you don't break clean."

He looked at her expressionless with what she called his poker-playing-face. "You don't mean it, you can't mean it. Leave me!"

"I have to mean it. It's not just you getting hurt. I've got an ulcer. Doctor Wooley has been treating it and it's not getting better."

"Laura, why didn't you tell me. Maybe we don't eat right . . . an ulcer!"

"I held it back from you, but I'm sick. It comes from a hell of a lot of agony, worry. You don't think all the pain's on your side. I'm sick!"

"Sweetie, sweetie, I had no idea. You look great. It's just . . . oh, God"—he grabbed her and sobbed—"I never figured. I'm a selfish sonofabitch."

"Now you know." She took the cup from him and sipped. "I'm not supposed to drink coffee . . . Nat, there's no other way. And I don't want to walk out."

He hugged her; it wasn't easy, with his arm bandaged and in a sling. "Look, I'll lay it out for you. You don't just walk out of the organization. It's a doublecross as far as the Spinellis and their people would see it. Monte is just a spokesman for a lot of biggies. Better you don't know who."

"We can't go away, change our names?"

"That's okay for a Cagney movie, but the organization is coast to coast and they have connections. I promise you this, sweetie, I'll begin making my move. Monte likes me. I've put them into some good things. Businesses, legit enterprises. Give me six months say and I can swing it. Break away. But no rush act or they'll think I'm changing sides. Six months, huh? Please?"

She felt the acid in her stomach, the big pain. She rubbed her brow, gave him a mirthless smile. "Don't lie to me, Nat. You lie a lot. It's second nature with you and you're good at it. You tell me what I want to hear."

"I didn't want to hurt you. I know the rackets are poison to you. We're both sick and we're all we have. Remember that."

"Six months?" She said it firmly trying to picture the image of her ulcer in the X ray she had seen.

"I swear it on my . . ."

She held up a hand, "None of that, Nat. Just six months from today. If you're still playing the old game, I'm walking, and don't come after me."

Nat, in despair, filled his cheeks with air and exhaled slowly. "Six months. Okay. I'll be in the clear or (a thumbs-down gesture) curtains."

"Bullshit. You're smart. You have angles. You can get out of the organization if you really try. God, don't you see I want us to stay together, live a decent life?"

"I know. I never meant anything more in my life. When I say six months, we'll do it. Now you don't get into any uproar, take your ulcer medicine. Easy does it. Once we get on the train I know you'll feel better."

She smiled. "Old Doctor Bendell the eminent quack says I'll feel better."

She smiled and leaned over and kissed him and they held each other close.

38

Doctor Wooley wasn't too pleased about Laura leaving Los Angeles, and taking a long train journey.

"Your ulcer is very advanced, and it could rupture the wall of the stomach at any time. And on a train trip—let me show you the X rays again."

"No thanks, Doctor, it's not my favorite art composition. You see the trip, it's something I can't avoid. I have to go. I don't want to sound like a soap opera but . . ."

The doctor, a young brisk specialist in his field, set aside the envelope of Laura's X rays, "I've found that soap operas are the only shows that really picture life today. I don't want to pry, Mrs. Bendell. I just want to save your life."

"Thank you. I'll watch the diet, I'll take the pills. I'll stay as calm as I can."

"You're either a brave woman or a fool."

The doctor looked at his desk pad and grinned. "No extra charge for that remark. I know about your husband's trouble from the newspaper stories. If you begin to bleed very badly get to a hospital no matter where you are and get a blood transfusion. Don't delay. Let me know how you do."

Laura left the office wondering if the doctor was not above making a pass at a patient.

So they took the train.

Nat tossed the magazine aside. "We forgot to send a message to S.S.'s kid. She got engaged today to this rabbi. We should have sent a telegram."

"We can still send a wire." She looked at her wristwatch. "The party is still on at the Silverthorns."

Nat rang for the porter and said to Laura, "Write something out, something an engaged girl would like."

The porter said they could send a telegram at the next town. One of the cars had developed a hot box; smoke was coming from the packing of one of the wheels. They'd be stopped nearly half an hour.

The dusty, sun-tormented town of Las Vegas wasn't very impressive, but there was a Western Union sign on the depot's late-nineteenth-century facade. While Laura filed a telegram—GOOD LUCK. HAPPINESS AND HAVE THE BEST LIFE THERE IS. LAURA AND NAT—Nat, lighting a cigar, talked to the Pullman conductor, a portly man with silver-rimmed glasses who said, "Not much hereabouts but Gila monsters and cowboys playing dime poker on paydays. Mormons settled here first but there were Indian raids, so they gave up, went back to Salt Lake City."

"You mean real Indian raids?"

"Oh, not much of a fuss. Place didn't really amount to much till round 1905. My father was here then. Land was all owned by the San Pedro, L.A. and Salt Lake Railroad. They were planning a division point here but it was all a come-on to auction off the land."

"Who'd want it?"

"They dumped it on a lot of suckers." The conductor looked down the line at a brake man signaling. "Better get the lady. We'll be moving on soon. Got twenty-two minutes to make up."

Nat puffed cigar smoke into the dry air. "Gambling is legal here?" he asked as Laura came out of the depot.

"Low stake faro, card playing, wheels of fortune . . . All aboard!"

The conductor helped Laura up the steps and picked up his little platform from the ballast. "Hasn't grown much since 1911, when it was incorporated as a city. Some city. Once Boulder Dam is finished and the work crews clear out, it's going back to the Gila monsters . . . all aboard!"

Nat ate a good dinner, finished two flavors of ice cream, sat in the club car talking to cattlemen, commission brokers of packing houses, tractor salesmen, engineers from the dam project.

Laura was in bed reading a dull Christie mystery when Nat came in whistling, "A Hot Time in the Old Town Tonight."

"Who did you flim-flam?" she asked.

"Honey, I have an idea." He removed his jacket, hung it up with care. "Gambling is legal in this state, and this whistlestop town Las Vegas is right on the main line, and a good road from L.A. crosses the Mojave. Why, it could become a fine place for a casino. Slot machines, dice, wheel tables. Maybe I can talk Monte into putting up a real posh hotel and gambling setup. That might get me off the hook."

Laura closed her book, took two pills, a sip of water, "You're running a fever, Nat, from that arm. Who would come to this dump, off to hell and gone? Nothing grows here, you'd need to truck in food, water, pave the streets. Even suckers aren't dumb enough to trek out here."

"All right, all right, just a thought."

The *Super Chief* hooted in the night; an echo came back as the train climbed to the distant mountains. A crossing warning bell rang out and there was a flash of orange outside the window, the hurried image of an old

383

man under an oscillating arm swinging a red disc, then the night was inked in darker than before.

Laura awakened in the night to the sound of the train laboring up some twisting gash cut through the mountains. Nat was asleep, snoring not too loudly, but as he turned to favor his hurt arm he would mutter something she could not make out. He appeared bitter at someone in a ruined dream. He quieted down and Laura lay, sleep not returning. She thought, against her will, of Teddy Binder, her stepson. Clearly she mustn't see too much of him in New York. It was more than being susceptible. There was something shameful about it, like the breeding of young collie dogs to their mothers. Also she had enjoyed their time in bed, sensed in herself again the wild desire for sensual delight, to feel in a younger man the full vitality of romantic physical passion, to hold close a person nearly her own age. Nat had become fully a middle-aged man. Still handsome, solidly sure of himself, but sexually she didn't fully hold his attention. It was not likely that he was unfaithful to her. With his duties to the organization on his mind, with other crises and problems that existed in his world, his physical needs for her were less. Once or twice a month he would turn to her in bed and stroke her head, her hair, talk amorously, and make love to her in a noisy but not gross manner. For a few moments it was like it had been in the beginning. But just . . . and then he was off her, a last wet kiss, and he turned on his side and went to sleep. It occurred with such haste that at times she didn't have an orgasm.

She often had a feeling that even those rare lovmaking times were forced by Nat to show his affection, which she never doubted.

She slept in snatches as the train reached a gentler grade. Very early she got up and dressed and went into the diner for coffee, orange juice, and French toast. She sat in the back of the observation car watching the high umber and pale lavender country unroll like a great rug of gorges, the slab sides of the peaks, the little stunted trees struggling to exist at such heights. Overhead large white clouds lay flattened, twisting, churning in a driving wind. When she was a child she had looked at clouds and seen horsemen and dragons and the lofting hills of heaven. But this morning they were just clouds.

Arthur Bogenstein had no intention, never had, of becoming a fashionable rabbi. He listened to S.S.'s talk of a good new temple in the valley: "Not just golf players. But savings and loan officials, dental surgeons, screen writers. Perhaps something a little more with *tom*—taste—near San Francisco, across the bay in Sausalito, a congregation of second-third-generation Jews. Marin County art collectors, Berkeley professors, supporters of opera. I don't say I guarantee you a *bema* there, but people know I'm a man of my word, of charity—a hospital needs a new wing, an old-age home needs a clinic, they come to me. Call me old-fashioned, I offer my daughter a *noddin*—a dowry."

Arthur listened, went to Sari, asked did she love him. She said of course. So they didn't wait for the big wedding that S.S. would insist on.

As Ira said, "When Sid wants something, he could milk a cow without waking her up."

So they got Rabbi Esserick from his storefront shul on Fairfax Avenue. The wedding was held in a small Hasidic shul in Ventura. S.S., Nora, Harry, Ira, and Paul were given half a day's notice to attend. A dozen Hasidim and Arthur's parents also attended the ceremony. Arthur broke the ritual wine glass under his foot and there were cries of *mazel tov*! Wine and honey cake were served. And so Arthur and Sari became man and wife.

385

Then after backslapping and earnest kisses, the newlywed pair was gone. S.S. threw up his hands in mock despair. "I had this check—enough for a house, furniture, a car—and they're gone."

Ira poured wine for Rabbi Esserick and Paul. "They just want to get away alone. Family farewells are harrassing."

Nora, fanning herself with lace, asked, "Where are they going?"

Ira said, "Just went off with no plans. Maybe they're right. After all, the rabbi gave them a full service."

He nudged Martha. "Not like us—a justice-of-the-peace and a honeymoon of unloading bread for your stand in the Farmers Market."

Martha nudged him back. "A marriage is more than some obsolete desert gibberish mumbled under a flower canopy. It's the merging of two tempers, two understandings, not this—oh, pardon me, Rabbi, I didn't see you."

Rabbi Esserick combed his beard with his fingers, then brushed honeycake crumbs from it. "No, no, Mrs. Silverthorn, you're so right. But it's our secret, eh?" He winked, lifting a bushy eyebrow.

"There was no music," said Nora, "no catering. But they looked so happy."

S.S. reached for his cigar case. "It didn't seem a wedding."

Paul, who had been talking of the desperate conditions of Jews in Germany with the rabbi's wife, went up to Harry, who was telling a ribald joke about a rabbit and an elephant to one of the Hasidic girls.

"Harry, sorry to interrupt you, but I need some film footage from the *Crystal Night* when the Germans smashed up storefronts."

"I'll have one of Pop's cutters edit it for you soon."

386

"I need it tomorrow. There's a big Zionist protest meeting planned. I want to show it."

Arthur's mother and father and two brothers in their dark suits went around solemnly shaking hands. "We have to go. Fine wedding. There is a tomato crop must be picked right away. One day's rain and it's kaput."

Rabbi Esserick decided to have another glass of Silverthorn's wine, a good wine, tangy and fruity. As he sipped, he offered up a prayer to God who gave us the vines, a prayer of the eighteenth-century thinker Moses Hasid of Prague: "Let melancholy and passion, born of spleen and bile, be banished from hearts on this day."

Rabbi Bogenstein did not encourage his father-in-law to find him a social prominent bourgeoisie congregation. Two weeks after the wedding, he and Sari were settled into a cottage down the coast at Mesa Springs. He became the spiritual leader of the Hasidic shul, a former fruit processing plant that with a new roof, a coat of white paint, and the installing of the ark of the Torah served the spiritual needs of the two dozen Hasidic farmers who disdained decor and lived for a successful culmination of joy in God.

Arthur would accept nothing from the Silverthorns for their cottage, supplied by the shul and furnished by a departed Hasidic rabbi who had gone with a pregnant wife and six children to try to enter Palestine.

But for the shul, the place of worship, Rabbi Bogenstein did accept from S.S. a rare eighteenth-century Torah, the Five Books of Moses called the *Humash*, handwritten on parchment.

Sari learned to cook simple dishes (Arthur had a queasy stomach), and was astonished how well she did—Arthur was gaining weight. If she fell from grace at times and went shopping in San Diego, she would lunch on a gourmet Chinese meal—a Lun g-ha fu-ying, lobster omelet, egg rolls chuen kuen; feel guilty for at least half an hour, usually salving her sins by bringing home for Arthur a dozen bagels and half a pound of lox. Sari was very happy and desired a child. But as yet no sign.

BOOK SIX

ECCLESIASTES

39

May I go first, had been Malka's silent wish, her unspoken prayer to God. But it was not to be. The fierce, possessive Jahweh had other plans. Clearly Aaron was slipping away from them here in his son David's apartment on West End Avenue. The group seated in the living room could hear the cries and shouts of children playing in Central Park, the roll of traffic going on its way.

What did it matter that an old man was dying? The drapes had been drawn. Malka, silent, solid, dry-eyed, sat surrounded by her sons David and Nat, Nat's wife Laura, and his son Teddy. All felt the rueful loneliness, aware of the impending death in a family, of mortality, of the futility of human endeavor.

Nat, his arm still in a sling, felt the most guilt: his father was dying, he was sure, with a sense that his younger son was a misfit. For this son he had fled Poland for the unknown, escaping like a convict, a fugitive from the Tsar's grip, attempting to remove the boy Nathan from brutal military service. So much sacrifice, so much hope put into a dream of a new start on the streets of a new world. To what end? An outlaw son against society, against all the ideals, principles the old man held to.

I'm another generation, Nat thought as his mother sighed. Perhaps she understands that we don't make the destinies we live, that we all don't see the world as described by the Torah, disciplined by the Talmud, but as a rat race, a wolfish world, a struggle against pressures, perversities.

Nat took Laura's hand. He would change his life; beginning today, he would begin firmly to break away from the organization. Nat was not a man given to pessimism; he had survived a rough life as a soldier in the Philippines after the Spanish-American war, existence as a partner in a fine gambling house, trying to sidestep crooked police, dishonest city government—enough to make a man a cynic. But no, he had seen life as a desperate struggle and also exciting in all of its capriciousness: the thrill of gambling, the bodies of women to pleasure with in the past, the bootlegging, the hijackings, his life on the line, a hair's breadth away from death. To him, life's uncertainties meant a freedom that the ordinary citizen never feels but only dreams about, experiencing vicariously in the movies' thrillers.

Laura was what now mattered to him. Her sensitivity and perceptiveness meant everything. Her ulcer was a calamity. But modern medical science could cure anything, prevent anything, except, of course, the death of an old father.

The nurse in crisp crackling white came out of the bedroom, put a finger to her lips as if to hush a conversation among the family, talk that didn't exist. David's stiff leg itched; he had almost forgotten the boyhood accident that had injured his knee and the villagers saying how lucky he was that he didn't have to be a soldier. Lucky, he thought—my wife died in a dreadful factory fire, my son Karl with the AEF lost in the World War. And here I am dry as a reed, lost in the chaos that is called justice. I am beset by despondency, for I see that even here in this wonderful land there is one kind of law for the rich and the other kind for the rest of the citizens. Damn all lawyers. How right the Shakespearian character: "Let us begin by killing all lawyers."

Easy to say, but what would replace the shysters, the big-time corporation legal perverts? I've given my life to a bookcase of legal tomes, to torts, briefs, to causes that never had a chance. I should have remarried but I lack now the stamina and vitality for a domestic partnership. I should have been closer to my parents, to *Yiddisheit*, worried more over Nat. Henry James was so right: if you don't live your life fully now in this existence, when will you?

Teddy was staring at Laura; she was avoiding looking at him. Beware what you desire, he remembered some wise guy saying; you will get it. I desire my stepmother and a chance to fully act the scoundrel to my own father. She has this cockeyed loyalty to my old man, who never gave a damn about anything, anybody. The selfish bastard. Look at him sitting there, still gracious, shameless, handsome, tall, looking like a goddamn hero with his arm in a sling. He neglected me, my mother Sonia, used her when he was in trouble with the bootleggers, and she hid him after he had deserted her all those years. Maybe Freud is right. We all want to deep-six our old man. Does he have a reciprocal dislike of me? Grandpa in there, already halfway to the dark place. When I was a kid, I thought I'd never die. It was something that happened to strangers in another country. Well, how many years have I got left? I'm forty now. With taking care of myself, not too much chasing of showgirls or hitting the sauce hard, not overworking on a new show, a new song, sixteen hours a day on tryouts in New Haven—maybe fifteen years? Less if I live on a dozen cups of coffee a day on work in progress, bolting corned beef sandwiches and booster pills.

Please, God, could I have twenty? (Teddy began to sweat.) I'll have a checkup tomorrow.

Malka wiped her brow with a folded handerchief, stood up, and went into the bedroom to meet *Molochhamoves*, the Angel of Death, face to face. Aaron lay very still, sunk deep in pillows. He had a bit of difficulty in breathing, the white beard trembling as he twitched in his sleep; was it sleep, wondered his wife? Was he already on the other side? She wasn't too sure there was another side. A rabbi of Temple Sherith Israel had said life is like a pencil you use up writing down wonderful thoughts, hopes, ideas; you have to keep sharpening the pencil and in the end you use it up and what you hold then is a stub. Was that stub the remains of life, old age, and was it traded in for a promise of another place, another world?

She remembered the cabala, its hints of worlds beyond this one, of flying angels brushing you with their wings, of miracles done with secret incantations to lift one beyond this earth without death. If so, why should so many grow old, die? No, it's nonsense. What had Aaron based his life on? He'd say, "To do what is good is the true answer." How often he'd repeated it, drinking a glass of tea while holding a small lump of sugar between his teeth. Malka could never get him to take his tea from a cup. Now there he lies; nothing matters to him. May it be nothing is felt in the trance of a last sleep. She permitted herself a dozen tears standing by the bed. She didn't allow herself to sit; it would in some way be disgraceful.

Clouds were visible to the dying brain as cell by cell it receded into a trancelike darkness . . . I am rising slowly like bread dough; there is peace coming to me. How much I have suffered since I was a child; the hard poverty in the *Zhid*-hating villages of Poland, the pogroms, the blows on my back, Christian spit I wiped off my beard, the insults heaped on me, and all the time smiling, bowing . . . Job only had boils, and God spoke directly to him. I had only blind faith, hopes. Ah, this wonderful new land. The burdens still were heavy but one could eat the bread of liberty, never mind the sweat; one could seek a fine future if not for oneself for the children and their children. This is their birthright—sheeney, kike, yid, ikey; insults slipped by like water off a duck's back. There is a great dark curtain and a hand pulls it aside to reveal a sky all stars and a whispering—a *bentshin*, "*Ha Shem Yishmerahu*"—and he was young and Malka was young. They lay under the flowering apple tree, a gentle warm wind stirring the branches, and they were engendering their firstborn, yes, there in the grass, and a great face filled the world. It is the face of God a million miles long and wide counting the beard, and a voice says Aaron, Aaron . . . he adjusts his prayer shawl, tries to say *Gottenyu, Gottenyu*, dear God, and so the spark goes out of him, leaves no clue of what comes after.

Malka came out of the bedroom, her head up; now the tears were there. She said firmly, "It's over, he's gone. *Alva hashalom.*"

There was a cry of agony from Nat. David sat very still, his heart pounding, a ringing in his ears. Teddy went to his grandmother and hugged her, buried his face between her breasts as he had done as a child.

The nurse came from the kitchen, wiping her mouth, took in the scene, started for the bedroom. Malka put out a hand to stop her. "Leave him alone for a little while."

"But I have to . . . oh, very well."

The nurse caught the look in Malka's eyes and went to the hall to phone the doctor. David saw that for once in her life Malka did not serve food and drink at a gathering.

Oh, Brooklyn, thought Teddy as he rode with Nat and Laura to the cemetery, city of tombstones, the markers of Jews and Christians. Such blocks of heavy stone. As though they don't want the dead to rise, come home, the living pile up slabs of marble and granite, add railings, angels and crosses, stars of David, grow gloomy trees that hang their heads over costly sleeping grounds. Observe the sleek features of the funereal profiteers so smug, oily with guile.

By the wound in the ground sat the casket: plain pine. Aaron had left orders that he be covered by only a linen shroud and his *tallis*. No cosmetics, no evening attire slit up the back, no bow tie. Just a naked old Jew in the shroud.

Now the family stood around a mound of earth discreetly covered with false grass.

The rabbi, unknown to most of them, was a hawk-nosed beanpole of a man dressed in worn black-green clothes speaking in Hebrew, alien to them. Only Malka knew a few words.

"May God remember the soul of the departed who has gone to his rest . . ."

Malka's atention wandered to the nearby graves. There was David's wife, Josie, and their daughter Lilly, who had died organizing a textile strike some place in the deep South; no one was ever found of those who took her life with hunting rifles.

"May his soul enjoy eternal life with those of Abraham, Isaac, Jacob, Sarah, Rebecca, and Leah, and all of those righteous men and women now in Paradise."

Overhead, high up, a plane flew with a faint buzzing. From beyond the wall of the stone city of the dead came the sound of traffic. A truck passed with letters spelling out:

WONDER BREAD

The Staff of Life

The rabbi, an independent soul from the small shul, the Beth David, that Aaron had supported now spoke in English:

"May God whose rule is everlasting, He who delivered in ancient times David, His servant from the destroying sword, who made a way through the sea, a path through the great waters, may He bless the departed, also preserve, safeguard, aid, and exalt on high this nation America, its glory be enhanced. May the King of Kings in His mercy prolong its life, protect it, deliver it from sorrow and trouble and loss, cause its foes to fall before it. Let us say Amen."

"Amen." Malka turned away, holding Laura's arm, and walked from the graveside. She said to the group behind her, "You will all say the *Kaddish*, the prayer, three times a day."

Nat added, "We'll also sit *Shivah*."

And for a week, as is ritual, the men sat on low benches, shoeless, unshaved, reciting the *Kaddish* prayer. The maid served them poor food; they tore the lapels of their jackets. And so was held bereavement for Aaron Bendelbinder.

Malka, alone at night in the big bed, only then did she weep.

The view of the East River from Teddy's sixth floor apartment in the Beekman Towers was dramatic— tugboats nosing barges under the bridges, an island rimmed in the stone of prisons. Across the way were the historic shapes of Brooklyn Heights where Washington had once done battle with the British and lost.

Neither of the two people in the bed were at the moment interested in the view or the apartment, which was done in that period's idea of fashionable decor—bull fight figures and two original Lautrec posters, the first of the pre-Columbian Mayan figures from Mexico, Swedish-modern furniture, figures of glass and porcelain, a black Steinway grand, a Beidermeyer side table on which stood signed photographs of both Gershwins, Cole Porter, the mayor, Nelson Eddy, Scotty and Zelda Fitzgerald, Ruth Etting, a sheet of an original score and lyrics by Gilbert and Sullivan. Also a large photograph of Laura and Nat at one of S.S.'s costume parties, he made up as Groucho Marx, Laura as Harpo.

The bedroom was simple, a pearl-gray Japanese wallpaper hung with large colored etchings of lean women walking greyhounds or getting into their underwear.

The bed rested on a low platform. For half an hour Teddy and Laura had been lying there, their nakedness covered chest high by a buff-colored sheet. Their conversation had faltered as if they had, Laura thought, lost the definition of things.

They lay listening to the *hoot-hoot* of a riverboat, the building elevator's whining hum down the hall.

Teddy raised himself on one elbow. "I'll be damned if talking to you gets anyplace. It's like trying to find a bone in a bowl of mush."

"Teddy, it all comes down to you refusing to accept the word no."

"The yes isn't enough. Making love to my stepmother."

"You used to say 'screwing my stepmother'. Hell, love's a trap, Teddy. A trap."

Teddy beat a pillow with his fist. "It's not as if my old man was a husband you could trust, believe in. He's in thick with the organization, more than ever since he got this idea the mob should build big-time gambling casinos in the West Indies, in England, even in Nevada."

"Got any milk?" She sat up with an expression of pain.

"I thought your ulcer was better."

She got out of bed, not trying to cover her nakedness. "I feel it kicking up. Our talk was no help."

She went to the kitchen and opened the door of the frig to survey its contents: an end of a salami, an opened tin of caviar, some wilted mixed salad in a bowl, various cheeses. She lifted out a half-filled bottle of milk, sniffed it, and poured herself a glass. Slowly, with a sense of fear, she drank. Teddy came into the kitchen, wearing his shorts.

"It bad?"

"I was trying, damn it, to get away from the atmosphere that caused the ulcer. Distorted relationships."

She put down the glass and wiped her mouth with a finger.

"Nat and I are leaving for Miami tomorrow. That will get the kinks out of you, me."

"And this was to be my goodbye gift, an afternoon of sex?" His tone suggested that he was a sad mass of frailties, that out of his fashionable tailoring he was vulnerable. He was aware he lacked the handsome strength, the well-muscled body of his father. Only when clothed and at his craft did he feel vibrant and energetic.

Laura put her arms around his thin shoulders. "All right, Teddy, it was just sex between us, if that's the way you see it."

"It's more than Nat can give you these days."

"Don't be cruel, Teddy. To me, or worse of all, to yourself. We both came into this because we ached for something shared, needed each other. But we both knew from the first how transient our relationship would be."

Teddy rubbed his head against her neck and shoulders. "Jesus, I thought we'd go on and on and get to a point where we couldn't go back to the old insecurities."

Laura brushed back her disordered hair with the palms of both hands, aware that this gesture was lifting her torso, her over-ample breasts, that she was standing there naked like some enticing postal-card Venus. She went back to the bedroom, reached for her scattered garments: intimate, flimsy silk, a tweed skirt, sheer gunmetal-colored stockings hung on the back of a chair. She felt Teddy come up behind her, grab her; his arms tightly locked over her breasts.

"Laura, Laura, give way, be real." His voice was taut with an emotion almost grotesque in its intensity.

She felt the sensual trembling of his body, the rhythmic flow of his blood. She broke free, retreated, stepped into her drawers with the gesture of one of the ladies on the wall. "No more bed time, Teddy. Right now I'd vomit."

"It's that revolting?"

She sat on the chair and took up a stocking. "Not revolting. I just can't have any want of it at this time." Skilfully she gathered up the stocking and put a foot into it.

"Don't you want to shower?" he asked.

"I want to go away feeling we are as we were the few times we were together—warm, good people, understanding, with simple, honest intentions." She put on the other stocking, adjusted her garter belt, hooked up the nylons. As she struggled with her bra, twisting and turning, Teddy adjusted it for her, kissed a shoulder.

400

"Know how I feel? I feel like Columbus with no America, ha ha." And he wept on her shoulder.

She turned and took him in her arms. "Teddy, accept, you must learn to accept. We all have to. That's the way the world runs. I can't ever leave Nat. I say I will. I make promises, threats, take oaths I'll walk. But I lie. I know deep down I lie, that I'll always be there with him."

"Until he's knocked off, maybe you with him."

She nodded, hiccupped. "Get me a glass of water. I have to take some ulcer pills. Don't look so sad. I'm not going to drop dead."

She finished dressing. Being in clothes was living another life. Teddy saw her to the elevator. There was a last kiss. His face seemed frozen into a sense of loss and a smile that showed a bit of rancor. Laura suddenly felt shy, disordered, unreasonable. Their hands unlocked as the elevator doors closed, and the Philippine youth at the controls looked up from his copy of the *Daily News*.

"Nice day," he said.

"Nice day," Laura replied.

In the taxi going to the Plaza she felt virtuous and sad as she saw the citizens of the Republic rushing about in their late afternoon business.

40

With new danger signals appearing in the world and Hitler bellowing in louder tones, Harry decided to go back to Europe to supervise the SWP Newsreel operations. Before leaving he wanted to say goodbye to his sister Sari, the new Mrs. Bogenstein.

Harry drove down the coast, Rabbi Esserick at his side humming some ancient tune:

> *"Yismach Moishe bematnass*
> *Bemat nass chelkoy . . ."*

He turned to Harry. "You'd maybe rather have me sing like that *kocker* Perry Como?"

"No, you do fine enough, rabbi."

"I often go to the Hasidim for good chanting."

A noncommittal wind blew all along the coast. The sky had become a prodigious emptiness as the last night-seeking birds passed.

The car turned off and began to climb an easy bluff. Soon they were in Mesa Springs, a collection of low, weathered structures in need of paint, gas stations, cola signs, a shopping center, a Chinese eating place, two packing sheds. Further up there was an old cement mining compound, long abandoned.

Under tattered pepper trees was the building the

403

Western Lubavicher Hasidic Colony used as its meeting place and for holiday ritual doings.

Harry parked among a collection of old cars, pickups, a rusting steam thrasher, and other castaways. The building was lit up festively. A dozen men and boys in long black coats and wide fedora hats were gesturing and talking at the double doors. They all cried out greetings of *"Farbreingung!"* Inside Harry saw a big cave of a room noisy with gaiety.

A festival of joyous celebration was in flow. There had been drinking; Harry could smell the whiskey and wine fumes. Candles were burning, attached by their own wax in huge seashells. People were praying in happy abandon. All was movement, gestures, voices. Rabbi Esserick said, "A happy sight."

There were many young boys who could not yet grow beards but like the adult men wore the *payas*, long earlocks of hair. The women sat in one corner of the upper balcony, gossiping, blowing the nose of a child, waving a finger in warning of a coming slap on the head. Harry tried to find Sari's face among the women.

In the center of the hall was a lowered section of the floor where about two dozen men were huddled in attentive concentration. A dozen old men were seated at a long table covered with a white cloth, and among them Harry saw his brother-in-law Arthur. In front of him, a hairy man with heavy eyebrows was at a public address mike into which he was speaking in Yiddish, his voice amplified by four speakers under the roof.

Rabbi Esserick said to Harry, "That's Reb Halavi Gorshom Eliezer, the representative of Menachim Mendel Schneerson, the Lubavicher rebbe. Listen! Ah, the *tomm*, the grace of that voice."

The loudspeakers ground out Yiddish in overamplified tones: "With God's warning goes advice, the ways of the world are wrong. They seek to explain. All mean nothing, *nothing*, I tell you. For us there is only the faith in God. That is all there is. The only truth is in an absolute unfailing faith in God. Rest in the *Aron kodesh*."

From the congregation came muttering and an approving response: *"O-main!"*

The rabbi switched to Hebrew and there were groans; Rabbi Esserick grinned. "You see, they feel comfortable only in Yiddish, these *yiddels. Sh'ma Yesroel, Adonnai Elohenu Echad.*"

The wine glasses were passed to the table of the seated people and the rebbe brushed aside his thick beard, muttering a prayer as he sipped the wine. Arthur followed his example.

The ring of men and boys around the table began to clap hands. *"Daa daa da . . . Daa da da da."*

They stomped on, the sound loud and clear, the dancers rolling across the floor, heads dipping and rising, knees pumping heels into the floor; the whole place echoed with fervor. The women chanted, the children joined in a shrill chorus with handclaps: *"Daa daa . . . Da da da."* The candles quivered, their flames shook.

The rebbe cried out, *"Baruch ata Adonai!"*

All answered, *"Elohenu melech ha-alam asher!"*

Harry was carried away by the movement around him. He became part of the dance. He saw the rebbe and Arthur, too, eyes closed, dancing. The long line of dancers circled and chanted, banged heels on the flooring. Here and there someone went into a trance, a holy sign, someone screamed. A lean, black-bearded youth was led off, eyes rolling, nose running, mouth open. Harry saw his sister Sari up there with the women and he broke away from the dancers and went up to her.

405

Her head was covered with a large kerchief, as were all the women's, and she was laughing and shouting.

"Harry, Harry, oh, good to see you."

He pulled her to one side under a white-washed rafter. "It's really rolling. They'll wear themselves out."

"Isn't it all a cockeyed wonder? Look at Arthur. He's having a grand time. He'll sweat through his jacket."

"How are you?"

She whirled around and did a mock curtsy. "I'm fine, Harry."

"I'm leaving for London tomorrow. I thought I'd come see the old married dame. Pop still expects you to get over this and come back to the nest."

"Up his . . . but you should have brought Pop. He'd make a movie of all this."

"Jewish producers don't make films about Jews. They keep the profile low. I have some stuff in the car Ma sent: pillows, sheets, a crate of Helena Rubenstein goop. Anything else you need?"

"What else is there? as Reb Halavi Gorshom Eliezer once asked."

"The machos might let you women go downstairs, let you dance with them."

"We like it as it is, Harry. We dance up here. You see, at home we lead these guys around by their ear-locks and . . ."

The noise of chanting and shouting grew too loud for conversation. Now on the balcony the women were dancing around each other, circling the balcony, heads back, shouting, *"Daa da da Da!"* A delirium of dancing seized them, and Sari, eyes flashing, limbs active, joined them.

Everyone who could reach for a wine glass was drinking. Some voices sounded now like plaintive oboes. Harry went down to sip a sour kosher wine.

406

He reached Rabbi Esserick among a pack of dancers. "I'm going to leave here in about an hour."

"In good health." The rabbi's homberg was cocked to one side. The old boy was clearly a bit looped.

"*Daa daa da*," answered Harry.

"Harry, dance."

"I'll dance."

The Hasidic men in their huge brimmed hats, some trimmed with fur, were in a frenzy; the scene grew wilder, everyone dancing, drinking, sweating, crying out prayers.

Arthur began to speak in Yiddish: "The Pharisees upheld the virtues of obedience to precept, but shunned exercises of ritualism. They maintained strict rules for the Sabbath, but saw them fulfilled in joy and good cheer in family life."

Harry wondered as he twirled how the older men kept it up.

After a while the lights began to go off center for him and he felt he had danced enough. He and Rabbi Esserick tried to say goodbyes to Arthur and Sari, but they couldn't get close. At the door a young bearded man came up to Harry. "*Bist a Yid?*"

"*Nu woo-den.*"

The young man showed a fist full of silver coins. "*Eppis?*"

"Begging?" asked Harry as he pushed some coins into the boy's hand and smiled.

"Begging is honorable when one does it for God."

"That's an angle."

Harry could hear the sound of frenzied merriment from the old building. Outside in the cold night under the bright moon a group of young boys and girls were whirling in the *hora*, circling the few watchers, while youths with tin canisters moved about asking for funds for tools needed for the kibbutzim in Palestine where they soon would be working. Harry stood with Rabbi Esserick, looking at the scene, feeling a sense of tradition.

Indoors someone was playing a record of the Hasidic cantor Moshe Kamakendra. As the chant, clear and loud, came to Harry, a feeling of understanding surged over him. Even agnostics, *goyem*, perhaps even anti-Semites could understand what was here being said by these dancers: *I am a person.*

Rabbi Esserick said cheerfully, "Moses, you know, was a very parochial man, a dancer, a Fred Astaire from the *pupik* down. I'm sure of that, *very* sure of that."

Harry was soon back on the coast highway driving north. The land was steel-gray in the night, the sea an almost motionless chrome-plated surface but for the chalky surf outlining the shore. Huge trailer rigs were moving south like monsters let loose into the night, carrying in their entrails milk and fresh bread, the morning's newspapers, sides of beef, the delicacies advertised on the radio sets.

Harry slowed as a Shell tanker roared up and passed him, its row of ruby tail lights like a gleeful remake. Harry was in no hurry to get to Europe.

Rabbi Esserick, in sleepy tones, said, "A man in Prague once wrote: "What does it all matter as long as the wounds fit the arrows?"

A professor of economics at UCLA, active in Zionism, who wrote articles on the Middle East, had lent Paul the use of his beach house in Malibu, a small pleasant place on stilts. The professor was on a sabbatical in Turkey. Paul would swim in the surf in the morning, watch the lone fishermen cast into the tide. Often two or three surfers would appear in the afternoon, paddle out on their boards and come riding them to shore on the crest of a wave topped by white foam to end in the hissing surf among the cast-up kelp. At night hyped-up jocks would light fires and get drunk on beer.

Paul was reading his way slowly, and without much interest, through *The Tale of Genji* and writing a long short story about gun-running by a mysterious agent working out of Cairo. Somehow the short story never grew much longer.

Weekends a slim blond girl called Dedee, a model, came out to stay, usually with a three-pound steak, a boysenberry pie, and a bottle of Dewars White Label scotch. After a swim and making love and another swim, they would broil the steak over charcoal on the outside grill on the patio facing the Pacific. They would drink scotch and water, eat the steak and the pie. As the day died in the west, the sandpipers gave up probing the sand; pelicans and seagulls massed, seeking night shelter. Paul and Dedee would listen to Eddie Cantor, Jack Benny, or Fred Allen on the radio. During the commercials Dedee would tell Paul about her work posing for ads for shoes, stockings, and underwear, and how she suspected all photographers of duplicity.

Later she would stand naked on the bathroom scale and moan that the weekend was ruining her figure. Paul would go out to see if the charcoal in the grill had burned itself out; if not he'd pour water on it and look up and down the beach where there had also been grilling of steaks. There was a party or two going on, but mostly the beach houses were quiet, the occupants usually being, Paul knew, weekend fornicators, double-gaited or straight, alcoholics or sun-tanned hermits who avoided the night.

Dedee would be waiting on the king-size studio bed, and they would make love again. Dedee was a very sweet girl, nineteen, and she cried when one night he told her how he got the scar, the war wound in his hip. She cast his horoscope and it showed he had contradictory moods and fidelity. Dedee had a brother who was a naval officer on the *Arizona* in Hawaii, and he sent her a painting on black velvet of a native girl, which she gave to Paul on his birthday. They liked the amiable informality of their relationship.

Paul went down the highway one morning to a shop to buy a bottle of chili sauce for the steak Dedee would bring out the next day. He stopped to get his mail at the post office's general delivery window and there was an airmail letter with a royal head on the post stamp.

It was from Joyce. He sat in the sunlight on a parking lot's low cinderblock wall and opened it carefully as if it were a new kind of bomb:

Dear Paul,

There has been great confusion here. Some insist they will wait, others see it all as just a lot of jockeying and pathological international posing. There is talk of civilian safety in case. They did dig trenches around town and build some shelters. But that's all neglected now. It was only a gesture anyway, to give people a sense somebody cares.

There is a move on to send the younger tykes to the country. Some people are sending their children to America. I have also come to the conclusion that it would be best and safest to send Shana to you in the United States. We are living near Regent Park and Tony thinks if there should be air attacks where we are in the heart of London this place would be very vulnerable.

I am working in the Mediterranean section of a military office of information. Tony has gone to the RAF airdrome near a Spitfire factory for some technical work. So it is best that Shana go to you as our lives here are in disarray.

Shana is very clever, a bit petulant at times, but with a firm hand she has great charm, is a very loving child. No subterfuge or gaucherie about her. I would have given you more time to think about this, but a group of children is going over in care of nannies, and they will take Shana. She will be coming by air to Los Angeles, TWA Flight 16 on the 22nd.

She is no bother—housebroken, likes American cornflakes. She is to have no sweets, only a half bar of chocolate a week. She likes to listen to the wireless, to be read to. No fantasy stuff but adventures of animals that act like people. She is much attached to a battered doll she calls Pawka that sleeps with her. If it's ever lost or mislaid there is hell to pay, as we knew for two days last month. I'm sorry, Paul, if this should break in on your way of life or if you are married. But you said in your last letter on Shana's birthday, you aren't ever likely to. I don't think I ever will either. The Tony thing has run its course.

I hope you don't hold any too strong a grudge against me for the way things went in Italy. I've no excuses and don't intend to present any. This business of loving and living and doing, also being irrational, is the way the world runs. And right now it's running madly. What a sad decade it's been.

Not having Shana with me, I shall be living alone near my work. I shall like that, to gather myself together, rediscover myself, as our parents used to say. As I write there is the doleful drone of rain overhead; what would England be without rain? Also they have just begun to test the air raid sirens just in case, a sound that suggests the end of the world. They say time brings definition to most things. I am still waiting. Cordially,

J.

Paul refolded the letter, unfolded it, read it again . . . Two girls in halters, driving a red Studebaker roadster out of the lot, gave him the eye, and he shook his head. The 22nd? Four days and he would see his daughter. Would she like him? Would he prove a good father? Would he . . . The hell with questions. Grasping the bottle of chili sauce in its brown paper bag, he headed up the highway for the beach house to clean out the junk-filled guest room.

41

Ira Silverthorn had once quoted Alexis de Tocqueville to S.S., " 'In democracies nothing is greater or more brilliant than commerce. Its leaders participate not only for the sake of profit it holds out for them but for the love of the constant excitement occasioned by that pursuit.' "

S.S. was delighted to hear that. "Jesus, he hit it right on the schnozz. I'd be willing to give films away if a way could be found for me to have the excitement, keep on getting the kicks I get from making pictures, forgetting the money."

"You'd want a little spending money to keep up your racing stable."

"I'm getting damn near the age when the grace of a running horse is more beautiful to me than a woman taking off her clothes." He grinned, winked. "Well not for a bit more, Ira."

"As St. Augustine prayed, eh? 'Make me chaste, O Lord, but not just yet.' "

The relationship of the two men had grown closer over the years. In a city where it was easy to falsify sentiment, they managed to remain sure of each other; this hard, driving, tough head of a major studio (as Ira put it, "Sid can piss ice water when he has to") and the one-time citizen of Holland, a casual observer of people and events.

413

S.S. and Ira Silverthorn relaxed this afternoon in the studio head's private steam room, sweating and naked, pouring dippers of cold water over their heads and bodies. They felt fully at ease, away for an hour from the turmoils of the studio, the problems of a changing era, this 1939 of rumors and threats. From time to time they sipped Le Tanneur Grand Fire champagne brandy from a bottle in a bucket of ice cubes.

"I tell you, Ira, sometimes I feel I'm living in a world of falling leaves; Chamberlain and his peace, Austria, the Czechs swallowed up. Such mad change, and I ask myself, can I move with it?"

"You're still worried Lowitz Corporation will put the pressure on you, take away some of your studio power?"

"You're damn right." S.S. rubbed his stomach. "God, I'm getting fat as Patty's pig, have to exercise more."

"Right now they need you. You're the golden goose."

Ira poured a dipper of water over his head, sputtered. "You're expanding the studio, putting on more production. Fine. You'll have to have more space. I suggest you buy yourself a lot of land, set up a ranch, a SWP location site. You need it."

"I do, but those bastards in New York will send their fancy half-assed lawyers out and badger me about costs."

Ira sipped his drink, leaning back against the warm wood wall. "Sid, *you* buy the land for exterior shooting areas. Let them lease it, build the standing sets. They'll go for it. Save a couple million in land costs."

S.S. winked. "A company in which I'm a major stockholder and own the land? Whatever is built on it I control. Ira, you're a genius."

"No, I always remember Mark Twain's crack, 'Buy land, they're not making it anymore.' "

"Maybe I should find time to read more, as you do . . . But I'd have to put up a lot of money I don't have. I mean in cash. I've got big trust investments for Nora and the kids. How big a spread should I buy?"

"Five hundred to a thousand acres. Say you borrow on your share of the pictures in work, on income due from releases here, overseas. In twenty, thirty years it's going to be runaway inflation. Ever since Columbus landed on the Indies there's been a steady rise in costs. And, Sid, land is the biggest hedge against it. You'd have Lowitz by the balls right in your fist. All you've got to sell them is the idea; their only cost is the rent."

S.S. beat his fists together. "Ira, find me those acres."

"I'll set up a company—say, Orchard and Farm Land Company—Just looking for groves and places to grow melons. No hint to sellers it's for a studio ranch. No ostentatious project."

"It sounds better and better."

Ira was well aware of the real estate world's games and ruses. He would have to get options, soil tests, bring out orchard experts, play the game by feel. But how to find the acres he wanted without alerting the land sharks? Not by asking around or advertising. He decided to do it through the air. Hire a pilot and cruise Southern California, map open space rugged enough to serve as background for western films, places with a stream, flat areas to set up facades of villages or city streets, also lots of extra land to just be there increasing in value year by year.

Martha Silverthorn was feeding gruel to their son Robert in his highchair. The child refused to open his mouth wider. She said to Ira, "A horse I'd trust you on, Ira, but in an airplane? It's not for you . . . Bobbie, open the mouth or you'll feel my hand."

415

"Don't wanna."

"Don't be stubborn, Bobbie," said Ira.

"Like his father."

Ira hired a crop-dusting pilot and plane out of Burbank Airport. Joe Wallcott had flown in China for the Nationalists, had a broken nose, a six-foot-three body and when not hired out as a crop duster was often a stand-in for Gary Cooper.

They took off on a clear day in a reek of motor oil, hardly any breeze stirring the wind sock. Already there were hints of the smog that was to plague the city in later years. Seated in the open cockpit, a helmet and goggles in place, Ira looked down on the checkerboard landscape and tried to coordinate what he had marked on the map with what lay below at three thousand feet. Over the sea sailboats tacked in the glass-green ocean off Long Beach. On land traffic moved like rushing beetles along the main arteries that connected towns with the expanding city. Already citrus groves were disappearing. Land where the busy little Japanese-Americans had cultivated their bean fields were being filled and leveled by bulldozers. Entire canyons were being filled by the garbage of several million people. Huge trash trucks, clearly visible from the plane, were emptying their loads, followed by hundreds of gulls and other birds waiting to pick up tidbits.

To the west of Beverly Hills was Bel Air, more fashionable than Beverly Hills in the last few years. It had gates, was still wild in spots. Beyond Bel Air was the University of California at Los Angeles, and beyond it, Brentwood, a charming middle-class section of the city, cheap to live in.

The coast highway north of Santa Monica was flanked to the east by cliffs three hundred or four hundred feet high made of decomposed granite that had been eroding for ages. In the wet season a house or two would come down with a section of cliff. People still lived up there with part of their yards hanging over in space.

Up the coast a few miles was Malibu, the new "in" place with a private gateman. The hell with it, Ira thought. Actually it was a kind of low sandbar, not very interesting as a sight; there were a dozen better spots to build a beach house. But it was the fashion among motion picture actors, rich tax lawyers, retired industrialists turned art collectors to refer to "my Malibu beach house."

The plane swung south over Huntington, "right wing and square," money and class without any flashy settings, the politics high Tory, the decor genteel; Laguna about thirty miles south of Los Angeles, a kind of California Coney Island and Cape Cod combined, an art colony that had not accepted anything painted since 1900; Newport with its crowded waterfront. The beaches were marvelous all along the coast, long and white and still relatively clean.

For several days Ira continued his bird's-eye view of Los Angeles and its surroundings. Fred Allen had claimed, "It's a great place to live if you're an orange."

On a fairly clear day they flew past the dark outlines of mountains, then a stretch of desert and soon lines of roads, then superhighways and the green groves of oranges and lemons, the cubist shapes of fields laced with the silver sprays that water the dry land.

Over LA and environs, he studied clusters of houses, scattered on hillsides and along canyons; factories, too, shopping centers, stadiums and playing fields and swimming pools, bright blue coins blinking in the sun. Even the slums looked fairly decent, the misery hidden away inside.

At home in the evenings, Ira searched out the owners of acres he thought would do. Martha, listening to a

417

radio and smoking a cigarette, was knitting something in blue for their son Bobbie.

"How's my *luftmensch* tonight?"

"What Lindbergh could do I can do."

"Don't mention that anti-Semitic sonofabitch in this house. You heard, Ira, that speech he made for the America Firsters? And he never did give back that Nazi medal Goering gave him."

"Roosevelt will kick his Fascist ass for him. How's Bobbie? I'm neglecting the kid. If he were older I'd take him with me."

Martha coughed, expelled cigarette smoke. "You know that big pistol you got in the closet? I'll take it and give you the whole six bullets you ever try to take Bobbie up in one of those machines."

Ira laughed. "Knit him a small parachute."

After a week's study from the air and another week seeking out owners, estates, pricing, making offers of options, looking bored and shaking his head at counter offers, Ira appeared in S.S.'s office at the studio with a battered briefcase full of notes written out in his looping script.

"Sid, I think I've got some prime stuff." He laid out maps marked in red crayon. "Near Riverside, below Diamond Bar, six hundred acres. Abandoned groves, citrus, avocados, trees too old to bear. And here below Anaheim, three hundred more acres. We can combine it with the Riverside stuff. Now we can get the land company options for a layout of, say, two hundred thousand down, to buy say maybe an added million from bank loans. You'll go into escrow after Lowitz signs a lease."

"What the hell am I doing? Raw land, not even good for farming. And I'll have to really do a selling job on Lowitz."

"You're not going to farm. Anyway, it's the future you're buying, Sid. The future, the whole damn coast, LA, the shitty little towns are swelling up like a poisoned pup, expanding, and it's all moving west. Defense industries will need a hundred thousand homes for workers, whole developments. I want you also to buy acres in Tarzana, Sherman Oaks, Van Nuys. The San Fernando Valley is going to burst its seams in ten years."

S.S. waved off Ira's excitement. "No, no. Let's just stick to the two sections, work enough for me to get Lowitz Corporation to go along."

Ira sat back, lit one of S.S.'s Havana's, put his cowboy boots on the edge of the desk. "You've bought this big best-selling novel about the South and the New Orleans sporting houses after the Civil War. Going to put—what—several million in it?"

"Between you and me, it will come to more . . . Yes, I come to the Lowitz boychics with plans to build New Orleans, the levees, the southern mansions. And an option for them to lease the ranches for ten years."

"It's a money saver for them."

"I'll still have some shit-kicking in the dust to do. We'll put good ol' California boys on the board, pioneer names, and the shares properly registered. This is no fast-buck setup. I want it properly done. You're sure this whole idea is really kosher?"

"Legal? How do you think the Chandlers, the Italian bankers, the big oil crowd, all the rest worked the water deals in Owens Valley, got their big ranches incorporated? It's as legal, Sid, as sex on a wedding night."

"I'm putting my *tocus* in your bear trap, Ira."

"Make it a beehive, offer the Lowitz people honey— some shares in the ranches through a third party."

S.S. began to dictate a presentation of the project.

42

Dear Uncle Paul:

I am at the moment at the Hotel Engematthof in Zurich, meeting a camera crew from the newsreel here to photograph some festive gathering of Swiss women in costume. I've had a hell of a time trying to help work out that idea of exchanging five hundred American-made trucks for five thousand Jews held in German prisons and camps.

I met Charles H in Leipzig. He's been representing U.S. auto companies in Europe for many years. And while he's no lover of Jews, he is a good and I think an honorable man. He was to come with me to the place where I would meet with that Nazi economics colonel who had indicated the trade was feasible. I got to the Reichshof in Leipzig and I found Charlie in bed with a broken leg in a fresh cast. He, this overweight, middle-aged man, a sports nut, had been in a racing car accident. I said we had to go on with the plan and he said he'd like to but with the painful cast on his leg he doubted he could. I explained it was the last chance, the way things were going, to get a large group of Jews out of Germany. I also mentioned what his commission would be on five hundred trucks. I can honestly say it wasn't just the commission but a hatred of the brutality of the Germans toward the Jews that got him out of bed onto the train. Along the way we were to meet two underground people who have lists of imprisoned Jews in grave danger and the places they were. The Germans wanted to be assured by Charlie that the whole idea was no pipedream or a scam.

Charlie insisted, to avoid too much attention, that we take a second-class train compartment. His broken bone with its bandages and plaster had become an instrument of torture. There was nothing out there beyond the streaked train window to help him through this agony, and there was nothing inside but his stern control of himself—and my company—to keep him from crying out.

By the time we were in sight of the rise of the Zugspitze near the Austrian border, he was running a temperature of at least 101, by the sweat and warmth of him. And his mind had a habit of leaving him. I had a vivid picture of it—hovering like a bat on the stained ceiling of the train compartment before it came back inside his head. (Yes, we had been drinking Steinhager and Kummel.)

The oily darkness turned to rain outside the streaked glass of the Leipzig-Regensburg-Munchen night train, then to sleet. The trains were shabby and the rolling stock was old and neglected. This car, I thought, had been on the Arlberg-Orient Express run in the years before the old war. It was not put into service, the station guard said, except in weather like this, when the airfields were closed in and there was an influx of grounded passengers going on with their journeys by rail.

The train tore through mist and rain past the black shapes of moored trees, a crossing of galloping bells, and a few specks of orange light from houses crouched against the rain on the right of way. The car smelled of *Aalsuppe* (eel soup, which I detested), *knoblauchwurst*, and the lavatory at the end of the car—echoing ancient crap going back to Emperor Franz Josef.

Charlie's leg must have been on fire. It would most likely have to be reset when he got to Garmisch-Partenkirchen and our contact with that high Nazi official. I had begun with the thought the whole idea was insane—and then felt it was possible with such mad people as the Nazis.

The train slowed as we entered Munich, for me only memories of swinish cheers for German supermen, dead Jews in little looted apartments; from the train window, it looked merely dark and wet with a dank Teutonic heaviness. The stone roofs that had survived, the spires of churches, St. Catherine Hospice, all stained by the gray misery of a just-stopped rain; all the shitty Meistersinger scenery out of howling opera. I thought it was badly drawn, out of kilter.

Our first contact was to meet us here. The train entered the echoing *Bahnhof* and the car porter left in a hurry, setting his brass-fronted cap solidly on his straw-colored head. The doors opened to cold dampness and the odor of wet pigeon droppings and stale grease, the empty hulls of sunflower seeds, old newspapers scattered about. The train shivered to a stop. Charlie held his fists buried deep into the plush seat, and when the air

423

brakes were released he let words escape him: '*Jesus, Maria, und Josef.*"

"That's right, Charlie, pray."

I will not go into details of the little man in the brown fedora who came aboard and handed Charlie the material I needed, which I at once hid.

The station was loaded with soldiers, S.S. men and types who could only be Gestapo (if I read my Graham Greene right).

We saw two poor wretches dragged off, their bust-open suitcases disgorging old clothes and phamplets.

Brown Fedora left with a whispered "*Ani maamin,* I believe."

The train soon was gaining momentum past red and green signal arms, trees with rain still nesting in their branches. The old coach began to joggle and shake. I tried to wedge Charlie's plaster cast more firmly with newspapers and small bundles.

By morning the train was running through the clear highlands, spires of peaks, far blue distances incredibly clean. In the passageway two young climbers ate ham on thick rye bread. A section of Swabian strudel on a paper tray waited to be devoured.

The doors opened and a dining car steward came in, a pot of coffee in his hand. He gave us a cheerful Italian smile as he bent to pour. "Only Italians know how to brew good coffee."

Charlie spoke through his sinuses. "Hot anyway."

I sat eating ham and sipping the black coffee, looking out over the mountain slopes and the blue shadows and the deep green of the pines. Ahead was the Zugspitze, impressive, solid, placid. Landscapes have a pleasantly narcotic quality for me.

"How high would you say, we are, steward?"

"Nearly ten thousand feet," Charlie said.

"Nine thousand seven hundred and twenty," said the steward.

He offered Charlie the tray of rolls and ham.

"No, I slept a little but I don't want to eat. Just coffee."

"I've wired ahead for an ambulance, Charlie. You're going right to the hospital for an X ray. It may be set badly."

Charlie pursed his lips and looked out the window. "It's clean up here, isn't it?"

The train slowly made a great turn. Overhead there was a rushing of earth down a slope and a wind blowing.

I stood up. "I'll collect our things and take them to the hotel. Then I'll come to the hospital and see you don't pinch the nurse's ass."

Charlie tried to smile. "You do that, Harry, and bring the colonel to talk to me."

Here in the station I made the second contact, a big sleepy-looking fellow in red hiking boots. He spoke in Yiddish, of which I am not, as you know, an expert, but when I shifted to Spanish it worked fine. No going into more details of this meeting here . . . The next item was to present Charlie's letter to the Nazi colonel and begin talks on the truck deal.

The village was solidly built in that fool German Hansel-and-Gretel style. There were a great many people in colorful sweaters, tasseled caps, and hats with chamois brushes. The little bars were active and the Konditorei were doing well serving their overrich cakes and little sandwiches. Walking back from the hospital after seeing Charlie admitted to get his leg X-rayed, I inhaled the crisp air. I was happy I was not older, that I didn't have a broken bone, and that there were still maybe a few years ahead for me. The sterile philosophy of Sartre and Camus, mere negation, is popular among the young intellectuals. It gives me the grue.

I entered the Salzhaus, suddenly less cheerful as I thought of my mission, and was engulfed by a smell of malt and lentil soup with *Wurstchen*, also the special odor of well-cared-for wood all these cafes had. At the bar I ordered a glass of Lowenbrau. A man in a loose brown alpine and a dark hat was soon seated next to me. He smiled and pleasantly inquired how I was.

Would you believe the sonofabitch, young and slim as a dancer, baby-blue eyes, no dueling scars, was the Nazi colonel? Looked more like a Santa Barbara tennis pro than a nasty German dealing in human cargo. He was cool and simple—trucks for Jews, he said—and we went over to the hospital where Charlie was in a better mood and talked over details. Charlie got out a catalog from his suitcase, and Colonel K (how like Kafka this all is) said he would pass it on to the higher people and we would hear in a few days. I was to go to Zurich, and here I am. The message I got from Berlin over the phone this morning was: "It would appear the matter of the trade exchange is making progress" and that it was up to us to see that the money for the trucks was on deposit at the Suissede Geneve Bank on Freistrasse. So Uncle Paul, *Prosit, und zum Wohlsein!*

Harry

To this letter at a much later date someone had added the lines: *Events, and the United States State*

*Department, decided not to approve of this humane
project, so it all came to nothing. Brown Fedora was
hanged by a piano wire after being captured, leading a
band of partisans near Kiev. Red Hiking Shoes runs a
book store in Haifa.*

Epilogue

S.S.'s private projection room at the Silverthorn World Pictures Studios had very comfortable club chairs and a console on which S.S. could regulate the volume of sound. There were standing bronze ashtrays for the staff and guests that usually accompanied the head of the studio in viewing the dailies, the rough or finished cut of a feature film.

In the throbbing darkness of the room was running the first cut of a new film: *Win Or Lose*, a romantic melodrama of gamblers and lovers set in Monte Carlo. S.S.'s cigar end was a dot of color, its smoke rising to touch the ray of light that projected the film onto the screen. S.S. felt at ease. On his right was Lou Zucker: on his left was his secretary to take down any notes he might suggest while viewing the film. Also present were the director, the film editor and his assistant, and Ira Silverthorn, legs extended and cowboy boots crossed. S.S. was recognized as one of the most expert doctors of a film before its release. He knew where to cut, what scene to redo, where the music failed or was too loud. His creed was: "If the customers are amazed by the camera work it means we've moved to being merely pretty, the story isn't holding them, and if they are aware of the music then it's showing off, taking away interest from the actors and what they're doing."

To directors who felt they were producing art, S.S.

had an answer: "The good directors are those who know if the actors don't move, the camera does. And if the actors move, the cameras don't have to."

Very simple, *too* simple, people said, but the ideas were more than arbitrary rules. Sidney Silverthorn loved making motion pictures, felt he had some duty, nearly sacred, in bringing a film from story treatment to final prints for release around the world. His world was logical in its simplicity of purpose.

As he was about to dictate a note to his secretary about inserting the motor boat scene, the sound suddenly was cut off and the images of the actors were left moving their mouths and jaws in silent animation.

S.S. grabbed for the phone that connected him to the projectionist in his booth.

"Charlie, what the hell is the matter with the sound? You asleep?"

The public address system overhead came on with an electric hiss:

"Mr. Silverthorn, something has happened. I thought you should hear about it."

Ira laughed, "Another San Francisco earthquake?"

"Charlie!" shouted S.S.

"Sir, it's NBC radio. I'll plug it in."

Lou Zucker asked, "He been drinking?"

The radio voice was serious, dramatic: ". . . At 4:45 a.m., September 1, with no formal declaration of war, the German Army has violated the Polish frontier. The German Wehrmacht crossed the frontier at several places with fifty-three divisions under the command of General von Brauchitsch; Polish defenses are said to be overrun. German tank columns are penetrating deep into Polish territory. There are also reports of heavy air bombing of the cities of Warsaw, Lodz, Krakow and the port of Danzig . . ."

S.S. felt as if someone were pounding his chest with a

heavy mallet. There were exclamations of surprise and shock all around him. He pressed the light button on the console and the blinding glare of the overhead lighting revealed strained faces, dazed expression.

Ira beat his hat on the arms of his chair. "The fat's on the fire."

Lou Zucker watched the film still moving silently on the screen. "S.S., the news services will be wanting a statement about this from you."

"That will be a big help. It's the start of a new world war."

The director said, "Not if it's kept just to the Germans and the Russians carving up Poland."

S.S. shook his head. "There are three million Jews in Poland and millions and millions of Christians. Hitler is a sack of venom, no man to respect the Old or the New Testaments. As for Stalin, he'd shoot his mother and bet you which way she'd fall."

Ira stood up and knocked out the fire in his cigar in an ashtray. "It all depends on how the other European countries see their pacts to defend Poland. It's like a promise made in bed at night—do you give a damn in the morning?"

"It could be over in a couple of weeks," said Lou Zucker. "The Poles still depend on their horse soldiers and the saber."

S.S. held up a hand. "Quiet, let's hear the radio:"

" . . . In all capitals of the world there is a sense of collapse of reason. Neville Henderson, His Majesty's ambassador in Berlin, is expected to inform the Germans that England will live up to its pledge to come to the aid of Poland unless Hitler withdraws his armies. Robert Coulondre is also ready to express the same view on behalf of France. It is expected that Hitler will ignore the ultimatums and that World War II is almost certain to break out."

S.S. drummed his fingers on the console, looked about him, then stood up and started for the door. He felt a world was ending and a new one was forming: bestial, degenerate, unimagined evil. He sensed that they *all* had been guilty, had some small part in what was happening at that moment in the burning villages on the Polish plains. He could visualize the camera's view of dead women and children, the brutal movements of the Germans in their coal scuttle helmets, their grinding machines, smashing through walls and forests. He recalled going to his father Alex for aid. The old man had quoted Isaiah: " 'Every valley shall be exalted and every mountain and hill shall be made low; and the crooked shall be made straight and the rough places plain.' " After chagrin and bafflement, after compulsive hatreds, after a misspent age that failed its opportunities, can the crooked be made straight?

In the now deserted projection room the film ran on, voiceless and moving in some desperate, meaningless urgency. Forms without words, tones without logic, mouths without language. Ira, who had gone back to pick up his hat, looked at the screen and thought: why, *this* is Plato's cave whose inhabitants thought the shadows on their cave wall to be the true pictures of things.

No, he thought as he picked up his Stetson, nothing has ever been clearly understood; only the fact that somehow there has always been survival. Perhaps, just once more.

TO THE READER

What is never-ending is the personal human interest in our times. Our emotional, sensual relationship to those men and women, each with a personal joy, agony, or dream that touches us.

The Silverthorns and the Bendelbinders continue their stories in The Golden Touch, where we will pass through the raucous 1920s, the flapper and gangster age, to see them all—Sidney; his son, Harry; his nephew, Paul—in their romantic, glamorous relationship with the women and the turmoils of the Florida land boom, the age of silent films, and the talkies, with Silverthorn World Pictures becoming the greatest studio—until the Depression of the 1930s causes Sidney to fight for survival.

And what of the women's world—Nora, the silent film star; Laura, the New England-raised puritan entering the modern, bohemianism of flashy journalism; and Joyce, an early terrorist fighting for a 2000-year cause, like a new Joan of Arc.

All come together in epic storytelling; vital, real, as all their lives are changed while the wolf cries of a new war . . . as the characters we have lived with so far move so. . . .

Stephen Longstreet